Praise for *Magic to the Bone*

"Loved it. Fiendishly original . . . a stay-up-all-night read. We're going to be hearing a lot more of Devon Monk."
—Patricia Briggs, *New York Times* bestselling author of *Bone Crossed*

"Highly original and compulsively readable. Don't pick this one up before going to bed unless you want to be up all night!"
—Jenna Black, author of *The Devil's Due*

"[A] gritty setting, compelling, fully realized characters, and a frightening system of magic-with-a-price that left me awed. Devon Monk's writing is addictive, and the only cure is more, more, more."
—Rachel Vincent, *New York Times* bestselling author of *Rogue*

"*Magic to the Bone* is an exciting new addition to the urban fantasy genre. It's got a truly fresh take on magic, and Allie Beckstrom is one kick-ass protagonist!"
—Jeanne C. Stein, national bestselling author of *Legacy*

"The prose is gritty and urban, the characters mysterious and marvelous, and Monk creates a fantastic and original magic system that intrigues and excites. A promising beginning to a new series. I'm looking forward to more!"
—Nina Kiriki Hoffman, Bram Stoker Award–winning author of *Spirits that Walk in Shadow*

"Monk's reimagined Portland is at once recognizable and exotic, suffused with her special take on magic, and her characters are vividly rendered. The plot pulled me in for a very enjoyable ride!"
—Lynn Flewelling, author of *Shadows Return*

Magic
in the
Blood

DEVON MONK

RoC

A ROC BOOK

ROC
Published by New American Library, a division of
Penguin Group (USA) Inc., 375 Hudson Street,
New York, New York 10014, USA
Penguin Group (Canada), 90 Eglinton Avenue East, Suite 700, Toronto,
Ontario M4P 2Y3, Canada (a division of Pearson Penguin Canada Inc.)
Penguin Books Ltd., 80 Strand, London WC2R 0RL, England
Penguin Ireland, 25 St. Stephen's Green, Dublin 2,
Ireland (a division of Penguin Books Ltd.)
Penguin Group (Australia), 250 Camberwell Road, Camberwell, Victoria 3124,
Australia (a division of Pearson Australia Group Pty. Ltd.)
Penguin Books India Pvt. Ltd., 11 Community Centre, Panchsheel Park,
New Delhi - 110 017, India
Penguin Group (NZ), 67 Apollo Drive, Rosedale, North Shore 0632,
New Zealand (a division of Pearson New Zealand Ltd.)
Penguin Books (South Africa) (Pty.) Ltd., 24 Sturdee Avenue,
Rosebank, Johannesburg 2196, South Africa

Penguin Books Ltd., Registered Offices:
80 Strand, London WC2R 0RL, England

First published by Roc, an imprint of New American Library,
a division of Penguin Group (USA) Inc.

First printing, May 2009
10   9   8   7   6   5

Copyright © Devon Monk, 2009
All rights reserved

ROC REGISTERED TRADEMARK—MARCA REGISTRADA

Printed in the United States of America

PUBLISHER'S NOTE
This is a work of fiction. Names, characters, places, and incidents either are
the product of the author's imagination or are used fictitiously, and any resem-
blance to actual persons, living or dead, business establishments, events, or
locales is entirely coincidental.
   The publisher does not have any control over and does not assume any
responsibility for author or third-party Web sites or their content.

*For my big, crazy, wonderful family.
I couldn't do this without you. Thanks for
believing in my dream and helping me
to make it come true.*

Acknowledgments

I am so grateful for all the help I received while writing this book.

Thank you to my wonderful agent, Miriam Kriss, for your unflagging excitement and support. My deepest gratitude also to my editor, Anne Sowards, who took the time to call and talk with me about the book. Though you may not know it, in that one hour you showed me a new way to approach writing not only this novel, but many novels yet to come. A big thank-you also to assistant editor Cameron Dufty, designer Ray Lundgren, and artist Larry Rostant. You made this book shine.

I am lucky to have the best, most supportive, and most persistent first readers in the world. Thank you, Dean Woods, for always asking when I'll have something for you to read and following up with such insightful questions. You are brilliant. Thank you, Dejsha Knight, for being there for me from the very first story. I wouldn't be here without you. Thank you, Dianna Rodgers, for your friendship, and for giving such honest feedback, even on short deadlines. Thank you, Sharon

Thompson, for all your encouragement, support, and advice. And thank you to Deanne Hicks for everything. I love you, girl.

I'd also like to thank the fabulous readers who read *Magic to the Bone* and liked it enough to try this sequel. I hope it doesn't disappoint.

Lastly, all my love to my husband, Russ, and sons, Kameron and Konner, for all you are and all you do. Thank you for being the very best part of my life.

Chapter One

I dunked my head under the warm spray of the shower and rubbed shampoo into my hair, wondering where my next Hounding job, and paycheck, were coming from. I hadn't been using much magic since I got back to town, and the bills were piling up. It was time to get on with my life, time to get on with tracking spells again.

I heard a distant pop, like a lightbulb blowing, and all the lights in my apartment went out. I opened my eyes just as a stream of soap dripped into them.

"Ow, ow, ow."

Outside, the wind howled past my bathroom window. We'd been having some bad storms lately—plain old windstorms, not wild magic. Probably a tree or landslide up in the west hills had knocked out the line or blown a transformer, throwing this part of Portland into a deep early-morning darkness. The wail of an alarm from a nearby business started up, and then an answering siren, and then two, joined in on the noise. A couple car alarms got busy.

I rinsed as much of the soap out of my eyes as I

could, turned off the shower, and stumbled out of the
tub. I hit my shin on the toilet bowl.

"Ow!" I groped for the sink, found the cool surface
with my fingertips, and looked over my shoulder at
the single frosted window behind me. No light, which
meant the magic grid was down too. There were backup
spells to power the streetlights in case of blackout—
spells the city paid the price for. Weird they hadn't kicked
in yet.

I felt my way along the sink, the wall, the light
switch, and the towel hanging on the back of the door.
I knew there was no one in the room with me, no one
in my apartment. Still, I did not want to be alone and
naked in the dark.

"Allie," a voice whispered so close to my cheek I
could feel the cold exhale.

I bolted out into the hallway and turned. It was so
dark I couldn't see anything.

I traced a glyph for Light in the air in front of me,
completely forgetting to set a Disbursement for the
pain that magic was going to put me through. Pain, I
could deal with later. Light, I needed now.

The hallway, hells, the entire apartment, lit up like
sunlight on snow.

I was not alone.

My dead father stood right there on the yellow
ducky bath mat in front of my shower. It didn't look
like death had done him any favors.

Sure, he still wore a dark business suit—I'd rarely
seen him out of business dress—and he was clean
shaven and gray haired. Other than that, he looked
like a hastily drawn interpretation of himself—his skin

too pale, his green eyes gone so light as to be white. Dark, dark shadows caught beneath his eyes and pooled in the hollows of his face. He scowled. He was angry.

Angry at me.

Well, apparently death didn't do much for a person's mood either.

He stretched out his right hand, traced the first strokes of something in the air—maybe a glyph—and then moved fast, faster than any living person, until he was standing in front of me, close, so close his hand pressed against my forehead.

I raised my arms to keep him away, push him away, make him stay away from me. I could smell him—or maybe it was just the memory of him—and taste him, leather and wintergreen, on the back of my throat.

I yelled, tasting more wintergreen as he leaned in closer, all ice and bone—cold and damp against my naked wet skin. The Light spell flickered out, probably because I was too busy panicking to concentrate, and magic does not tolerate that sort of thing.

The apartment plunged back into blackness. I could still feel my dad's hands on my arms.

I ran backward, scrambling to get away from the cold and wintergreen of his angry touch. My back hit the hall wall and I had nowhere else to go.

"Seek," he whispered against my cheek.

Streetlights snapped on—the city's spells finally kicking in—and poured blue light through the windows.

My dad was gone. Cut off midsentence like a dropped call.

Holy shit.

I gulped down air, shaking with more than cold, and

backed into my bedroom, needing to be dry, dressed, covered, protected, safe, and the hells away from here as quickly as possible.

I'd been groped by a ghost. My dad's ghost.

My hands shook, and my heart beat so hard, I couldn't breathe. My dad touched me. And I'd been naked.

I fumbled into a pair of jeans, my bra, a T-shirt, and a wool sweater. Then socks and boots. I picked up the baseball bat I kept near my bed. I didn't know if a baseball bat would work on a ghost, but I was willing to find out.

I stood there, breathing hard, the bat over one shoulder, and stared through the empty hallway at my empty bathroom.

"Dad?" I asked.

Nothing.

Let's just go over the facts: I'd seen a ghost. My dad's ghost.

And he had seen me. Touched me. Spoken to me.

Okay, that was so far down Creepy Lane that it had intersected with Scaring the Hell Out of Me Avenue. I hated that avenue.

I shook out my hands, switching the bat from one to the other, and tried to calm my breathing. *Take it easy, Allie,* I told myself. *Ghosts aren't real.*

Yeah, well, that felt real.

Maybe seeing him was some sort of weird leftover guilt from not being there when he died. Not being there for his funeral or his burial. No, I know I wouldn't have gone to his funeral even if I'd been able to. I was still angry at him then, angry that he had let his hunger for money and power hurt everyone in his life, including me.

As a matter of fact, I was still angry about that.

The lights in my apartment—regular electric—weren't working yet. I didn't want to pull on magic again for light because when you used magic, it used you right back. There was always a price—always a pain to pay. Why give myself a headache when I could just light a candle? Problem was, my candles were all the way across the apartment in the living room.

I strode into the hallway, bat ready to swing. I looked in the bathroom—no one there—and walked (not too quickly, I'll add) over to the side table next to my ratty couch. I put down the bat and found a box of matches. I lit several candles on my bookshelf, on top of the TV, and on the little round dining table by the window. For good measure, I pulled back the curtains, letting in as much light from the street as possible.

Blue light from the streetlamps caught in the whorls of metallic color that ribboned around my fingertips and up my arm and the side of my neck to the very corner of my right eye. It was still strange to see the marks magic had left on me—brighter and more iridescent than tattoos. Stranger to feel magic heavy inside me, a constant weight that moved and stretched beneath my skin.

Even though my right arm didn't itch anymore from the magic flowing through me, my left arm, banded black at my elbow, my wrist, and at each knuckle, was always a little cold and numb when I used magic too much.

I wasn't sure what all of it meant—because no one I'd talked to had ever seen anything like this, like me. People who try to hold magic in their bodies die from it. Horribly. And I'd done my best to stay away from doctors who might be curious enough to want to take me apart to find out why I wasn't dead yet.

I rubbed my arm—the right with the whorls of colors—and scanned the street below.

Rain and wind? Yes. Ghosts? No.

The last room to check was the kitchen. There were no windows in the kitchen, so I picked up a candle in a glass jar and paused in the entryway to the kitchen. My apartment door stood to the right of me, my kitchen lost in shadows ahead of me. I lifted the candle. Yellow light pushed aside blocks of shadow. Nothing.

The phone rang. I jumped so hard, wax sloshed over the candle's wick and smothered the flame.

The phone rang again, and a wash of cold sweat slicked my skin. It was just the phone.

It rang again.

I didn't want to answer it.

Another ring.

Could ghosts use the phone?

Okay, now I was being ridiculous.

I put the candle down on the half wall between the kitchen and foyer and jogged to the phone in the living room. Caught it on the fourth ring.

"Hello?" I said, my voice a little too high.

"Allie Beckstrom?" a low male voice asked.

I recognized that voice. Detective Makani Love had spent a good deal of his childhood in Hawaii and still hadn't lost that particular rhythm to his words. Plus, I could hear the ring of phones behind him and then another voice, female, and likely his partner, Lia Payne. I think the police department had stuck them together for a laugh—Love and Payne—but they'd turned into such a good team, they hadn't asked to be reassigned.

"Hey, Mak," I squeaked.

"Is everything okay? Are you okay?"

I swallowed and worked hard to get my voice down an octave or so.

"Yes. I'm fine. Just, uh . . . kind of startled when the phone rang. Is the power out over there?"

"No," he said. "But we heard part of town was down. You dark?"

The lights flicked back on, and my computer on the desk in the corner hummed back to life.

"Not anymore," I said. "It just came back on. So, what's up?"

"We need you to come down to the station to give your statement regarding the death of your father."

Oh.

I'd never filed an official report. See, I'd been there the day my father died. I may even have been the last one who saw him alive—except for his killer. But since I'd spent the next several days being chased by the people who killed him, I hadn't had a chance to actually talk to the police about the last time I'd seen him.

Well, the last time I'd seen him alive.

I wondered if Mak believed in ghosts.

"Can it wait until later? I haven't had breakfast yet and was hoping to hunt down some leads on Hounding jobs this morning."

"No. It's been long enough, yah? You've been back in town, what, a week now, almost two? That's patience on our side, you know. We need you this morning. Can you get here in an hour?"

"Will there be any decent coffee in the building?" Love and I weren't best buddies, but I usually ended up going to him when I worked Hounding jobs that involved someone doing something illegal. He and Payne were two of the few police officers I knew who were cross-trained to handle magical crime enforcement.

"Oh, sure. Best coffee in the city, yah. Dug a pit this morning, roasted it with my own hands over the fire. Fresh just for you."

"Right." I glanced out my living room window and through the bare tree limbs that spread across my view of the street and buildings on the other side. It was six o'clock on a late-November morning and still dark. Rain gusted sideways past the window, flashing like gold confetti in the headlights of slow-moving traffic crawling toward downtown Portland, Oregon, and the freeway beyond. The police station wasn't all that far from my apartment, but I didn't have a car. The bus ran every half hour and would take me straight to the station doors.

It was doable.

"I'll be there in about forty-five minutes."

"Good. And, Allie?"

"Yes?"

"Don't leave town. And be careful."

A chill ran down my arms. Why would he say that? I wouldn't skip town. And I was always careful. Well, as careful as the situation allowed. "I'll be there in forty-five."

I hung up the phone and scowled at it. Okay, maybe

he had a reason to worry about me not showing up. I'd gotten myself into some weird stuff a few months ago, not that I remembered much of it. My friend Nola, who lived three hundred miles away on a non-magical alfalfa farm in Burns, had taken me in afterward. She tried to tell me what she knew about the days I no longer remembered and the weeks that had gone by while I'd been in a coma. But her information was sketchy too.

The one thing that had become abundantly clear to me was just how much memory I had lost. It still gave me nightmares.

I glanced over at the table by the window. The blank book where I wrote everything just in case magic took my memories was there. I walked over to it, flipped it open. The most current pages were the basic itinerary from the last few days—me settling into my new apartment, the phone messages from my father's accountant I hadn't returned. The sandwich shop I discovered a couple streets over that made really good paninis (I give the salmon rosemary five stars), and the name of a song I liked on the radio.

But as I flipped back toward the front of the book, I found the blank page. The corner of it was worn from me going back to it so often in the last few weeks. Right there on that blank page I should have written everything that had happened to me between when I last saw my father alive and when I woke up at Nola's farm a month later.

Blank.

No matter how hard I stared at it, the notes I should have written were not there.

Things I really wish I could remember, like what

had happened between me and a man named Zayvion Jones. I remember him hanging around St. Johns neighborhood in North Portland. I remember him asking me out for lunch, and I remember him going with me to see my father.

What I didn't remember—the things my friend Nola had said happened—was falling in love with him, so much so that I'd sacrificed myself to save him.

It just didn't sound like me.

Slow to trust, slower to love, I couldn't figure out how I had fallen for him so completely in such a short time.

I shut the book and pressed my fingers against my forehead. Magic is not for sissies. Sure, it can do a million good things—keep cities safer and hospitals going, and even just make a bad paint job look good— but it always comes with a price.

Sometimes magic makes me pay a double price— pain for using it, and loss of memory. Yeah, I'm just lucky that way. It was almost enough to make me want to give it up altogether. Almost.

The phone rang again, and I looked through my fingers at it, trying to decide if I really wanted to talk to anyone else this morning. It might be a Hounding job, which would mean money, or, heck, Nola checking in on me.

I picked it up.

"Hello?"

"Hello, Allie." A woman's voice this time. I searched my memory and came up with nothing—see how annoying that is? "I'm sorry to call so early, but I've left a few messages on your cell phone and thought I'd try to catch you before you went out for the day."

I flipped my book open again. Who had been leaving me messages? Just my dad's accountant, Mr. Katz. I glanced at my cell phone—no light at all. The battery was dead, blown. I'd had it only a couple days, and it was currently plugged in to the charger.

I'd had zero luck with cell phones lately. Any electronics that worked through a line, like my computer, seemed to hold up okay, but anything wireless self-destructed when it saw me coming.

"Allie?" the woman said.

"Yes," I said, still trying to place her voice. "My cell isn't working. You might want to leave messages here on my home phone."

"Do you want me to have Mr. Katz set you up with a new phone?"

And that was when I knew who it was. Violet. My dad's latest wife. She had a young voice, and from the newspaper articles Nola had shown me, I knew she was about my age. I think I had met her, but that memory was toast too.

"No, that's fine. It's still under warranty. Sorry I haven't gotten back to you. Why are you calling?"

She hesitated, just a pause, an inhalation, but it made every instinct in my body rise up.

"Are you in trouble?" I asked.

She exhaled with a sort of laugh. "I'm fine, just fine. I was hoping you might want to get together for lunch today. I haven't heard from you since before the coma. You didn't contact me when you came back into town. I know we've only met once, but . . . well, since you weren't able to come to the funeral . . . and there's still so much unfinished business with Beckstrom Enterprises and your role in managing the company . . .

I just thought . . . I don't know. I thought we might want to get to know each other a little better. Talk about some things."

My dad had been married six times. Years ago I'd stopped trying to make nice with the women who attached themselves to and were discarded by my father. Which is why I surprised myself by saying, "Sure. Let's do dinner instead, if that's okay. I have a lot of things to get to today."

Violet sounded just as surprised. "Oh. Good. Dinner's fine."

We settled the time and restaurant—not one of the exclusive swanky spots in town, but Slide Long's, known for its seafood—and then we said our good-byes.

I stared at the phone for a minute, trying to sort out how I felt about getting to know her.

I guess I was a little curious but mostly just lonely. My best friend lived three hundred miles away. The man I was supposed to love was nowhere to be seen. I didn't even know any of my neighbors.

And my dad was dead.

I wondered when I'd stopped liking being alone. Maybe somewhere in the days I couldn't remember, I'd given up on the solitary woman bit and had actually let people into my life. And maybe I had really liked it.

Or maybe I just wasn't in my right mind. Which might also explain the whole ghost-in-the-bathroom bit.

Well, whatever. Right now I had to get down to the police department and tell them what I knew about the day my dad died. After that I'd scout around town and see if there were any Hounding possibilities.

I picked up my journal and quickly wrote that I was giving a statement and had dinner plans with Violet. I paused, wondering if I should write that I'd seen a ghost. Common sense won out, and I simply wrote: *Saw Dad's ghost in the bathroom. Not fun.* And hoped that would be that.

Chapter Two

I blew out all the candles and checked to make sure my windows were locked and my heater wasn't turned up too high. My apartment looked like it always did: sort of half-decorated, a few boxes still out from my move a week ago, laundry piled on one corner of the couch waiting to be folded, and empty coffee cups perched here and there amidst a half dozen paperbacks I was reading.

The place was coming together. Pillows on the couch and a couple pieces of artwork I'd bought at the Saturday Market did some good to add color to the off-white walls and tan rug.

And best of all, not a ghost in sight. If I managed to stay here long enough, it might even feel like home someday.

I gathered all the empty cups and took them to the kitchen sink. I was procrastinating, and if I waited any longer I was going to miss the bus and miss my appointment with Love and Payne. Then they'd be on my doorstep, wearing their not-at-all-amused faces.

Going in to see the police before coffee wasn't my idea of fun.

I took a nice deep breath and put the last cup in the sink. I could do this. Go downtown, give my statement, and then head over to Get Mugged—my favorite coffee shop in the whole town—and get me a decent cup of joe and something for breakfast.

All the normal stuff normal people do. Normal people who use magic only occasionally because they don't want to pay the physical price of pain. Normal people who use magic only to make themselves look thinner at their high school reunions or to keep their cars shiny in the summer. Normal people who use magic only to get high on Friday nights.

Normal people who don't see ghosts.

So what if I wasn't good at normal? Didn't mean I couldn't have some fun.

I turned out the kitchen light and walked around the half wall, snatching up my knit hat on the way. I tugged the hat over my head, thankful my hair was short enough I didn't have to tuck it up. I headed to the living room and pulled my coat and scarf off the back of my couch and put them on. I put my journal and dead cell phone in one pocket and then checked for my gloves (black leather driving gloves that were actually warm and stylish, wonder of wonders) in the other pocket.

The gloves served two purposes. One, they kept my fingers from freezing—it had been cold the last week or so. I was amazed the rain hadn't turned to snow yet. And two, the gloves hid the marks magic had left on my hands. Which meant I didn't have to put up with the stares and questions.

Yes, I get tired of making up excuses for something

most people wouldn't believe. That magic, magic in my bones, painted me, marked me, scarred me. Most days I liked how it looked but some days I didn't want the attention.

With my keys and wallet tucked in my pockets, I went out the door, locking it behind me. The delicious spice of cinnamon and yeast caught at the back of my throat and made my empty stomach cramp in protest. I inhaled deeply and sighed. Sweet torture, someone was baking cinnamon rolls. I put one hand over my stomach and picked up the pace a bit. I hadn't eaten since my peanut butter sandwich for dinner yesterday, and I was suddenly very hungry.

I marched down the hall and noted the last apartment door was propped open. The tenants had moved out about a week after I moved in, and it looked like someone had rented it already. I passed in front of the door and inhaled deeply again, this time picking up on the more subtle scent of almond and deeper spices—a man's cologne, the slightest tang of sweat and something sweet like licorice—as I passed by the door. I didn't hear anyone moving around in there, but clearly, moving was going on.

There were no elevators in the Forecastle, which was one of the reasons I practically begged the landlord to let me rent. I had a serious thing about small spaces. I seriously hated them.

Elevators, changing rooms, even small cars set me off in a panic. I'd rather walk a million stairs than push a single elevator button. The other thing the Forecastle had going for it was it didn't reek of old magic every time the weather got bad. And in Portland, the weather got bad a lot.

I headed down the central staircase, my boot heels silent on the carpeting. The lobby was cold and quiet and dark except for the ceiling lights. There were windows next to the doors that led to the street, but dawn hadn't knocked the night out of the sky yet.

I pulled my hat closer over my head and tucked my chin in my scarf before opening the door.

Rain fell in huge heavy drops, cold as ice melt on the gusty winds. I pushed my hands into my pockets and tipped my head down, trying to keep my face out of the worst of the wet. I tromped up the sidewalk to the bus stop. The good thing about being six feet tall is I can cover some serious ground in a short time. But even though the bus stop was only a few blocks up the hill, I was out of breath by the time I hit the first curb.

Nearly dying had taken a lot out of me. I hated being reminded that I wasn't as strong as I liked to be, but it was true.

Time. All I needed was a little time to finish getting well and then I'd be healthy and strong. I'd be normal again.

Magic pushed under my skin, stretching and making me itch a little. Reminding me it was there, ready to be used, to be shaped, to be cast. Reminding me it would do anything for me. So long as I was willing to pay the price.

Okay, maybe normal was too much to ask for. Right now, I'd settle for healthy.

I ignored the push of magic and kept a steady pace to the bus stop. I was drenched by the time I arrived. The bus stop itself was a cozy little Plexiglas closet of death beneath the glaring eye of a streetlight. My palms broke out in a sweat inside my gloves.

Oh, no way. No matter how wet and cold I was, there was no force in this world that could make me stand under that tiny roof with the other six people who were already crammed inside. Freeze to death in the driving wind and rain instead? No problem.

Five or six men huddled on the other side of the bus stop, between it and the curb. They faced the street, hands in their pockets, heads bent against the gusty rain.

Typical to Oregon, no one carried an umbrella, though everyone had on a hat or hood. We all waited, silent, a mix of old, young, and odd.

I scanned the faces, wondering if I knew any of them. It was possible they could be my neighbors. But no one made eye contact, and no one looked familiar. What everyone looked was wet, and tired of it.

The bus rumbled up to the curb and screeched to a stop. The curbside men got on first, and then a few of the speedier bus stop huddlers, myself in the mix. I reached the door and flashed my bus pass. The smell of people—lots and lots of wet people—hit me full in the face.

That was one of the disadvantages to being a Hound. Not only was I able to track spells back to their casters, but I also had a pretty sensitive nose, even without magic enhancing it.

I tucked my nose a little deeper into my scarf and beelined to the empty back of the bus. I took a seat near the door and leaned my head against the window behind me. That let me stare across the aisle and out the other window while the rest of the riders got on the bus. Across the street, a man pulled free from the shadows. He stood there, in the open and the rain, a darkness against darkness. He stared at the bus. He stared at me.

I felt his gaze all the way down to my bones.

I knew him. I was sure of it.

Zayvion Jones. The man I had fallen in love with— the man I might still be in love with. The man I hadn't seen for weeks.

The doors hissed shut and the engine growled as the bus pulled out into traffic, leaving Zayvion lost to the rain and darkness behind me.

Loneliness hollowed out my chest. What had he been doing there on the street? Was he looking for me?

Well, if he was, he'd have to wait. My cell was toast. If he had a phone, I didn't think he'd given me the number. I'm sure I would have written it in my blank book. Or at least I thought I would have.

I shook my head and tried to push Zayvion out of my mind. He knew where I lived. Obviously. He could leave me a note if he wanted to get ahold of me.

"Mind if I sit?"

That voice sent my stomach down to my shoes and left nothing but fight or flight rising up through me in a hot wave. I suddenly wished I'd brought my baseball bat with me.

I looked up.

Lon Trager, the kingpin of drugs and blood magic, smiled down at me. I'd saved Martin Pike's grand-daughter from his blood-and-drug den a while ago. My testimony had put Trager in jail.

He was supposed to get thirty years. Thirty. It hadn't even been three.

He wore a nice business coat, expensive French cologne, and a hat straight out of a 1930s film. He didn't wait for my answer before folding into the seat next to me, his shoulders brushing mine. His face was long, dark, his cheeks hollowed out so the bones cut a hard line under his eyes. He was a predator. He was violence. A dealer, a pusher, a killer.

"Great day to be alive, isn't it, Ms. Beckstrom?"

If he thought I was going to sit there and make nice talk, he was out of his mind.

I stood.

Six other men in our immediate vicinity rose out of their seats just a little and glanced at Trager. They each had at least one hand in a pocket. I pulled my nose out of my scarf and caught the faintest scent of metal and oil and gunpowder.

"I'm sure you are a very busy woman." Trager put his hand out, and his thugs sat back down in their seats. "Please sit, Ms. Beckstrom. We wouldn't want anyone on this bus to have an unpleasant experience."

I was so screwed. If I yelled for the bus driver to call 911, or even if I silently traced a glyph to cast magic, Trager's men would pull their guns. Everyone on the bus could be killed.

Magic is fast.

So are bullets.

Think, Allie, I told myself. There had to be a way out of this.

But the only other thing I could think of was to sit down, listen to his threats, and maybe oh-so-casually trace a glyph that I could use on him before his goons killed me.

Life or death before coffee. Welcome to Monday.

I sat on the edge of the seat and half turned so I could meet him eye to eye.

His eyes were brown enough to be black. Cool, flat, and alien in a way that made me squirm inside.

"Cops know you're out?" I asked.

"Oh, yes. Yes, they do."

That sent chills over my skin. He had gotten out legally. Or maybe he had bought his way out. Either way, he was free. Really free.

Holy shit.

"Does it worry you?" he said. "You know, this . . . bad blood between us"—he smiled, and it made him look hungry—"could be wiped away. I'm willing to call it clean, done, over, no harm, no foul, so long as you do one thing for me."

I had no intention of doing anything for him. But he didn't have to know that. "Really? Must be my lucky day."

His smile wasn't doing anything for his looks. Unless he was going for the crazy psycho-killer thing.

"Ms. Beckstrom," he chided, "you don't know how lucky you've been. I will kill you." He shrugged his shoulders as if he were discussing which pizza to buy for lunch. "Today, tomorrow. If not by my hand, then by my voice and the hands of my people. My people are everywhere. Even your rich, dead daddy knew that. Even your rich, dead daddy bowed to me."

I blinked like I wasn't the least bit intimidated. And in some ways, I wasn't. He could insult my father all he wanted—I didn't care.

"Is this going to take all day?" I asked. "My stop's coming up."

A flicker of raw anger flashed in those alien eyes. "Bring me Martin Pike," he said with such emphasis that his spit peppered my face. "Bring him to me alive. By tomorrow night. Tuesday, no later than midnight. If I don't see both of you strolling across my floor, you will be dead before the sun rises on Wednesday."

The bus grumbled and slowed, kneeling toward the stop at the curb. His goons all stood.

I should have seen it, should have sensed the change in his body language. But when six guys with guns stand up at the same time, I am all about keeping an eye on them.

The bite of a needle plunged deep in my thigh hit me like an electric shock. I grunted but didn't have time to yell, didn't have time to cast magic or even punch him in the face before Lon Trager was on his feet. In his hand was an odd double-chambered glass syringe wrapped from tip to plunger in a fine metallic cagework of glyphs. And in that syringe was my blood. Six guns from his goons were pocketed and pointed at me.

Subtle. Deadly. "Tomorrow by midnight." Trager deposited the syringe in his pocket.

I stood to throw a spell at him, regardless of the stupidity of taking him down with all his gun-buddies ready to waste me, and thumped back into the seat on my ass. A wave of dizziness washed over me. The sickeningly sweet taste of cherries exploded in the back of my mouth, and the entire bus slipped sideways while a flood of heat spread out over my thigh.

What was on that needle?

By the time the dizziness passed—maybe a full minute and a half—Trager and his men were gone, the bus was no longer at the curb, and the seat across from me was now filled with a mother and two kids sitting on their knees so they could look out the window behind them.

Sweet hells. I was so screwed.

Lon Trager had my blood.

And I didn't know what he was going to use it for.

I thought about calling the police on my cell, but it was beyond busted.

Magic shifted in me, pressed to slip my tenuous hold on it. It promised anything, promised to destroy Trager, if I was willing to pay for it.

No. I'd find a traditional way to throw his ass back in jail. Some way that he wouldn't be able to plea or bribe his way out of.

I'd be at the police station in just a few minutes. Enough time to calm my pounding heart and regain my cool.

Tall buildings slid through the branches of trees that lined the streets as the bus continued into downtown. At the next stop, a man wearing a ski hat, a gray trench coat, and a black scarf walked up the two stairs and paused to scan the bus like he was looking for someone. He had a newspaper folded under his arm. The brown paper cup in his hand sent out the scent of coffee like strains of music from a caffeine angel's harp.

He paid, glanced again at the mostly full seats, and caught me looking at him. Okay, I was really looking to make sure he wasn't carrying a gun, but still, he caught my glance.

Here is something else that's weird about me. I do not look away when people catch me staring at them.

I'd spent too many years staring down my father even though I hadn't ever won. My father had a deep need to control people—his only daughter perhaps most of all. Still, it taught me not to back down from confrontation.

The man with the coffee smiled, just the slightest curve of his lips, and walked my way. He didn't look away either, and I found myself staring into a pair of eyes the color of winter honey. He had a square face with heavy brows and eyes framed by very dark lashes. I didn't think he'd shaved this morning, and it looked good on him.

"This seat taken?" he asked.

What was it with me and strange men today?

"Yes."

He frowned, looked toward the front of the bus. No other empty seats. But instead of pushing it, which would have gotten him a broken nose because no one was screwing with me again, he took a couple steps forward. He switched his cup into his left hand so his right hand was free to hold the overhead bar. With the newspaper pinned under his arm, he took a sip of coffee.

I sniffed him out, searching for a hint of Trager's French cologne. Instead of Trager's overpowering scent, this man's cologne—sandalwood and sweet oranges— mixed with the fragrance of coffee. A delicious combination made more delicious because he didn't smell like Trager, didn't smell like the goons, the guns, or the danger that had suddenly pushed its way into my morning.

My gut said he was just a regular guy.

Well, Regular Guy would just have to ride the bus on his regular feet.

We rode awhile in silence, me looking out the window across the aisle, keeping him in my peripheral vision, him looking ahead. He took a sip from his cup, and the smell was sweet torture.

At the next stoplight, he let go of the bar and extended his right hand. "Paul Stotts," he said.

I did not shake his hand. "Good for you."

"I know you," he said. "Allie Beckstrom, right?"

I did a quick search through my memories. I didn't remember him, but instinct told me he wasn't as Regular Guy as he appeared to be. "How long have you been following me?"

"Hmm," he said around a swallow of coffee. "Just today."

He didn't hold himself like a Hound, didn't have that desperate look of a Hound, and was wearing too much cologne to be a Hound. He also didn't look or smell like he was into blood magic or drugs, so maybe he wasn't a part of Trager's game. But with Trager's "my people are everywhere" speech ringing in my head, I did not want to chance it.

"Police," he said. "Detective Stotts."

Oh. I hadn't expected that.

"Police? Where were you two stops back?"

"Waiting for the bus. Why?"

I hesitated. Did I really want to go into this in public? Just because the goons got off the bus with Trager didn't mean someone else wasn't here acting as his ears. If Trager had any brains—and I had to assume he did, since he had not only created the largest blood-

and-drugs cartel in the city, but he had also pulled a get-out-of-jail-free card—he would have left someone behind to watch me and report back.

Hells, for all I knew Stotts could be his guy.

I rubbed at my forehead with the tips of my gloves. "Never mind. Are you here to make sure I get to the station?"

He glanced at me and then away. "Well, we didn't want to leave anything to chance."

He had no idea how chancy it had been. Still, that was interesting. I'd never had police protection or escort. At least, I didn't remember having it. So far, I wasn't all that impressed.

"Didn't think I could manage it on my own?"

He smiled, that soft curve of his mouth. Okay, this close, I noticed that his bone structure had a Latino influence: arched cheekbones, square jawline, but soft eyes and lips. A very nice combination.

Yes, I looked at his left hand. Saw the wedding ring. Can't blame me for being curious.

"We thought it might be better if you had an escort." And I could tell by the tone of his voice, and the rhythm of his heart, that he was telling the truth.

So it was a friendly gesture. The police were looking out for me, not against me.

"How thoughtful."

He took a drink of coffee, nodded. "You haven't exactly been living on easy street lately. Pegged for murder, shot, chased, nearly killed by wild storm magic."

"And the coma," I said.

He nodded. "It just seemed like the odds of you getting to the station unscathed were pretty low."

"Thanks for the vote of confidence," I drawled.

"Could be worse," he said.

The bus pulled to another stop, and I caught a glimpse of the police station through the rain-pebbled window. This was our stop.

"Worse?"

"Decker could have been on duty."

I winced. Officer Decker and I did not get along. Not since the time I'd Hounded a drug deal back to his brother's girlfriend and found out I'd been mistaken. It was his brother, not the girlfriend, who was dealing and Offloading the price of magic onto a retirement home. It had been my testimony that put his brother in jail. Since then I mostly tried to avoid Decker.

Detective Stotts stepped backward and waited for me to take the place in front of him.

"Aren't you chivalrous?" I asked as I stepped into the aisle.

"No," he said from close behind me. "Just trying to keep my eye on you."

"Get in line," I muttered. Actually, I appreciated his honesty. I would appreciate it even more as soon as I confirmed he really was a police officer.

I checked the people still sitting on the bus as I shuffled down the aisle. One woman, who I thought had been asleep, lifted her head and opened her eyes to watch me go by. She smelled like sweet, sweet cherries. Blood magic. One of Trager's people, watching, listening.

I couldn't get off the bus and out into the freezing rain fast enough. I tucked my head and jogged toward the station doors, too many threats too early in the morning making me want to run.

But I knew better than that. One, it would exhaust

me. Two, whoever was still watching me would know how spooked I really was. Instead of going faster, I slowed my pace, my boots slapping through dark puddles. I strode past the concrete blast barriers and up the steps to the front door of the police department. Other people milled along the stairs with me, too many people and too many scents for me to know which of them was part of Trager.

I pushed through the doors and expected Stotts to be right there with me, but once I made it to the lobby and wiped the rain off my face, I realized he wasn't there. My police escort was gone, like a ghost in the wind.

Chapter Three

Before I'd taken more than three steps across the lobby, a man's voice called out. "Hey, Tita!"

Detective Love, who, if you believed his stories, had a mama from Samoa and a daddy who was a Scottish pirate, strolled my way. Love was six foot three if he was an inch, and almost as wide. His dark wavy hair fell down to ox-thick shoulders as broad as a city bus. He wore a bright blue button-down shirt and tan pants, a combination that made me think of sand and sky on a distant, sunnier shore.

Tita, I'd learned, meant tough girl. Love had called me that since the Hounding job I'd done that put Lon Trager in jail.

"Why'd you have to make it in on time?" he asked with a wide, white smile. "Now I owe Payne ten dollars."

"You should know better than to take bets against me," I said.

He laughed. "Yah, yah. Come on this way."

He started off toward his office, and I fell into step next to him, absorbing the sunlight good humor he radiated. "There's coffee, right?"

"Oh, yah. Coffee's onolisicious today." He glanced over his shoulder and rolled his eyes.

So much for coffee.

"You like the new apartment?" he asked as we left the lobby behind us for a maze of cubicles and desks. "I heard you moved away from the river."

"I like it okay. It's better than the Fair Lead."

"Yah, yah. That place's a pit. Don't know why you stayed there so long." He opened a door to the small office he and his partner shared. He lumbered around the desk to the right and sat. Payne was not in the room.

"It was cheap." I pulled off my coat and hung it on the coatrack that leaned against the file cabinet. With me and Love in the office, I was fast running out of breathing space.

Think calm thoughts, I told myself. There was plenty of room for me, plenty of room for Love, and plenty of room for lots and lots and lots of air.

"You okay?" Love asked.

I nodded and took the seat in front of the desk. "Small spaces." I shrugged like it was no big deal.

He raised his eyebrows. "Want me to open the door?"

"No. I'm good."

He gave me a considering look. I (of course) met his gaze straight on.

"Okay," he finally said. He pulled a file folder off of a stack to his left, opened it, and tapped his computer keyboard. "Right." He looked over at me and gave me a nod. "You ready for this?"

"Sure."

He pulled out a tape recorder and turned it on and then held it close to his mouth while he said his name, the date, and some other things I wasn't paying attention to. What I was paying attention to were the pictures on the wall. Him towering over a group of kids at a school, him and a police dog. And one of him and his dark, lean partner, Lia Payne. Other than that, the walls were off-white cracked plaster.

There was something odd about the walls, a cool dampness that emanated from them. I looked closer. Those weren't cracks in the plaster. They were very fine, very subtle Blocking spells, placed there by adding lead and glass to the paint or plaster and then drawing out the glyphs with Intent. Pulling a magic fast one in here would rebound back on the caster. The glyphs seemed strange to me, since I didn't remember ever noticing them when I'd come in to talk with Love before. I wondered if they'd created the spells recently, or maybe if they'd done it because of my spectacular meltdown a few months ago.

Magic shifted in me, stretched so hard I had to take a deep breath to make room for it. I hoped Love didn't notice.

The door opened and Detective Payne walked in, three coffee cups in her hand. The door stayed slightly ajar behind her, offering a tantalizing glimpse of the space behond it.

"Hello, Allie. I knew you'd make it. No sugar, right?"

She handed the coffee over my shoulder and I smiled up at her. The woman never smiled, but I liked her anyway. Clear, efficient, and not afraid to make hard choices on a moment's notice. She must have a soft side since I knew she had a couple of kids at home that her husband took care of during the day.

And, hey, she remembered how I liked my coffee.

"Right. Thanks." I took a drink and shuddered. It was really and truly horrible, but it was hot and caffeinated, and I was desperate. I held my breath and went for another gulp.

She gave Love his coffee, which smelled like powdered hot cocoa mix, and held her hand out to him.

"Pay up."

Love sighed and shifted his weight to access his wallet in his back pocket. "Fine. Fine." He sifted through a couple bills. "We said five, right?"

"Twenty."

"Ten." He slapped a bill in her hand. "You tired of robbing me yet?"

"Just look at it as my way of keeping that superhero collection of yours under control."

"Superhero?" I asked. "Which one?"

"Deadpool," Love said.

"Who?"

"See?" Payne said. "No one even knows him."

Love just shook his head. "He'll be bigger than Batman, I'm telling you. People love him."

Payne drank her coffee and gave him a level stare. "People love Batman because he's a good guy."

"Really? You read him?"

She blinked a couple times like that was the stupidest thing she'd heard all day. "I don't read comics."

"See how she is?" Love shook his head sadly. "No heart for the art."

I took another drink of my coffee. Winced at the horror of it. "I think it's the coffee. It could make anyone mean."

Payne did not smile, but her eyes twinkled. She

pocketed the cash and sat at her desk. "Yah," Love said, "That's why I drink the cocoa. Keeps me sweet."

Payne just raised one eyebrow.

Love thumbed the recorder back on. "State your name, please."

I did so. Love took a nice, noisy slurp of his cocoa and wrote something down on the yellow legal pad in front of him. Then he asked me to state where I was the day my father died and to tell him what happened in as much detail as possible.

So I did. The entire statement didn't take longer than fifteen minutes. I'd Hounded for Mama Rossitto a hit that was killing a five-year-old out in St. Johns. I thought the magical Offload was my father's signature and had taken a cab to my dad's office, where I told him I was advising Mama to contact the police and then sue my father for illegal Offloading practices.

I told Love my dad denied that he or his company had Offloaded on the kid. I told Love I stabbed my dad's finger—and my own—with a straight pin and worked a blood magic Truth spell at his request. Even under the influence of Truth, my father had told me he and his company were not involved with the Offload.

"Were you angry?" Payne, who was also taking notes at her desk, asked.

Okay, here's where I realized it might have been smart to have an attorney come in with me. Hells, how stupid could I be?

Still, honesty was the best policy, right?

"Yes, I was angry. I thought my father had Offloaded a huge magical price onto a five-year-old kid and that the kid was dying."

"Was that the only reason you went to see your father that day?" Love asked.

I knew what he was getting at. I'd managed to avoid seeing my dad for seven years before I'd gone storming into his office. And on the one day I did go see him, he was killed. It was a pretty hard coincidence to swallow.

"That was the only reason."

Love nodded. "Did you see anyone else while you were there?"

"His receptionist. I . . . uh . . . cast Influence on her so she would show me into my dad's office without making me wait."

Love's eyebrows went up. Influence came naturally to my family. With a smile and just the barest whisper of magic, a Beckstrom could make almost anyone do almost anything. Still, any spell cast legally on another human being had to be done with their consent. That was a damn hard thing to actually enforce, but the spirit of the law ruled in magic-related cases.

Cases like murder.

"Did you Influence anyone else in the building?" Love asked.

"No."

"So other than your father, his receptionist was the only other person you spoke to while in the building," Love said.

"No. Zayvion Jones was there too."

This time it was Detective Payne who gave me the weird look. She held so very still I realized she had the bones to make a lovely marble statue. Then she looked down at the pad of paper in her hands and wrote something.

But it was more than just the weird look that had me wondering what the big deal was about Zayvion. It was the sudden scent of surprise, lemon sour, and something else—a confusion of anger or maybe just worry—that radiated off of her. She knew Zayvion. Or knew something about him.

Wasn't that interesting?

"Do you have contact information for Mr. Jones?" she asked.

"No. If I did know where he lived, I don't now. I don't have his phone number either."

She nodded and went back to writing. News of my coma had been all the rage while I'd been sleeping it off. There probably wasn't anyone in Portland who wasn't up on the latest disaster in the Beckstrom family.

"Okay, then," Love said. "That's it. Thank you, Ms. Beckstrom." He turned off the tape recorder and made another note on his paper. "So. You seen Zayvion Jones since then?" he asked without looking up at me.

"From what I can remember, I've talked to him once since I've been back."

"How long ago?" He still wasn't looking at me, still had his pen on the paper, and I was pretty sure he wasn't actually writing anything, just going through the motions. No more sunshine and sandy beaches. Makani Love was nothing but rain-cold police procedure now.

My personal life was none of the police's business. Except, of course, when it was.

Zayvion had been noticeably absent. It was possible he didn't want to see me anymore. Possible he had changed his mind about us. I wouldn't blame him. My life was full of complications. And so far, it didn't look like it was getting less complicated anytime soon.

I had seen him this morning—on the street, watching the bus go by. Or at least I thought it was him. But maybe I was just seeing something, someone, I wanted to see in the rain and darkness.

"The last time I spoke to him was about two weeks ago, when I first got back to town."

Love looked up from his paperwork. No smile this time. "If you do see Zayvion Jones, we'd appreciate knowing about it."

"Why? Is he in trouble?"

"No. We just need him for some paperwork. Nothing serious."

Right. It didn't take a Hound to know he was lying.

"Okay," I said. "Is that it? Can I leave now?"

Love looked over at Payne, and she closed the pad she'd been writing on.

"How much do you know about the Magical Enforcement Response Corps?" she asked.

I knew nothing—didn't even know the police had a separate department to deal with magical crimes. I just thought some of the police officers were cross-trained to deal with magic, like Love and Payne. "Have we talked about it before?"

"No."

"Then I don't think I've heard of it."

Love grunted and took another slurp of his coffee. "We don't go out of the way to make the MERC public, yah?"

"So why tell me?"

They didn't say anything. I looked between them,

at Love's wide, usually happy face, at Payne's thin, perpetually scowling one.

"Is there a case you need my help with? A Hounding job or something?"

Love sat back a little, his chair groaning. "You've had some problems with magic, yah?"

Besides blowing my brains out with magic and doing a three-week coma? I thought. *Besides these lovely colorful tattoos down my right arm and bands across my left? Besides carrying magic in me instead of just drawing on it from the stores beneath the city like sane people? Besides Trager stabbing my leg for a syringe full of my blood and the magic it contained, and of course, that freaky visit from my dad's ghost this morning? No, no problems at all.*

"Define *problems*," I said.

"We want you to know you can call us—any of us—if something goes wrong again," Love said. "The law is here to protect you."

"What makes you think I need protection?"

"In this city, everybody needs protection." He smiled, but it was the grim look of a man who had seen the worst of what people could do—with and without magic.

Here was where I should lay my cards on the table and tell them about Lon Trager on the bus. I opened my mouth, but nothing came out. And it wasn't some sort of Silence or Choke spell.

I hesitated because if I told them Lon Trager wanted Pike, I'd end up whisked out of town under police custody, thus killing any chance of me convincing Pike he should come to the police to make sure they could take care of Trager aboveboard and legally.

I did not want Pike to go vigilante and get himself killed or thrown in jail.

And if the police didn't rush me out of town, they might just tell me to take out a restraining order on Trager, which wouldn't do me any good if one of his unrestrained "people" decided to kill me. Barring those two options, Love and Payne might decide instead to tail me 24/7, which I would hate. I don't like people watching me.

I took another drink of coffee to cover my pause. Pike. First I'd talk to him, find out what the old Hound knew. Then I'd drag his stubborn hide down here to the police to make sure he was protected from Trager right along with me. If I was getting whisked out of town by the cops, Pike was coming with me.

"So, just in case you need protection," Love continued, "we want you to meet a few people on the MERC force. You have time now, yah?"

"I guess."

"Good. Come on this way."

He stood, filling the free space in the room, and I stood too because even with the door propped open, the room suddenly felt much too small for the three of us. I stepped aside so Mr. Island Warmth could walk past me, and then grabbed my coat and exited the room right behind him. Payne followed, a blade of dark shadow on our heels.

Love led us through the maze of cubicles again, and the tightness in my chest squeezed harder. Getting out of that room hadn't done much good for my claustrophobia. Even here it seemed too small for so many people, and so many desks, and so many walls. There wasn't enough air.

I gritted my teeth and thought calm thoughts about big open fields and big open oceans and big open skies, where there was plenty of room and plenty of open and plenty of me breathing slowly and smoothly and not hyperventilating like a moron.

Then we were out into the lobby, into high ceilings and echoes and room to breathe, and no more hyperventilation. A hall to the left took us to another door that was card-locked and also had a hell of a Diversion glyph on it. Most people probably wouldn't even see the door with that big of a Diversion operating. Behind the door was a stairwell. We went down at least two flights, the only sound the squeak of Love's right sneaker, the clomping of my boots, and the ghostly hush of Payne's sensible loafers.

Love stopped on a landing and turned toward a wall with a peeling paint job. It smelled strange here, a weird blend of hot epoxy and dill. Love pulled a card out of his pocket and held it waist high—as if there were some sort of scanner embedded in the flaking paint.

And look at that, there was.

A laser read his card, and then he fingered the motions to a glyph, which I couldn't see since he was wide enough to block his hand and most of the stairwell from my view. He unlocked the Diversion glyph, and the wall with a crappy paint job became a wall with a door.

"Buckle up, Beckstrom," he said as he stepped through the open door. "You must be this tall to ride the ride."

I strolled into the room. Payne stepped in and locked the door behind us. I smelled the burnt epoxy stink of the Diversion spell snapping back into place as the door closed. Someone was doing a lot to keep this room beneath people's notice.

For good reason. The room was large, windowless, and crammed full of so much magic and magical equipment, I literally felt it like a punch to the gut. An ant-bite rashy tingle washed over my skin and made me want to scratch every inch of my body.

As if that weren't enough, magic twisted inside me, pushing against my bones, my muscles, my skin. My ears started ringing and the edges of my vision shaded. I took a deep breath and cleared my mind of the panic that was coming on fast. Panic was bad. Panic would make me lose control of the magic inside me.

I am calm. Calm as a river. Calm as blue sky. I held still, intent on my own breathing. Inhale, exhale. I did not need to lose control of the magic inside me right here in front of the police. They'd have me locked up in a glyph-warded room faster than I could say hocus-pocus.

That is, if I didn't burn the whole place down first.

I am a river, river, river.

"You okay?" Love asked.

"Good," I lied. I even put on a smile. It must have been close to convincing. He nodded. Magic inside me twisted, pushed to get out, to be used, licking hot along the whorls of color from my shoulder to my fingertips, cooling each band on my left hand and arm. It begged to be used. It would be so easy to draw on magic and cast it—not that I even knew what I'd cast it for. And then I'd pay the price.

No way.

Magic turned again, pushed at my skin. I did nothing. Nothing. And magic slowly ebbed.

Go, me.

"So here's where a lot of it takes place." Love waved his hand, gesturing at the room as a whole. I had no idea what he was talking about.

He did not step forward. The room stretched back farther than I could see, but as though I were looking through a fishbowl, I could not focus enough to actually make out the back wall. They had heavy Diversions in the room, probably some Glamour or Illusion, keeping my eyes believing what they wanted me to believe.

There could be an entire three-ring circus back there, elephants and all, and I wouldn't see it through those spells. It was the most effective magical version of a one-way mirror I'd ever seen.

"All what takes place?" I asked.

Love pointed to my left. "Watching the city for magical crimes. Over there we have surveillance equipment in the most heavily populated areas of the city." He pointed to my right. "Over there we have a magic-blocked holding cell, and back there"—he pointed at the fuzzy end of the room—"are restrooms." He smiled.

Restrooms. Right.

"Okay, so you're equipped to detect magic and crimes dealing with magic. Why show me?"

"Because, Ms. Beckstrom," a new but familiar voice said from the fuzzy side of the room, "we need your permission to let us keep you safe."

Paul Stotts, my bus buddy, appeared like, you know . . . magic, out of a thick fog that was the other side of the room. Well, well. He really was a cop. Let the show begin.

From Love and Payne's body language, I figured he must be the boss here and maybe not a very well-liked man. Something about him made them uncomfortable. Something I just wasn't getting.

Three people walked up behind him. Of the two men, one looked like an aging hippie gone bald with a pigtail of hair at the nape of his neck, and the other was about four feet tall and sandy-haired. He gave off a clean-cut accountant vibe. The woman was heavy and looked like she'd just come in from working as both fry cook and bouncer at a truck stop. They were all dressed in street clothes. Like everything else in the room, their scents were overpowered by the strong smell of magic.

"This is part of the team from Magical Enforcement Response Corps," Stotts went on. "Officers Garnet"—the hippie nodded—"Julian"—the accountant smiled—"and Richards." The woman held up one hand. "They have all been specially trained in magical abuse investigation, control, and regulation."

"Nice to meet you all."

Stotts walked forward. The rest of the MERC team went back to the fuzzier side of the room, chatting quietly amongst themselves where I could not hear what they said.

"I asked Detectives Love and Payne to bring you here after you gave your statement so you would better understand the lengths we will go to make sure you are safe."

There it was again, people thinking I was in danger. "Are you telling me I need you to look after me?" I did not like people telling me I couldn't handle myself or my life. Hells, I'd been mauled by my father's ghost just this morning and managed to come out of that okay.

"Not at all," he said smooth and nice-like. "I am asking for your help."

Well. I had not expected that. My witty retort about not needing bodyguards or babysitters died on my lips.

"Excuse me?"

"We'd like to hire you to Hound a case we're working on."

"Why me?"

"It involves magic."

If he had said it involved juggling ostriches, I wouldn't have been more confused. All Hounding jobs involved magic. He wasn't smiling, but I could tell he was enjoying himself. I gave him a dirty look and tried again. "Why not hire Martin Pike or one of the other Hounds who contract with the police?"

"We think you would be the best person for the job."

Okay, there was more behind that. They wanted to either keep an eye on me, keep me in the city, or what? Maybe all the other Hounds were busy. Maybe I was being called in for a second opinion. That happened a lot—using several Hounds on one job to make sure the results were the same.

And here's the deal: I hadn't done any Hounding jobs for weeks. If I was ever going to make a living at it again, I needed to stop being afraid of what might happen if I lost control of the magic inside me and take the damn job. Plus, I needed the money.

"You know my rates?" I asked.

He nodded.

"Then okay. I'll take the job. What is it? Where is it? Who is it?"

"Before I get into those things, we need your permission to tag you."

"What?" I said a little too loudly. "No. Absolutely not." Tags were the polite way to tell someone they were going to be under constant police surveillance. Spied on. Wired. Well, wireless. Magic had brought some amazing advancements into the spy biz too. Which would also mean someone was going to have to Proxy the price of the magic used to follow me around.

There was no way in hell I was going to let someone spy on me.

Stotts looked like he'd expected that. He rubbed at the edge of his jaw.

"Ms. Beckstrom," he said, all business now, "because of the volatile nature of this case, the police feel it would be in your best interest for us to know where you are and who is with you at all times while you are on the job. We will be able to respond much faster to any threat, whether it be a common crime or magically based. We will be able to keep you safe. It would be a smart move on your part to let us do this for you, and you would also be doing the MERC a favor."

"By giving you permission to spy on me?"

"By helping us find the criminal we're looking for."

"If I find whoever is doing whatever, I will report it to you. I don't need to be tagged. As a matter of fact, tagging me might interfere with my ability to Hound." For one thing, I wouldn't be able to get the stink of their spell off me, and that would make me trackable to more people than just the police.

Magic twisted in me, pressed up, out, wanting to be used. My right arm itched, stung. I held still and held Stotts' gaze. I forced my thoughts to quiet, settle, become smooth like glass. He couldn't make me do this. That was also against the law.

Magic pushed, so I let it pour up from where it was held in deep natural cisterns beneath the city, into my feet, bones, body, rushing up my right side, webbing out beneath my skin, then like a loop, a battery, let it flow out of my left hand's fingers to fall back into the ground again.

I knew no one could see the magic flowing into me. Magic is fast, invisible to the naked eye. Which was why Hounds were needed to trace back the burnt remains of spells.

And all the time that we stood there glaring at each other, I didn't draw on it, didn't mutter one mantra or wiggle so much as a single pinkie.

I was a frickin' poster child of self-control today.

And this poster child was done with the stare down.

"Good-bye, Detective Stotts. Thanks for the offer." I turned and headed to the door. Got there too. Payne had her hand on the handle and turned it for me.

"Okay," Stotts said.

I looked over my shoulder. "Okay what?"

"Okay, we won't tag you, although I'm strongly against it. Will you still take the job?"

I thought he'd put up more of a fight about the whole tagging thing. Still, the money would be good, and I would be back on my feet, Hounding again. I liked that idea. "Yes."

"Good." He walked over to me. "I'll take you out to the site tonight."

This was the part I didn't like about Hounding for the cops. To not contaminate evidence or influence a Hound's opinion in any way, the cops kept you in the dark until you were actually on the job.

"Can it wait that long?" Spells got cold pretty fast, which was why so many Hounds were on call for the police.

"For what you're looking for, yes. Can you be back here by five?"

I paused like I was thinking that out. It was an old habit. My social calendar hadn't been booked in years. Oh, wait. I actually did have a dinner planned with Violet. Hounding usually left me pretty tired, even more so if it involved something the police were interested in. Like dead bodies.

I'd have to call Violet and reschedule. I nodded. "I can do that."

"Then meet me here," Stotts said.

"Right here?" I pointed at the floor.

"Outside."

"All right. See you then."

Love, who had been silent through this, cleared his throat. " 'Kay, then. Anything else, Detective Stotts?" he asked.

"That's it. Thanks for coming by, Ms. Beckstrom." He didn't offer to shake my hand, which I thought was pretty smart of him. I was not going to carry around the scent of the cop who was sending me in on a job. Just because Hounds worked for the police didn't mean they didn't work for anyone else. And I was getting the feeling there might be people in town other than the police who were interested in keeping an eye on me.

"I'll see you in a few hours," I said. I turned just as Payne unlocked the Diversion spell.

I looked at Love. The big guy didn't seem worried, but he wasn't his happy self either. He nodded and pointed at the door. I followed his cue. Payne leaned against the open door, scowling like normal.

"Thanks." I strolled through the doorway and took a deep breath on the other side. The prickly ant-bite rashy tingle I'd felt from the moment I stepped into that room eased up. I didn't care who was watching— I scrubbed at my right shoulder and down my arm, trying to relieve the ghostly itch.

Love came through the doorway, and Payne followed and locked it all up again so that it looked like a wall full of bad paint. That was a hell of a spell. Really masterfully cast. If I had the time, I would totally want to Hound it and see how it was made.

"You think that was smart?" Love asked.

"What? Taking the job?"

"Not the job," Love said. "You're a good Hound. I mean going into it without being tagged."

"Do you know which investigation he's hiring me for?"

"Classified," Payne said. "MERC doesn't have to share files with city police."

"Okay," I said. I didn't know that, but it wasn't what I had asked. "Has he told you what the job is?"

"No," Love said. "But Stotts doesn't tag every Hound he uses. Just the ones who might be in danger working his cases."

"Like who?"

"Piller."

"I don't know a Hound named Piller."

" 'Cause he died six years ago," Love said. "Hounding for Stotts."

"Listen," I said. "Hounding is risky—with or without the police or MERC involved. One death in six years isn't enough to make me let people spy on me."

"Sixteen," Payne said.

"What?"

"Sixteen Hounds have died in the last six years. All of them were working for Stotts."

Whoa. That was suddenly a whole different thing. How could I not know about that?

I could not know about that because Hounds are insular, solitary, suspicious people who didn't talk to one another, didn't help one another, and didn't want to be around one another for any reason. Not even to talk about their own dead.

"Is he making them walk through fire or something?"

Payne scowled, and I had the feeling she wasn't in the mood for a smart-ass.

Luckily, Love answered me instead.

"It's like bad luck, yah?" He walked up the stairwell, his shoe squeaking. "When it comes to Stotts, he's got more bad luck than good. Bad magic, bad cases, bad survival odds. He's cursed."

"Is that supposed to scare me?" I asked. "Maybe you don't know the kind of men I've dated. Or—oh, here—did you ever meet my dad? How about all those fabulous women he married? Cursed doesn't even begin to cover my life."

Love grunted and called me some name in Hawaiian I didn't understand.

I followed him up the stairs. "I'm not going to let him spy on me," I said. "Do you know what being tagged would do for my business? People won't hire me if they think the police are watching me. A girl has to make rent."

"Thought you had your daddy's fortune," Love said.

"Well, don't believe everything you read." The fact was I did have some money from his estate, but there were so many legal complications and roadblocks to me actually getting my inheritance, I was still living pretty much month to month. And on top of that, I had some hefty guilt about using money my dad had earned by twisting, manipulating, and destroying lives.

Call me a softy.

"Hard to collect a paycheck when you're dead," Payne said quietly behind me.

"Fine." I stopped walking. Both of them stopped too and looked at me. "Tell me what I'm getting into and convince me it's worth getting tagged and ruining my reputation."

Payne crossed her arms over her chest and leaned one shoulder against the wall. "Stotts gets involved in some heavy stuff. Dark magics."

"Like blood magic?" I asked, resisting the urge to rub at the scars on my left shoulder. Those scars had been the result of some cranked-up gutter trash jumping me with a blood magic spell and a knife a few months ago. "I can handle that."

She shook her head. "Not just blood and drugs, Allie."

"How about giving me some specifics?"

She just gave me a hard look and said nothing.

Great.

"I'm a big girl. I know how to take care of myself."

"Yah, Tita, we know." Love didn't sound convinced.

Nice. Where was the love when a girl needed it?

"You have a cell we can reach you at?" He started up the stairs again, and Payne and I fell into step behind him.

"I did," I said over the echo of our footsteps. "I will. I'm getting it replaced today." *Again*, I thought. Ever since I'd turned into a walking receptacle for magic, cell phones worked for about a day, and then the battery burned out and the wires fused, or melted, or just quit working. It made me a little jumpy about other things failing—like elevators, or, hells, car engines. But so far it was just the cell phones and wireless connections that went belly-up on me.

"That'd be good," he said. "Make sure you call in and give us the number, okay?"

"Sure."

"And you have your will in order, right?" he asked.

"Ha-ha. Funny."

He looked down over his shoulder and gave me a wide smile. "Naw, we won't let anything happen to you. This job will be a piece of cake. You help Stotts this once, walk away alive, and maybe find some other way to make rent, yah?"

"I like Hounding. It's what I do best."

Love reached the top of the stairs and paused before carding open the door. "You can be strong as you like, Tita, be the best Hound there is, and still get your ass kicked in this town."

"I know," I said. "I'll call you when I get a new phone. Promise."

Love smiled, and it was all sunshine and breezy beaches again. "That's all we ask." He slid his card through the reader, unwove the Diversion spell—this one much smaller than the one on the bottom floor—and opened the door for me.

I walked out into the brighter fluorescent-lit hall, the smells of too many people coming in out of the rain, the sounds of too many people in too small a space closing in on me. I needed fresh air. Now would be good.

"See you soon," I said to Love and Payne.

"Be careful," Love said.

I intended to do just that. Which meant I needed food and a decent cup of coffee to keep my strength up. I knew the perfect place to get both—Get Mugged.

I pulled my scarf closer around my nose and chin. Time to leave the secret police, magical crimes, and cursed dead Hounds behind me. At least for as long as I could.

Chapter Four

Outside the station, I took a deep breath and got a noseful of diesel, fish cooking in hot grease, and the wet concrete and mold that pervades Portland from October through May. The wind gusted, pushing hard between buildings and bringing me nothing except the smell of rain and cold.

Daylight was making some progress against the cloud cover, washing the sky in steel gray light. In the strange half-light and rain, everyone looked a little surreal and ghostlike, their forms and features lost to the haze.

I headed down the stairs and strode toward the bus stop that would take me nearer the river and my favorite coffee shop, Get Mugged. After a morning like this, I wanted some real coffee, good coffee, dark coffee. Then I'd start looking around for Pike. I made it all the way to the curb before a man stepped up behind me.

"Allie."

The scent of hickory overtones and soap—not French cologne, just plain soap—rolled on the wind to me, and

I knew who it was without even turning. Perfect timing.

"Morning, Pike," I said. "Want coffee?"

Martin Pike and the guy with him stepped up beside me, and we all crossed the street together. Pike was shorter than me by at least six inches. His gray hair was shaved down to a tight buzz, and the lines etched at his eyes, cheeks, and forehead mapped all the wars he'd served in. Former Marine, I'd always assumed, and a damn good Hound who did a lot of work for the police.

The other man I'd never met. He had a head of black hair and had a pencil-thin mustache beneath a nose that had been broken more than once. He was younger and slighter than Pike, and wore a jacket that reminded me of the gangs out on the east side of town.

"No, thanks," Pike said, his words carrying a hint of the South, where I thought he'd grown up. "This is Anthony Bell, Hound."

"Hey," Anthony said around a piece of gum.

I nodded. He smelled like sweet cherries—which meant blood magic and drugs. For the split second he managed to hold eye contact, I noted his pupils were pinpricks. Raging high.

That was the easiest way to spot a Hound. Nine times out of ten, a Hound was whacked out on painkillers, booze, drugs. Anything to cut the pain of using magic for a living.

"So how's your granddaughter?" I asked Pike.

"She's dead."

I stopped. Turned. Pike stopped too and faced me. Anthony got one step farther down the sidewalk and then glared at us. He shifted from foot to foot like holding still hurt. He swore and then shrugged the hood on his light gray jacket farther over his eyes.

"She committed suicide," Pike said. "Couldn't handle life after . . . that." His voice was emotionless, but his eyes narrowed in anger or grief—it was hard to tell with him. Pike never let much show. And even though I thought he was a good Hound, there were moments—moments like this—when I wondered if he Hounded for the money or for the killing thrill of the hunt.

I swallowed against a knot of nausea. She had been so young. Strong. I thought she had a chance. People can shake blood magic addiction. People can pull themselves up from abuse. But Lon Trager had done more than abuse her. She'd been tortured. Raped. Broken.

"I'm sorry, Pike." Then I did something Hounds don't do. I reached over and touched his hand. Physical contact meant leaving some of your scent on someone else. Not a desirable thing if you didn't want to get tracked down via the people you'd been around. Like I said, Hounds have a fierce need to keep their scents to themselves.

He nodded and pulled his hand away. But not before I noticed gauze wrapped around the edge of his wrist. Not before I smelled the slight tang of his blood.

I tipped my head toward his hand. "What's that all about?"

Anthony stopped pacing and looked over at us, suddenly interested in our conversation.

"It's nothing," Pike said.

And that was a lie. Okay, fine. He didn't want to

talk about his wounds. I didn't want to talk about mine yet either.

He said, "Lon Trager is out of jail."

"I know." It was still raining, and the wind was blowing so hard, I had to correct my stance every time it let up. Still, my face flushed with heat. Nausea pushed up the back of my throat and burned. "Thirty years, Pike. Trager got thirty."

"That's not the way the courts see it," Pike said. "Mistrial. Contamination of evidence. He's out, Allie. And he's going to be looking for you."

"About that . . ." I began.

Anthony homed in closer to us and stood there, staring at me, smiling now, and chewing something that was not gum. "You're gonna be one popular lady, eh?" he said. "All his people, they're gonna be asking around about you, looking for you. Real popular. Until he finds you." He laughed. "Ain't nobody gonna want you after he gets done with you."

Pike threw him a hard look.

I glared at Anthony, who, I decided, was a prick.

"Can you and I talk alone?" I asked Pike. "Somewhere indoors?" I was freezing cold again.

"We could," Pike ventured. "But this has been on the news. In the papers. I know you don't keep up with those things, so I thought I'd find you. Don't know what else we'd need to say."

"Can't handle the real world, can you, rich girl?" Anthony said. "And now you don't got no rich daddy looking after you no more. Keeping you safe from dirt under your nails. Dirt like Trager."

"Shut up, Ant," Pike growled.

Anthony kept chewing, kept smiling, but his eyes

narrowed. "Why? Rich girl ain't never been one of us. She too good for that, right, Beckstrom?"

"I said shut up," Pike said.

So, that quiet killing vibe Pike gave off? Right there, hot and dangerous between him and Anthony. Anthony was either too stupid or too wasted to notice it.

I resisted the desire to back up a step while they squared off. If I had to bet, I'd say Pike was going to come out on top and beat the living crap out of the kid, but Anthony had that drugged edge of crazy going for him that said he wasn't going to feel the pain of a fight until days later.

"Side with the rich girl, white girl, gonna jump her bones, old man?" Anthony said. "Fuck her. Get a piece of rich bitch, daddy's money, and never have to work again?"

Pike, who I thought was going to punch the kid, instead pulled back. He turned his shoulder toward him, dismissing him with body language as clearly as a fist in the face. He shook his head slowly. "That's the blow talking, boy. If you're gonna be a dumb ass, get out of my face and go home."

Anthony bared his teeth. "You afraid? Think you can take me? You don't know what I can *do* to you, old man. You don't know me at all."

"You're making me wish that was true," Pike said. "Go home to your mama. Tell her I won't teach a boy who doesn't have the brains to keep his nose clean."

Anthony's face burned a dark red, and he clenched his hands into fists. "Fuck you." He growled. "I didn't fucking ask for your fucking help." He spun and stormed off.

"When you get your head on straight," Pike called out over the wind and rain, "you know where to find me."

Anthony punched both fists in the air and flipped him off. But like a dog on a chain, he did not go far. He stopped just a couple yards away, jerked as if he knew better than to walk any farther, and began pacing. If his ears were good enough for Hounding, he was still well within hearing range no matter how quietly I spoke.

I didn't want to talk about Trager in front of the kid. He might be a prick, but there was no need to get him mixed up in this.

Pike started walking again, slowly enough that I caught on he was waiting for me to follow. I strolled along beside him, both of us passing Anthony, who trailed behind us a couple yards back. We walked beneath the awnings of buildings as much as we could. Shield spells—the kind of thing that would keep you dry even without stretching an awning over the sidewalk—were not used here. I guess they figured it wasn't worth the Proxy price. Oregonians were used to the wet, and since these buildings were mostly offices, not shops, old-fashioned umbrellas or hats just had to do.

"Get Mugged?" Pike asked, as though nothing had happened.

I nodded. We were headed that way, toward the bus stop a few streets down. "So," I said after we'd been walking awhile, "I see you've been making new friends."

He chuckled, a short, low sound. "Took him on for a friend on the east side. His mama thought I could keep him off the streets and out of the gangs long enough so he could finish school. She wanted me to teach him to Hound." He glanced over at me, shook his head, and then looked back at the rain coming down so hard, I was pretty sure I'd have to wring out my underwear by the time we made it to the coffee shop.

"I told her I'd do what I could," he said.

"I don't think he likes you very much."

"I don't give a crap if he likes me or not. He'd make a decent Hound if he'd stay clean. He's got a hell of a knack. But I don't see that happening any-time soon. Ought to just haul his ass into juvenile detention. Let them take a whack at that thick skull of his."

"How old is he?"

"Fifteen."

"Damn." I tucked my hands in my pockets. "Maybe juvie isn't a bad idea."

Pike sniffed. "We'll see if he can pull it together. Then. Maybe."

"So, other than telling me that Lon Trager is out of jail, why are you following me?"

He was a step or so ahead of me, so he gave me a curious, sideways look.

"For the police?" I asked. "Did they hire you to follow me?"

"Not doing much Hounding lately," he said. "Think-ing about retirement. Twenty-five years is about enough pain for me."

I never thought I'd hear Pike say that. He was the toughest Hound I knew—not that I knew a lot of Hounds. He'd not only been chasing down magical signatures for at least twenty years; he was one of the original Hounds to hire out almost exclusively with the police. I guess I'd always looked up to him for that and figured he was going to Hound until he was old and gray.

Well, older and grayer.

I wondered if he'd ever hounded for Stotts. Since he was still alive, I guessed the answer to that was no.

"Hate to see you call it quits."

He looked a question at me.

I shrugged. "It's like seeing a legend end."

He chuckled again. "Well this *legend*'s thinking about warm beaches where pretty women wear more flowers than clothes."

"You? Warm beaches?"

"Don't think I'd do it?"

"Oh, I think you would," I said. "But you'd get bored, and you'd be back."

He stopped beneath the end of an awning. There weren't very many people on the sidewalks—too early, too cold, too windy, too wet. The light was red anyway, so we stayed there.

Pike watched the traffic crawl past. "Every legend has an end, Allie. And a beginning."

"How very poetic of you," I noted.

He scowled and fished a card out of his pocket. "Here." He handed it to me. "I want you to join."

I pulled the card close to try to keep it dry and read the plain white letters set against the black background. "The Pack?"

"Call the number and they'll let you know where we're meeting next. We move around."

"Who's *we*, Pike? You and Anthony? What's the Pack?"

"Hounds. Those who work with the police, and those who work against them, and any others who will join. Not all of them are as stupid as Ant."

I heard Anthony mutter, "Fuck you."

My ears were good too.

"You put together a support group for Hounds?" I asked. "That's just . . . that's just so . . ."

"Allie . . ." he warned.

". . . sweet." I grinned.

He gave me a level stare and I was glad he didn't have a gun in his hand, and that he and I were, if not on the same side, not on opposing sides.

"Things are changing in this city, with magic. With everything," he said. "We either watch each other's backs, or we'll be used up—used against each other. Dead. If you're on our side, call and come to a meeting."

"And what if I don't want to be on any side? I like being on my side—alone."

"Then don't come." The way he said it, he made it sound like a threat.

"Nice. So I don't come," I said, dead serious myself now, "what will you do? Hunt me down?"

"I won't have to." He held my gaze long enough that I knew what he meant. Someone else would find me, like Lon Trager's men, or maybe I'd just bite it working for the cursed Detective Stotts. Hounding alone meant I'd end up dead eventually, maybe even anonymously, like the sixteen I hadn't even known had died in the last six years. And even though I liked the idea of living on my own, having my own independence, and not being held responsible to anyone, the idea of dying alone, with no one to even know I was gone or how I'd died, made my chest hurt.

He was right. Things were changing in the city. The strange tension of something—a fight, a fire, a storm, something—hung heavy on the air. I had felt it after I saw my dad's ghost, I had felt it at the police station, and I felt it now.

I leaned in and whispered, "I need to talk to you alone, Pike. It's about Trager."

He didn't show any change of emotion. Just nodded. "Come to the meeting, and we'll talk."

"How about I skip the meeting and we talk anyway?"

"Nope."

I rubbed at my face. I didn't care what he said. Nothing could convince me meeting up with a bunch of Hounds would make my life any kind of easy.

"Have you ever seen a ghost?" I asked.

Pike's eyes widened. I was pretty sure this was the first time I'd ever seen him surprised. "Don't believe in them," he said, dead flat and poker-faced.

"That's not what I asked."

He looked down at his shoe, his body language turning inward, as if trying to dodge an old pain. When he straightened and squared his shoulders, he was nothing but steel cold killer again. "Can't live as long as I have without seeing things."

"Like ghosts?"

"You want to talk, call the number and come to the meeting."

"Oh, come on," I said. "When did you give up on talking straight?"

The light changed; traffic stopped. My bus had pulled up on the other side of the street. Passengers were getting on. I really wanted some coffee and a chance at being warm and out of the wet. I took a step, but Pike did not follow. I glanced over at him. He had already turned and was walking away, back the way we'd come.

"What? You giving up on coffee too?" I yelled.

"Call the damn number," he yelled back without turning.

I shook my head and then jogged across the street before the light changed again. I didn't care how many times he ordered me to do something. I wasn't going to join his little club.

I got to the other side of the street but not soon enough. My bus pulled away from the curb, gunned the engine, and rolled through the yellow light, leaving me behind.

"Damn it!"

And all I heard was Anthony's shrill laughter.

Chapter Five

Okay, so far today I'd been haunted, stabbed, strong-armed by an ex-con, interrogated by the police, hired by a cursed criminal-magic-enforcement guy, and threatened and/or invited by a Hound to join a secret union/army/tea party/club thing.

And I'd missed my bus.

I hated missing my bus. That, most of all, officially put me in a pissy mood.

I shoved my hands in my pockets and strode off toward Get Mugged. The coffee shop was maybe eight blocks away. Against the wind, of course.

I kept a steady pace, not worrying about getting there fast—it didn't matter now because I couldn't get any wetter—but instead working on getting there in one piece. I watched the people moving around me, looking for Trager's men; breathed through my nose, smelling for Trager's men; used all my nonmagical observation skills to stay aware of Trager's men. But seriously? Trager's men could be anyone, anywhere.

The few other people tromping through the crappy weather didn't make any strange moves. No one paid any attention to me. No one even made eye contact. My teeth started chattering, so I picked up the pace, hoping faster would make for warmer.

By the time I'd made it to Get Mugged's cross street, I was wetter and warmer, which is not as sexy as it sounds.

I turned down the street and spotted the roofline of Get Mugged. The neighborhood had gone through some heavy reconstruction. Buildings had been torn down, leaving behind dirt, concrete, and gravel. There were two buildings left standing: Get Mugged and an empty warehouse with boarded-up windows.

Get Mugged held down the corner of the block, a coffee-scented old broad wearing too much paint and plaster to cover her age but still turning over clients like a dime-store hooker. The warehouse looked like Get Mugged's meth-mouthed sister, broken, rotting from the inside out, spongy, and frail.

For years, people had wanted to turn this area into boutique shopping. A building would go up, something would move in, and before there was time to hang curtains, the business would bankrupt. Enough of that had left the whole block looking a little like an unmade bed. Nothing seemed to survive here for long. Except Get Mugged.

I jogged across the street and walked beside the empty gravel lot, heading toward Get Mugged on the far corner. On this side of the street there were no awnings to keep me dry and no buildings to block the wind coming up off of the Willamette River. I was tired, and the cold, wet, and weirdness was catching up with my lack of stamina.

Neat.

A flash of color caught my eye.

One windowless wall of the empty warehouse faced the gravel lot. Magic glyphs I'd never noticed before were painted across that wall, running from the second story's rusted gutters to disappear somewhere behind the piles of dirt at the foundation.

I slowed. The glyphs were strange, bright whorls of color ribboning from one spell into the next. I couldn't read them, not exactly, which was a little weird. It was like there was too much rain between me and the wall, even though I was only about half a block away from it. The glyphs looked washed out, faded. The bricks cut ridges through them like ribs stretched beneath pale skin.

My gut told me they were protection spells, warnings of some kind. I blinked, wiped rain out of my eyes, and squinted to see them better. No, not exactly wards and warnings. The glyphs were a study in opposites. Several glyphs for Healing and Thrive and Life were painted on the wall. But what caught my eye was the glyph repeatedly drawn around all the others.

Death.

Over and over again.

Death by magic. A glyph and spell no one ever drew, and never cast, since the price for casting it was death not only to the target but also to the caster.

Sure, you could trace it out, but if you so much as flicked a speck of magic on it, Death would ricochet back on you so fast you wouldn't even have a chance to swear before you were done breathing. I can't believe someone hadn't complained about the glyph on the wall, hadn't demanded the city or the property owner take it apart, paint over it.

That glyph was bad luck. Dangerous.

To say the least.

But as I came closer to the wall, I realized why the glyphs looked so strange.

They were in the style of my dad's signature. All of them. The Healing and positive glyphs and even the Death glyph were written in his hand. Written by him.

And just as my brain did a nice double somersault to try to wrap some logic around all this—that somehow my stern, corporate father had become a graffiti artist in his spare time four months ago when he was still alive—the glyphs were gone.

Gone. As in one blink they were there—pale watercolored lines of spells two stories tall, with no magic behind them—and the next blink, nothing but brick wall and rusted gutters.

Holy shit.

A chill dug nails under my skin as I realized there wasn't even a hint of color on that wall. I am not stupid. Slow, sometimes, but not a complete idiot. Something really weird had just happened.

I scanned the empty lot, looked behind me at the sidewalk, the street, and the buildings beyond. A few people moved through the rain, but except for a steady stream of cars on the street, I was alone out here. I inhaled deeply, my mouth open, to try to smell if someone were near enough to cast magic—Illusion, maybe—to make me think I saw those glyphs.

Nothing but the stink of the city and the sour bite of my own sweat and fear.

I walked the rest of the way to the wall, smelling, tasting the air. The wall looked like an old brick wall of an old brick warehouse.

Nothing, the world around me seemed to be saying, had happened.

But I knew better.

I stopped close enough that I could touch the wall if I wanted to. I didn't want to. Not yet.

Then I did something I do not love doing: I cast magic in public. Now that I carry magic in me, it takes a lot of concentration not to let it get out of hand. And I hate the idea of someone sneaking up on me while I'm in the middle of a spell. What if I lost control and hurt them? Casting magic also points me out to every other Hound in the city. To a Hound, cast magic is as clear as if the user ran around with a paintbrush and wrote: *Allie Beckstrom was here at seven o'clock in the morning, freezing cold and freaked out, so she decided to cast a Sight spell.*

Of course there was the whole angry ex-con thing that made me a little hesitant to put all my attention and concentration into casting a spell too.

But for this, to Hound my father's signature, it was worth the risk. I whispered a mantra, just a little child-hood jingle to settle my mind—*Miss Mary Mack, Mack, Mack, all dressed in black, black, black*—and set a Disbursement for the price of using magic. A head cold—maybe a headache—would hit me in a couple hours. I was starting small, with a little spell to pull a little magic into my sight, so I could see glyphs my father had drawn on the wall, or see the jerk who thought throwing an Illusion in my face would be funny.

I traced the glyph of Sight in the air with the fingers of my right hand. A few months ago, I would have been very conscious of tapping into the stream of magic that pooled naturally beneath the city, or the stored magic held in the special network of heavily glyphed lead and glass conduits that ran beneath the sidewalks and in and over the buildings.

But now I had all the magic I needed inside me, constantly replenished from the stores beneath the city. I was a sponge and magic filled me.

Handy, that.

Magic flowed warm and thick down my neck, pouring like heated oil over the curve of my breast and down the length of my right arm to settle hot against my palm. I traced the final lines on the glyph for Sight and pushed magic out of my fingertips into the spell.

Like pulling a blindfold from my eyes, the world was suddenly too bright and too clear.

Vivid lines of color shot through the air, draped like lace shrouds over buildings, flickering at the corners of streets, clinging to people who moved in the distance. Magic was everywhere in the city. From spells for bad breath to intricate and subtle Influences luring consumers into shops, glyphs of individual spells lingered in the air, crouched on the soil, and stuck to the glass, steel, and stone of the city.

This was what I imagined it would be like to see on a more microscopic level—to see the germs that lingered long after a hand had touched a surface, long after a kiss, an exhale.

I scanned the empty lot, looking for a spell big enough to pull off the graffiti trick. A few faint, old spells lay on the ground, mostly protections to let the owner know if someone was messing with the chain-link fence. All of those were used up, and useless as tissue paper in the rain.

There was no sign of foolery. That worried me.

I looked at the brick wall, where magic had just a moment ago dripped in pale, chalky warnings. Warnings of death. Brick, just brick. There was no sign of magic being cast—no sign of my father's signature.

I leaned closer and inhaled, scenting rain, cold and clean, and the sharp counterpoint of dirt and mold. I could taste gasoline, the soap from the dry cleaners down the street, and the bitter hint of coffee that had roasted hours ago.

I traced a glyph for Smell and poured magic into it. I leaned in closer to the wall, close enough that I could press my palm against it without straightening my arm. Close enough my lips almost brushed the rough brick. Closed my eyes and inhaled again.

Just the faintest sour scent of leather flavored my tongue, but it was there—the smell of leather and wintergreen. My father's scents.

I opened my eyes and backed the hells away from the wall. I was breathing heavily, sweating despite the rain. And as I stood there with Sight still covering my eyes, I realized everything—the wall, the street, the city—had fallen beneath a fog of pale watercolors.

Ghostly images of people, who I knew had not been standing on the street a second ago, appeared.

Holy shit. This was not a good time to be hallucinating.

None of the watercolor people seemed particularly aware of me or of the traffic that moved by. Some seemed more solid than others, and they were interacting—talking, strolling, holding objects in their hands I couldn't quite make out. Some were only the faintest blur of movement at the corner of my eye. Others moved so near me, I could count the buttons on their shirts.

And all of them smelled like death—rank, fetid flesh.

Okay, this was scaring me now.

I blinked hard, but the watercolor people did not go away. Clarity. I could cast a spell of Clarity to strip the street of illusions.

I muttered a Diversion and pulled on magic.

All the watercolor people stopped. All the watercolor people looked at me with black, soulless, hungry eyes. All the watercolor people could see me. Then they started toward me slowly, as if they were moving underwater.

Oh, hells, oh, hells. Magic leaped readily to me— too quickly, too much, a flare of heat burning up my arm. I suddenly found myself working hard *not* to use magic, lest I burn up.

Calm, calm. I am a river. It wasn't working, because, hey, magic won't do what you want it to do if you're freaking out. Magic flushed through me, too hot up my right side, too damn cold down my left. Still, the watercolor people drew near.

I looked for my father among them—hells, I expected him to be leading the march. But I did not see him, did not recognize any of these people/ghosts/illusions/whatever they were.

And then it wasn't a march anymore. As if broken from a chain, the watercolor people sped forward, fast, faster than anything human, a blur of transparent colors anchored by bright, hollow eyes that were too far away and suddenly way too damn close.

I tried to yell, but they were on me. Hands grabbed

and stroked, dug into my skin, and pulled misty tendrils of magic out of me. They stuffed fistfuls of magic
into their mouths, moaned, and slapped at me for more.

Everywhere they touched, magic rose and broke
through my skin, like blood gushing free into their
hands. I swayed, dizzy from the loss of magic, and
pushed at their hands while I stumbled backward.

I yelled. The watercolor people followed me back
until I was flat against the chain-link fence. Ghostly
hands dug deeper for magic, burning down to my bones.

Then I did what I usually do in tight situations. I
got angry.

No more Mr. Nice Girl. I had magic—magic they
were pulling out of me, magic they were feeding on—
and I was not about to be anyone's all-you-can-eat
buffet.

I let go of the magic bolstering my sight and smell,
ending that flow of magic so I could recast something
to protect myself. I needed to pull magic into a new
spell, something that could kick watercolor ass—what
the hells *could* kick watercolor ass? A mop? A hose?
But as soon as I let go of magic, before I even started
to trace a new glyph, the world snapped back into
place.

The real world was the real world again. The watercolor people were gone.

"Allie?"

I traced a Hold glyph so fast, it was cocked and
ready to fire before my heart had a chance to slam
one more beat against my chest.

I didn't pour magic into it.

Good thing too. Grant, the owner of Get Mugged,
stood outside the door of the coffee shop in a T-shirt

and flannel shirt, cowboy boots, and dark jeans tight enough to show he had bragging rights.

The only thing he was doing was getting rained on and looking worried.

I didn't blame him. I'd be worried if a wild-eyed woman were pointing a Hold spell big enough to stop a rhino in midcharge at me too.

He slowly raised his hands to about chest high, while I stood there breathing hard, and blinking harder, and trying to think straighter.

"Easy, now. Are you okay? Are you hurt?"

What I had seen—the glyphs and the watercolor people—was not here. Or at least they were not here anymore. I sniffed and couldn't smell death. Couldn't smell the leather and wintergreen of my dad, couldn't smell anything except the city, coffee, and Grant's cologne that hinted at vanilla and something deeper, like bourbon and sex.

Grant didn't do anything else, didn't move any closer.

I pushed off the chain-link fence and was happy that my legs held me. I ached in my joints, ached where Trager had stuck a needle in my thigh, and my skin felt tight and sunburned.

"You're shaking," he said. "How about a cup of coffee to warm you up? Come on inside. It will be okay."

I lowered my hand, breaking the Hold glyph as I did so. Magic seemed a little dimmer in me, a little smaller. And my heart was still pumping too hard, like I'd been running or had just come out of a fight.

No surprise there.

But other than that, everything was fine. Normal. Fine. I was fine. Normal. Fine.

Oh, who was I kidding?

"I've had a really bad morning," I said, my voice catching at the end.

Grant nodded, like maybe he already had that figured out. He strolled over to me, all sweet and brotherly—if I had a brother who was a hot-looking cowboy coffee roaster—and put one large, warm, coffee-scented hand on my shoulder. "Let's get you inside. You can tell me all about it."

When all I did was stand there and shake, he slid over next to me and rested his arm across my shoulders. Then he gently propelled me forward toward the doors of Get Mugged.

Chapter Six

The smell of hot coffee and baked scones wrapped around me like a hug as we walked into Get Mugged. Grant's employee, Jula, was behind the counter, moving scones out of the oven and into the glass case below the counter.

There were about a dozen people seated at the mismatched wood tables and chairs, reading papers, their laptops, phones, handhelds. Get Mugged was bigger than it looked from the outside, and open up to the second-floor ceiling, with an overlooking loft at the back half of the shop. Ceiling-to-floor windows and strings of track lighting on the pipes across the rafters lit up the place, while the brick and wood walls made that light feel warm.

"Hey, Jula," Grant called out. "Get me a Shot in the Dark, would ya? And a towel?"

She looked up, the piercing in her eyebrow flashing blue and then pink as she looked from Grant to me. "Oh. Sure." She put down the tray of scones and reached for a big mug from the shelf behind her.

Grant, his arm still over my shoulder, steered me

farther into the shop, back to a table nestled against a narrow window on the other side of the counter. It was far away from the door and out of sight from most of the people in the shop but close enough to the counter that Grant or Jula could keep an eye on whoever sat there.

I had the distinct impression Grant didn't think I was doing so hot.

"Here now," he said. "Best seat in the house."

"Thanks," I said. "I'm okay." The heat of the place was working wonders for me, easing some of the ache. Even the intense sunburn sting from the watercolor people touching me was fading some. I was soaked through my coat, but still cold enough that I didn't want to take it off. Once I got home I really would have to wring out my underwear.

I tugged my hat off and ran my gloved fingers through my hair. Another good thing about short hair is it handles the wet pretty well. I tucked it back behind my left ear, but kept it loose on the right so it would swing forward and cover the whorls of colors that licked beneath my jaw and up to the corner of my right eye. I was feeling a little touchy about the whole marked-by-magic thing at the moment.

Grant sat across the small table from me.

"Rough morning, huh?" he asked.

"I've had better," I said.

Jula stopped by the table. "Here you go." She placed a mug of coffee and a plate with a hot scone in front of me. "The towel?" she asked.

Grant pointed to me.

She handed me the towel. "Anything else I can get you?"

"No," I said. "Thanks."

She looked over at Grant again. He was leaning back in his chair, his own short hair wet enough that it looked as black as mine instead of the light brown I knew it was. Drips of rain caught on the edge of his spiky bangs and ran a wet line down his temple and jaw. Grant had dark, dark blue eyes and that sort of rough and ready look that always made me imagine him in a cowboy hat.

Even though all I wanted to do was dive into that cup of coffee, I took the towel, pulled off my gloves, and inspected my hands. Black bands on all my left knuckles, whorls of metallic colors over every inch of my right hand. The black bands looked a little swollen, like they were bruising beneath, and the whorls of colors were darker than normal, dull, like someone had sanded the metallic shine off of them.

Or several someones.

I dried my hands carefully, though they weren't really hurting. The ache and sunburn had faded fast, leaving me cold. Just cold. And wet. I wiped my face. The towel was white, soft, and smelled of lemon dish soap.

"Thanks," I said again, lifting the towel a little before handing it to Grant. He rubbed it over his face, wadded it up, and put it on the table.

"You had me worried."

"Sorry."

"Want to talk about it?"

Oh, I so did not. I didn't like telling people I was going crazy.

"That's really nice. But trust me, you don't want to get involved in my troubles."

"I don't know. Everyone needs a little trouble now and then. Keeps things spicy."

"Running the coffee shop isn't spicy enough?"

He shrugged. "Business is business. But I want my friends to know I'll do what I can to help. Be there if they need me."

I shook my head but smiled despite myself. I'd been coming to Get Mugged for years, and I didn't know Grant considered our casual morning talks the basis for a friendship.

"Friends?" I asked.

"Anyone who gives me tickets to the Schnitz for my birthday two years in a row is officially my friend."

"I did that?"

Grant gave me a funny look. I knew that look—it happened when I had forgotten something in my past but the person I was with had not. Fantastic. I'd not only forgotten I was friends with Grant, but had also forgotten I'd given him tickets to the opera.

"You sure you're feeling okay?" he asked.

I rubbed at my eyes. "Sorry, Grant. Things . . . The coma did weird things to my memory. I have a lot more holes. I think I lost your birthday." And damned if that didn't make me feel like a heel.

"Hey, that's okay. I'll remind you. *The Phantom of the Opera*'s coming to town, and I do like me some *Phantom*." He patted the edge of the table and it suddenly felt like we'd just sealed a deal. We were officially still friends.

"So, tell all, girl. What's going on?"

I am not the kind of gal who falls for every nice smile she sees. But Grant's smile was like the shop—

warm, friendly, comfortable. I smiled back, and for the first time in what must be years regretted not putting on at least a little mascara.

Not that it would matter with Grant. Women weren't his thing.

"I just, well, I took a new job—"

"Hounding?"

"Right, for the police, and I guess my mind's on that."

"So, you're not hurt?"

"No."

"Not in trouble— No, let me rephrase that. Don't need me to call the police for you?"

"No."

"And you're feeling a little better now that we got you out of the rain and wind?"

"Uh-huh," I agreed. I took a drink of coffee and closed my eyes as it rolled hot all the way down to my belly. Hot, dark, rich. Heaven.

"Trust me," I said. "After a cup of this, I'll be perfect." I took a bite of scone. "Wait," I said around a mouthful of pumpkin spice goodness. "I'll be perfect after the coffee *and* the scone."

"Good." He straightened and put both his hands on his knees, ready to push up onto his feet. " 'Cause you looked like you'd seen a ghost out there."

I choked on the scone and coughed uncontrollably.

"You okay?"

I nodded and thumped at my chest to try to get the bite of scone either up or down. I picked up my coffee and took a slurp. That got me a burnt tongue and scalded the roof of my mouth, but at least the scone slid down my throat. I coughed a little more and then sneezed.

How graceful was I today?

Grant calmly handed me the towel again, which I used to wipe the tears from the corners of my eyes.

"Maybe I should stop filling those things with gravel," he said.

"What did you say?"

"Gravel. The scone. It's a joke."

"No. You said something about a ghost."

Grant gave me a long look and then leaned his forearms on the table, folding his fingers together. "I said you looked like you'd seen a ghost," he said calmly. "Standing out in the rain all pale and spooked. Why? Did you?"

I didn't want to talk about this. Not to Grant. As far as I knew, he didn't use magic, didn't really understand it, and wouldn't even care if I had seen ghostly glyphs or a whole herd of ghostly people stampeding outside his door.

"Did you see one?" he asked.

"What?"

He wiggled his fingers in the air. "A ghost." Those dark, dark blue eyes still held the echo of his smile, but he was not joking around. It was a serious question.

I took a drink of coffee—a little more carefully this time.

"Get Mugged used to be an old saloon and boardinghouse," Grant said. "It was built over the Shanghai Tunnels—did I ever mention that? Some people—especially people who use magic a lot—see things here. Spirits. I had a local ghost-hunting team come out and check into it a while back. Said there was a lot of activity. Ghosts of the men and women who were knocked out, locked up, killed, or sold onto pirate ships heading to China."

"You had ghost hunters in here?"

"Sure. Why not? You don't believe in ghosts?"

"I just—" I took a breath, exhaled. "I'm surprised you do."

"Well, now that I've shared my secret, it's your turn. Did you see a ghost?"

Hells. Why not?

"Yes."

"Here?"

I took another drink of coffee, which hurt the burnt spots in my mouth. Totally worth it.

"Outside," I said. "It was just for a couple seconds, but there was more than one."

Grant grinned. "I liked the sound of that. Haven't had multiple apparitions before. Were they full body?"

"Excuse me?"

"Did you see them clearly from head to toe?"

The memory of them turning, gazing at me with hungry, empty eyes, moving toward me slowly, too slowly, flashed through my mind.

"Every bit of them. And I don't know what you're so happy about. They scared the hell out of me."

"Haven't seen a full body myself. Always kind of hoped I would. The ghost hunters said they didn't think there was harmful activity here."

"You might want to rethink that," I said. Hells. Who was I to change Grant's mind? If he liked thinking friendly ghosts were Caspering about in his coffee shop, that was cool with me. He could probably capitalize on the haunted thing and bring in the tourists.

And since no one else had seen multiple full-body apparitions (see how quick I pick up on this stuff?), I was beginning to think seeing them—and being touched by them—had more to do with those Death glyphs out on the wall than with Grant's Shanghai victims.

"Oh, now. Don't go holding out on me. I can see it in your eyes. There was more. Spill it, girl."

I took another bite of the scone, which practically melted into sugar and spice in my mouth. "This is really good. Did you change bakeries?"

"It's my own recipe. Less scone. More ghost."

"You made this? I'm impressed. You should open a bakery or a coffee shop or something."

"Allison Beckstrom," he said. "Don't make me sic Jula on you. And don't think she can't take you—she's little, but she's tougher than she looks."

"Listen," I said. "I saw ghosts—a lot of them. And they . . . um . . . touched me. It hurt. Don't. Don't look like that. I'm fine. It was just for a second. Right before you came out. And before that I saw some kind of magic written on the warehouse wall. Glyphs that were for Life and Healing—good glyphs. But around all those was the glyph for Death. When I got closer to the building, they . . ." Telling the truth and watching Grant's expression go from excitement back to worry again was harder than I thought it would be. ". . . they just—"

"Disappeared?"

I nodded.

"And you're sure you're not hurt? I've heard of ghosts leaving marks."

"I think I'm fine."

He stared at me.

"I'll check myself over when I go home. After coffee." I picked up the cup and took another drink.

Grant didn't push me on that, for which I was grateful.

"Life and death, huh?" he asked. "Were they city-cast to keep vandals off the block?"

I blinked. "I don't know." I'd never even thought about that. "Do you know if the city has any standing spells here?"

"I can look into it. The company that owns the lot next to me went bankrupt. I'm thinking about buying it, though I don't know what I'd do with it."

"Open a bakery?" I suggested.

"Like I need two businesses to run."

"You could always rent the place out to the ghost chasers." I popped the last of the scone in my mouth.

Grant's eyes went wide. "That's a fabulous idea."

"Wait—I was joking."

"No. It's good. It's really good. They're looking to move out of their place—too small and not enough . . . you know . . ."

"Decay?"

"History. They were saying they wanted to move closer to the older part of town. This whole block's been trying to go high-end for years." He winced. "It hasn't caught on, which is fine with it me. I like things the way they are."

"And you think bringing in people who run around doing séances is going to bring the property value up?"

"Séances." He shook his head. "You really don't know anything about this, do you? But even if it were séances, do I look like I care?" He grinned and I could tell that no, he most certainly did not.

"Well, good luck with that. If things go well, maybe they can come de-ghost my apartment."

I was joking around.

Grant didn't buy it.

"Why? You seen ghosts there too? Ghost magic?"

"No. Not really. Not like here on the street. It's complicated. And what do you mean ghost magic? There's no such thing."

"Those graffiti things you said you saw, that appeared and disappeared. Ghost magic, right? Talk to me."

I could talk to him about the magic near his place, could talk to him about the ghosts on his street, but telling him about my dad, in my apartment bathroom, touching me when I was naked and alone in the dark . . .

Nope. Wasn't gonna happen. All I wanted to do about that was find some way to scrub the memory of it, and the echo of his touch, out of my brain and off my skin. Too bad magic didn't erase the memories I wanted to get rid of.

"I don't really want to get into it, okay?"

And he must have caught the "please" in my tone because he reached over and patted my hand.

"Does it have something to do with this?" He gently brushed the back of my right hand and the whorls of metallic color that webbed there.

"Maybe."

"That happened when you left town for a while, right? The coma and all?"

I nodded.

"When you feel like talking about whatever happened in your apartment, or anything else, you come back here, okay?"

"If you keep making these scones, I will."

But he wasn't about to be brushed off so easily.

"Allie. Listen to me now. I want you to know you can come here anytime. No questions asked. I have a place you could sleep—alone—if you need it. And I know how to keep my mouth shut about people's . . . business."

"Thank you," I said.

That, Grant accepted. He probably thought it was sincere. He had good instincts.

"Okay, so how about I get you a refill on that coffee?"

"That'd be great."

He gave my hand one last pat and then pushed up on his feet and walked off as the door opened.

I don't usually pay attention to opening doors. Not really. I mean, sure, when I was running for my life I jumped at every creak of door and slide of window. But that was over with now. This was my town. I was safe. Except for the released felon, the cursed cop, and the ghosts, everything was peachy.

Or not.

It wasn't just one person coming through the door; it was a half dozen, split four men, two women. They were all dressed in Sunday morning churchgoing clothes even though it was not Sunday. They all carried that earnest sincerity of those who feel a deep need to spread the Word.

I let out the breath I'd been holding. The last thing I needed to worry about were churchgoing people. They looked around the room as they took off their coats and hung them on the coatrack by the door. They were chatty, smiling, and making the "isn't this nice" noises of people discovering a new pleasant place to hang out.

But another movement caught my eye. A man sitting in the far corner of the building lifted his cup of coffee toward me in a sort of salute. I'd say he was in his mid-fifties, and he was bald except for a ring of hair that may have once been blond and was cut short behind his temples. He wore bifocals and a nice dark brown sweater. He didn't take a drink of his coffee and didn't look away from me. He just sat there and smiled and smiled.

Creepy.

People moved between our line of vision, so I went back to finishing my coffee. Since I'd told Detective Stotts I'd Hound for him tonight, I also needed to score a phone and call Violet to cancel our dinner date. Now that I thought about it, I wondered if Pike could tell me something about those weird glyphs. I still had the card he'd given me for the Pack. He said if I called, they'd tell me when they were meeting next. I pulled my cell out of my pocket, hoping it might have miraculously repaired itself, but no. Still dead. Maybe Grant would let me use the phone here.

A man walked up to my table.

"Good morning," he said as though he knew me and I should be glad to see him.

I looked up. Yep, it was the creepy guy from across the room. Didn't recognize him.

"So good to see you," he said. "My name's Frank. Dr. Frank Gordon. I believe we are neighbors."

"Oh?" I asked.

"Third floor of the Forecastle. I just moved in. I thought I saw you leave the building this morning. You're an early riser, Ms. . . . ."

"Beckstrom," I said. "Allie Beckstrom."

He held out his hand, and I reached over and shook it.

Frank's gaze shifted from my face to my hand. He tipped his head back so he could gaze through the bottom half of his bifocals. His smile went hard, his teeth clenched, and he held his breath. Surprised. Then, quietly, "Remarkable."

Okay, I was done with him staring at my hand like it was fresh meat. I tugged free of his grip.

"A remarkable tattoo, Ms. Beckstrom. Where did you go to find such an . . . unusual design?"

"The country," I said. "It was nice meeting you, Dr. Gordon, but my friend will be here . . ."

"Magic, isn't it? You do know that, don't you? I make it a hobby to study such things." He hadn't moved, hadn't stopped smiling, but everything else about him—the sudden stiffening of body language, the tone of hunger and anger just behind his pleasant words—meant I had a problem on my hands.

Well, not on my hands themselves, though that was also true, what with the marks and all, but the current problem was Dr. Creepy here.

I knew when things were edging toward violence of some sort—physical, magical, verbal. I checked his hands for weapons: a knife, needle, or gun. Nothing. But you didn't need anything more than your fingers and a few well-spoken words to draw on magic.

And magic could do a lot of harm. Trust me on this.

I inhaled to catch his scent—the smell of almonds and sweat with just a hint of licorice—and then I stood because I wasn't about to get into a fight sitting down.

"Hey, Allie," Grant called out, cheerful and loud.

I didn't look over, didn't look away from Dr. Gordon. Dr. Gordon didn't look away from me either.

Grant, however, wasn't caught in the showdown. He strode right over, all casual and cowboy, and leaned his entire body between us while he placed a fresh cup of coffee on the table.

"Here's your refill." He turned and stuck his hand out. "I don't believe we've met." He and Dr. Gordon were close enough, there was no way Dr. Gordon could get out of the handshake. And Grant had wide enough shoulders that he pretty much blocked my view, breaking off our glaring match. "Name's Grant. Grant Rhines. I'm the owner of this coffee shop."

Dr. Gordon had to take a step back to shake Grant's hand. "Pleased to meet you, Mr. Rhines. I'm Dr. Gordon."

Thank you, Grant. I did not want to become someone's pet project. Didn't want the doctor to get some kind of idea that he could take me apart to find out how I could hold magic in my body when no one else could. It was time for me to get out, move on, be done with being here.

"I don't believe I've seen you in my fine establishment before, have I, Doctor?" Grant asked.

"As I was saying to Ms. Beckstrom before you interrupted us, I'm new to the neighborhood." He wasn't even trying to be pleasant anymore. "Now, if you'll excuse us?"

"No," I said. I stepped out from where I was closed off by Grant and stood slightly behind him because there wasn't any more room to go past him unless I forced the issue. "We're done talking. Grant, could I use your phone?"

"Sure thing." He didn't move or look away from Dr. Gordon. "I'll show you where it is. Can I get anything else for you, Doctor?" he asked.

Dr. Gordon smiled, instantly a mild-mannered nice guy again. And it freaked me the hells out that he could do that—look so completely harmless in the blink of an eye.

"Oh, I don't think so, Mr. Rhines. You've done enough. Thanks for the offer." He stepped aside and glanced at me. "I'll see you soon, Ms. Beckstrom. Have a nice day." He turned and ambled over to the door. He paused and pulled a heavy coat and umbrella off the rack. Grant and I stood there, watching him until he was out the door and onto the street.

"Great guy. You really know how to pick 'em, don't you?" he said.

"Like you wouldn't believe," I said. "Can I really use your phone?"

"Sure, sure." Grant strolled even farther to the back of the shop, and I followed him through a door to the left. He pulled out a set of keys, unlocked the door, and pushed it open. Beyond the door were nice, carpeted stairs going down.

"A dungeon?"

"I did mention the Shanghai Tunnels, right?" He moved past me and started down the stairs. "Just give that door a good tug behind you. Wouldn't want a customer tripping down here."

I hesitated. I mean, how well did I really know Grant? All I had to go on was his word. The whole birthday thing could be a lie.

"Mind if I leave it open?" I asked.

"That's fine. I'll be back up in a sec." He had turned

the corner, out of eyesight from the top of the stairs. "Phone's here on the table. Allie?"

I took a deep breath. Hounds are not trusting people. But Grant had given me more than his word. He'd gone out of his way to run interference with Dr. Nosy up there. And besides, we were friends. I think. I shut the door and clomped down the stairs. "I'm leaving wet footprints on your carpet," I said. Then, "Wow."

The room opened up at the bottom of the stairs and was most definitely not a dungeon. A full apartment, it was nicely furnished in leather and linens, with accents of deep blues and greens and lights set along the walls and ceilings in just the right way to make it feel airy and spacious instead of like the brick basement it was.

"You decorate this yourself?" I asked.

"Mostly. Had some help from a friend or two. Do you like it?"

"It's fantastic." I meant that.

"Thanks," Grant said. "The phone." He gestured to an old-fashioned standing candlestick phone with a rotary dial.

"Serious?"

"Authentic. Works too."

I walked across thick carpet to the phone table next to a very comfortable-looking easy chair.

"Take your time. I'll be right back." He headed up the stairs, leaving me to make my call.

I dug in my coat pocket and pulled out my blank book and thumbed through it until I found Violet's number. I dialed the number and got her on the second ring.

"Beckstrom speaking," she said.

Strange to hear my father's name, my name, from

her lips. I wondered if I'd ever gotten used to that before, when I had known her, before I had forgotten her.

"Hi, Violet, this is Allie."

"Allie. Is everything okay?"

Note to self: start living the kind of life that would make that question no longer the first thing everyone thought to ask me.

"Fine. Except I need to cancel our dinner appointment."

"That's too bad. I was looking forward to it."

"Yes, well, I got a Hounding job that needs to be done tonight before the spell fades. Maybe breakfast?" I offered.

Violet hesitated. "I think I could do breakfast. What time?"

"Eight?"

"Eight should work," she said. "How about Kickin' Cakes?"

"I'll be there."

"Perfect," she said. "And, Allie?"

"Yes?"

"Be careful."

Note to self number two: start living the kind of life where people weren't always ending their conversations with me like that.

"Sure thing," I said.

I hung up the phone and dug in my pocket for the card Pike had given me.

I dialed the number. I was about to hang up on the fifth ring when a man's sleepy voice answered. " 'Lo?"

"I'm looking for the Pack?"

"Found it." He yawned loudly and I heard rustling,

like blankets being swept aside, and the wind-chime clink of a couple of beer bottles thunking onto carpet.

"Pike told me to call for the next meeting time."

"Yeah?" he said.

"Yes."

There was a long pause.

"Listen, if there's a secret password or something, he didn't tell me what it was," I said.

"Wait," he said. "Who is this again?"

And I thought Pike said not all the Hounds were as dumb as Anthony.

"Forget it."

"It's cool, it's cool," he said. "It's just early, right?" More sounds of him grunting as though he'd stood up, and then the plastic-on-tracks rattle of window blinds being pulled aside. "Damn," he said. "Not early. So what was your name?"

"Allie Beckstrom."

"No kidding." He suddenly sounded much more awake. And happy. That made me suspicious. "Nice to finally hear from you, Allie Beckstrom. Meeting's at noon at Ankeny and Second. You know where that is, right?"

"I'll manage," I drawled.

He laughed, and it sounded like a dog's bark. "Right. You got this town down, dontcha? Okay. Lower level. Today. Noon."

"Is there a room number?"

"You'll find us."

And then he hung up on me. Hung up. Fab.

I hooked the ear piece on the receiver and stood there in Grant's apartment, feeling a little less lost. At least I had a plan for finding out more about ghosts from Pike, and once I talked Pike into going to the police with me, we could take care of Trager too. The muffled thump of footsteps on the floorboards above my head was a comforting sound. Down here, in this place, I was alone, removed from the world. Hidden. Safe.

Safer than I felt in my own apartment. Which was all sorts of wrong that I didn't even know how to begin fixing.

No, that wasn't completely true. I knew why I didn't feel safe at home. My dad. Or rather, my dad's ghost. I rubbed my hands up and down my arms as the memory of being naked and vulnerable while my dad's ghost touched me sent chills down to sour in the pit of my stomach.

I thought about what Grant had said—ghost hunters believed spirits of people who had died traumatic deaths lingered here and that people who used magic were sensitive to them. Maybe I didn't believe in all that stuff, but I could not ignore what I had seen today. My dad's ghost. Glyphs that bore my dad's signature. The empty-eyed watercolor people.

Maybe I was seeing things because I carried magic inside me. Or maybe all the ghost stuff was my subconscious telling me I needed to face my father's death—something I had not done in any physical manner since I'd come back to town. I should just do the one thing I was avoiding and go to my dad's grave, and get it through my head that he was dead and gone.

And not hanging out in my bathroom waiting to ambush me.

I dialed the phone again and called a cab. They said they'd be by in about three minutes.

Just as I hung up, Grant came back down the stairs. "Everything okay?" he asked.

Sweet hells, there was that question again.

"Yes. Thanks. For everything."

"You leaving now?"

"Have an appointment at noon and some other things to do before then." I fished my wet gloves out of my wet pockets and thought briefly about going home first to change into something dry. Since I would be out in the rain anyway, it seemed like a waste of laundry. Hopefully I'd have time to go home and change before the Hound meeting.

"Need a cab?" Grant asked.

"Just called one." I started walking toward the stair.

Grant hitched his thumb in the opposite direction.

"How about I take you out the back way? Quicker than going through the whole shop again." He crossed the living room area, and I got a quick peek at a very nice modern kitchen before he opened a door revealing a freight elevator that had been redone in gaudy Gothic cage work. Not at all what I expected out of mister-casual-cowboy Grant. A set of brick stairs lit from above by the morning light stacked up to the left, wall-hugging sconces of sword ferns placed against both stairwell walls. A nice touch of green so far belowground.

Grant started up the stairs. "You sure you're going to be okay?"

"I am."

We reached street level. No great surprise—it was

raining. I pulled my hat out of my pocket and put it on. I zipped my coat to keep the chill wind at bay. I wondered if we'd have worse winds by tonight, wondered when the storm would blow through.

A black-and-white Radio Cab drove up. I didn't think it was the one I had called, but I waved it to the curb anyway.

"Thanks, Grant. Really."

"Any time." Grant crossed his arms over his chest, hunched against the gusty wind.

I opened the passenger door.

"And, Allie?"

Don't say it. Don't say it.

"Be careful."

Great.

I gave him the best smile I could manage and got in the cab.

"Where to, lady?" the cab driver asked in overpracticed English.

"The Riverloft Cemetery," I said.

It was time to face the one person I'd been avoiding since I got back to town. My father.

Chapter Seven

It was strange, but sitting in the backseat of a taxi that stank of spoiled milk and staring out the rain-splotched window at the wet graves made me more relaxed than I had been in days. Something about the rain softly falling made me think maybe it wasn't going to be so hard to face my dad's death.

"This is it," the cabdriver said.

I glanced up at him, caught his gaze in the rearview mirror.

He quickly looked away.

I didn't know him, or at least I didn't think I did. Losing my memories had really made for some awkward social situations.

But even though I didn't recognize him, he probably knew who I was. Maybe he didn't like the daughter of the recently deceased Daniel Beckstrom in the backseat of his cab. Or maybe he didn't like the marks magic had burned down the side of my face. I didn't think the marks were ugly. But scars, all scars—internal and external—drew attention. And I was trying my best to keep a low profile right now.

I self-consciously pulled my hat down a little tighter on my head, hoping the wool would hide the marks on my temple. Then I dug in my coat pocket for cash. I found a twenty.

"Thanks," I said.

The cabbie glanced in the mirror again and tipped his hand palm up over his shoulder. I pressed the bill into his hand, holding eye contact until he looked away.

Yes, I was petty like that.

I opened the door and stepped out into a world of gray. Icy wind speared down my nose and throat, and I fumbled with my scarf to get it up over the bridge of my nose.

Hells, it was cold out. The temperature had dropped several degrees on the cab ride over here. I wouldn't be surprised if the rain turned into snow. I stuffed my hands in my pockets, hunched my shoulders, and headed toward the open iron gates of the cemetery, the wind pushing and tugging at me.

The graveyard was set on the east side of the Willamette River, on a hill with a good view of the mountain on fair weather days, not that the buried probably cared about what sort of view was available. It was obvious the graveyard was not off-grid since patented iron and glass glyph-worked conduits caged the mausoleum at the top of the hill and allowed access into the magic that pooled so deeply beneath the city. Still, as most graveyards did, it had the feeling of quiet distance from the rush of real life.

Violet had sent me the invitation to my dad's funeral, even though I'd been in a coma at the time. On the back of the invitation was a map to his grave. I'd stared at that for days, and had the image of it burned in my brain. His grave was set to the far right of the cemetery, halfway up the hill and out of the way of foot traffic.

It was so unlike him to want to be tucked away out of sight, out of the attention of the masses. It made me wonder if there were things about my father that I would never really understand. Maybe his brutal business persona was not all the man he was. I hadn't attended his funeral or burial. I hadn't seen his ex-wives do the "grieving widow" show for the press. I hadn't seen Violet, who might be the only woman at his grave who actually cared for him, cry. I hadn't even had a chance to wonder why my own mother, overseas, had refused to attend the service.

I might not have loved my father, but for a long time, I wanted to.

My chest hurt. I swallowed against the tight feeling of tears and sniffed. I was not going to cry over this. Not out here in the cold and wet. There was no way I could change any of my father's choices, and no reason to change mine now. We had lived our lives as well as we could in regard to each other, arguments, hatred, and all. I had to accept that. Dead is dead. And my dad was definitely dead.

The modern flat-faced gravestones punched rectangular indents into the ground in long, orderly rows to both sides of me. The sound of traffic was muted by distance. I trudged along between graves, toward the older part of the cemetery where headstones carved of marble, granite, and metal stood like bittersweet poems against the cold sky.

Somewhere in this world of carved sorrow was my

father's grave. I squinted against the horizon. The graves seemed to reach out for miles, though I knew that wasn't true. Up a little farther rose a thin forest of trees beneath which headstones were planted like stone flowers, melancholy angels resting among them like earthbound birds.

Magic stirred in me, this time gently, stroking beneath my skin with soft, sensual pressure. It offered release, respite, anything I wanted. With little more than a strong thought, the right words, and a gesture or two, I could make magic do anything I desired.

My right arm itched, and I scratched at it—rubbed it really—with my stiff left hand. Magic here pooled deep beneath the ground, much deeper than the graves. Ever since I'd changed, ever since magic had decided to use me as a vessel, an open channel, I felt like the tables had turned.

I didn't struggle to use magic. I struggled not to use it.

And it was possible it was affecting my mind too. Like seeing the watercolor people, the magic on the wall. And my dad's ghost.

I tipped my face to the sky and took several calming, deep breaths as rain flicked wet against my exposed skin.

Magic was not as strong here, despite, or perhaps because of, the graves. But it felt slightly different, old with the scent of heavy minerals, like rich soil. Grave rich. I wondered if using magic left a residual in the flesh. If perhaps, even after we died, the scent of magic lingered within our bones or leaked out of spent flesh to flow back to the natural reservoirs deep in the earth.

I wiped rain off my cheeks and headed toward the trees.

I knew my father's grave before I was near enough to read the headstone. For one thing, the headstone was the tallest and most elaborate thing on this side of the cemetery. But mostly I knew it was his because it resembled a spindly, rune-carved Beckstrom Storm Rod more than a proper monolith. In a way I was relieved. Even in death he had to show the world that he alone had mastered the way to pull magic from the earth and sky. Total ego case, my father. He would be appalled at a humble marker above his head.

However, he might also be disappointed that the Storm Rod headstone was positioned so it was hidden from the majority of the graveyard. Blocking it from the rest of the graveyard was an old bare-leafed oak, trunk black as an artery, roots sunk into the soil, venous limbs spread against the gray flesh of the winter sky.

I tromped around the tree and stood at the foot of my father's grave.

I tried to get it into my head that my dad was dead. Gone. Buried. Murdered. And if it had been his ghost I had seen, his ghost should be here, graveside.

The sound of traffic bled away, the startled call of a crow smothered out beneath the rush of blood in my ears. My breath, my heartbeat were suddenly too loud.

My father was gone.

Really gone.

We hadn't been close—he too distant in his pursuit of wealth and power, me too young and grieving the loss of my mother and absence of him. And with age,

I traded grief for anger. Now that could never be different, could never change between us.

And I didn't even know if I'd lost the small bits of him most people got to keep—memories, maybe memories of us together, maybe memories of the good moments. I searched my thoughts, tried to dredge up images of him smiling, of times we'd spent not angry at each other. But all that came to me was his stern disapproval. If we'd ever been happy or gentle with each other, it was lost to me. And now that he was gone, I'd never have a chance to get those times back or to make new ones.

How could I say good-bye when he never gave me the chance to say hello?

I sniffed even though I couldn't feel my nose, and blinked hard until I could see the grave clearly again. Finally I stepped up next to his grave and knelt.

"Good-bye, Dad." I pressed my palms against his grave, pushing through the scrubby grass to the wet soil.

Magic shifted in me, maybe responding to the connection between my hands and the ground, and I realized I could use it, use a small bit of magic to reach out to my dad one last time and feel the physical presence of his life in this world. I could connect with him before finally and totally letting go of him.

I whispered a mantra and spoke the words of a Disbursement. I'd have a bigger headache later today or tomorrow, but that was okay with me. I traced a glyph for Sight and for Touch. I put only the smallest hint of need behind my action. I still didn't have the best control over all this magic, and I did not want to suddenly find myself feeling as though I were actually in the coffin with him.

A light touch was all I was looking for.

Magic responded with an almost sexual tingle, lifting into my senses, heightening my sight and sense of touch. Faded colors, like Christmas lights through fog, moved at the corners of my vision. I looked around me, looked at the graves. A watercolor haze lay over them like an aura. I expected watercolor people to pop up out of that haze, out of the graves, but nothing. And more important, no *one* moved.

Weird. I mean, if there was ever a place I expected to find a ghost, it would be here, in a cemetery. The hazy, faded colors shifted a little, as if an unseen wind stirred them. But that was all.

Good.

I directed the magic into my hands, into my tactile sense. I felt rather than saw magic wrap around my hands like liquid ribbons of warmth. I sent those ribbons down into the earth where my father's body lay at rest.

Maybe it was a creepy idea. Death makes people do creepy things. But I needed to acknowledge his life one last time. Maybe more than that, I needed to acknowledge the cold, hard reality of his death.

Then hopefully there would be no more of this ghost stuff for me.

I braced for the awareness of his flesh and bone, well on their way to decay and collapse. I braced for the sensation of a once-living man now reduced to an inert lump of tissue. I braced for the feeling of a body completely absent of life, of soul.

What I did not brace for was to feel nothing.

Nothing.

I frowned. I could sense the weight of dirt and stone around the casket. I could sense the casket, made of wood, still strong and whole.

And I could sense the emptiness within it.

There was no body in that casket. No decay. Not even a single bug. Nothing but stale air.

Was this the wrong grave? I glanced at the headstone, read my father's name, his date of birth, date of death. This was the right grave. His grave.

It couldn't be empty.

Wishful thinking? Delusional thinking? I closed my eyes, tipped my head down, and whispered a Seeking spell. My headache would last twice as long now, but I didn't care.

Magic jumped in intensity, spooled out of me, plunging deep into the frozen earth, brushing like hands around the casket. Wood and metal, smooth, whole. I sent it deeper. Soft, cushioned lining, silk casket dressing. I sent it deeper. Stagnant, stale air.

And nothing more. Nothing.

They told me he had not been cremated. They told me it had been an open-casket viewing. People—a lot of people—had seen him dead and had seen him lowered into the grave. This grave.

So where the hells was he?

Dad, I thought. *Is this why you came to me? Were you trying to tell me something about being buried or not being buried?*

"You picked a cold day to say good-bye," a man's voice said from behind me.

I'll admit it—I jumped. I hadn't seen anyone else

in the graveyard, hadn't heard anyone walk through the soggy, noisy grass.

I spun where I crouched and pulled magic up into my fingertips, ready to weave an entirely different kind of spell.

Black ski cap pulled tight over his head only made his golden brown eyes larger and warmer against the darkness of his skin. High-arched cheekbones, strong wide nose, and an undefinable cut to his features made me think Native or Asian flavored his family's blood.

Zayvion Jones, the man I might love.

He wasn't wearing a scarf, just that ratty blue ski jacket zipped up to beneath his jaw, jeans, and sneakers. Against the stark gray of the day, I found myself drawn toward him, toward a forgotten warmth.

I couldn't remember it, but I'd risked my life to save him once. Knocked myself into a coma. Still, emotional echoes of him remained within my subconscious. I remembered him being there when I found out my dad had put a hit on Boy in St. Johns. I remembered him following me to my dad's office the day my dad was killed. And then, all I remembered was finding him a couple weeks ago at a diner and asking him why the hells he'd left me a Dear John note.

We hadn't seen each other since then. I thought he'd givien up on us. Or that maybe there was no "us" to give up on.

Still, those echoes of emotional memory, of what his touch had made me feel like, resonated through me like a deep-tolling bell.

Oh, I had it bad for him once.

Maybe I still did.

"What are you doing here?" I tried to sound annoyed but it came out a little breathless and husky. Hells, I wanted him. Wanted him to touch me. Needed him to touch me. Not just because I was feeling a little alone and a lot spooked right now.

Okay, maybe just because of that.

Zay shrugged. "Lucky coincidence?" he said in that damn voice of his, low and easy, delivered with that damn Zen calm. "I was driving by and saw you get out of the cab. I thought you might need help finding his grave. It's out of the way over here."

I stared at his handsome face and didn't believe a word he was saying. Oh, he may have seen me get out of the cab. Probably because he had been following me. Maybe he'd been following me since I saw him outside the bus this morning. I had a feeling nothing was quite as it seemed with Mr. Jones.

If he'd told me he was stalking me, *that* I might believe.

"Why don't I think anything is a coincidence with you?"

He tipped his head to the side, giving me a nod. "Because you have trust issues."

"I don't think you know me well enough to say things like that."

He pulled his head back as if I'd just slapped him. His breathing changed, and I suddenly realized that Mr. Jones was a very dangerous man beneath that Zen calm.

I stood up, not liking the dynamic of me crouched down with him towering over me. And besides that, magic was pushing in me, filling me again too full, and I was having a hard time keeping control of it.

Even though I am six feet tall, Zayvion still had a couple inches on me. And standing this close to him, I could see he had width too. Though he managed to hide it, he was built like a brick wall under that ski coat—wide shoulders tapering down into a narrow waist, and all that relaxed body language doing little to conceal that that body knew how to fight, and did it often.

"My apologies," he said stiffly. "I see you didn't need help finding it."

I had no idea what we were talking about.

"Your father's grave?" he reminded me.

Right. He was talking about my dad's grave. What I was doing was trying to figure out why he was here, and getting all frickin' dizzy again. Magic was still filling me, filling me too full. I had tapped into it, used it to look for my dad's body, and now I couldn't seem to make it stop filling me up.

This was something I'd been dealing with a lot since I came back to Portland. Keeping a close hold on the magic in my body so it didn't just escape me and do something stupid like burn down a city block was getting to be a real pain.

I was a walking time bomb. But I really was getting good at keeping my finger off the trigger.

Well, except for right now.

Maybe the whole weird morning was starting to catch up with me. Maybe the magic-sucking watercolor people had damaged me in a way I didn't know. Maybe the price for the magic I'd used today was coming due.

Whatever. I felt like hell.

The gray day went dark at the edges, and the ringing in my ears harmonized with the thrum of my blood.

Oh, hells. There was no way I could handle this much magic. Magic pulsed and slid, pulsed and slid, filling me full, too full, too tight.

I held my breath against it, bit the inside of my cheek, and tried to think calm thoughts.

I am a river. Magic pours through me and back into the ground. It does not shape me. I do not shape it.

"Allie?"

What *were* we just talking about? I blinked. It felt like my eyes stayed closed for a long time. When I opened them again, I was on my knees.

Weird.

"Allie?" Zayvion's voice floated down to me from far, far away. "Don't try to stand. Lie back and take slower breaths. It's going to be okay. I got you."

That didn't sound good. Still, I had apparently lost the ability to speak, or breathe out, or really do much else, so Zayvion's suggestions were helpful in their way.

Even more helpful were his hands.

I exhaled as minty heat from his palms soaked through my heavy coat. Mint spread down through me, like water against a fire. The mint calmed the magic pouring through me, blanketed it, pushed it back to my muscles, my bones, and then down deeper—pushed the magic back into the ground from where it came. Zayvion's touch eased the ache of magic, giving me room in my own body to breathe again.

"Excellent," Zayvion said. "Slower breaths. Good."

I did as he told me, let the mint fill me, cool me, stroke soft and sweetly through me, leaving shivers of pleasure across my skin. Sensual. I wondered if he was like this in bed.

Now there was a memory I wished I still had.

"Can you open your eyes?"

I could and I did.

Zayvion's face filled my vision. His eyes were brown and burning with gold I did not remember seeing before. And beyond that, beyond the tiger brightness, was a vast, vast feeling of emptiness, of space. I could suck up all the magic in the world, pour it all out into him, and never be able to fill him up.

Nice.

"I don't know if you remember," he said, "about this. About us. I'm Grounding you, Allie. If you want to help, just clear your mind and think calm thoughts. Meditate."

Right. And after I did that I'd jump up and sing some show tunes.

That also must have shown on my face because Zayvion's lips quirked. "Whatever you're thinking—it's not helping."

Well, it was good to know he couldn't read my mind. I licked my lips, or at least I thought I did. I actually couldn't feel my mouth, couldn't feel my body other than in a distant, half-asleep, still-room-for-breathing sort of way.

That worried me.

But instead of panicking, I took a nice, deep breath and focused on Zayvion's gold, gold eyes.

I am a channel, a river. Magic flows through me but does not fill me, does not change me.

Zayvion could fill me, could change me. And I'd like it. That didn't help clear my mind either, so I went back to the river thing, repeated it to myself until it became a mantra, a meditation. Repeated it until I could feel my body—cold and wet down my back, butt, and legs; warm and dry down my front from Zayvion leaning across me, his wide back sheltering me from the falling rain.

Until I could feel the heat of him more than the heat of magic.

The mint sensation grew stronger, like I'd just been rubbed down with wintergreen leaves. Tingly, cool, and warm everywhere, inside and out.

"Beautiful," Zay said, soft and sexy-like.

I licked my lips and felt them this time. "Thanks."

"Sure." He didn't move. I didn't want him to. He was so close, the overpowering pine scent of his cologne mixed nicely with the smell of winter grass and wet jackets. Even though I probably shouldn't, I liked the combination. I gave myself a heartbeat or two to wonder what his lips would taste like.

Hells.

I kissed him.

I think he was surprised. But it didn't take him long to get over that.

His lips were soft, thick, and gentle. I opened my mouth for him, and he responded, deepening the kiss, making promises, or maybe just suggestions, that I completely agreed with.

I inhaled the heat of him and my body stirred with sensations and memories that had nothing to do with magic.

Zayvion made a needful sound at the back of his throat, and the magic within me rose up, coaxed higher by Zay's mouth on my own, his thumb tracing the whorls of magic that pulsed against my throat.

Wait, I thought. Something. Something wasn't right about this.

Zayvion's mouth moved to the edge of my jaw, and then his lips, soft, warm, opened against my throat as he sucked, nipped.

I moaned. Magic, oily and hot, pulsed through me, rising to Zayvion's tongue that gently stroked across the marks on my neck, easing the edge of my need in only the smallest degree and making me want more.

He knew me. Knew what I wanted.

"I've missed you," he breathed across my skin.

Then the rest of it—the reality of it, of where I was, of whom I was with, and why I was here—hit me.

I was making out with a man I couldn't remember, and wasn't sure I could trust, on my father's grave.

Talk about a mood killer.

"Let me up," I said, my voice a lot stronger than I'd expected. "Up. Now. Off." My voice rose with each word. "Off me. I can't. Not here. With you." I meant to say not on my dad's grave but I didn't get the chance.

Zayvion pulled back, studied my face, those gold eyes dark with hurt or anger—I so wasn't in the mood to suss out the difference. I didn't have to. He rocked back on his heels away from me.

The rush of cool air between us made me gasp so hard, it hurt. He looked away at the horizon, the muscle at his jaw clenched, while I gathered myself until I was sitting and then standing.

He stood too, with the kind of grace that comes from martial arts training. When he finally looked at me again, his face had settled into Zen calm.

"I'm sorry," he said. A shadow of hunger shifted in his eyes, gold, then brown, then was extinguished, leaving his gaze emotionless, flat.

I sniffed and rubbed my gloves over my butt, trying to brush off grass and mud, trying to pull myself together. Why did I feel so guilty?

"I needed the . . . that Grounding. Thank you. Sometimes . . . magic . . . It's not always easy, but usually I'm fine. Today's been"—*horrible*, I wanted to say, but instead I said—"long. So don't apologize for Grounding me."

"I wasn't."

Oh.

That flare of heat and desire flickered in his eyes. He blinked once, slowly, and gave me the Zen calm again.

"Oh," I said. "Good. And you're really good at that. Grounding," I clarified. "Studied much?"

His lips tightened at the corner. For some reason, that question brought him pain. "Yes. But Grounding isn't really my specialty."

"Really? What is?"

He nodded. "I don't think you want to know."

"I wouldn't have asked if I didn't want to know."

Well, could I be more awkward and standoffish? No, I think not. Before things could get worse, I took a deep breath and tried to say something that didn't sound like I was itching for a fight.

"What are you really doing here?" I asked.

"Looking for you. To ask you out. On a date." As he said it, his gaze flicked over my shoulder and rested just a little too long on the horizon.

So I turned and looked back there too. Close to the

mausoleum at the top of the hill, a figure moved, walking among the graves. Heavy knee-length coat, a hat. It didn't look like anyone I knew, but from this distance it was hard to tell.

"Is there a problem?" I asked.

See how I bought myself time to think about the whole date thing?

"Not yet." Zayvion had not moved, had not stopped squinting off into the heavy drizzle. "Maybe not at all." He wiped rain off his face and pulled his beanie closer to his head. "This place always makes me jumpy."

"Always? How often do you come here?"

Zayvion finally looked away from the figure, who had stopped walking between graves and was now standing, just standing there, staring in our general direction.

"I was last here at the burial," he said quietly.

I glanced down at my father's grave. The press of our bodies had left the image of a broken snow angel in the soft grass and soil. A mud angel. Oregon style.

"You saw him lowered down. Down into that?" *Into that empty grave*, I wanted to say, but didn't, couldn't, yet.

He nodded. "Are you done here?" he asked. "If you want to go, I have my car."

He didn't look cold despite the rain. Didn't look like he was in a hurry. Didn't look like he might be trying to avoid answering my questions too.

"Maybe," I said. "Will you tell me about it?"

"About what?"

"Everything."

"Everything might take some time." He tipped his head down a bit, his smile warm. More than warm— it was firelight in the damn cold world, a heat I wished

I could pull deep within me. Maybe I could overlook the darkness of the rest of the day if I could hold on to a little bit of that fire.

"I have some time," I said. "Until noon, anyway. You have somewhere you need to be?"

He held very still, so still I didn't think he was breathing. Finally, "No. Just with you."

And for no reason at all, those words made my stomach flutter, like he'd just drawn his hand down my back and pulled me close. Oh, yeah. There was a reason I'd been attracted to him. Still was. Even in a graveyard, even in a rainstorm, even after a crappy day like today, he knew what to say to make me feel like there was no one else in the world with him but me.

Well, me and the person standing by the gravestones, staring at us.

We walked toward the car, Zayvion crossing behind to position himself on my right and slightly uphill from me. The way someone would position himself if he wanted to put his body between me and, say, that person up there on the horizon.

"How about you start by telling me why you don't want whoever that is up there to see me?"

I could see his smile from the corners of my eyes.

"You're an observant woman, Ms. Beckstrom."

"You have no idea."

I let the sound of our boots in the grass take up some time. Zayvion didn't look worried. I couldn't smell anyone on the wind, couldn't smell much over the strong pine of Zayvion's cologne.

"Might be no one I know," he finally said.

"Or?"

He shrugged again. "Never hurts to be careful. You're a public figure right now."

"I've always been a public figure."

"Not like this," he said softly. "Not like now. People are watching you, Allie. Closely."

Like that was news. It would take more than a vague reference to scare me. Hells, as far as I knew Trager's men waited around every corner and even dead people had suddenly decided to watch my every move.

"I'm just lucky that way. Who do you think is watching me?"

"A lot of people. People in powerful positions."

I usually wouldn't put up with that kind of coy answer. But I had lost weeks to that coma, and a lot of memories. Zayvion had been with me for a lot of what I no longer remembered. He'd been there when I last saw my father. Nola said he'd even been there when I found out my dad was dead and when I'd turned into a living receptacle for magic.

If he had something to say, if he knew something about my life, then I wanted that information.

I could be patient when I had to be.

The raindrops fell, bigger, harder, a cloudburst now instead of a steady drizzle. The wind, which had never really stopped, picked up the pace.

"I'd like to hear more about those people," I said.

"Then it's a date?" he asked.

"It could be."

Zayvion brushed his hand along my bent elbow and guided me forward a little more quickly.

"My car is down by the gate. Let's get out of the rain first."

Out of the rain and out of earshot, or eyesight, of whoever was watching. Without looking over my shoulder, without breaking stride, I strained to hear the sound of footsteps, of movement, of breathing in the graveyard. Strained to hear or sense, without the use of magic, anything or anyone other than Zayvion and me.

"The car's over here." Zayvion pulled his keys out of his pocket and strode off ahead of me.

I glanced over my shoulder at where the figure had been. He—because I decided it looked more like a man than a woman—was still there, leaning against a tall pillar gravestone, black coat, black figure against a dead sky. And I knew, without using magic, that he was looking for me. Maybe even was one of those powerful people Zayvion said was watching me.

See how well I put two and two together?

Zayvion came back to where I stood and touched my arm. "Come on, Allie."

The click and thunk of his car door opening, and the promise of warmth and sanctuary it offered, got me moving. I crawled in and had a moment to worry about ruining the black leather seats, but was grateful for the shelter from the cold, the wet, and the overwhelming presence of death. I was freezing, soaked through, and tired. Really, really tired.

Like death warmed over. Ha-ha, not funny.

Zayvion walked around the car and slid in the driver's side.

"So who do you think that man is? Was he there when my father was buried? Does this all have something to do with his death?"

He put the keys in the ignition, started the car, and, thankfully, the heater.

"How about I drive while I talk?"

"Where are we going?"

Score one for the logical mind.

He looked over at me. Nothing but Zen. Well, a little wet. A lot kissable. And just unreadable enough that I didn't feel safe enough to risk getting too intimate. Yet.

"Where do you want me to take you?"

"Anywhere you're going to tell me the truth about that man out there, the powerful people watching me, and my father's grave."

He frowned. "What about your father's grave?"

"Did you actually see his body lowered into it?" I said it like it didn't freak me out that my dead father was missing in inaction. So to speak.

He looked out the front window like he was looking into his memories. Then took a very deep, loud breath. Let it out. "A lot of . . . people saw his casket lowered into the grave."

"Nice hesitation," I noted.

He put the car in reverse and backed out of the cemetery, out through the iron gates, then put it in drive and pulled onto the street. He didn't say anything more. I didn't let that stop me from talking.

"Listen, I know we said we'd try this . . ."

"This?"

"Us," I said. "At the deli when I came back to Portland. That we'd try us. But I am so done with the mystery-man bit. If you don't level with me, there is no way I'm going to trust you like—"

"Like you did before?" Zayvion gave me a sad smile. "Trust wasn't exactly what our relationship was built on."

"Really?" I said, not believing him. Trust was a big thing for me, and I didn't get into a relationship without it. "Then what was it built on?"

"Really good sex."

I had the unfortunate tendency to blush. And I think Zayvion Jones knew that.

He grinned. "Maybe there was some trust going on too. I know that I trusted you. Trusted in your strength. And your stubbornness."

"Watch it," I warned.

"Maybe it's not me you're afraid to trust right now," he said. "Maybe it's yourself."

I didn't know what to say to that. Because he was right. And I was too stubborn to admit it.

Chapter Eight

Zayvion guided the car down the hill, heading north toward downtown. My chance for a snappy comeback had passed about a minute and a half ago. Instead, I'd opted to look aloof and unimpressed while I waited for the hot rush of blood to drain from my cheeks, neck, and chest.

"As I was saying," I said, "I'd like you to level with me."

"That sounds fair," he said. "But it will take some time. Are you hungry?"

My underwear were giving me the wet wedgie of a lifetime. I really wanted to change into dry clothes before going to the Hound meeting.

"I just ate," I said. "What time is it?"

He nodded toward the car's dash and a digital clock. "Ten thirty."

I bit at the inside of my cheek. I had just enough time for him to take me home so I could score some dry clothes before the Hound thing. And besides, he'd said he'd talk while he drove.

"I have an appointment at noon. Could you take me home so I can change?"

"Sure."

He didn't ask what the appointment was. Didn't ask me where I was going or whom I was going with. I was simultaneously happy and disappointed that he wasn't interfering in my personal business.

"I moved to a new apartment," I said.

"I know."

"Have you been spying on me, Mr. Jones?"

"On you? No."

"Spying on someone else in my building?"

"That seems unlikely, doesn't it?"

"Way to dodge the question."

"Thank you. Speaking of questions, why did you go to the graveyard today? It's not exactly good weather for it."

"It's almost December. Of course it's not good weather. Who was that man back at the graveyard? Is he part of MERC?"

Zayvion frowned, and our little question volley took on a more serious tone. "Where did you hear about MERC?"

Interesting. So he knew about them.

"Friends on the force mentioned it. Is that it? The MERC team is watching me?"

They had wanted to tag me. Since I said no to that, it made sense that they might want to follow me in a more conventional manner. The weird thing was I had no idea why they wanted to keep such a close eye on me, unless it was because of Trager. I hadn't worked for them yet, hadn't Hounded whatever case might put me in the line of danger.

And all I kept thinking about was sixteen Hounds dead in six years.

"Maybe MERC is watching you," Zayvion said.

"Are you a part of that? Of them?"

He gave me a strange look. "Allie, you know I don't work for MERC."

"No. I don't."

"Ah." He Zenned.

No other reaction. Just that: "Ah."

"How about a little help here?" I said. "Who are the powerful people watching me and what are they watching me for?"

"I shouldn't tell you that."

"Because you work for them?"

"If I did, do you think I'd tell you?" He smiled, laugh lines crinkling at the edges of his eyes.

I groaned and thunked my head on the side window. "For all that's holy, Jones, talk to me. If I'm in danger, I need to know. Is it Trager?"

Zay tightened, looked at me. "Lon Trager?"

I shrugged. "I heard he's out of jail."

Zay nodded. "He is."

"Is that it, then? Trager's looking for me?"

"It's . . . complicated." He glanced at me, looked back at the road. He was no longer smiling. "I do some work for the . . . for people. In powerful positions. The man in the graveyard is a part of the . . . of what I'm . . . working on. He might have something to do with Trager."

"Does he have anything to do with me?"

"He shouldn't."

"But he could?"

"Anything is possible in this city." At my glare, he

added, "There are a lot of things going on—with people who use magic, with the people who police magic. All of them involve magic. What it is. How it's being used. Who can use it. And you use magic, so, yes. It could involve you. It could involve Trager, but I don't know that as a fact yet. It could involve anyone."

"Was my dad part of what is going on in the city? And before you answer, I know he's dead, but I know he was a powerful magic user. There's no reason you can't give me the truth on this. Was he involved in what's going on with magic in the city?"

"Yes." He looked like giving a straight answer hurt.

"So the danger to me—if there is danger to me—may be secondary? Because I'm his daughter?"

"Have I ever told you you are a very astute woman, Ms. Beckstrom?"

"Never hurts to hear it again." Sweet hells. People who might want to kill me were going to have to start taking a number and getting in line.

"Did you see my father's body before he was buried?"

If he was surprised by the change of subject, he didn't show it.

"I saw it at the viewing, yes."

"Are you sure it was his body?"

Now *that* surprised him. His heartbeat elevated, and this close, I could tell he held his breath.

"I'm serious," I said.

"I know you are." His lips pressed into a thin line. He wove the car through traffic, heading closer to the downtown area.

"I didn't touch the body," he finally said. "I did

lean in close to it during the viewing. It wasn't an imposter."

"Not a fake? A mannequin or wax dummy?"

"No. The man in that coffin was dead."

"Are you sure? Absolutely sure he was dead?"

"Allie, I know a dead body when I see one."

Under other circumstances I might have asked him why, exactly, he was that familiar with corpses. But right now, I just wanted to know what he knew about my dad's death and burial.

"Why?" Zayvion asked.

"Because his grave is empty."

No more Zen Zayvion. No more calm and quiet Zayvion of the cool mint fingers and sexy smile. He stopped the car—good thing we were at a stop sign—and didn't move through the intersection even though there was no other traffic.

He turned toward me. He was wider through the shoulder than he looked, so there wasn't much room for him to really turn.

Images, no, memories of his body against mine—not on my father's grave, but some other time, when the heat and strength of his body pressed against me—came back with a quick flash of fire. My stomach fluttered and I swallowed to keep from making any small sound.

Then the image—and the emotion behind it—was gone.

The man before me wasn't the same as the lover of my memory. Blackness poured like ink through the brown of his eyes, filling his gaze with killing darkness. Then he blinked, and his eyes looked brown again—

just brown—and I really, really hoped I was just imagining things.

"How?" he asked.

"Do you think I know? That's why I'm asking you."

"No," he said. "How do you know his grave is empty?"

"I wanted to touch him." Okay, that sounded creepy.

He blinked a couple more times, like either the sentimental me or creepy me wasn't lining up.

"Physically?"

"Did you see me carrying a shovel? Of course not physically."

"So what did you do, Allie?"

"I touched him. With magic. Because, you know, grave robbing is so last season."

"Allie. This is serious."

"I know. My dad is dead—or so everyone tells me. But he is not in that coffin. Nothing is. Nothing but stale air."

Zayvion rubbed a hand over his face and scrubbed at the back of his neck. He glanced out the windshield and seemed to notice we were not moving. He straightened, took his foot off the brake, and rolled through the intersection.

"How can you be sure?" he asked. "A dead body doesn't feel the same as a living body. Even when touched with magic." There it was again—his casual acquaintance with dead people. And how they felt when touched with magic. Interesting.

"There would have been bacteria, not to mention bugs of all sorts, so, yes, there would have been something alive if there had been any flesh in that box. There wasn't anything in the coffin except air."

"People don't bury empty coffins."

"Someone did."

He didn't say anything.

"Is this a part of the whole dangerous magic going on thing?" I asked.

The image of the magic glyphs on the warehouse wall came to me. Warnings. Life magic. Death magic. All in my father's signature.

"Does it have something to do with death magic? Was my dad involved in some sort of . . . dark magic?" Now that I thought about it, it wouldn't surprise me a bit if he were involved in whatever passed as the dark arts.

And no, I didn't know what that was. It wasn't exactly covered in my college Business Magic 101, where you learned the proper Proxy-to-potency ratio for advertising illusions.

The line of Zayvion's shoulders tightened. I'd hit a nerve.

"Where would you get that kind of idea?" he asked, all low and calm, like it was silly to even think there was dark magic. He totally did not fool me.

And that was when it occurred to me that he might be a part of this—whatever *this* was. He might be a part of the reason why my father was not in his grave, might be a part of the death magic glyphs, hells, might be a part of why I saw my dad's ghost, or—and at this I felt a chill all the way down to my wet panties—he might be a part of my dad's death.

It was clear Mr. Jones could be a dangerous man. He'd admitted working for powerful people dealing with "complicated" things.

Even though he remembered our relationship, and

I'd asked him if we still had a chance together, I realized I didn't know him—didn't know enough about him to warrant trusting him so soon.

Plus, I just was so not up to fighting for my life at the moment.

"Allie?" he asked when I'd been a little too quiet a little too long.

"Never mind," I said. "It's just been a long day. I'm jumping at shadows."

He took a deep breath, let it out. Okay, he wasn't buying my bluff either.

Note to self: do not play poker with this man.

"Allie, don't ask me about . . . dark . . . about your dad and . . . things. Things I'm working on. It's being taken care of by people who want things right . . . good. For the city, for people. Things I want right. For you. Us." He squeezed the steering wheel, growing more frustrated with each word of his staccato explanation. "I can't say more without putting you in a compromising position."

"Maybe I want you to put me in a compromising position."

Oh, groan. What was I doing flirting with him? Hadn't I just decided I couldn't trust him?

He smiled, a flash of straight white teeth, curve of thick lips, and then gave me a sideways glance. "When you put it that way . . ."

Yes, I was blushing. Fabo.

Time to reestablish some boundaries here.

"Listen. Just tell me: do you know where my father's body is?"

No matter how bright those tiger eyes burned, he could not lie to me. I could smell a lie as easy as I could smell other strong emotions, as easy as I could smell the lines of cast magic. I was a Hound. And good at it. *So go ahead*, I thought, *tell me a lie, Zayvion Jones.*

"No."

Not a whiff of change, not a scent of a lie. He was telling the truth.

"But you have some idea?"

"Not yet. Soon."

Okay, this honesty thing was working for me. I just needed to know one more thing before he closed up again.

"I'd like to know what kind of people I should be worried about spying on me. The police? MERC? My dad's ex–business partners? My dad's ex-wives? Lon Trager?"

He didn't say anything, but his knuckles went yellow from squeezing the steering wheel.

"You don't have to name names," I said, "but right now it feels like everyone is after me. And before you tell me paranoia will at least keep me alive, I have a job to do, Zayvion. I'm doing some Hounding for MERC. It's possible I'll be putting myself out there in dangerous ways. If I know where the heat's coming from, I will do my best to avoid it."

Still nothing.

"If you want me to stay safe, give me the tools to keep myself safe. Tell me who I need to avoid." *Trust me*, I thought. *Please.*

I waited. I am not a patient woman. But I knew if I pushed any harder, he'd close up for good.

"There are . . . magic users . . ." he said so quietly, I almost couldn't hear his voice over the drone of the engine and the rhythmic swipe of the windshield wipers. "Magic users who specialize in knowing when someone is over their head with magic."

"Like a regulatory agency?" I was thinking FBI or some sort of secret black ops.

"No. Not like that. These people know when a person is using too much or more than they can handle. Know if they're addicted to the rush, the pain. Know if they're . . . abusing magic in ways harmful to themselves or others. When that happens, these people step in. Handle things. Discreetly. Without the involvement of the police, MERC, or the law."

Holy shit.

"There are magic users out there who decide if other magic users should . . . what? Be forbidden from using magic?"

He didn't say anything.

"Be put in jail?"

Still nothing.

"What, Zayvion? They decide if magic users should be—"

"Killed," Zay said softly.

Holier shit. Magic vigilantes. Worse—secret magic vigilantes.

I took a deep breath and waited for my heart to start beating again.

"Are those people watching me?"

"Yes."

Holiest shit. I really was going to need to start a Kill Allie Here line.

"Are those the people you're working for?"

He didn't say anything.

I took that as a yes. My mind spun with possibilities

of who could be spying on me, waiting for me to use magic wrong, use it too much, or make one bad choice. Violet, Grant? Pike, Stotts? Zayvion? How secret were these secret magic vigilantes?

"I want you to promise me you won't go anywhere in this city alone," he said. "I want you to promise me you won't go looking for your father's body. And that you won't use magic more than you have to."

"I'll do what I can," I said.

"Allie. Listen to me. These people don't see the world in any manner but black and white. If you fall anywhere near the gray, they will not hesitate to—"

"Kill me. Yeah, I got that part. Holy crap, Jones. You could have told me."

"When?"

I opened my mouth to answer him, but maybe it was the blur of movement that caught my eye. Whatever it was, both Zayvion and I took that exact moment to look away from each other and back at the street. More precisely, to look at the red light we were running. And the crosswalk. And the man striding across it.

A man wearing a dark business suit with a lavender hanky in his pocket. He was tall like me, looked a lot like me, but had gray hair. He strode across the middle of the crosswalk, headed right for us, right in front of the car.

My father.

"Stop!" I yelled.

Zayvion slammed on the brakes. I put my hands on the dashboard to brace for impact.

Then I screamed as Zayvion ran over my dead dad.

Chapter Nine

Time has a weird way of slowing down when I'm in high stress situations. I had plenty of time to study my father, to note that, yes, indeed, that was a lavender handkerchief in his pocket; yes, indeed, he turned so he could see into the car; and yes, indeed, he wasn't looking at Zayvion but at me.

He didn't look particularly surprised that I was killing him. He just looked very, very disappointed in me.

And then he was close, his face right in front of my face, much closer than should be possible with all the metal and glass between us. And yet he was still standing as if even a speeding car wasn't enough to knock him down.

I yelled and didn't hear the thunk of his body hitting metal, didn't hear anything but the brakes locking up and tires screeching as my dad slipped down somewhere beneath my line of vision, beneath the hood, beneath the tires.

Or maybe I just couldn't distinguish him from the blur of the city outside the window. I tasted leather and wintergreen on the back of my throat, felt the stink of it smack my skin like a cold sweat.

I heard him, I swear I heard my father's voice, close as my own thoughts: "The gates open, seek death." Words that bore the push of Influence, the magical knack we Beckstroms were known for using on people to make them do what we wanted them to do. Influence forced those words into my head until my stomach clenched with the need to follow, to do as he said, even though I was still yelling and had no idea what he meant.

All that, as the car came to a stop in the middle of the intersection.

"What the hell?" Zayvion yelled.

"You hit him! You hit my dad!" I fumbled with my seat belt, the door latch, and then was out into the cold and rain, running back, cars honking and swerving around me, back to where my father must have fallen as we ran over the top of him.

There was no one there. Not a mark across the pavement except for the car tires, not a splash of blood against the rainy, dirty asphalt, not a body. Not so much as a single lavender hanky thread.

I blinked and blinked and could not believe what my eyes were telling me. My father was not on the ground, not wedged beneath the car (yes, I turned and looked), not anywhere.

"Shit," I whispered.

Zayvion was beside me now, standing just out of swinging range. "Allie?"

I couldn't stop staring at the pavement. Couldn't unsee what I know I had seen.

"You need to get out of the street," he said.

Maybe my eyes couldn't see what I knew must be there, but I had other ways to sense. Other ways to see.

I took a deep breath and drew a glyph for Sight, Taste, and Smell, and let the magic that pooled in me slip up through my bones, my veins, my flesh, and into my fingers to fill that glyph. Magic pulled like a hood over my eyes and senses.

The world broke open in a wild storm of smells, tastes, colors, and shades.

Old lines of magic cobwebbed the buildings. As cars drove around us I could see smaller spells attached to them like vibrant jellyfish, tendrils trailing behind to link to the people in cars. Sharp-edged geometric glyphs pulsed on the light posts, doorways, edges of alleys.

And there, at the corner of my vision, were the watercolor people. They had no magic tied to them, maybe because magic can't tie to someone who is translucent—I don't know. They walked along the street, through buildings and cars, as if the city itself did not exist.

They all paused and looked at me.

Again.

Seriously, I just don't think I'm that interesting.

They moved toward me in slow underwater steps, homing in like sharks scenting blood.

I stayed calm, because magic cannot be cast in high states of emotion. I didn't flinch, didn't doubt.

Go, me.

Show me, I thought, my fingers tracing an intricate

glyph for Reveal. In any trained magic user's hands, a Reveal spell would uncover the illusion of a thing, strip away its magical covering and let you see the aged skin, the brown grass, the old paint beneath.

But in my hands that glowed with magic, hot on the right, cold on the left, the Reveal spell intensified the world, showing the hard edges of black, white, color, shape, angle, shadow.

Everything was stripped down. Paint seemed to be composed of hundreds of layers, individual raindrops were sharply outlined, and the tread marks from the tires turned into a mosaic of rain and stone and heat.

I looked at my hands.

Wow.

My right hand was luminescent, glowing with fire in neon colors. When I moved my fingers, magic poured out in ribbons, hovered in the air, and then floated back down to wrap around my fingers, where it sank in, beneath my skin, coursing through the heavy swirls of colors up my arm, my chest, to the silk-slender neon threads at the corner of my eye.

My left hand was white and black, the bars of a prison, bands of ebony ringing each joint, the flesh between pale as death. My left hand felt numb, cold, dead. A memory, slight but clear—like a faraway radio tune—came to me. Of Zayvion holding my hands.

"Positive," he said while lifting my right hand. *"Negative,"* he said while touching my left. *"Very sexy."*

And then he had kissed both of my palms. The electric sensation of his lips on my skin made my knees weak.

Oh.

I glanced over at Zayvion.

But I did not see Zayvion standing there—or rather I saw him in a way I never had before.

Even though he was just over six feet tall, Reveal gave him another half a foot, made him appear wider at the shoulders, thicker through the chest and thighs. More than dark, he was a blackness. His skin flickered with blue-tipped black fire, radiating a cold deadlier than the icy air.

Beneath the night-sky flame of his body was something that resembled glyphing.

Spells in ebony, silver, and coal carved elusive against his skin, even with Reveal. His eyes burned Aztec gold shot through with sharp cracks of obsidian.

"What are you?" I whispered.

My words were like a soft breeze, stirring the flames against his skin so that they shifted and flared blue, indigo, black. He reached for me, and I raised my hands to hold him off.

He touched my right shoulder, and the familiar heat and mint of him washed through my body. He Grounded me, easing the ache of the magic I held.

It felt wonderful. It felt right. And I knew instinctively that this was the way magic was meant to be used.

"Allie," he said, and it was Zayvion's voice. Straining to stay calm, but still him, still a man. "Your dad isn't here. We need to go now. Come with me."

His words were sweet, seductive darkness. I wanted to walk to him, fall into him, let his darkness fill me.

I took a step back, and his hand fell away from my shoulder. "I can't. I have to see."

"Allie." He looked past me, looked at the watercolor people who were closing in, still slowly, too slowly. If these watercolor people were like the ones outside the coffee shop, as soon as they got close enough, they'd start moving fast—too damn fast.

And I was pretty sure Zayvion could see them. Wasn't that interesting?

The flames against his body washed blue, indigo, black over the silver glyphs of his skin. "Hurry."

I knelt where my father's body should be, pressed my fingertips through the standing water until I touched pavement. I whispered another mantra while a car honked and blinding headlights swerved around us. I opened my mouth and breathed in, getting the smell, the taste of the rain, the pavement, car oil, dirt, on the back of my palate.

I sifted scents for my father—searching for the notes of leather and wintergreen. I smelled all the common odors of the city—the chemical tang of cars and oil and waste. And I smelled the strangely antiseptic odor of falling rain. Beyond that, the stink of diesel, the rubber of tires, the heavy pine of Zayvion's cologne, and my own sweat mixed with the cheap soap I'd used in the shower this morning.

But I did not smell my father. Not even a hint of him.

"Now, Allie." Zayvion wove a glyph—something that was in the Shield family but twisted toward the center in a way I had never seen before.

He pulled magic from the stores deep beneath the city, and it flickered like electric ribbons up into the invisible glyph in front of him, filling it in until I could see the glyph too.

Magic is fast. Too fast to see until it has been cast.

Well, normally that was true. Apparently when I was using Reveal, I could see magic while it was being used.

How cool was that?

Zayvion glanced down at me. The flames over his skin had gone bloodred, tipped with a silver so dark it hurt to look at. I didn't know if he was trying to keep from casting a spell or getting ready to Shield the hell out of himself.

I stood. Rain and magic dripped from my fingertips and swirled in metallic colors, joining the stream of water pouring into the storm grate. Magic rushed up into me, through me, from deep below the earth, hot and fast, while I remained cool and calm.

"Can you see them?" I asked.

"Get in the car, Allie," he said.

"Can you see them?" I asked again.

I really needed him to say yes, to tell me that I was not crazy, not losing other parts of my mind besides my memory. I really needed him to say, yes, there are a bunch of hollow-eyed see-through people marching our way.

"Allie—"

I blinked rain out of my eyes. That was all the time they needed. The watercolor people broke forward, moving fast, so fast that I didn't get my hands up in time to cast anything.

Zayvion, however, did.

The watercolor people hit the Shield he cast around us in an explosion of sparks that would have made a special-effects director proud.

They all stepped back.

Then one of them—a man in clothing that looked

like it belonged to the previous century—extended his hand toward the Shield.

Zayvion's Shield, a ten-foot-tall and -wide lattice of blue glyphing that strummed with power, stretched out and out toward the man's hand. The Shield distorted until the edges became a fine mist, and finally the vibrant blue magic became a watercolor fog that streamed toward the man's hand like smoke from a chimney.

The man opened his mouth wide, wider, empty black eyes unblinking, and inhaled. The mist that had just been a Shield spell flew forward and filled his mouth. He swallowed in huge gulps, throwing his shoulders back and arching his spine as he swallowed and swallowed.

All the watercolor people moaned, low, hungry, like a hard wind blowing over an empty grave. They wanted that. They wanted magic.

They rushed.

Zayvion drew a second glyph.

I was faster.

I traced Hold spells with both hands (yes, I'm spellambidextrous; have I not mentioned that before?) and threw them at the mob ahead and behind us.

Magic licked up my bones, pushed against my skin, and unleashed into the spell.

The watercolor people froze.

They did not look happy about it.

I, frankly, was hella impressed.

"Good," Zayvion said, like I was a pupil who had just figured out how to concentrate so that a Light spell will reduce weight, not illuminate.

"Now get in the car."

I had to give the guy props. He didn't sound the least bit concerned that my spell was dissolving into mist even faster than his had. Didn't sound worried that it too was being devoured by our ethereal company.

And, as far as I could tell, he didn't seem bothered by the large crowd of new watercolor people who were trudging in slo-mo down the streets toward us.

I was pretty sure they weren't just stopping by to cheer on their home team.

"Car, Allie. It's safer."

I didn't move. Call me crazy, but I was not going to leave him out here to fight these things alone. Hells, for all I knew the car wouldn't do me any good. These things walked through walls.

Zayvion finished the glyph—an intricate, thick-lined beast of a thing—and began chanting.

Chanting.

Okay, I'd done two years at college studying magic. I'd been around magic and my father for most of my life and had watched him do all kinds of spell casting. Ninety-five percent of the people in the city use magic.

And I had not once ever heard anyone chant.

Chant.

What. The. Hell?

The words didn't sound like a language I recognized, but the magic—oh, sweet loves, the magic—poured up out of the ground, leaping to Zayvion's body, sparking the glyphs and symbols on his skin to catch with a secondary fire so they seemed to shift and undulate across his skin. Magic rolled up his body in metallic colors like the marks on my arm, bright against black fire.

The man was raw, controlled power, and I wanted

to touch him. Wanted to be that with him. He drew his wrist and palms together and then separated his hands in one smooth motion. He spoke a word. It sounded a little like "not" or "nunt." My ears stopped working for a second—nothing but white noise and a high-pitched ringing.

Then the air in front of Zayvion became hard—I don't know how else to explain it. The space around him, around me, turned into a thick glass wall, and in that glass wall, currents of gold mist swirled and shifted. Just as I almost made out the glyphs the gold formed, it would change into another glyph, fluid, flowing.

The watercolor people slammed into the glass wall, grappling at it with fingers that could find no purchase.

Zayvion spoke another word, and I could tell he was pouring magic through that word. His leaned forward, both palms extended but not touching the wall. He shifted his stance, leaning into something that looked vaguely tai chi, knees bent, one leg stretched back, torso and arms forward, as if he were pushing against a great weight. And still the magic rushed up his body, molding, whirling through the glyphs and flames against his skin, pouring through his hands into the wall. Raw power I had never seen before.

The glass wall darkened in front of Zayvion. A hole—no, a door or a gate—appeared there, so dark, it hurt to look at it. So I looked away to the edges of the wall that were still snaked with gold glyphs.

Beyond the wall, the watercolor people gathered in a huddle. They weren't moving now, not even their arms. They did not look happy. Worse, they leaned, no, stretched out toward the black gate thing Zayvion was casting, faces and bodies elongating in a manner that defied the laws of nature. Like watercolor flames caught in an updraft.

Another word from Zay, and the dark gates filled with a rushing stream of light, filled with the watercolor people pouring in off the streets around us and funneling into that black hole. Zayvion slammed his hands together in a resounding clap, and the gate thing closed and was gone, leaving the glass and gold wall still standing.

He chanted again and brought his hands together. Another resounding clap that broke the glyph. The wall shattered into a million translucent droplets of magic that fell from above us, around us, and mixed with rain to splash against the street, where it disappeared into the rain, swirling, down the storm drains.

The watercolor people were gone. Sucked into that black door in the wall that was no longer there.

"Wow," I breathed.

Zayvion tipped his head to the side, working out stiffness. Then he put both his hands in his pockets and turned to face me. Zen Zay. Now that I wasn't pulling on magic, he just looked like a guy in a knit hat and ratty blue ski jacket.

And he was so damn much more.

"Let's get out of the street," he said. "We're going to get run over if we're not careful."

He took a step toward the car, and I did too. My mind wasn't doing so good keeping up with everything that had just happened. For right now, I decided to cut myself a little slack.

I got into the car, even wetter than I'd been just minutes before. I glanced at the clock on the dash.

That entire altercation had taken less than a few minutes.

Zayvion got in the driver's side and put the car in gear. Traffic behind us honked, and a car passed on the right. The driver gave us the middle finger.

Zayvion rolled through the intersection, taking the normal street into the normal city, driving through the normal rain.

When we were just a few blocks from my apartment, he spoke. "Are you okay?"

Why did people always ask me that?

"I'm fine. That was some . . . spectacular magic you threw around back there."

"Hmm."

"So what are they? Those people?" I asked.

He double-parked next to my apartment building. "We're here."

I glanced at the clock again. I had just over an hour until I needed to be at the Hound meeting. Plenty of time to shower and change. And I was not about to let Zayvion wander off without coming clean about what had just happened.

"Why don't you come on up?" I said.

He took a deep breath, leaned his head back against his window, and looked at me. "You're going to grill me about all this, aren't you?"

"Have I told you lately that you are a very astute man, Mr. Jones?"

"No." He paused, seemed to be weighing something. "You saw them?"

"Yes, I did." I gave him a level gaze.

"And you saw your father?"

"Why don't you come up and we'll talk about it?"

It took him a moment more to decide. "I want to. How about we make a date of it instead?"

"What?"

"A date. It's a custom that's been around for a long time. It usually involves two people going out for drinks, dinner, and companionship."

"Ha-ha. You're just trying to dodge me, aren't you?"

"No." I knew he was not lying. "There are some things I need to take care of. Appointments I have to keep. I'm free tonight. Does that work for you?"

"No, I'm Hounding tonight. Tomorrow?"

"For dinner?"

I hesitated. Did I have time for dinner with him? I didn't know what Pike would want to do once I told him about Trager. I didn't know if I'd be in protective custody. But I didn't want to miss my chance to get information out of Zayvion, or miss what might be my last chance to be with him.

"Maybe around five," I said. "You might want to call first." I made it sound all hard-to-get instead of worried, and apparently, he bought it.

"That should work," he said. "I'll call at five."

"Good. See you then."

It was still raining, but it wasn't like I could get any wetter.

I opened the door and got out.

"Allie?" Zay called after me.

I ducked down to look at him.

"Be careful." He was dead serious.

I wanted to crawl back into the car and stay with him. Instead, I shut the door, and then strode across to the sidewalk, under the awning, and into the familiar surroundings of my building.

Chapter Ten

I jogged up the three flights of stairs, maybe because I wanted to get to my apartment and shower and change in time to pull myself together before the Hound meeting. Or maybe because that fight with the watercolor people on top of the rest of my day had shook me in a deep way that made me want to scream just a little.

Yeah, mostly it was the second thing.

Running up the stairs in a totally dignified and not scared of my own shadow kind of way let me release a little of that pent up panic, let my body burn while my mind rolled out the fear carpet and took a nice leisurely stroll.

Whatever those watercolor people were—they had been a lot harder to get rid of this time. And despite not wanting to tell Zayvion, I was sure—positive—I had seen my father in the street. I was positive I had heard him.

He had said something about gates opening and seeking death.

Why did ghosts have to be so spooky? I mean, it

had been a while since my dad and I had spoken to each other. He could have talked about the weather, asked me how my job was going, or maybe explained why even though he was dead he still felt the need to meddle in my life.

Honestly, he could have just told me why he wanted me to seek the dead and what seeking the dead meant.

I made it to my apartment door. All the other doors down the hall were closed, including the one where my newest neighbor, the creepy doctor from the coffee shop, lived. I unlocked my door, and then, because I was feeling more than a little jumpy, I drew a glyph to enhance my senses of hearing and smell, set a Disbursement this time (oh, hells, I hadn't been setting Disbursements when we faced the watercolor people; I was so going to have magic pound that price out of me), and leaned close to my door to listen for any movement, any breathing beyond it. I sniffed and got only a noseful of the smells I am used to in my building, along with the slight smell of almonds that I decided must be my new neighbor.

A motion at the corner of my eye caught my attention and I looked down the hall. I thought, for just a second, that someone had been standing there. Even though I had not enhanced my sight with magic, the pale green and blue tremor of fog—watercolor fog— at the end of the hallway near the head of the stairwell was enough for me to let go of magic.

The hall was just a hall again. No fog. No movement. No sound.

And nothing seemed to be moving in my apartment either.

I walked in, flipped the lights on, locked the door

behind me, and strode through the entire place, just to make sure I was alone.

And I was.

I wanted a shower, but that would mean getting naked in my bathroom again, and as good as hot water sounded, I just didn't have it in me to get all naked and vulnerable yet.

Last time I was in that bathroom, my dead father had seen me, touched me.

"C'mon, Allie," I said out loud. "Get over it. You've gotten over every other screwed-up thing that has happened to you."

Maybe I needed a cat. Or a dog. Something that would sense if there were anything out of the ordinary going on in my apartment. But a cat or dog would take time to care for, and I barely made time to take care of myself.

Maybe something smaller that needed fewer walks in the park and less one-on-one time. A goldfish? How about a ghost-sniffing hamster?

Ha.

I took off my coat, hung it on the hook behind the door, and decided I could stall the whole get-naked thing while doing something useful. I pulled out my notebook.

I wrote down everything that had happened today— the bus ride with Trager, the visit with Love and Payne, Stotts and his secret magic police, the Hounding job I'd go on tonight, Pike and the angry young Anthony, and of course the watercolor people, magical disappearing Life and Death glyphs, Grant's opera tickets, my re-date with Violet for breakfast tomorrow, my dad's empty grave, his appearance in the intersection, the encounter with the watercolor people, and the surprisingly powerful Mr. Jones. I noted that I was going to a Hound meeting and that I had a dinner date with Zayvion, who had said there were magic users out there, watching me, waiting for me to make a mistake. And that the price for that mistake might well be my death.

Listed like that, my day was shaping up fan-damn-tastic.

I pulled off my knit hat, dropped it on the half wall between my entryway and kitchen, and scratched at my wet, itchy head. I had delayed it as long as I could. Time to shower. I picked up a candle I had left there on the half wall and stopped in the living room to light it.

A headache was looming, pressing at the back of my skull, not bad yet, but I knew in an hour or two, it would probably be a migraine.

"Disbursements, Allie," I said out loud, trying to fill the emptiness of my apartment with my voice. "Why do you always forget to set Disbursements? You are such an idiot sometimes."

I set the candle on the edge of the sink and left the door open. If the lights went out again, I wanted something to see by and a clear escape route. I took a deep breath and pulled back the shower curtain. Nothing but my empty shower. Good. I turned on the shower to give the water time to warm up. I undressed and kept glancing out at the hallway and peering at the corners of the bathroom.

I tossed my clothes in the hamper and checked myself for bruises and cuts in the full-length mirror standing next to the hamper.

No cuts, which was great. But the site where Trager had shoved the needle in my thigh was a hard, sore, hand-sized lump. A bruise spread out in thin tendrils that looked more like a broken spider web than a bruise. A glyph? I ran my fingers over it carefully and didn't sense any magic left in it. But, yes, it was a glyph. Blood magic, though not any kind I was aware of. It had to be the thing that had made me feel so dizzy after he had stabbed me.

I swore.

But the glyph wasn't the only new mark I carried. There were four dark red circles down my neck, a lot more on my left shoulder, and several on the outside of my hips, thighs, stomach, and what I could see of my back. They looked like finger-bruises, only they weren't the right color for bruises. I gently rubbed the marks on my left shoulder.

Ouch.

Sticky moisture clung to my fingertips. Those red spots hurt. I wasn't exactly bleeding, but I was sort of weeping fluid. The marks burned like someone had peeled my skin off. I touched the ones on my neck more carefully. Same thing—raw and painful.

I didn't think Trager could have caused these marks. I would have known if he touched me like that, no matter how glyphed and dizzy I was.

No, I knew where I must have gotten them from— the watercolor people touching me outside Get Mugged. I had felt light-headed after that—drained and sort of sunburned. And these were the marks left behind from their attack.

I didn't have any Band-Aids.

I wasn't even sure I had any painkillers in the house.

I bet this was going to sting like hell in the shower.

I could do this. I could get in the shower, wash off despite being afraid my dead dad was going to show up again, and despite the pain it might cause my new wounds.

I stepped in the shower and did not pull the curtain closed. So what if I got a little water on the floor? It probably needed to be mopped anyway. With the curtain open I had a better chance at that clear escape route.

The water hit my shoulders, and sure enough, it stung like mad.

Fabulous.

So instead of taking a nice relaxing soak, I shivered in the heat of the water and made it quick. I washed my hair with shampoo that stung, then rubbed soap that stung over my skin, and patted myself dry, which also stung.

Not that I was bitter about it or anything.

I got out of the shower, wrapped the towel around me, and brushed out my hair, tucking it behind my ears. Then I opened my medicine cabinet. That lingering headache was moving in, sinking down into the back of my head and squeezing at my temples. All I had in the medicine cabinet were some cold pills, cotton swabs, a bottle of aspirin, and Bactine.

I pulled out the painkillers, tipped four tablets into my palm, and then swallowed them down. Next I uncapped the Bactine and squirted the antiseptic over each of my raw marks. It helped some—took the sting out—but the cold rivulets of antiseptic that snaked down my body made me shiver.

I blew out the candle and took the aspirin with me

into the bedroom. If I was going to get through tonight, I would need to chew down at least another eight of these things.

I didn't keep prescription painkillers in the house for a reason. Being a Hound and using magic for a living made it way too easy to fall into abusing substances for pain relief.

I dressed in an extra layer, a soft cotton long-sleeve shirt so that the raw marks wouldn't get scratched by my wool sweater, and wore a pair of tights beneath my jeans for the same reason.

Next on were wool socks, a black scarf my friend Nola knitted for me, a spare pair of leather gloves, and the only other coat I owned: a short black leather trench. It wasn't as warm as my other coat, but it would keep me dry. I pulled on a new slouchy knit hat.

Back in the living room I picked up my journal, and my wallet, and after locking the front door behind me, I strolled back down the hall and stairs to catch the bus to the meeting.

I looked good. Very secret agent–ish.

I made it to the bus stop just as the bus pulled up and found an empty seat near the door. For the next twenty minutes of stop and go, my headache thrummed along merrily. The painkillers weren't doing squat so I went over everything that had happened today and what I understood about it.

A lot, and not much.

I was apparently being haunted by my father. He wanted me to look for dead people or dying people, or the just plain dead. If he wanted me to "seek the dead" by doing something stupid like killing myself, he was so outta luck. Still, he had said those words with Influence, so even while I was sitting on the bus tapping my foot impatiently, my mind kept going back to his words, to the need to seek the dead that he had put on me.

Thanks a lot, Dad.

Meanwhile, Zayvion, who I still had feelings for and really shouldn't trust, all but told me he was part of a secret group of magic users who went around killing people. I should tell the cops about them, about him, but first I needed to find out what he knew about my father's death. I didn't want to tip off the people who might be watching me that I had caught on yet— people, for all I knew, who might be involved in where my dad's body was. I wasn't going to do anything drastic until Zayvion gave me the information I needed. If I could find my dad's body, make sure he was all buried and happy, he might stop haunting me.

So much for me not believing in ghosts.

But I wasn't the only one. Grant believed in ghosts and was all buddy-buddy with the kooks who hunted them. Okay, maybe not kooks, since I myself had seen some weird shit today. But I was so not going to let any ghost chasers check out my apartment. After all, I'd seen my dad in the freaking middle of a freaking intersection today—I didn't think this ghost problem was limited to my shower.

And even though the watercolor people must be ghosts, they were different from my father's ghost. For one thing, they didn't speak and use Influence on me. For another, they had those empty black eyes. And they could pull apart perfectly good, perfectly strong spells and eat them.

Freaky with a capital "eeky."

Sure, my dad had touched me in my bathroom, and I'd smelled his familiar, living scents, but his touch hadn't hurt, hadn't left marks. The watercolor people's touch sucked.

Literally.

So maybe there was more than one kind of ghost running around the city.

Pike had said he'd talk to me at the meeting. And since he ran with the cops I figured he might know as much or maybe even more than Zayvion.

The bus stopped in Ankeny Square. Today wasn't Saturday, so the open air market that usually drew people to this area, even in bad weather, was not set up, leaving empty parking lots, a handful of old and renovated brick buildings, and, beyond more buildings toward the east, the Willamette River.

I got out and took a good sniff of the place. Dirt, diesel, oil fumes, river, and the stink of people, restaurants, and garbage. Too many smells for me to know if I were being followed by anyone.

The wind was still blowing, gustier here, so I crossed the busy street at a good clip, walked up to the building, and walked in.

A thick, heavy cloud of smells hit me as soon as I stepped into the building that was currently occupied by several clothing stores, restaurants, and other retail outlets. Got a nose full of incense, hot dogs, candles, soap, garlic, frying oil, espresso, and more.

Why in the world would Hounds want to meet in a place that was so overloaded with smells? It didn't make any sense. But the more I thought about it as I wandered around, the more I realized it actually made a lot of sense. Too many smells was a better cover than no smell at all. I couldn't distinguish any one person's scent. I simply could not Hound without magic here. It was the perfect way to ensure a level playing field, a way to disguise our scents from each other.

Tricky.

And since Mr. I'm-not-awake hadn't told me where, exactly, they were meeting other than on the lower level, it made this whole thing into one big smelly treasure hunt.

If only my head weren't hurting so much, I might actually have enjoyed wandering down the mazelike hallways, lit with "vintage" (i.e., dim) lighting, and passageways that led to bricked up doorways or maintenance closets. This was no place to be wandering around tired, hurting, and irritated.

So what was I doing? Yeah. D. All of the above.

Anyone could be lingering in the shadows. Anyone could be waiting behind the jogs of brick walls. It looked like the kind of place Trager's men would hang out. How great was that?

"Beckstrom?"

I slowed my pace. A man, the owner of the voice, stepped out from where he was indeed hanging out behind a jog in the wall. He was a little shorter than me, thin in a smoked-leather sort of way. His face was sallow and clean shaven, his blue eyes startled pinpoints beneath light brown hair combed back slick. He had that ruddy bloodshot look to him that spoke of too little sleep, too much whiskey, and too many years of chain-smoking.

"Yes," I said.

"This way." He turned and walked halfway down the hall and then leaned his shoulder into the wall to pushed open a door I would not have noticed on a casual stroll by.

He kept walking through the door. I paused on the threshold. A narrow corridor stretched out from here, dirt floor to either side of an uneven wooden walkway. The walls were bare studs with a random scattering of drywall nailed into place. At the end of the corridor was another hall that ran to the right, toward the river, though we were belowground and there were no windows to confirm I had my bearings straight.

Was there any chance he actually wasn't a Hound and wasn't taking me to the Hound meeting? The way my day had been going, yes. Yes, there was a high probability he could be anyone taking me anywhere for any reason. Right down Lon Trager's gullet, even.

"Where are we headed?" I called out, still standing in the doorway.

He glanced down and back at me like I was stupid. "Hound meeting."

Okay. Was that so hard? I shut the door behind me and followed my whiskey-drinking white rabbit all the way down the corridor and then down the next, which opened up—and I mean there was no door, just a wide-open wall with the rough edges of bricks sticking out like bad teeth—to reveal a room beyond.

"Vintage" didn't begin to describe this room.

Stained wallpaper that may have once been yellow and green but now leaned toward brown and browner covered the three walls, curling back in the corners and torn at the seams. The lighting was a huge brass and glass chandelier that was probably worth a small fortune, and the floor of the room was covered by several layers of threadbare rugs that looked like they'd grind down to dust if you put too much weight on your heels.

Old-timey. Funky with the stink of mold and rotted wood. And likely the cheapest, crappiest meeting space in Portland. While one part of my mind took in the room, the other part of my head was tallying the people and details.

Ten people in the room, six men and four women. Most of them stood against the walls, equidistant from each other like they were holding down territory. At the table, which was four sawhorses supporting a plank of plywood in the middle of the room, sat Pike. Anthony, still in his gray hoodie, glared at me from the far right corner, where he was getting his slouch on. Other than my guide, Whiskey Guy, who wandered over to my left to claim an empty spot of wall, I didn't recognize anyone else.

Okay, this was where my jaded outlook on being a Hound kicked in. It was easy to identify a Hound in a room—all you had to do was find someone who looked completely antisocial, yet became too curious too quickly, and of course was hiding an additction.

"Allie Beckstrom," Pike said in his gravely voice, "meet the Pack. I'm only gonna go through this once, so pay attention. That's Sid Westerling." He pointed to the first man standing on my right.

Heavyset and blond enough to have Norwegian ancestors, Sid wore wire frame glasses and looked like he should be sitting behind a computer, not sniffing down spells. I guessed him for prescription painkillers. He nodded a hello. "I think you and I worked the Spatler case a few years back."

I frowned, dug for the memory, found it. "Right. You were fast."

He grinned and tucked his thumbs in the sides of his Dockers. "Yes, I was. Still am."

"That's Dahlia Bates," Pike said, indicating the woman who sat on a metal folding chair next to Sid.

She was motherly looking and had short hair colored from a box that was probably called Glorious Sunset. She exhaled like she thought holding her breath would make her invisible. Or maybe she just hated the stink of mold as much as I did. Downers, I guessed. Maybe Valium.

"Davy Silvers."

A young man, thin, also sat in a metal chair, the back of his head resting against the brick wall, dark circles beneath his closed eyes. His skin was a little too pale and green. Out of the bunch, I figured he was the one who answered the phone when I called.

He lifted one hand in a wane hello but did not open his eyes. Alcohol. Probably something else in the mix too.

"Anthony Bell."

I glared at Anthony, who still stunk of the sweet cherry scent of blood magic and drugs, probably coke or speed. He sniffed and spit on the floor. Nice.

"Theresa Garcia."

She stood slightly away from the wall and, from my vantage, studied me from just above Pike's left shoulder. She wore a suit jacket and black slacks over her solid build. Her hair was pulled back in a braid. She couldn't be over five feet tall but looked like she could wrestle a bull elephant to the ground. Her hazel eyes were sharp and inquisitive, and she did not break eye contact. I figured her for hard core exercise and maybe the occasional weekend bender.

"Tomi Nowlan."

A girl who looked like she was twelve going on twenty-one leaned hip and shoulder against the wall, and chewed gum. Her dark hair was tucked behind her ears but a lot of bangs hung in a heavy curtain to edge her eyes. She had on a hoodie and low-waisted jeans that showed a thin glimpse of hipbone where three thin razor scars shone white against her white skin. Her belt was wide and black, anchored by a heavy silver buckle shaped like a doggy bone. She gave me a flat stare, blew a big pink bubble, and bit it with her back molars. A cutter.

"Beatrice Lufkin."

Beatrice was also standing, wearing jeans and a nice beige sweater. Walnut colored hair stuck out in wild curls barely kept in check by her wide flower-pattern headband. Her eyes were too large in her round, freckled face, but she smiled, revealing dimples, and surprise, surprise, she seemed genuinely happy to see me. "I've hoped to meet you for some time now," she said. "You've done some really great jobs in the city."

"Thanks," I said, feeling like I might have a chance at making friends with her. I guessed her drug of choice was probably weed, mushrooms, and wine coolers.

"Jamar Legare."

Jamar was at least three inches taller than me and wore his mustache and beard in a circle around his mouth, his dark curls shaved close to his scalp, and a pair of thick-rimmed glasses that did nothing to hide his deep brown eyes. He had on a jean jacket with a hoodie under it and seemed comfortable surveying the room, one thumb tucked in his front pocket.

"Afternoon," he said.

I nodded to him. Tough call, but I'd guess alcohol. "Jack Quinn."

Whiskey Guy, the closest person on my left, was in the middle of lighting a cigarette. He gave me a brief nod.

The prospects of me having my own bit of wall to lean against were pretty low, since the room wasn't very large, something made worse by the low ceiling. Everyone was scattered to maximize the distance from each other. So I just stood to one side of the door, nearest Whiskey Guy—I mean Jack—and blond Sid on the other side of the door to my right.

"Davy," Pike said, "is this it?"

Davy, the Hangover Kid, opened his eyes and looked around the room. "Yep. Everyone who said they'd come."

I was right. He was the one who answered the phone.

Okay, so my theory that Hounds didn't know one another had been seriously thrown out the window in the last minute or so. It looked like all these people knew one another and knew other Hounds working in the city. Maybe I was the only one disinclined to hang out. Maybe in my push to be free of my father and his expectations, I'd taken the concept of solitary into every other aspect of my life. Maybe Hounds hung out all the time at special Hound bars, had Hound parties, and, hells, did Hound job-share and babysat one another's Hound kids.

"Anyone have any news?" Pike asked.

No one spoke. Not even me. I had no idea what they considered news. Did ghosts count? Being hunted by a blood and drug lord? Magic assassins?

"Anyone have any complaints about an employer?"

Silence.

"How about leads on jobs?" he asked.

Nothing.

At this rate, the meeting was going to be over in about thirty seconds.

Pike pulled a small notebook and pen out of his shirt pocket. "Who's working where?"

Sid cleared his throat. "Gotta job with the cops. Don't know where yet."

Pike noted that in his book and then looked expectantly at motherly Dahlia next to Sid.

"Nothing that I know of," she said.

"Davy?" Pike asked.

Davy didn't even bother opening his eyes. "The college wants me to run the halls for a couple days. Probably do it this week."

"Do it sober," Pike said.

Davy shook his head like he'd heard that before and hadn't listened last time either.

Anthony spoke up. "I'll be wherever you are, old man."

Pike noted something in his book. From the motion of the top of his pen, I was pretty sure he'd just written "ass."

Theresa the elephant wrestler said, "I'm still on retainer with Nike." She shrugged. "It's been quiet."

"Good," Pike grunted. "Tomi?"

"Jesus, Pike," the cutter girl said, "do we have to do this every week?"

"Every week you show up. Every week you want someone to know where the hell you are and who the hell you're putting your life on the line for."

She chewed, blew, popped. I noticed Davy's body language changed, and Tomi glanced from beneath her heavy bangs over at him, at his still-closed eyes, at his just-a-little-too-shallow-to-be-relaxed breathing, at his hands that had clenched, probably unconsciously, into fists.

She bit her bottom lip and looked away.

"I have a private client," she said in a dull tone. "In the West Hills. That's all I'll say."

Davy's fists went white at the knuckles.

"Bea?" Pike asked, shifting the tension in the room.

"Me?" Beatrice smiled, and those dimples nipped her cheeks. She nodded, her wild curls bouncing. "I'm still pulling morgue duty for at least the rest of the month. And if I get killed there, at least you'll have plenty of witnesses on the slab. If you can get them to talk!" She giggled.

My eyebrows shot up. Okay, she wasn't all freckles and sweet strawberries and cream like she looked. I made a mental note: never underestimate Beatrice. Or anyone else in the room for that matter.

Jamar just shook his head and smiled. "Damn, girl. You gotta get a different job. You sound like you're starting to enjoy sniffing corpses."

Bea, still giggling, gave him a huge smile and shrugged, her hands up, like who could blame her.

"I'm working a new section of MLK Boulevard for

the police," Jamar said. "Mostly day work, looking for trap and trigger spells, illegal Offloads. Gang crap. Nothing I can't handle."

"They going to open that up for another Hound to work it with you?" Pike asked.

Jamar pushed his glasses back up on his nose. "I asked maybe a month ago. Don't think they have it in the budget."

Pike noted that and then waved his pen at Whiskey Guy. "Jack?"

Jack exhaled smoke. "City called me in for some piddly things. Public nuisance illusions, screwing with the art in the parks, stink spells in public halls, that sort of shit."

"Okay," Pike said.

And that left me.

"Allie?" Pike looked over at me.

"I have a job for the police. Tonight. With Detective Stotts."

At the mention of his name, the body language in the room changed. There wasn't a person in that room who liked Stotts. Interesting. Apparently his cursed reputation had proceeded him.

"Has anyone ever worked for him?" I asked.

Sid, next to me, rubbed at the side of his nose. "I Hounded for him. Once. Spooky shit happens around him. People die."

"So I've been told," I said. "But since I've been out of the loop with all this"—I waved my hand to include them all—"Hound bonding stuff, I was hoping someone here could tell me what's so dangerous about working for him. Maybe give me a couple examples of what happened to other Hounds."

No one said anything for so long, I figured the Hound bonding stuff didn't include sharing the details with the new girl of how one another died. Or maybe they didn't know.

Then Jamar spoke. "I heard about a guy, name was Piller, I think. He worked a serial murder case for Stotts. Some lowlife robbing old people, killing them, and dumping the bodies up in the coast range. Used a lot of Binding, Hold, and Influence spells. There was always a mark of magic left behind in the old people's houses. The killer liked to leave a 'note,' you know? Anyway, on the third time out, Piller was Hounding back a spell—getting close, real close to the killer. But just before he could pin the guy, Piller walked off the Steel Bridge and died."

"Walked off the Steel Bridge?" I asked.

"That's what I heard."

Bea piped up. "Remember Rosalee? She took a job with Stotts. Illegal tapping into the cisterns of magic beneath the city and Offloading the price of using that magic onto some unregulated S and M joints—killed a few politically influential customers while they were doing some back door 'negotiations.' "

She giggled, and several other people chuckled. "I would have killed to see that! Anyway, Rosalee took her money and left the state the day after the job was finished. They found her dead at a truck stop in Nebraska."

"That could be a horrible coincidence," I said with little conviction.

Sid snapped his fingers. "Wasn't Herm— Har— What was his name? The Swedish guy?"

"Herlief," Dahlia chimed in.

"Right," Sid said. "Herlief. He worked a couple cases for Stotts—maybe three or four. Did okay. Until his head fell off."

"Oh, come on," I said.

Sid put one hand over his heart. "I swear, it's true. He was Hounding for Stotts. I don't remember what the case was—" He looked around the room.

Jack stabbed his cigarette toward Sid, leaving a trail of smoke behind. "Magical coercion—someone trying to make people join something, give all their money to something. . . ."

"Right," Sid said. "So it wasn't even dead body and kinky sex stuff. Herlief traced the spells back to the perps, and then the next day while he was getting coffee, a cable from a construction site snapped, whipped down, and bam!" He snapped his fingers again. "Severed his spine. Took his head right off." He chuckled.

Okay, this was one sick group of people. Still, I understood the laughter—gallows humor. It could have been anyone of them, anyone of us, in those Hounds' shoes.

As a matter of fact, tonight, it was going to be me.

"But no one actually died during their Hounding job, right?" I asked.

Pike shrugged. "It's happened. Death is a risk when you work for the police. Any of them."

And his understated acceptance of that did more to calm me than if he had told me there was no chance anything would go wrong. After all, Pike had been Hounding for the police for years. And he wasn't dead yet.

"Okay," I said, bracing myself for my next question. "Any of you ever seen a ghost?"

The easy smiles stalled out, and even Davy opened his eyes and leaned forward to give me a weird look.

"I have a possible client who says he's seen a ghost," I said with a straight face, because Grant might someday be a client, and he told me he'd seen a ghost once. I know, I was lying and justifying my cowardly behavior. But I didn't feel the need to come off like one hundred percent wacko at the first meeting.

"He's seen full-body apparitions and glyphing that appeared on a wall and then disappeared. He thought the glyphs were warnings." I left out the Death glyph part.

Davy was the only one who spoke. "You Hounded a ghost sighting?"

"No. Look, I'm just asking if any of you have had any experiences involving ghosts."

Everyone shook their heads. But it did not escape my notice that they had all become awfully quiet and sober at the change of subject. Strange. Ghosts could startle them to silence, but people's heads popping off—that was comedy.

Or maybe asking about ghosts meant I was nuts. I mean, I had a reputation too. Besides my being the daughter of Daniel Beckstrom, it wasn't exactly a secret that magic knocked holes in my memory. It didn't take a genius to wonder if magic took potshots at the rest of my mental facilities.

Screw it. I so didn't care what they thought.

"Okay," I said. "Thanks."

Pike gave me an I'll-talk-to-you-later look. That, at least, was something.

"Anything else?" he asked the room in general.

More head shaking.

"Good. Anyone Hounding for non-police want backup?" No one answered, including me, because I didn't know what he was talking about.

"Looks like we have Sid, Jamar, and Allie doing police work," Pike said, referencing his notes. "Who volunteers for backup?"

"I'll take Sid," Jack said, exhaling smoke. "I'm on call, but I already did a job today. Don't think they'll call me back until tomorrow."

"That's okay with me," Sid said. "So long as you keep a low profile. And stay downwind with those cancer sticks, okay? They kill my sniffer."

Jack just gave him a crooked-tooth smile. "You won't even know I'm there."

"Theresa," Pike asked, "do you have time around your Nike duties to take Jamar?"

"This week, sure," she said.

"Don't know that I like that," Jamar said. "It can get dicey in that part of town. Lots of drug movement over there."

"You do your job," Theresa said, "and I'll do mine."

Jamar just took a deep breath and let it out while shaking his head.

This looked like some sort of weird buddy-system, job-shadow matchup.

"Anyone want to tell the new girl what's going on?" I asked.

Pike continued as if I hadn't spoken. "Who wants to take Allie?"

"Take Allie what?" I said.

"I'll do it," Davy said.

"Do what?" I asked again.

Tomi stiffened and stopped chewing her gum. She glared at Davy.

Davy looked across the room, made eye contact with her. "I'm not doing anything tonight," he said to Pike, though it was obviously aimed at Tomi. "And the college doesn't need me for a few days. I'm free."

Tomi held very still, her face blank. But she was young. She hadn't figured out how to keep the pain out of her eyes yet.

She did know how to recover quickly though. She tossed her bangs and muttered something that was ninety-five percent obscenity and five percent poetry. She looped her thumbs in her belt and stared Davy down, daring him to challenge her.

Pike broke up the little lovers' spat by speaking up so Davy would have to look at him. "Drink and eat something first. I don't want to hear about Allie tripping over you or her worrying about you being out there."

"Wait," I said. "Out there? Do you mean when I Hound for Stotts tonight? No. Absolutely not. No way. I work alone. I always Hound alone." I so didn't want this kid on my tail. Especially if Trager were after me.

"Settle down, Beckstrom," Pike growled. "He's not going to do any Hounding. And you don't owe him a cut on the job or any favors, unless maybe someday you want to volunteer to shadow him. He's just going to be in the neighborhood while you're doing your job. An extra pair of eyes and ears. Someone to call for help if things go wrong, that's all."

"That's all?" Okay, why was I the only one in the room who thought this was a massively bad idea?

"People die when they Hound for Stotts, remember? Heads fall off?"

"I'm not Hounding for Stotts," Davy said. "You are. All I'm going to do is be on the same street or block when you're working, keeping an ear out in case something comes up."

"Well, good luck, because I'm not going to tell you where I'm Hounding."

Davy grinned, and some of the pale sick look seemed to leave him, revealing a mischievous, disarming twinkle in his eye. He was young—maybe as young as seventeen—but he was also very clearly a smart, ambitious man. "You won't have to tell me. Finding you will be half the fun."

I opened my mouth.

"And," he said, cutting me off, "I'll stay so far out of your way you won't even know we're in the same city."

"That's it, then," Pike said. "We're done."

Everyone pushed away from walls and chairs and started toward the door. They all filed out, no one touching each other, not even inadvertently. No one talking.

Too damn weird.

Pike was the last to get up, which was good. I had some talking still left in me.

He pulled his coat off of the back of the chair and put it on while he strolled over to me. "Glad you could make it."

"Pike," I said. "This is crazy."

He paused in his effort to zip up his jacket and gave me a hard look. "You have some problem with me trying to make sure people stay alive?"

"No."

"Then I don't want to hear it. You don't like it, don't show up next week."

He walked past me, waiting for me to leave the room so he could turn off the light and shut the door.

"Until then, you're stuck with Davy keeping an eye on you tonight. Don't underestimate the kid; he's good." Pike started down the half-constructed hallway.

"I work alone," I grumbled behind him.

"Allie." He sighed and stopped. He turned to me. "We all work alone. Having Davy watch you isn't about the job. It's about you. He'll have a cell phone on him. If something goes sour, he'll call 911. Easy as that. So stop whining and shut the hell up. You kids drive me batshit."

I laughed. I don't know why. I guess it was I'd never thought Mr. Tough Guy would willingly set himself up for babysitting duty.

"I bet you're a real hit with the grandkids," I said.

Pike nodded. "I am." He started walking again. "So talk to me about seeing ghosts."

"I didn't say I'd seen a ghost."

"You can't fool a nose. Lies stink." He glanced over his shoulder. "You stink, Beckstrom."

"Gee," I said, "if I knew I was going to get such a great pep talk, I would have come to one of these things a long time ago."

"Fine. Don't talk." We had reached the door at the end of the corridor, which the other Hounds had closed behind them. He rested his hand on the latch to pull it open.

"Wait." I rubbed at my forehead and gave up on trying to decide if I should be honest with Pike. Who else could I trust? At least I knew he wanted what was best for Hounds. And I was a Hound. So maybe he wanted what was best for me. And if not . . . well, I'd just deal with that.

"I have seen a ghost."

Pike let go of the door and crossed his arms over his chest. He leaned back on a bare stud, patient as a stone.

"I saw my father's ghost. He said, 'Seek the dead,' and he touched me. He smelled like wintergreen, Pike. Just like when he was alive." I kept my tone and gaze level, even though thinking about it made me feel like I needed to wash again. I was sure Pike noticed my elevated heartbeat, the acrid smell of my cold sweat.

"I saw more ghosts too, but they were different from my dad. Sort of pale pastel colored, with black holes where their eyes should be. But they were still people. I could count the buttons on their shirts, see the laces on their shoes. They touched me too, and it burned. . . ." I pressed my lips together and then let out a frustrated sound. "Don't just stand there and stare at me. Do you know anything about ghosts? Do you know anything about them messing with magic?"

He frowned. "What do you mean?"

"They, some of them, the watercolor ones, suck. Magic," I amended. "Spells. I could see them when I cast Reveal, and they pulled my spell apart and ate it like it was cotton candy."

The silence that stretched between us would have been comical if I wasn't worried that there were things out there—ghostly things—that could do that kind of shit.

"What are you using to manage the pain, Allie?" he asked.

Sweet hells. He thought I was hallucinating.

"Aspirin. Tylenol. Bactine."

He sniffed but could smell no lie on me.

"I'm not joking, Pike. And believe me, I don't like standing here in front of you and sounding like an idiot. I prefer to be an idiot in the privacy of my own home."

Pike looked down at his shoe. "I've seen . . . things. Ghosts, I suppose you could call them. Heard voices, all that." He looked back up at me. "But I've been in wars, Allie. And wars either blind a man or open his eyes to things he can never look away from. I figure some of the things I've seen have more to do with that than actual spirits. You seeing your father, I can understand. It's hard to lose a parent."

"He said, 'Seek the dead,' " I said. "Does that mean anything to you?"

He shook his head. "Not enough to go on. Maybe he was trying to tell you we all end up there—dead—someday. No way to know."

"I guess not," I said.

"Now, the other ghosts you've seen—the magic eaters? I've been around this town for almost as long as magic has been in use, and I've never heard of such a thing."

"I know what I saw," I said.

"Didn't say you didn't. So let's assume you saw ghosts—or something—that could take apart a spell like cotton candy and eat it. If there really is something out there like that, then we might just have a problem on our hands."

Had a real flair with the understatement, that man.

"Have you talked to anyone else about it?"

"I mentioned ghosts to a friend of mine. I didn't talk about the magic eating thing."

He stared off in the middle distance, obviously rolling options around. "I'll ask some people I know. But I think the best way to find out what you're experiencing might be to ask Stotts about it."

"Yeah, that doesn't work so good for me," I said. "I have a strict rule: only one person per day gets to find out how crazy I am. Plus he's signing my paycheck. I don't need him thinking I've gone insane."

"I see," Pike said. "When you decide to stop being such a pansy ass and worrying about what people think about you instead of your own safety, talk to Stotts. He has the inside track on a lot of the weird shit that happens in this town."

"Anyone ever tell you you're a jerk?"

Pike grunted, but it sounded more like a laugh. "At length. Now talk to me about Trager," he said.

"First tell me what happened to your hand. It was bleeding this morning."

"That's none of your business, Beckstrom."

We stared each other down until I got tired of it. Jerk.

"I had a little meeting with Lon Trager today. On the bus."

So much for Pike the jerk. Even though he didn't move, didn't twitch, he transformed into Pike the killer.

"Explain." Cold as steel.

"He sat next to me. Had six of his thugs with guns with him. Told me he wanted me to do him a favor, and all the bad blood between us would be forgotten.

He said he wants to make nice." I waited, but Pike didn't say anything.

"He wants me to bring you to him. By midnight tomorrow."

"And?"

"And he got some of my blood."

We both knew what that meant. Trager intended to use my blood with magic. I, however, didn't know what he might want to do with it other than cast that glyph thing he'd left on my thigh. I hadn't studied blood magic in school. Probably because it was illegal.

"What do you think he's going to do with it?" I asked.

Pike was looking straight at me, but I could tell from his unfocused gaze that it was not me he was thinking about. He was weighing possibilities, costs, outcome.

"Nothing good," he finally said. "I want you to let me take care of him."

"Like hells I will. Weren't you just saying we have to watch each other's backs? Hounds don't Hound alone and all that crap? Trager wanted both of us there. Wanted me to deliver you to him. I'm not going to be left behind and killed because you want to take him mano a mano."

Pike's face flushed, and I could see the veins at his temples. He was very, very angry. At me. I braced myself, ready to yell it out or, hell, fight it out with him until he realized how stupid it would be for him to take care of Trager alone.

But Pike did not yell. He closed his eyes and rubbed his palm over his face. "Allie. This is between him and me."

"No, Pike. It's not. I know you want to kill him for what he did to your granddaughter. But it's time to stop being pansy asses and acting like we don't need help. We should go talk to the police about this. We should get protection—both of us. I have proof that can put him in jail—he threatened me and stabbed me in the leg. No one can tamper with that evidence, and I can't be bought. Let's get him legal, so legal he'll never see the light of day, never hurt anyone's granddaughter again."

Pike pulled his hand away from his face. He didn't look angry. He looked tired.

"Allie . . ."

"Legal, Pike. Let's do this right. Let's get this bastard for life."

He looked down. Stared at the floor. Finally he nodded. Slow. Beaten. Old.

He tipped his head back up. "You're right," he said, his voice tired. "That's the smart thing to do. Get the police on it, help them if they need it. I could find him if they want me to. I'll never forget that devil's stench. But I can't go down to the station today. I promise I'll meet you there tomorrow afternoon."

A wave of relief, a knot of fear released in me. "Morning would be better, don't you think?"

"I got crap to do with Anthony—for his mother. It will take most of the night tonight and part of tomorrow."

"What kind of crap?" I was afraid he was evading this, evading me, trying to find a way to ditch on our deal.

He winced. "Handyman crap." He tugged his sleeve back to reveal his wrist. The gauze bandage was wrapped up his forearm about six inches, and thick gauze pads lay across the inside of his wrist. It looked like a poorly executed suicide attempt.

"Pike, you didn't try to . . ."

"Christ, Beckstrom. What are you thinking?" He tugged his sleeve back down. "I damn near took my hand off with a goddamn circular saw this morning. And I still have to fix the sink, take care of a broken window, and patch a hole in the goddamn roof. I'm going to get that done before I deal with the cops. And you can wipe that smile off your face."

"I always knew you were a good guy, Pike."

"Shove it, Beckstrom."

"Noon tomorrow at the station?" I asked sweetly.

He nodded. "Might be as late as one, but around then."

"You do know I'm going to talk to Stotts about Trager tonight, right?" I said.

"Figured you would."

"He'll want to put you under protective custody," I said.

"He'll know where to find me, won't he?"

I nodded. "I'm sorry."

He didn't say anything. That was almost harder, seeing him give in like that. It was another sign of how ready he was to retire, to be done with all this, to let the police take care of the city without him.

"Thanks for doing this the right way," I added.

"You don't think I'm going to do this without asking for something in return, do you?" he asked.

"Seriously?" Not that I should be surprised. Nothing without a price in this town. Not even friendship. "What do you want?"

"I want you to promise me you'll stay here in the city. After I . . . retire. 'Cause this damn sure is going to be the last time I work with the police. And when the Hounds contact you, if they need you—even if they say they don't—that you'll go to them. Look after them."

"You know," I said, "we're friends." I stumbled a little on the last word, but it was true. Of all the Hounds I knew, Pike and I had hit off a strange sort of dysfunctional teacher-student, or maybe even father-daughter relationship. "But you are so not my boss. No one tells me what to do."

"I'm telling you what to do. And I expect you to listen to me." Then, a little softer. "Just this once."

What would it matter if I said yes? I didn't think Pike was going to be retired for long. He'd be back, after he got tired of the sun and sand. Back to boss me and all the rest of the Hounds around. Back to take a kid under his wing and try to set him straight.

"Okay," I said. "I'll look after your little sewing circle for as long as it lasts. That's all I'm promising."

"That's enough."

He leaned away from the stud and opened the door. The heavy smells from a restaurant mixed with the perfume of the candle shop. I realized I hadn't eaten lunch yet. But the smells were overwhelming and triggered my headache. Add to that a nice helping of brighter light out in the main hallway, and my hunger turned to nausea in three seconds flat.

Neat.

I walked past Pike into the light and stink of the rest of the world. It was still early afternoon. I had time to go home, chew down some more painkillers, maybe sleep off some of the get-a-clue-and-set-a-damn-Disbursement-next-time headache before I had to meet Stotts at the station at five.

And right now, a little sleep sounded fabulous.

"See you tomorrow," I said to Pike as I headed toward the nearest set of stairs that would take me up into the retail space and on to daylight.

"Allie?"

"Yeah?" I looked over my shoulder at him.

His pale blue eyes burned in the shadows from the hallway. "It was worth it."

And then he walked away, down the corridor quiet and quick.

I hoped he meant getting the Hound group together was worth it. I hoped he meant Hounding for twenty-five years was worth it. I hoped he meant deciding to retire was worth it.

Or maybe he meant putting Trager in jail once was worth it, and it would be worth doing it again. The right way.

Chapter Eleven

I emerged from the building just as the bus pulled to a stop across the street. I swore and jogged for it. I caught the bus, scanned the people there, and didn't see anyone who looked like they were going to stab me. Just in case, I chose an empty seat near the driver and sat down.

Unfortunately, it was the wrong bus. That meant I got to spend an extra twenty minutes lurching from stop to stop, nursing my headache made worse by the stink of diesel that poured in the doors every time the beast belched its way back into traffic. And just in case that wasn't fun enough, once I got off the bus, I had an eight-block trudge—uphill—to get to my apartment. The rain had let up, which was something, I guess, but the wind was still blowing out of the Gulf of Alaska, too cold and too strong.

Okay, yes. I was feeling a little sorry for myself.

And the headache made it impossible to pay close attention to the people around me. It wasn't like I was wandering in a blind fog; it was more of a set-jaw determined slog up the hill, and I just didn't have it in me to twitch at every little sound. If Trager's men decided to jump me, I would beat them senseless with my shoe.

So when I paused to catch my breath outside a restaurant with big glass windows, it probably took me only a full thirty seconds to notice the man waving at me.

Apparently Davy had taken Pike's words to heart. He was sitting at a table at the window, alone, half a huge burger demolished on the plate in front of him.

I frowned. There was no way it was a coincidence he chose this restaurant this close to my apartment on this day.

He was planning to stalk me. The little twerp.

I didn't waste my energy glaring at him. I started up the block.

Davy jumped out of his seat. From my peripheral vision I watched him continue to wave his hands at me while he dodged tables, heading to the door and getting there faster than me since he was inside and didn't have to deal with the incline. I hoped someone stuck out their leg and tripped him.

No luck.

Just as I passed the restaurant door, it flew open. Out strode Davy. The wind shifted and I got a hint of his scent. Beneath the cloud of burgers and onions from the restaurant, Davy smelled like warm cedar and lemons. The taint of booze lingered on his sweat too, adding a sour note.

"Here," he said, closing the distance between us in a few loping strides. Kid was all leg. He stepped in front of me and shoved something at my face.

I knew what it was before I even looked down.

French fries stacked in a cardboard carton, two packs of ketchup, and a napkin tucked down one side.

"Ordered an extra for Tom—" He swallowed the rest of what he was going to say and tried to hack it back up before I noticed. "—for a friend who didn't show up. I think you and I started off on a bad foot today. No hard feelings, okay?"

Ordered for a friend. Right. His angry cutter girlfriend, Tomi.

"Did you spit on them?" I asked.

"I thought about it." His mischievous twinkle was back.

I'd promised Pike I'd look after the Hounds. And even though Pike wasn't retired yet, this was a part of it.

I took the carton. Still warm. He either hadn't been waiting for his "friend" for very long, or he had ordered the fries late into the meal. He might have called her and asked her to eat lunch with him after he was already at the table. She might even have said yes and then called back to bail on him.

I so did not miss my high school relationships.

"Tomi?" I asked just to make sure.

He tucked his hands under his armpits and shrugged. "Not anymore, you know?"

"Yeah," I said, not knowing what else to say. I didn't know him, didn't know her, and didn't have much luck with my own relationships anyway. Even though my stomach was still queasy and my head hurt, I pulled out a nice thick fry and took a bite. Hot, crunchy, salty, and greasy. Really, really good.

"Thanks," I said, lifting the carton a little. "I think I was starving." I popped another fry in my mouth.

"Next time we start off on a bad foot, could you bring me orange soda, too?"

He grinned. "No prob."

I shoved another fry in my mouth and walked past him. "Excellent," I mumbled. "See you tonight."

"Not if I'm any good, you won't."

"I expect you to be very, very good, Davy," I said over my shoulder, thinking about Trager. "There are bad men out there. You stay out of their way, out of my way, and I'll give you a cookie."

"Gee, thanks, Mom."

I ignored that and kept walking, stuffing my mouth with hot, salty fry goodness. I didn't even hear Davy walk away until the door to the restaurant closed behind him.

He was good.

The last few blocks went by quickly. I devoured the fries like I hadn't eaten this century, hoping against hope that my headache would let me keep them down.

I made it to my apartment without any other interruptions and clomped up the stairs and down the hall to my door.

I paused outside my door and listened for movement on the other side before opening it. Some old habits are worth keeping. There was no one in my apartment. I checked every room, including the bathroom, where I swallowed a couple more aspirin and wished I had something stronger. Then I tugged off my coat, hat, gloves, and boots and left them in a pile on my bedroom floor.

Standing next to my bed, I took off my jeans but left my tights on. I wanted nothing more than to crawl into my bed naked and be wrapped up in the softness of my sheets, but I had to get up in a few hours to Hound. Getting undressed and comfortable would only make me sleep too deeply.

It had nothing to do with not wanting to be naked and asleep if my dad's ghost popped in to pay me another visit. It had nothing to do with an ex-con blood magic dealer looking to break my neck.

Okay. It had everything to do with that.

The tights stayed on. I did take off my sweater but left my long-sleeved T-shirt on too. Good enough.

I crawled under the covers and remembered to set my alarm for three thirty. I closed my eyes and counted each beat of my headache until it lulled me senseless and, finally, to sleep.

Three thirty showed up far too quickly.

But even that much sleep helped shave away the edges of my price-for-using-magic headache so now it was just an uncomfortable tightness at the back of my neck and temples. That, I could deal with.

I got up, got dressed, brewed a pot of coffee, and took my time drinking half of it before calling a cab. I had plenty of time to get down to the police station and meet Stotts by five. I looked out my living room window. The winter day was fading fast and would be dark soon. I checked the sky. It wasn't raining, but I didn't see any blue out there either.

My gaze wandered to the street. People just getting off work or done with class for the day hurried along the sidewalks, trying to beat the rush hour crowds. A couple hearty bicyclists pumped up the hill. And there, in the shadow of an awning, two men stepped forward.

They stopped at the edge of the overhang and looked up at my building, at my window.

There was just enough light left in the day for me to make out their faces. Trager's men, two of them, from the bus.

Shit.

They stared at my window, stared at me, because this building didn't have fancy tinted windows. No, with the curtain pulled back, anyone could see into my living room. Anyone could see me.

A cab pulled up in front of the building and I let the curtain drop. If I missed my cab, I'd have to take the bus. And I was not going on another ride with those goons.

Hands shaking, I tucked my hair up in my knit hat and patted my pockets to make sure I had everything I needed. I took a deep breath and calmed myself. I was going to be fine. Let the goons watch me. Hell, let them follow me all the way to the police department; I didn't care. All I had to do was get in the cab without letting them touch me.

Feeling a little more settled, I left my apartment and jogged down the stairs. Before I pushed through the door to the street, I looked up and down the sidewalk to be sure no one was waiting to jump me. All clear.

The wind gusted at my back as I hurried to the cab. I ducked into the backseat and glanced across the street. Trager's men were still there, still under the awning, still watching me.

"Evening," the cabdriver said.

"Hey." I didn't look over at him. "Police station, please."

The cab slipped into traffic. I watched the goons watch me drive away and was really, really glad I'd called the cab.

Once they were out of sight, I sat back and waited for the police station to show up. I didn't know what case Stotts wanted me to Hound. I hadn't read a newspaper in a month, and I didn't watch news on TV, so I wasn't even sure what crimes had been committed lately.

Well, except that Trager was out, and I'm sure his men had been keeping busy.

Whatever Stotts wanted me to do, I planned to survive it with my head still attached, curse or no curse, Trager or no Trager.

I wondered if Davy was already following me. Unless he had a car, he was going to have a hard time keeping up with the cab. He might just be waiting for me at the station. After all, I'd said I was working for Stotts tonight. It was what I would do if I were him.

The more I thought about it, the more I thought Davy was probably a pretty smart kid. Driven. He'd have to be to Hound for a living and to be good enough to get hired on by places like the college.

But despite Pike's assurance that Davy could take care of himself, I was going to watch out for him too. I didn't know how far Stotts' curse reached, and I did not want to see Davy walk off a bridge or get shot by one of Trager's people.

The cab dropped me off in front of the station. I paid and strode up the stairs and through the door. The cavernous lobby was bustling with people. I paused inside the door, trying to remember where Stotts had wanted me to meet him. Not down their secret staircase to their secret door and their secret lair.

Maybe I should go find a receptionist to let him know I was here. Luckily I didn't have to do anything. Detective Paul Stotts pushed through a door across the lobby, carrying two paper cups with lids.

He caught sight of me, smiled, and strolled across the lobby.

"Allie, good to see you." He offered me one of the cups. "Nothing fancy. Black."

"Is it from the break room?"

"Oh, God, no." He faked shock. "You haven't drank that, have you? You know we only use it for interrogation."

I shook my head and smiled.

"This is from the place on the corner. The good place."

There were two places on the corner. One, a little mom-and-pop coffee shop that really did have good coffee. The other was a big corporate joint. I'd never much liked the corporation's coffee—they seemed incapable of roasting beans without burning them.

I accepted the cup and took a drink. It was from the mom-and-pop shop. He had good taste in coffee. Well, he and I had at least one thing in common. "Thanks," I said. "You know your beans. You must be from around here."

"Portland?" he asked.

"The Northwest."

He gestured toward the doors behind me, indicating we could start walking. "Seattle. Moved down to be with family when my mom lost her job. I was about sixteen. And you?"

We reached the sidewalk and strolled against the wind up the street.

"Here," I said. "My dad's business kept us in the city." Honestly, it had been years since someone asked me where I grew up. My family name was almost synonymous with the Storm Rods and the lead and glass lines that conducted magic throughout the city.

He stopped next to a dark green sedan parked along the street. "This is mine. Are you ready?"

"It would be nice to know what the job is exactly."

He pressed a button on his key chain and unlocked the doors. "Go ahead and get in. I'll tell you."

I slid in the passenger's side, grateful to be out of the wind and out of the open. My cheeks and nose felt stingy-hot, windburned. With my pale skin, I probably looked like a snowman with a head cold.

Detective Stotts' car looked and smelled brand-new, with a light leather interior and several high-tech policelike things mounted under and out from the dashboard. The only ornamentation in it was a rosary with a small charm hanging from the rearview mirror. If you judged a man by his car, Paul Stotts was neat, paid attention to detail, and did his share of praying.

Who wouldn't in his line of work?

He put his coffee in the holder, and I kept mine in my hands for added warmth through my gloves.

"I don't know if you keep up on the news," he said as he started the car.

"Not much," I said. "I got used to avoiding the media in my teen years when I was rebelling against my father."

"Just your teen years?" He turned on the blinker and eased the car into traffic.

Well, it looked like one of us kept up on the news. I shrugged. Let him figure it out.

"Does the job have something to do with the news?" I asked.

"It does. There have been a lot of disappearances on the northeast side of town. Mostly teen girls."

"How many girls?"

"Between six and eight."

"You don't know for sure?"

"A lot of the girls were involved in gangs. Some might be runaways, skipping town on their own."

"So I'm going to Hound places they were last seen?"

"Something like that."

Okay, so at least I wouldn't have to Hound any dead bodies. I was happy to leave the corpse sniffing to dimpled-and-bubbly Beatrice.

"And you think there was something magical about the girls' disappearances?"

"I've had a couple Hounds sniff out the sites. It's possible magic was used to either sedate the girls, harm the girls, or transfer the girls."

"Possible? Magic is a pretty clear yes/no thing," I said.

Hounds were experts at seeing, tracing, and smelling the difference between every kind of spell, even when the spells decay into ash. A good Hound could tell you where the spell came from to within a few yards of the caster. An excellent Hound studied signature variables and could tell you exactly who cast the spell by the "handwriting." I knew there were excellent Hounds who worked for the police, including Pike.

Stotts just shook his head. "We want another opinion."

"Does this have something to do with Lon Trager?"

He glanced over at me. "So you do keep up with some news."

"Not really. I ran into Trager on the bus this morning."

"Is that so?" Stotts looked calm, even his breathing was still normal, but the rest of his body language screamed at me. He was worried.

"He told me he and I could live and let live if I did him a favor. He wants me to bring Martin Pike to him by tomorrow midnight."

"And you didn't report it?"

"That's what I'm doing now."

He took a breath, let it out. "Do you know why he asked you to find Pike?"

"He hates Pike. Hates me too. Mentioned he'd be willing to kill me. Since he also mentioned that he has men everywhere, I figure he has the resources to find Pike. Pike and I don't see each other much. So if I had to guess, I'd say Trager really wants both of us in the same room at the same time for some reason.

"You don't look surprised," I added. "Did you already know about this?"

"Lon Trager is a person of interest. We keep an eye on him."

"That wasn't exactly a yes," I said.

"No," he said. "It wasn't. Have you talked to Pike?"

I nodded. "Today. Told him about Trager. He's willing to cooperate with the police."

"Interesting," he said like it really was. "I don't suppose you might know where we could find him."

"Pike? He's helping a friend on the east side of

town do some house repair. I don't know her name, but her son's name is Anthony Bell."

Stotts nodded and took a sip of coffee.

"Does the job tonight have something to do with Lon Trager?" I asked again.

"I'm not going to say anything more about it," he said. "I don't want to influence your opinion."

Yeah, that's usually the way the police played it.

"So," I said. "I've heard people die when they Hound for you. They say you're cursed."

Stotts drove for several blocks in silence. He didn't even reach over to take another drink of his coffee. It started raining, big, intermittent drops. He flicked the windshield wipers on low.

"The cases I deal with always involve magic being used to harm others," he said. "There are risks when anyone Hounds for me. But I think my . . . reputation has been exaggerated."

"Sixteen Hounds in six years?"

"People who Hound tend to live short lives. I think it's from using magic so much and from not buying Proxies for relief from the pain. Most people who Hound use the money for drugs instead. So if you run the facts, you see I only hire experienced Hounds, which puts one mark against them—they've been using magic and probably drugs for a long time. And if you run the numbers you see a national average of twice that many Hounds who work for the police dying in that same amount of time."

"Sounds like you've done a lot of thinking about this."

"It's clear the odds are against most Hounds who work for me before they begin to work for me."

"So there is no curse?"

He picked up his coffee without looking at me. "I didn't say that." He turned a corner onto the bridge, and the rosary on his mirror swung in silent counterpoint.

Chapter Twelve

The wind whipped up off of the river and blustered hard enough to rock Stotts' car and throw rain that sounded like rocks against the windows. It was going to be miserable out there.

"I don't suppose there's any chance the girls were last seen indoors?" I asked.

"One of them," Stotts said. "They all disappeared from the same general area—about a four-block radius. There are two places that are still hot. One's on the street; the other is in a parking garage."

"Well, at least one's out of the rain." I drank my coffee, letting the warmth and caffeine bolster my confidence and clear my mind. I could do this. I could go stand out in the rain with a cursed magic cop, Hound an old hit and not lose control of magic, and keep a lookout for Trager's thugs. Oh, and Davy.

I'm sure it was all going to go just fine. I mean, nothing weird had happened to me all day, right?

"We'll go to the parking garage first. Maybe we'll get lucky and get a break in the rain before you Hound the hit on the street."

The neighborhood shifted from office buildings and fast food joints to tumbling down apartments and warehouses, mostly concrete fitted with the older, heavier iron pipes with almost no glass showing. Crouched beneath a blackened sky in the driving rain, the neighborhood gave off a dark, wary vibe. Here and there a few houses huddled amongst the industrial-looking buildings, less than half the windows lit with yellow light. Even in the rain, people moved on the street, or sat smoking beneath edges of roofs, or leaned under eves. A lot of those people seemed very interested in our car as we cruised by.

"You come out here a lot?" I asked. I didn't think the northeast had more magic crime than anywhere else in Portland, but I might be wrong.

"Sometimes. I have family here."

"Family, as in mob connections, or family, as in crazy uncles who drink too much?"

"There's a difference?" He smiled. "I'm kidding you. I got Latino roots, not Italian."

I noted that he didn't really answer my question. "How long have you been a police officer?"

"About ten years now. Specialized in magic crimes and been part of MERC for eight. This is it." He turned the car into a parking garage that looked like it had been built in the seventies. He did something to the tollbooth with a card, and the bar lifted and let us in.

Lights hung in cages bolted to the concrete beamed ceilings. Every other light had been busted out, creating pools of darkness and not nearly enough light. I was feeling pretty good right now about being in the company of a police officer who knew the neighborhood and carried a gun.

Magic shifted inside of me, stirring, pushing to be released. That headache that had been nothing but a tightness now shot pain along my temples and jaw. Apparently the aspirin had worn off. Great. I rubbed at my temples and wished I'd taken more painkillers before leaving my apartment.

"Here," Paul said. "She was last seen right here." He parked the car, the headlights shining on the elevator door.

"She was in the elevator?"

Paul took a drink of his coffee and put it back in the holder. "She was."

Oh, holy hells. I hated small places. Hated elevators. I think that came through my body language, or maybe the oh-so-subtle look of terror on my face clued him into my phobia.

"Is that a problem?" he asked.

"No." My voice was a little too high and that annoyed me to no end. "It's fine. Fine."

It would be fine, I told myself. I'd go out, get in that tiny closet of death, Hound the spell in that tiny closet of death, and then I'd get out of that tiny closet of death before anything could happen to me—like maybe death. And, hey, there was a chance I wouldn't have to go into the elevator. Maybe the spell had been cast on the outside.

After I did this, I was going to lobby for a new law: no spell casting in small places. Ever.

"Let's do this," I said, trying to pep talk myself into it.

I took off my gloves because I could learn things by touching the spell, and my gloves would make that impossible.

I opened the door and stepped out into the cold air. The temperature must be near freezing. I could smell the ice in the wind. I took a deep breath and let the cold take the edge off my headache.

Paul shut the door but did not lock it. He left his coffee in the car and unzipped his coat to allow easy access to his gun.

I was beginning to like this man.

"Witnesses say they saw her there." He pointed to the elevator. "The story breaks up as to whether or not they saw anyone on the elevator when she got in it. No one's seen her since."

"How long ago was that?"

I walked over to the elevator with him. It looked like every other parking garage tiny metal coffin of death. An orange number three was painted on it, big enough it would split in half when the door opened. The wall next to it was tagged. Gang symbol, not magic glyph.

"Three days. Do you mind if I record this?" he asked. He had a small tape recorder in his hand.

"That's fine," I said.

I heard the recorder click. He said something in it, and then he sort of faded from my awareness. I could feel the lingering weight of the old spell in the air. I whispered a mantra, set a Disbursement. This time I was going for general muscle aches and fever to Proxy my use. I hoped that wouldn't kick in until I got rid of this headache.

I drew a glyph for Sight, Taste, and Smell and pulled it toward me. I very carefully drew upon a small amount of the magic coursing through me and poured it into the glyphs.

My senses heightened.

The parking garage shifted. Lines of burnt magic, faint and far between, threaded through the air. People rarely cast spells in parking garages. Maybe a Locator so they could find their car or a Shield to keep them dry once they stepped out into the rain, but other than that, a concrete parking garage was just a concrete parking garage. There weren't even any lead and glass lines to channel magic through here.

Which was why I was so surprised to see the heavy gold knot of burnt magic webbing the door of the elevator. Someone had cast a hell of a spell here.

Paul said it was three days old, yet it still pulsed with the slow throb of magic in rhythm to the city's heartbeat. That was strange. Unless someone was paying the price to maintain it—to come back and pour more magic into it—it should have burned out by now.

I walked over, not caring that Stotts was taping me, not caring that the spell was centered around an elevator, not caring that a low pastel fog was gathering at the edges of the garage and slowly, slowly lifting.

The spell wasn't complicated. It was clearly an Illusion glyph, cast to hide actions from another person. Under a strong Illusion spell, a herd of hippos could roll down Main Street and no one would notice.

If I were going to smuggle something or kidnap someone, this is the kind of spell I would use.

I leaned in toward the elevator door and took a

deep breath, my mouth open so I could get the smell and taste of the spell on the back of my palate and sinuses at the same time.

It stank of burnt wood and something sweet I couldn't quite nail. I drew my fingers gently along the thickest line of magic. A snapping tingle resonated up the marks on my arm.

I traced the glyph, memorizing the strokes, the turns, the twists. The signature was familiar. I traced the full glyph and then pressed my mouth against the strongest pulse of the spell, at the spell's heart, to taste it. Cool metal of the door met my lips.

The flavor of hickory and sweetness bloomed in my mouth and spread out through me like I was drinking it down.

Magic stirred in me, and I wanted more, needed to taste the spell, the magic. I knew I had Hounded this signature before, knew I had been around this caster. There was more to it, more of the spell I needed to unravel, more of the rank sweetness hidden inside the lines of magic. I wanted to taste that, smell it, lick it.

Closer. I needed to be closer.

I pressed the elevator button, impatient and not caring that I'd have to get in the damn thing. The door opened. I took a deep breath.

And nearly gagged. There was Glamour here. A blocking and shielding that burned with anger, with strength.

Someone had hurt that girl. Hurt her and then taken her. I could smell the slippery musk of violence in the lines of the spell.

There was blood here too, but not on the floors, not on the walls. The blood was in the spell. I knew blood magic was usually cast by dipping the tip of a silver or gold needle or knife in the caster's blood, and often the victim's blood, and then drawing the glyph in the air with the knife instead of the fingers. Great care had to be taken that the blood didn't touch any other surface while it was tracing the glyph; otherwise magic would not flow into the spell.

Blood magics hurt. Blood magics scarred. And mixed with drugs, blood magics could be the highest high ever obtained.

Which is why they were illegal except for during certain medical procedures performed by well-trained and well-regulated doctors.

It was very difficult to sniff out and separate the mix of blood cast in this spell. Every person's blood carried its own unique scent, but the differences were so minute, it would take a better Hound than me to untangle all of them.

I stepped into the elevator, into the tiny space with no air and no room, walls closing down around me, magic clogging my nostrils, burning my throat, hurting my lungs.

Pain. Violence. Glamour. They didn't see anyone on the elevator with the girl because the attacker had been hiding. In plain sight. But he had been there. He had been right here.

I knelt down, pressed my palm to the floor. She had fallen here. She had been frightened here. Hurt.

This is where the true center of the spell was located. In the faint burnt ash of the caster's handiwork, I could finally recognize the signature.

A Hound had cast this spell.

A Hound I knew.

Pike.

I didn't want to believe it. I traced the lines of the spell again. Inhaled again. Hickory, just like Pike; the glyph drawn just like Pike's signature. And the blood, at least one of the bloods involved, was Pike's. I was sure of it. He'd been bleeding this morning. I'd had plenty of time to learn the smell of his blood.

Damn.

But the sweetness that lingered in the spell, I had never smelled on Pike. It was the tang of sweet cherries, blood magic. Maybe Pike wasn't doing house repair. Maybe he'd been bleeding for another reason. Maybe Pike was teaching Anthony, who always smelled like cherries, how to use blood magic.

But why would Pike kidnap the girl?

Maybe he didn't think he was kidnapping her. He might think he was saving her. Saving her like he couldn't save his own granddaughter who had been about her age. Saving this girl before Lon Trager could get his hands on her.

Or maybe Trager had already found Pike, cut his wrist, and told Pike this was the favor he owed him. I didn't like any of those ideas, didn't want to tell Stotts that my friend might be behind the disappearance of these girls.

My heart thumped against my chest as I looked over my shoulder at Stotts.

A wave of watercolor people gathered behind him. They took one slow step, two, slid past Stotts, slid *through* Stotts, hollow blackness where their eyes should be, mouths open and hungry, hands reaching out for me. For my magic.

"Shit!"

"What?" Stotts said. "Allie? What's wrong?"

The watercolor people lunged.

They filled the elevator, smelling like fetid death. Cold fingers stabbed me and I yelled at the pain. Fingers pulled magic off my bones like meat from a turkey. They stuffed the magic in their mouths and moaned for more.

I yelled again. Fingers slid into my mouth, sucked at my tongue and inside my cheeks. The taste of raw, rotted meat filled my mouth. I rocked back on my heels, hit my head on the elevator wall. I pushed at them, at their hands, but it was like pushing air. I let go of the glyphs for Sight, Smell, and Taste. I wanted, I needed a spell, another spell. Something to make them go away.

As soon as I let go of magic, the watercolor people were gone.

I breathed in short, shallow gasps. Everywhere they had touched me burned. And they had touched me—all of me—inside and out.

"Allie?" Stotts said from somewhere far away.

I needed air. I needed to be out of this elevator.

I got up to my feet and ran out of the elevator, ran past Stotts, ran across the garage. I heard footsteps behind me, chasing me, but I didn't stop until I slammed into the concrete railing at the edge of the garage. Air. Space. I was going to puke.

I leaned over the edge.

A fist grabbed the back of my coat and yanked so hard I landed on my ass on the floor. I groaned. Too much. It was too much. I rolled up on my knees, and then I lost everything in my stomach.

"Shit," Stotts said from close above me but not too close.

I heaved and heaved, trying to get the taste of death out of me, trying to get their rotten touch out of me, trying to forget them reaching inside of me and pulling me apart.

Why didn't magic ever take away the memories I wanted to lose?

A hand, Stotts' hand, pressed gently on my back. "Here," he said.

I swallowed until I was sure nothing more was coming up and sat back. Stotts kept his hand on my back, a comforting weight. He offered me a handkerchief, and I took it, wiped the tears from my eyes, blew my nose, and used the last dry corner of the cloth to wipe my mouth.

"Think you can stand?" he asked softly.

I wondered if he had kids. He seemed like an old pro at this.

I stood, and his hand came under my elbow to help support me. "I'm fine," I said. "I'm good." My legs, however, didn't believe me. Exhaustion rolled over me, and I stubbornly locked my knees to stay standing. Even so, I was trembling.

"You're doing just fine," Stotts said. He helped me walk maybe six or seven steps away from the mess I'd made. I was breathing hard, like I'd just climbed Mt. Hood. Darkness closed in at the edges of my vision, and the whole garage slipped away down a far tunnel.

"I'm going to help you sit. That's good," Stotts said from somewhere farther away than the ringing in my ears. "Now I'm going to help you lie down. That's good. I'm going to go get the car. I will be right back. You are going to stay right here. No trying to jump off the building again, okay?"

Jump off the building? Did I look like I was in any shape to jump off the building?

As soon as I could open my mouth, I was going to ask him what he meant.

Maybe I blacked out. I don't know. The next thing I knew, his hands—warm, human, living hands—helped me up.

"I'm going to help you into the backseat so you can lie down."

"No," I mumbled. What do you know, I could talk. "The front. The front's fine."

"Are you sure you can sit?"

"I'm feeling better," I said. Even I could tell my voice was gaining strength. He helped me into the front seat, closed the door. The weight of the car shifted as he got into his seat. He twisted to pull something out of the back and then handed me a blanket.

"Thanks," I said. I draped the blanket over my lap and leaned my head against the headrest. I was feeling stronger, but the magic that usually filled me so full was distant, dulled. I felt empty but not in a good way.

The watercolor people had done more than just eat the magic of my spell. They had pulled the magic out of me, and magic was having a hard time filling me back up.

The absence of it, the absence of its weight and motion, made me feel raw inside. Knowing those people could do that scared the hell out of me.

"Sorry," I said.

"Tell me what happened." The engine was running, and the heater was on full blast, but we were not driving anywhere yet. "Tell me what you saw. Could you trace the spell?"

I nodded. "It was still strong. Even after three days."

"Do you know who cast it?"

"I want to Hound the other site before I say."

"We aren't going to Hound the other site. Not with you trying to leap tall buildings back there."

"I wasn't going to jump."

"Uh-huh."

"Listen." I took a deep breath. Pike told me to confide in Stotts. Even though I was feeling a little shaky about Pike's loyalties at the moment, he was right about one thing—Stotts knew about magic and magical crimes. If anyone in this city would know what those watercolor people were, it might be him.

Well, and maybe Zayvion, but Zayvion wasn't here, was he?

"Listen," I said again, keeping my voice calm. "I Hounded the spell and it's very strong. Blood magic was involved. There was more than one blood used for it. Those things I would swear to in a court of law. I have a suspicion of who cast it. But I want to Hound the second site so I can be one hundred percent sure. And me freaking out back there?"

Do it, Beckstrom, I told myself. *Don't be a pansy ass.*

"I saw people. I think they're ghosts. They attacked me, and pulled apart the spells I cast, and ate them." I didn't tell him they sucked the magic out of me too, because as far as I knew, he didn't know I could carry magic in me. As far as anyone knew, I pulled magic out from the stores deep beneath the city and poured it directly into the glyphs, just like every other magic user.

No one was stupid enough to try to draw magic into their bodies—magic always demanded a price, and the price of holding it in your body was organ failure and death. At the very least.

Take that, Pike. Now who you calling pansy?

Detective Paul Stotts had a good poker face. He gave me a considering gaze, and I returned it. I was beginning to get my strength back and might even be capable of walking when I got out of the car. But the sunburn from the watercolor people's touch was worse than the last time they'd attacked me. I wondered how many more raw circles would be on my skin when I next looked in the mirror. It felt like a lot more— dozens more.

"Can you describe what you saw?" he asked.

This was the calm and controlled police and procedure thing I could really appreciate right now.

"I saw a pastel mist rise at the edges of the parking garage before I got in the elevator. I finished Hounding the spell, and when I turned, several people who were not solid were walking toward me. I could see their clothes and I could see their faces, except for a blackness where their eyes should be."

"Could you smell them?"

I nodded. "They smelled like death. Rotten flesh, compost pile, matter breaking down."

"Did you recognize any of them?"

"No."

"When did you stop seeing them?"

I frowned. "What?"

"When did they disappear? I'm assuming they *did* disappear?" One of his thick eyebrows twitched upward.

"Yes. They did. They disappeared as soon as I stopped using magic."

Oh, crap.

"All right. Did you first see them when you were using magic—Hounding?"

"Yes."

"And have you seen them before?"

"Just today, but yes."

He didn't have to say it—I'm not stupid—but he said it anyway.

"You see them when you cast magic, and they disappear when you stop casting magic. It might be some sort of side effect you're experiencing from magic use. A hallucination, an afterimage—I don't know. I haven't ever heard of this before. But you're a Hound. You use magic a lot, and I'm not surprised something like this might happen. I think you need to see a doctor."

No, I thought. I most certainly did not need to see a doctor. "Okay," I said. "Well, that's a place to start."

I knew I wasn't hallucinating. Zayvion had seen them too. Zayvion had fought them with me. If I was hallucinating, then so was he, at the same time, and about the same thing. Not likely.

"I'll take you back to the station," he said. "I'll get your statement and the paperwork started, and then I'll take you home." Stotts didn't wait for me to answer. He put the car in gear and followed the exit arrows.

"I'd rather finish the job first." I was tempted, really tempted, to put Influence behind my words. With no more effort than breathing, I could make Stotts do what I said.

I'd seen my father use that power far too often—

on others and on me—to think it was a moral action. Still. I really wanted to Hound the second site to see if Pike's signature was on it too.

Stotts picked up his coffee, drank the cold dregs. "I don't think that's necessary."

"Let me tell you why you're wrong," I said. *That* got his attention. He smiled and glanced over at me before looking back out the front window.

"All right."

"I think I know who cast that spell. But I am not sure, not certain enough that I would testify in court. If I Hound the second site and it looks like it's the same person, then I would be happy to stand in front of the law and point fingers. But if I don't have a second site to compare to, I will not feel comfortable taking the stand."

"Who do you think it is?"

"Not until I see the second site."

"Are you trying to bribe me, Ms. Beckstrom?"

"If I were trying to bribe you, you wouldn't have to ask that question," I said.

"So you won't tell me what you found, even though I'm paying you for your services and you are legally obligated to tell me?"

"Oh, I'll tell you. But I won't testify to it."

"Tell me."

I didn't have a choice. If I wanted a stab at that other site—and I did—and if I wanted a chance to clear Pike's name—and I did—I would have to trust Stotts would give me that chance.

"Martin Pike."

I felt like a complete jerk, but Stotts did not look surprised at all.

"Interesting," he said.

"I'm not the first Hound to indicate him in this, am I?"

"No. But you're the first one who has doubts."

"Something about the spell doesn't smell right," I said.

"And you're not the first one to say that." We were on the ground floor of the parkade now. He paused and then turned right. "I'll take you to it," he said. "But if you see anything strange while you're using magic, anything like back there—ghosts, or whatever—you will stop and we'll call it a night."

"Thanks," I said, and I meant it.

It was dark now and still raining. The drops were smaller, icier, driven by the wind like a sandblaster.

We drove through the neighborhood and I worked on calming my mind. Magic stirred in me, sluggish, distant, but it did respond. I might have been drained by the watercolor people, but it was not permanent.

Good. I didn't care what Stotts said. I was going to pull on magic for as long as I wanted and Hound this spell no matter what the watercolor people did to me.

Now that I was expecting it, I could handle the pain. The watercolor people had hurt me, but they hadn't killed me. Yet.

Stotts parked at the curb. "This is the second site."

More people moved around in this part of the neighborhood despite the rain and cold. Shadows hunched in doorways and overhangs, light catching the cherry embers of cigarettes, the flash of teeth, the glitter of eyes.

This, I decided, was not the kind of place to be alone in the dark. Stotts pulled his gun, did something with it, and then reholstered it. Good thing I'd brought a buddy.

Hells, what about Davy? Was he out there, skulking in the shadows? If he was, he should be easy for me to spot. I glanced at the street, at the houses and abandoned shops and boarded-up buildings. I didn't see Davy. I hoped he had stayed home.

Stotts took a deep breath and traced a glyph too quickly for me to see which spell he was casting. Then he closed the thumb and forefinger of his left hand, creating a circle and holding magic there like a trigger, ready to pour it into the glyph when he needed it.

Well, well. He wasn't just a by-the-books gunslinger after all.

"Ready?" Stotts asked.

"Damn straight." We both got out of the car.

Stotts didn't need to point out the place where the kidnapping had happened. I could tell even without pulling on magic. Someone had built a small, hand painted cross and nailed it to the side of the building and written "My baby" across it. This girl may have been running with a gang, but she was also someone's daughter. Someone who still remembered her.

"She was last seen two weeks ago." Stotts walked around the car to stand next to me.

"Two weeks? Have there been any leads?"

"Nothing I can disclose."

Magic bucked in me, burning slowly up my bones. It felt like my limbs had fallen asleep on the inside, my bones numb. Magic burned, stung, tingled painfully from the soles of my feet upward, as if it were trying to reestablish blood flow.

Holy hells, that itched and hurt.

You can do pain, I told myself. *It won't last forever.*

"How old was she?" I asked.

"Fifteen."

The same age as Pike's granddaughter. The grand-daughter who was used by Lon Trager. The grand-daughter who committed suicide.

Oh, Pike, no.

I walked to the middle of the sidewalk. The soles of my feet felt bruised, but at least they weren't burning numb. I hoped the pain of magic refilling me would be over soon.

Stotts stayed near the cross, his coat open. His right hand was free so he could easily pull his gun. He stood with his middle finger and thumb obviously together, a clear symbol to anyone watching that he was holding a spell in check and could cast it in seconds.

I hadn't bothered putting my gloves back on. But I needed to stall just a little until my arms and hands stopped itching and hurting so much. I couldn't cast magic if my fingers weren't working.

"Did you do anything with the spells?" I asked Stotts.

"No. You're not the first one to Hound them, but no one's contaminated the site."

"No kind of Holding or Stasis put around them?"

"That's contamination. These are just as we found them. Can you get to this now or is there a problem?"

I shook my head. No more stalling.

If Stotts was that uncomfortable standing out here on the street while he had magic and a gun, I needed to get this done quickly.

I calmed my mind, putting my expectation and fear of Pike being involved aside. I needed my judgment to be absolutely clear if I were to see the truth of this hit.

I muttered a mantra and set the Disbursement spell—that fever would last a little longer now. Probably ought to stock up on my chicken noodle soup supply. I pulled on the magic inside me.

Like lighting a fuse, magic burned through my bones, my muscle, my flesh. I gritted my teeth and let it flow, not using it yet.

It filled all the empty places in me, replaced the numbness with warmth. I was sweating. Shaking. Talk about a hot flash.

I sent a small amount of magic through the lines on my arm and felt the familiar cold numbness creep up my left arm. I let my breath out in relief. That was normal.

Well, normal for me.

Magic filled the glyph I traced for Sight, Smell, Taste, and my senses opened.

The street was lousy with old spells that hung like a miasma of smoke in the air. Some were faded ash; some were new and bright as neon fire. Cheap sex spells that never worked; spells of illusion, of coercion and influence. Spells of protection, warding, warnings.

And there were other magical things out on the street too. The watercolor people with hungry, empty eyes walked down the sidewalk and street, unaware of the rain, unaware of the cars, unaware of the people moving in the night.

They were aware of me, though. Like zombie moths to a flame, they turned.

I stepped closer to the strong spell that drifted in the air, tendrils of gold draping outward, thinning like a golden spiderweb spun onto nothing but air. It was the same as the one in the elevator. A Glamour intended to hide and conceal. And it was still burning strong.

Which was strange because it should have looked older, should have smelled older, should have faded. Time mattered in Hounding spells. Weak spells were older; strong spells newer. But these spells looked like they could have been cast within hours of each other.

I flicked a glance at the watercolor people. They were still moving slowly toward me, more of them appearing in the distance like fog—hells, like ghosts. I needed to either Hound this spell fast or get ready to fight.

I voted for speed. I opened my mouth, breathed in. I could smell hickory, could taste the sweetness of cherry behind it, could scent the mix of bloods. The spell looked like something Pike could have cast. It could be his signature.

I needed time.

Fine. I'd buy it. I leaned away from the spell so I had room to cast another glyph. I added a little more heat onto that damn fever I was going to come down with, hoped the combined Disbursements of three spells wouldn't mean I'd have to be hospitalized, and cast a Shield the size of Cleveland.

Magic pushed up through me, poured out of me fast, faster, building the spell around me and around the spell I was Hounding. Magic is too fast to see with the naked eye.

But I could see it, catching fire through the metallic whorls of my arm, leaping from my fingertips in ribbons of color, arcing and weaving into the twisting, tight glyph of Shield.

The air around me warmed. I no longer felt the wind. I no longer felt the rain. As a matter of fact, I didn't hear the cars going by either.

I glanced at the watercolor people. Still slow, but I knew they'd break forward and start eating the Shield at any second.

Stotts' mouth was moving. I was pretty good at reading lips. He was calling my name. Asking me what I was doing, what was wrong.

I tapped my ear and shook my head, letting him know I couldn't hear him, and then I turned back to Hounding the spell.

Hounding while also feeding a constant flow of magic into a defensive spell was harder than I thought. Zayvion had done this and more—he had put up a shield and opened something within it to swallow the watercolor people.

Zayvion chanted. The cheater.

My heart was pounding, and a little voice in my head that sounded a lot like fear just kept saying, "They're coming, they're coming, they're coming. . . ."

Stupid voice. I knew they were coming. It was all I could do not to look up, not to run away.

I traced the lines of the gold Glamour spell with the fingertips of my right hand. The spell's magic resonated across my skin, mixing with and ever so slightly altering the magic I was using for the Shield and for my senses.

Could this get any harder?

The lines of the Glamour spell were distinctive, cast

with the basic north, south, east, and west boundary lines I knew Pike always used.

It had to be his signature.

But the sweetness, the cherry, wasn't anything I'd ever sensed on Pike. Anthony, yes, but not Pike. Pike had never done blood magic in all the time I knew him. And he was plenty strong enough as a magic user to cast Glamour without using blood. So why would he do so? I followed the lines of the spell, trying to taste the wrongness on the back of my throat.

All I got was the scent of blood. Pike's blood.

The watercolor people slammed into the Shield.

And I felt it. Pain shivered through me.

Don't look at them; don't look at them. I knew I shouldn't. Knew I shouldn't look away from the Glamour spell.

But I did.

Holy shit.

People, and there were dozens of them, pressed against the Shield. This close, with magic still enhancing my vision, I could see that they were indeed people— tall, short, heavy, thin, pastel skin tones of varying shades, facial features distinct. They had no eyes, and yet I knew they saw me.

They leaned on the Shield, and I could feel the weight of them like a press of a storm about to break. Their fingers scrabbled across the Shield. Scraped, found purchase, and dug into the magic. They pulled at it like cold taffy, trying to bend it, stretch it, shove it into their mouths.

They hadn't broken the Shield yet. But they would.

Hound, Allie, I said, forcing myself to look away. *Get the damn job done.*

I pulled a little more magic from within me and added it to my sense of smell. I hissed as magic leaped up in response.

Magic rushed from the ground and filled me. I used it as fast as I could. I diverted most of it into the Sheild, pouring it out so fast, I was breathing hard with the effort.

And I was losing ground.

No matter how much magic I poured into the Shield, the watercolor people consumed it.

A pastel finger pushed through the Shield; another followed. I could smell death.

A hand broke through, and then another. A finger slid down my spine, thunking over each vertebra, hooking the magic in my bones and pulling it out of me.

Pain rolled over my body.

I gritted my teeth against a scream. *I am almost done, damn it. If they'd just leave me alone for a fucking second more.*

I reached with all my senses toward the Glamour spell.

And the Shield broke.

I was buried by them, smothered by their rotted stink, suffocating, breathing them into me, tasting them as they scraped through my skin, digging in like worms through my soft flesh, sucking, consuming.

Let go of magic. Let go, let go, let go.

But I couldn't.

Magic pushed up out of the ground and into me, following the burnt pathways down my arm, pouring out to fall again back to the ground, where it surged back up into me. I was an electric circuit.

I was stuck in a loop, trapped by magic.

I couldn't let go.

Come on, Allie. Do something.

I was being eaten alive.

I am a river. Magic cannot touch me. Magic cannot change me.

Burning alive.

Where the hell is the off switch when I need one?

Fuck this.

If I couldn't let go of magic, then I'd hold on to it with both hands and shove it down their throats.

I called magic up into me, more, all the magic that flowed beneath the city, all the magic flowing through the network of lead and glass lines, all the magic stored in deep cisterns. I spoke a word, ready to rain all bloody hell and destruction down upon them.

Something hit the back of my head. Hard.

Even though I hurt everywhere, that hurt more.

My vision went dark, and the ringing in my ears followed a rushing throb of blood. I think I landed on my knees.

And everything went black.

Chapter Thirteen

My dead dad stood above me. He was less transparent than the last time I'd seen him. I saw through him enough to make out the corner of the building and white wooden cross where his chest should be. He still, however, looked annoyed with me.

"Always set a Disbursement," he said, so close that it sounded as if his voice were in my head. "Every time you use magic. Every single time. How many times do I have to tell you that?"

I opened my mouth to tell him to bite me. He was dead. *Dead.* And that meant I no longer had to lie here and listen to his lectures.

He might be dead, but he was also fast. Fast like the watercolor people. Before I so much as inhaled, he bent over me and stuck his hand on my heart.

Not on my coat.

Not on my skin.

He stuck his hand *into* me. Deep. And touched my heart.

Magic slipped up his fingers. He squeezed my heart and I arched my back in pain.

Magic poured out of me. He pumped my heart again and pushed magic out through my veins like bad water coming out of a swimmer's lungs. A strange wintergreen warmth and the taste of leather at the back of my throat filled me.

I blinked. And my dad was gone.

In his place, Paul Stotts bent over me. Sirens screamed in the distance. "Can you hear me?"

"Yes," I said, baffled. I was lying on my back, on the ground. Stotts looked worried. That made two of us.

I sat, using my elbows for leverage, and then pushed Stotts' hands and protests away and looked around me.

"Allie, you shouldn't move. You should wait—"

"Right." I put my hand on his shoulder and pushed myself up to my feet. I wobbled a little, but he rose with me. I was confused but also full of energy, like I'd just had a brisk walk around the block.

Except it looked like I'd fallen on the ground, roughly right beneath the spell I was Hounding. The white cross was still on the building. A crowd of people—real people—were gathering on doorsteps and under roof eves. The watercolor people were gone.

And so was my dad.

"Where's the fire?" I asked Stotts.

"Ambulance," he said. "When I called, they already had a unit on the way."

I was still scanning the crowd, looking for my dad, looking for Trager's men, hells, looking for anyone and anything.

A leggy figure detached from a patch of shadow behind a car and strolled into the glow of a dull yellow streetlight. As soon as he hit the light, he turned and walked backward. He held up his cell phone toward me briefly, pulling it to his forehead and then away in a salute. And then he was part of the shadows again.

Davy Silvers, the Hound.

So much for the mystery of who called 911.

The ambulance rounded the corner and slowed as it neared us. Its siren switched off midwail, and the lights rolled through white, yellow, red, making the whole wet neighborhood look like a greasy disco hell.

"Why an ambulance?" I asked Stotts. "I feel fine."

He gave me the strangest look.

"What?" I said.

"Allie," he said, holding on to one of my arms like he was betting I was about to run or, you know, throw myself into traffic or do some other kind of curse-worthy thing. "Your skin was smoking."

Oh. Wow. Weird.

I met his eyes, gave him my most convincing look. "I feel much better now. I can tell you who cast that spell."

A man and a women hopped out of the ambulance and strode over to us.

"Did you call?" the woman, about my age but half a foot shorter, asked.

Stotts nodded. "She was out cold. Hounding magic. Says she feels fine now." The tone of his voice said he obviously didn't believe me.

That was the last time I let him talk for me.

I took a deep breath, surprised when my heart hitched with a twang of pain. Maybe I wasn't all right. But I was right enough that I wanted to get home, get clean, and sleep off the touch of the watercolor people, the touch of my dead dad, and most especially the fact that I was about to rat out my friend to the police.

All I had to do was convince the nice emergency medical technicians that I didn't need their services and was good to go. I'd be home within the hour.

Influence would be so *easy*. And so wrong.

"It was a pretty heavy spell I was Hounding. I got light-headed," I told them. "But I feel fine now."

The EMTs were very nice and helped me over to the back of the ambulance, where I sat down and let them check my vitals.

They asked some questions, took down all my information, recorded the results of blood pressure, and flashed lights in my eyes.

Everything checked out within normal ranges.

I threw Stotts, who had been waiting nearby, a told-you-so look, and he grunted.

Actually, I was surprised. I felt okay. Not great. I had a headache that could pound a mountain to sand, and the raw spots on my body—spots I did not point out to the EMTs, and spots that were not on my face or arms and therefore not seen by the EMTs—hurt like hell.

Sunburned and bruised down to the bone, even my heart felt sore. Kind of like someone had squeezed it.

Everywhere else, I was just stiff. Magic had taken my name and kicked my ass.

But I had survived it. Was still surviving it. And I had questions.

Why the hells had my dad showed up? What had he done, touching, *squeezing* my heart? And what did Pike think he was doing, throwing around blood magic, which he hated?

The EMTs and Stotts talked while I rested there on the back bumper of the ambulance, thinking. At every soft sound, at every shifting shadow, I felt my breath quicken, my heart hurt. I strained to hear if the water-color people were out there. Coming to get me. Coming to slide their fingers beneath my skin, to tear the flesh from my bones, to suck the magic from my blood.

To leave me empty, broken. Dead.

I heard nothing but the rain drumming like impatient claws against the ambulance roof. And even though I had a police officer armed with a gun and magic standing just a few yards from me, I was afraid.

Move over, bogeyman. There was a new hell in town.

Stotts strolled over. "They say you can go. How about I drive you home?"

Home sounded good. No, home sounded great. And once I hit my sheets, I wasn't coming back up for hours.

Maybe days.

"I'd like to give my statement so I can get some sleep."

We strolled over to the car, and Stotts opened the door for me. He probably didn't think I had enough strength to do it. And even though I'd never tell him, he probably thought right.

Stotts got in after me, turned on the car and heater, and eased out into the flow of traffic.

"What did you see back there?" he asked.

"Can't we wait until we get to the station?"

He dug in his pocket and held up a tape recorder. "How about I record it while I drive you home?"

And I swear, that was the nicest thing I'd heard all night.

"Do you treat all your Hounds this well?"

He looked over at me. Looked away. "It doesn't always work out that way."

Right. The curse.

He turned on the recorder and spoke his name, my name, the case number, and some other things I only gave half an ear to. That burst of energy I'd had was wearing off. I was tired. Damn tired. I felt like I'd run a marathon. Through a tar pit.

The drone of the engine, the heat of the car made it hard to keep my eyes open.

"Please tell me what you saw." Stotts put the recorder on a little spot between the cup holder that must have had Velcro on it to keep the recorder in place.

"Both spells at the hit sites were Glamour," I said. "The boundary lines were consistent with those I've seen Martin Pike use. There was also a taint of blood magic—a mix of more than one blood. I've never seen or heard of Pike using blood magic."

"Did you smell Martin Pike's blood in the spell?"

Don't make me do this.

"Ms. Beckstrom? Did you smell Martin Pike's blood in the spell?"

"Yes." *I'm so sorry, Pike.* "But there were other bloods involved too. And something else, something more. The spell doesn't smell right."

"Deterioration?" he asked.

"No. That's another thing. The glyphs and spells should have faded within a couple days. They were as strong as if they'd been cast an hour ago. Something or someone is feeding those spells."

"Do you think Pike would do that?"

I shook my head, rolling the back of my skull

against the headrest. "I don't know why anyone would want to do that. And Pike wouldn't be that sloppy. He's been using magic for years. Before that, he served in the military. If he wanted to make someone disappear, he wouldn't leave a giant glowing trail behind. He wouldn't use magic to do it. It doesn't make sense."

Stotts exhaled. "Hounding is hard. On the body and the brain. Maybe he's finally hit his limit. It happens."

I didn't know what to say to that, because it was true. Pike was tired. Worn-out. Moving on. Maybe he just got desperate. And stupid.

But Martin Pike had never been a stupid man.

"Both girls were hurt," I said woodenly. "I could feel the violence used against them, could feel their fear. There might have been more than one person involved. The mix of blood means there were probably more than two people involved."

"Could you identify any of the other blood?"

"No. Only Pike's."

"Could you identify the caster's signature?"

"I am not one hundred percent sure who cast that spell."

"If you had to make a guess?"

"I don't make guesses."

"I appreciate that, Ms. Beckstrom. But in your educated opinion, who do you think cast those spells?"

"Martin Pike." The words felt heavy in my throat.

Stotts reached over, the leather seat creaking as he turned off the tape recorder.

We drove awhile in silence, each caught in our own thoughts.

"Will you be all right on your own tonight?" he finally asked.

"I'm looking forward to some alone time."

Stotts slowed as he approached my apartment building. "I want to thank you for Hounding this, Allie. I know it's a tough thing, fingering a fellow Hound. It was hard for the others too."

I didn't want to think about that. Didn't want to know which Hounds had already told Stotts that Pike was guilty of kidnapping. Didn't want to think it might even be some of the Hounds I met today.

"You are the first Hound to identify his blood in the spell," Stotts said. "That could be the piece we need."

Nail in the coffin, that's me.

I was unable to drum up any enthusiasm for ruining an old man's life. "I'll send you my bill."

Stotts double-parked on the street.

"Do you want me to walk you up?"

"No. I got it." I wasn't kidding about that being-alone thing. I pulled on the handle of the door. Managed to get it open on the second try.

"Allie?"

I stood up into the rain, paused.

"Is Pike your friend?"

I faced away from him. It was raining, but the wind had let off a little. I heard the train call in the distance. I closed my eyes for a moment.

No. Not anymore, I thought.

To Stotts, I said, "Hounds don't make friends."

Chapter Fourteen

I made it up the steps to my building, where I let myself in. It was warm and dry and quiet in the lobby. I stood there a moment, dripping on the floor, content in the silence and not quite ready to face the three flights of stairs I had to haul myself up.

Sweet hells.

I put my hand on the wall and my foot on the first stair. I could do this. I could climb three stories after a day of being jumped, poked at, poked through, and squeezed. Darn right. I could climb these stairs with one foot tied behind my back. On a pogo stick. Blindfolded.

I headed up, one slow step at a time.

Okay, so this was the downside to living in a building without an elevator.

By the time I made it to my floor and my door, I was sweaty and tired. I didn't pause to listen for anyone in my apartment. I didn't pause to cast magic. I just shoved my key in the lock and walked in.

My apartment looked and smelled the same as how I'd left it. Nobody home but me.

I kicked the door shut, locked it, and tugged off my wet hat and jacket. The red light on my answering machine blinked, but I just didn't have it in me to listen to my messages yet. I did one circuit of my house, turning on all the lights. Then walked into the living room and sat on the arm of the couch, where I groaned my way out of my boots and wet socks.

Barefoot, I shuffled over to the window and looked out at the street below to make sure Stotts wasn't spying on me. His car was gone.

Across the street, a flash of blue in the rain caught my eye. A man stood beneath the awning. The blue light—a cell phone screen—angled to illuminate a face, a smile.

Davy waved at me, tipped his fingers in another salute, and then palmed his cell, smothering its light and throwing his face back into shadow.

I shook my head and watched him trot down the street, long legs lending him speed. There was a bar not too far from here. I figured he'd make it just in time for happy hour.

If the kid tracked spells even half as easily as he tracked me, he really was a good Hound.

I let the curtains fall back in place and thumbed on the answering machine. Three phone calls. One from a credit card company, and one from my father's accountant, Mr. Katz, politely reminding me that we had not yet met to go over the next round of papers to settle my father's estate.

As Katz spoke, I tugged off my sweater. It was wet and smelled of my own sweat and fear. I threw the sweater on the floor on top of my boots, skinned out of my long-sleeved T-shirt, threw that on the pile, and was just unbuttoning my jeans when the third message clicked on.

"Ms. Beckstrom," said a man's voice I could not immediately place. "I am sorry to be calling your home number. This is Dr. Frank Gordon, your neighbor. We recently ran into each other at the coffee shop. I have a Hounding job I would like to hire you for. It's . . . of a delicate nature. I hope you will call me so we can arrange a time to meet. Please return my call at your earliest convenience."

Instead of hanging up, he remained on the phone, breathing. Just breathing.

After a minute or so, the call disconnected.

Strange.

Standing in my living room with only my bra and jeans on, I felt a chill roll down my skin. I rubbed my hands over my arms and hissed as my palms crossed raw spots. Sure enough, I had more circles of raw burns on my left arm and shoulder and, now that I looked, on my belly too.

I shivered. There were more sores on my back, my legs. A lot more. I needed to shower again and put more antiseptic on them.

I was hungry. I was tired. And nothing was going to get done if I just stood there in my living room whining. I dragged myself into the kitchen and started a pot of coffee. I didn't care how late it was; it was never too late for hot caffeine.

But first, I wanted to be clean.

I walked into the bathroom, slicked out of my wet jeans, and turned on the shower.

I steeled myself and looked in the mirror.

Lovely. I looked as horrible as I felt.

More circles mottled my skin, down my left arm, my belly, my thighs, and what I could see of my shoulders. I opened my mouth and leaned in. Raw red spots marked the inside of my cheeks and both sides of my tongue.

I looked like I'd just done three rounds with a gang of octopuses and lost.

All the wounds were weeping. I checked the older raw spots. They had not healed, not at all. If anything, they looked bigger, the red gone a ghastly white-blue, like frozen dead flesh, spread out in wider circles. They were still leaking in the center and sore in the middle, though less sore on the edges. I didn't know if that was a good sign or a bad sign.

Fabulous. If the watercolor people got all slap-handsy again, I'd be a giant walking scab.

The bruise on my thigh from Trager's needle was the same size, still spidery and glyphlike with a red, needlepoint center.

With my crazy color marks wrapping from my right temple to the edge of my breast, down my shoulder, arm, and hand, and with new moist red circles poxing the rest of me like a medieval plague, I looked . . . strange . . . foreign . . . inhuman.

Even my eyes looked darker.

My stomach clenched. That scared the hells out of me.

Time to stop staring in the mirror.

I got in the shower and scrubbed from my scalp to my soles. I wanted to be clean. Really clean. Inside and out. I wanted to be healthy. I wanted to be myself. I didn't want to be changed by the watercolor people. Or by anything else, for that matter.

The soap stung and burned. I adjusted the water so

it was tepid and kept scrubbing. The combination of cool water and pain woke me up a little.

I got out of the shower and did what I could to apply antiseptic spray to my hurts. I left the light on and changed into the only pair of pajamas I owned: flannel with ladybugs and dragonflies. Usually I wore nothing to bed, or a slip nightgown. Tonight I was bringing out the big guns of comfort, though: flannel jammies, woolly socks, and a big mug of coffee that I wished were cocoa. Note to self: buy cocoa.

I shuffled into the living room again.

My front door knob turned. I froze, watching it. The knob turned back and then stopped. It was locked. Whoever was on the other side of the door drew on magic. The prickly discomfort of a spell ready to be cast—a big spell—poured over me like unwelcome rain.

Oh, hells.

I whispered a Disbursement—that little fever I had in store for me was now going to knock me out for a week. I traced a glyph for Shield, hoping that would keep me safe long enough to deal with my intruder.

I picked up the hammer I'd left on my bookshelf when I was hanging pictures, held it in my left hand, magic in my right, and waited.

Footsteps pounded up the stairs, as if purposely trying to be noisy, accompanied by loud, cheerful whistling.

The prickly spell unraveled. Broken before it was cast. Gone. It was hard to hear over the footsteps and whistling, but I think I heard an apartment door open and close somewhere down the hall.

What the hells? A knock made me jump. The knock rapped out again.

I thought about pouring magic into the Shield glyph but decided the hammer would probably solve my problem quicker. I let go of the glyph, switched the hammer to my right hand, and approached the door.

I looked out the peephole.

Zayvion Jones stood on the other side of the door, warped by the bend of glass. He was whistling loudly and holding something that looked like a pizza box in his hand.

He stared straight at the peephole like he knew I was looking at him and, without breaking eye contact, knocked on my door again.

I unlocked the door, opened it.

In front of me, smelling like pine and pepperoni, stood six feet plus of Zayvion Jones.

"Mr. Jones," I said, trying to think of what had really just happened. "What brings you by?"

His eyebrows hitched up while he looked me over, from my fuzzy socks and buggy pajamas to my wet, uncombed hair. His gaze lingered on the hammer.

"I brought you pizza."

"I thought our date was tomorrow."

"It is. This is just a late night snack. I thought you might be hungry."

Now that he mentioned it, I was starved. The delicious scents of basil, rich cheese, and spices wafted up from the box.

My stomach growled. Loudly. Traitor. Should I trust him? Let him into my house after the day I'd had? I thought it over. Realized I didn't care. I wanted food, and here it was, hot and delicious, on my doorstep. And Zayvion Jones wasn't hard on the eyes either.

"Come on in." I walked away from the door and

into the kitchen, putting down the hammer, pulling out napkins, and getting a couple glasses.

Zayvion closed the door behind him.

"Just put it in the living room," I said. "We can eat there."

I didn't hear him walk across the floor, but I did hear him put the pizza down and lift the box lid. I strolled out of the kitchen, napkins and two glasses of apple juice—the only beverage in the house besides water and coffee—in my hand. "All I have is apple juice. Hope that's okay."

He moved away from the window. He had taken off his ratty coat and black beanie, hanging the coat on the back of one of the chairs at the round table. He wore jeans and a dark gray sweater that looked like cashmere. The flex and movement of his chest and torso beneath that thin fabric made my heartbeat quicken.

I remembered him, remembered his body. An image flashed behind my eyes. He stood in a doorway, naked except for his boxers, his dark skin tiger-striped with yellow light, his eyes burning gold with passion. He had waited. Waited for me to say yes.

I blinked. And the memory was gone. A sad hunger lingered at the back of my mind and echoed through my body. I wondered if I'd said yes.

I realized Zayvion was silent, his thumbs hooked in his belt loops, watching me, waiting.

I blushed. "Sorry."

"That's okay," he said softly. "Do you want to talk about it?"

"No." I sat in the coatless chair. "It was just— maybe—a memory or something. It's gone." I tried to keep the frustration and embarrassment out of my voice.

He sat in the chair across from me silently, even though that chair usually creaked, and turned in his seat so he could see both the front door and the window. "Was it about me?"

I fished a piece of pizza out of the box, pulled it up until the strings of cheese broke. "Yes."

"Was I naked?"

I couldn't help it—I laughed. "I can't believe you asked me that. No comment."

He smiled, laugh lines curving at the corners of his eyes. "So I was naked."

"Shut up and eat your pizza," I said around a mouthful. And that was the end of my side of the conversation. I wiped out two pieces of pizza before coming up for air. Zayvion paced me, piece for piece. He got up, found the apple juice, and refilled our cups.

After the fourth slice I felt like I could think again. Hounding always made me hungry; drawing on magic always made me hungry. I'd been doing a lot of both of those things on nothing but a scone, coffee, and french fries, most of which I'd lost in the parking garage.

"How did the job with Stotts go?" he asked.

I tore the crust off another piece of pizza, leaving the topping portion still in the box. "I didn't tell you I was working for Stotts."

"No, you didn't."

"Were you spying on me?"

"Define spying."

"Were you on the street watching me Hound for him?"

"No. I was . . . working."

"And that involved keeping an eye on me?"

"In a roundabout way. I noticed you were with him. How did it go?"

"My Hounding jobs are between me and my clients," I said. "And this is police business. Confidential." I did not want to tell him about Pike. Didn't want to tell him I had ratted Pike out and that he would be charged with kidnapping—or more, if the girls were found injured, or dead.

Time for a subject change.

"So what was up with that chanting and light show you put on earlier today?" I asked.

"That?" He wiped his mouth with a napkin and nodded. "That was magic." He leaned back in his chair and stretched his legs out under the table like he was used to being comfortable around me and in my apartment.

"Genius. What kind of magic? What did you use against those things? The watercolor people things?"

He considered me for a second then. "What is the first rule of magic?"

"You're kidding me, right?" Zayvion did not look like he was kidding. As a matter of fact, if I had to describe how Zayvion looked, I would use the word *intense*. Something important was riding on this conversation. Or maybe riding on my response.

"The first rule of magic is if you use magic, it uses you."

"Yes," he said. "There is always a price to pay for using magic. Always. And when you spend a lifetime using it, it spends a lifetime using you. It leaves its mark on you"—he motioned toward my hands—"and you leave your mark on it."

"What do you mean, you leave a mark on magic? It's hard enough just to touch magic. Magic isn't solid."

"Neither are the Veiled."

"The who?"

"This doesn't apply to the casual magic user. This doesn't even apply to someone who uses magic once a day. But for those of . . . us . . . who use magic constantly, it is believed that our minds, our souls, our life essence, can impress upon the flow of magic. Like an image on film. Or maybe more. Some people believe that if you use magic too much, you will impress certain parts of your life into the flow of magic permanently. You can lose bits of yourself to it."

I suddenly wasn't hungry.

"But they're wrong, right? Because *I* have magic *in* me. Inside me. Tell me there aren't . . . parts of people's spirits and lives in the magic. Tell me I'm not full of dead people." It came out just as horrified as I felt.

I suddenly wanted to crawl back into the shower and scrub myself again.

Zayvion straightened and leaned forward without making a sound in my creaky chair. He reached across the table and put both of his hands over mine.

His hands were warm, wide, heavy like a blanket. "You are not full of dead people. But there are theories that magic is. And that sometimes when the gates between life and death are opened, those bits of dead magic users—the watercolor people, the Veiled—can rise."

"Like ghosts?" I could handle ghosts. There were people who got rid of ghosts. Exorcists and such.

"No, not like ghosts."

Well, that was just fantastic.

"Then what are the . . . what are the Veiled?"

"They are parts of dead magic users who don't know they're dead because they are still tied to—fed, if you will—by the flow of magic."

"That's the theory?" I asked.

"That's the theory."

"And the gates between life and death?" I asked.

"Theory."

Right.

"What happens if they touch you?"

Zayvion shook his head. "They can't see most people."

"They can see me."

"What?" Zayvion's hands tightened on mine. He tipped his head down, catching my gaze. "Did they see you? Did they touch you?"

I nodded.

"Where? When?" He was still calm, but his breathing was quicker, and I could smell the peppery edge of his fear. Theory, my ass.

I pulled my hands away from his and unbuttoned the top buttons on my shirt. His eyes flickered with another kind of light—desire—down to my collarbones before he schooled his face into that calm Zen expression that gave nothing away. I pushed one shoulder of the shirt down, revealing a patch of old and new burns.

He held his breath and sat there like I'd just slapped him.

I squirmed, really uncomfortable with the look in his eyes.

"Oh, baby," he breathed.

"It's nothing. Forget it." I tugged the shirt back up over my skin, hiding my wounds, hiding my pain. But Zayvion stood, walked around the table, and knelt in front of me.

"May I see it closer? Please?"

My heart was beating too fast. I didn't know why, but I felt like crying. Okay, it was probably because I'd had a shitty day. Or maybe it was because I felt like I'd been touched, violated in ways I didn't understand and couldn't guard against. I wasn't even sure I should trust Zayvion, if I should trust in the intimacy he assumed was between us.

"I might be able to ease the pain," he said gently. "Does it still hurt?"

I nodded.

And he just waited. Didn't touch me, didn't push, didn't ask again. He just knelt there on my carpet, in the pose a man would take to offer a diamond ring and the rest of his life. Except Zayvion wasn't asking me for forever. He was asking me to trust him. Just for now.

Sweet hells.

I unbuttoned the top button again and pushed the material aside to reveal my shoulder. I gave him a level gaze.

Zayvion leaned in a little closer and studied the marks without touching them. "Some of these marks look older than others. Have you been touched by them more than once?"

"Once outside the coffee shop. Once in the parking garage with Stotts, and once on the street. In that order."

"So you've seen them three times today?"

"Four. With you."

Zayvion nodded, very Zen, although I could still smell the fear on him. "Did you put anything on the wounds?"

"Nothing but soap, water, and Bactine, Doctor."

Zayvion glanced up, smiled. "Okay. That's good. I can ease the pain some too. Help speed the healing a little. Is that okay with you?"

"How?"

"I'll need to touch one of the marks. I can soothe them with . . . magic."

"Nice hesitation there," I noted.

He took a deep breath. "It probably isn't the kind of magic you were taught in school."

"Does it involve chanting?"

"No."

"Good."

"You don't like my chanting?"

"I don't *get* your chanting. The unknown plus magic always equals dangerous in my life."

"Hmm. So am I known or unknown?" he asked.

I held his gaze and remembered the black flames and silver glyphs that covered his body. There was more to Mr. Jones than met the eye. "Unknown. Especially when you are mixed with magic."

He smiled, and heat of a very pleasant sort stirred deep in my belly. "Fair enough," he said. "Maybe we can do something about that. Get to know one another better."

"Maybe we can."

This close, it would be easy to touch him, to kiss him. And even though I didn't remember us, my body responded to him like fire to oxygen. Zayvion could stir emotions in me with a soft word, a sideways glance. Sweet loves, he did such things to me.

"May I?" he asked.

I blinked, trying to remember what we were talking about. Oh, yes. The burns.

"Touch one of the marks?" I asked to make sure.

A smile quirked the corner of his mouth. "Yes."

"Will it make any difference? They'll heal on their own, right?"

He leaned back and tipped his head to the side. "They should. But if you continue to use magic, it could take a very long time for that to happen."

"Why? They're just burns."

He stared at me, waiting.

"Okay, fine," I conceded. "They're not just burns. They're dead-magic-user-ghost-finger-burn things."

"Death magic," Zayvion said, "is nothing to mess with. If you don't want me touching you, I could call a doctor I know—"

"No," I said a little too quickly. The idea of a doctor creeped me out right now. "It's fine. You can do it."

He leaned forward again and placed the fingertips of his right hand next to the marks on my shoulder. Whisper soft, he traced a glyph against my skin. Mint flowed out from his finger, warming in small circular motions as he retraced the glyph again, guiding the mint and magic to spread a pleasant heat up my neck, across my skull, and then down my other shoulder.

Oh. Nice.

"Mmmm," I said.

Mint flowed deeper, trickling and then pouring down

my body, my bones, my blood, soothing, stroking the pain away, leaving warm waves of pleasure behind. The fevered ache inside me eased. The catch in my heartbeat eased. The tight sunburn sting of my skin eased. Even though he touched me with only one finger, it felt like his hands were everywhere, drawing gently across my skin, touching me, holding me. Making me clean, whole, and myself again.

Finally he drew his hand away. "Better?" he asked.

"Please don't stop." It came out smaller than I wanted it to. "Don't go. Yet." I put my hand on his left arm, keeping him from going away.

Instead of pulling away farther, Zayvion gathered me into his arms and held me. His palm softly rubbed the center of my back and I breathed in the pine of his cologne, the sharp male bite of his sweat.

I put my arms around him and relaxed into him. Touch, human touch, felt so good. It had been a long time since anyone had touched me like this.

"What aren't you telling me, Allie?" he asked. "What's wrong?"

"My dad's dead."

Okay, that was a stupid way to start, but my brain was losing ground to the emotions I'd kept in check all day. Zayvion nodded, the stubble from his jaw rubbing against my cheek.

"I've seen him," I said. "In my bathroom when the electricity went out. Out on the street with you, and then after I Hounded. My dad was there. But he didn't look like the Veiled. He looked like himself but transparent. He spoke to me."

"Do you remember what he said?"

"That I always forget to set Disbursements, and 'the

gates, seek the dead,' or something like that. Do you think he meant the gates between life and death? In theory?"

Zayvion stiffened and then relaxed again, like a string being plucked. He pulled back just enough so I could look into his eyes. Gold eyes burning tiger bright.

"Did he say anything else?"

"No?"

"Did he do anything else?"

The memory of his hand sinking into my chest and squeezing, flickered behind my eyes.

"He touched me."

"Did it burn like the Veiled?"

"No. But it hurt."

The line of his lips tightened. He did not look away from me. "I'd like it very much if I could stay here tonight."

"Why?"

"If your father comes back . . . comes to see you . . . I might be able to communicate with him."

"And why do you want to do that?"

"Your father was a powerful man. A very powerful user of magic. I am worried he may have . . . planned for his death."

"You're not talking funeral arrangements and wills, are you?"

"No. I'm talking magic. You father may not want to stay dead. And I don't want him hurting you."

"Are you serious?" I asked.

"Yes."

And he was so not joking.

"So by 'communicate' with my dad, do you mean

casting a Shield spell and then sucking him down a black hole like you did to the watercolor—the Veiled?"

"If I have to, yes."

Great. My ex-maybe-still-current boyfriend was going to get into a magical battle with my dead-maybe-still-kicking dad.

"And that's the only reason you want to stay? To protect me from my father? Because let me tell you, Jones, I can deal with my father."

He blinked, and his gaze softened. "When he was alive, yes. But he's dead now, Allie. And I'm worried about you. I know what it's like to try to sleep with all the lights on because you're too afraid to turn them off."

"Calling me a sissy isn't winning you any points."

"I'm not looking for points. This isn't a competition; this is real. This is life. And I know what it's like to be afraid of the dark and all the things inside it."

"I'm not afraid of the dark," I said.

"You should be."

Silence stretched out between us. He meant it. He believed it. And if Zayvion Jones said I should be afraid of something, I'd be stupid to not at least consider the validity of that.

"Just for the night," I said.

He visibly relaxed, his shoulders lowering and loosening. He had been really worried I'd say no.

"Thank you," he said. He stood and so did I.

"I'll get you a blanket for the couch." I walked to my hall closet and found a spare blanket and a pillow. "I'm going to leave my bedroom door open, but it isn't an invitation." When I turned around, he was next to my couch, watching me.

"Here." I walked over and handed him the blanket. "What? What's that funny smile?"

He shrugged one shoulder. "This just seems familiar."

"Does it?"

He looked at me, looked for something I apparently didn't have. Then he became very interested in slowly unfolding the blanket and spreading it across the couch. I've seen that kind of reaction before from people who knew a part of my life, who had experienced something with me that I'd forgotten.

"I've slept on a lot of couches in my day; that's all," he said.

"That's not going to work for me," I said.

"What?"

"Lying. If you're in my house, I want honesty. Hells, I want it when you're not in my house too."

"Honesty," he said, tasting the word. "When you and I went to Nola's farm, she made me sleep on the couch. I could see the open door to the room you slept in. I could hear you breathing, moving, dreaming. And when you cried out, I came to you. So this"—he held his hand toward the couch and then my bedroom—"and this"—he pointed to me and then himself—"feels very familiar."

I'd asked for honesty and I'd gotten it. I liked that.

"Oh," I said. I handed him the pillow. He took it, his fingers brushing mine and pausing there.

Instead of letting him pull the pillow away from me, I held on to it and stepped toward him. Close. We didn't have to say this was forever; we didn't have to say this would last. We didn't have to say anything to understand the moment. We leaned toward each other, drawn like metal to magnet.

And kissed.

His lips were soft and thick and tasted of salty pizza and sweet apples. I opened my mouth to him, wanting to taste more of him, wanting to say with my body what I could not say with my words. That he was right. I was afraid and alone. And I really wanted to be touched by him.

His tongue drew gently along the inside of my lip and electricity thrilled through me, settling like a solid heat deep in my stomach. The kiss was hot, sweet, needful.

And I wanted more.

I pulled back enough to catch my breath. "Please. Come to bed with me."

Zayvion was breathing hard. His nostrils flared. I could feel the thrumming of his pulse through the pillow we both still gripped.

He closed his eyes. Licked his lips. "I can't."

"Can't?" I asked. "Or won't?" I suddenly wondered if he had another girlfriend or a vow of celibacy.

He opened his eyes and met my gaze. "The last time . . . out at Nola's. You . . . we . . ." He exhaled and rubbed the back of his neck. When he looked back at me, he seemed a little calmer. "I promised myself if I ever had a chance to be with you again, I would wait. Wait until you said yes because you wanted me. Wanted this. Wanted us. For more than one night. For more than one reason. And right now it isn't about us. It's about uncertainty. It's about death. That's not enough for me. It shouldn't be enough for you."

I didn't know if I should be frustrated, flattered, or furious.

So I was all three.

"A simple no would have been fine."

"Nothing is ever simple with you, Allie. That's what makes you so interesting."

What was I supposed to say to that? I let go of the pillow. "So this is good night?"

"Yes," he said, "it is. Sleep well."

I doubted that was possible. I walked to my bedroom, turning out lights as I went. I listened as Zayvion stretched out on my couch. I crawled under my covers and waited to see if he snored. But I never had a chance. As soon as my cheek touched the pillow, I fell into a dark, and thankfully dreamless, sleep.

Chapter Fifteen

Morning came too early and brought with it the fever I'd been hanging my magic use on. And the fever brought along its friends Body Aches and Bastard of a Headache.

Since I was already dealing with sticky, stinging skin and an ache somewhere deeper in my chest that I was pretty sure was my heart, I was just all sorts of joyful about waking up.

I rolled over and looked at my clock.

Six thirty. Hells. I was supposed to meet Violet in an hour and a half.

Double hells.

I sat up slowly, shielding my eyes from the light, and walked very, very carefully into my bathroom. I opened my medicine cabinet and pulled out the bottle of aspirin with hands that would not stop shaking. My hands shook so hard, I spilled pills into the sink. I caught three in my palm and then held my breath and focused on them so I could count and make sure it was only three pills. Overdosing would be too damn easy right now.

Three. I put them in my mouth, swallowed them
down with water from the sink. All I needed was a
little time. A little time and I'd be okay. I turned
toward the shower and took a couple steps, holding
on to the sink, the wall, the toilet. My teeth chattered.
I felt burned, and burning, inside and out.

Fabulous. Today was going to be a big ol' bucket
of happy.

A warm hand touched my left shoulder, and a wash
of mint made the jackhammers in my head take it
down a notch. So help me, if it was my father standing
there behind me, I was going to kill him, dead or not.

"You're burning up," Zayvion's soft voice said.

"Disbursement," I mumbled. "Should only last an
hour or two." Or all day. But right now I couldn't stomach that possibility, so I decided to ignore it instead.

"Mmm," Zayvion said. With his hand still on my
shoulder, he somehow turned on the shower and
simultaneously helped me over to it.

I plucked at my pajamas and wanted to growl in
frustration. Why had I worn a shirt with buttons on
it? Buttons were too complicated. Buttons took coordination. Why didn't I have a pajama shirt with snaps
or Velco or something?

Then Zayvion's hands were there, unbuttoning my
shirt. I squinted up at him, even though the only light
in the bathroom was the ghostly gray coming through
the frosted window and the wedge of yellow that the
hall light cast across the floor and wall.

Zayvion's gaze did not stray. He looked me straight
in the eyes while he unhooked the last button and
pulled my shirt away from my shoulders.

I was naked beneath my shirt.

I should be feeling all sorts of things in this awkward, embarrassing, needy moment. And even though a bunch of emotions lined up for attention, I ignored them all. I had been doing this alone for a long time now, nursing myself through the pain of using magic. And right now, I was grateful he was there, grateful to have someone helping me when I was sick.

Besides, if he made one funny move, I'd knock him upside the head with the plunger.

He placed his fingertips on either side of my hips. Even through the pain, I noticed his hands trembled slightly, noticed his breathing was mechanical and even, as if he was having to think about it. Still holding my gaze with that calm, Zen expression, he drew the elastic of my pants down over my hips, off my butt. He paused at my thighs and frowned, probably realizing that he was going to have to kneel and that oh-so-polite eye contact was about to be blown.

I eyed the plunger.

"Can you lift your legs?" he asked.

I had no idea. I put one hand on the wall to steady myself. "Sure."

Zayvion knelt and I lifted one leg. The heat from his body, so near my skin, was a mix of pain and pleasure as he tugged off my pants and panties.

Not a stitch of clothes on me. I did not remember getting naked with this man before, though I know I had. Still, getting naked when I was shaking with cold and fever and felt like a steaming pile of something the dog had left on the yard was not exactly how I had pictured our sexy encounter. Even if I could feel the warm exhale of my maybe-ex-boyfriend's breath high on my thigh.

He inhaled sharply, surprised. "Allie, where did you get that?"

I pulled my hand off of my eyes. What did I have down there that would get that kind of reaction out of him? "What?"

His fingers pressed gently at the edge of the mark on my thigh, the glyph Lon Trager had stabbed into me.

Oh. Right. That. So much for sexy.

And I swear, if I didn't get into hot water right this damn minute, I was going to shake apart. "Got jumped on bus," I chattered. "C-cold, Zay. Move."

He stood, and his wide hands steadied me through the last few steps and then into the warmth of the shower.

I wrapped my arms around my ribs and stuck my head under the water.

"How many aspirin did you take?" he asked.

"Three."

"Think you can take one more?"

One? I'd chew through a case of them. "Yes."

Zayvion left. I thought about soap but didn't want to move from beneath the water's warmth. Then Zayvion was back. "Here," he said.

I looked over, realized the shower curtain was open—had been open the whole time. Water was splashing out over towels I had not put on the floor. Zayvion held a cup in one hand and a pill—blue, and not aspirin—in the other.

"What?"

"It's for migraines. It should be fine with the aspirin. And this is orange juice."

I stood there staring at the cup like it was made of snakes. I didn't have orange juice in my house.

He interpreted my expression correctly. "I went out. Thought you'd be up for breakfast."

"You cooked?"

"If you count bagels and orange juice cooking, yes."

I took the pill out of his hand, read the tiny ink stamp on it. Brand-name painkiller. Stronger than aspirin. "Buy this?"

"Those, I keep on me. You aren't the only one who uses magic."

I popped the pill and drank down the rest of the orange juice. I needed all the energy I could get. I had a breakfast date in an hour, and then a meeting with Pike and the police, and quite possibly a drug and blood magic ex-con to find. I pushed the cup back at him, looked him straight in the eye. "Thanks." And pointedly closed the shower curtain.

"Do you know who it was? On the bus?" he asked.

Apparently closing the curtain wasn't enough of a hint that I wanted a little "me" time.

"Trager," I said. "Lon Trager." I dunked my head back under the water, shampooed and rinsed my hair, and rubbed soap over my skin. It didn't sting as badly as the last time I'd washed. I didn't know if I owed that to Zayvion's soothing fingers, or if the aspirin was kicking in.

When I came up for air and turned off the water, I still didn't feel fabulous, but the aspirin and migraine meds had hit really fast. I pulled back the curtain just enough to look out. Zayvion's wide back was to me. He stared in my medicine cabinet.

"A little space, please?" I asked.

He closed the medicine cabinet. "Do you have a needle?" he asked without turning around. The mirror in front of him was fogged, so I couldn't see his reflection.

"No."

"No?"

"Do I look like someone who sews?"

He made a frustrated sound. "Allie," he said, still not turning around. "I need to unbind that glyph from your leg. Since you aren't the sewing type, I'll need to use a knife."

Well, hello, Mr. Psycho-Killer. What'd you do with my maybe-ex-boyfriend?

"Like hell you will," I said.

He turned. Yep, that was a knife in his hand.

"If you use that on me, Jones, I will kick your ass with that plunger, fever or no fever." Sure, I talked a big fight, but right now, all I had at my disposal was a bar of soap and a loofah. Well, and magic.

"What do you know about blood magic?" Zayvion asked. He leaned his hip against my sink and kept the knife low. "Have you studied it?"

"It's illegal."

"Have you studied it?"

"No."

He closed his eyes and scrubbed at his face and then the back of his neck. "Why didn't your father want you to know these things? He knew you had great potential with magic. He had to know you would use it in ways that were not taught in college. Why wouldn't he want you to have the knowledge so you could keep yourself safe from shit like this?"

I shrugged one shoulder. "I think he expected me to stay dependent on him for those kinds of things. He never thought I'd leave him, leave the life he wanted me to live. He never thought I could stand on my own two feet without him."

"And you had to go out there and prove him wrong, didn't you?"

"I'm just full of disappointments like that. Now put down the dagger and hand me a towel."

How had my life changed so that I had to say those words before breakfast?

Zayvion put the knife on the countertop, found a clean towel on the linen rack, and handed it to me.

I took the towel, keeping the shower curtain between us. "No blood magic, no lectures, no stabbing, no knives, no nothing until I'm dry and dressed. Get out of my bathroom, Jones."

Zayvion picked up his knife and walked out of the room.

That was too easy.

I dried quickly, checked that he wasn't outside the door waiting to jump me, and then went into my bedroom and got dressed. My head hurt, but the chills were gone, leaving me feeling dizzy. I was probably still running a fever, but at least my teeth weren't chattering.

I found Zayvion at the window in the living room, looking through the curtains. The knife glinted silverbright in his dark hand. On the round table next to him was the carton of orange juice, some bagels, cheese, and strawberries.

Strawberries in late November. I could get used to this.

"Lon Trager has your blood." Zayvion turned away from the window.

"I know. I was there when he took it."

He nodded, as though maybe he was just making sure I remembered it.

Oh. He probably was making sure I remembered it.

"And the spell he worked, the one on your leg, will let him draw you to him any time he chooses."

"Excuse me?"

"It's a form of Binding. That glyph—" He nodded toward my thigh. "—and the blood he took from you are connected by the magic in your blood and the magic in the glyph. If he wanted you, there would be nothing you could do to resist going to him."

My stomach clenched. I was a dog on Trager's chain. How damn great was that?

"And you know how to break it?" I asked.

"Yes."

"Will Trager know it's broken?"

"What?"

"Will Trager know the Binding is broken?"

"If his blood was on the knife or needle, he'll know. Blood magic is . . . intimate."

I'd bet my boots Trager's blood was all over that damn needle. Great. Not only did I have to deal with blood magic; I'd need to go get screened for diseases too.

"Let me break it," Zayvion said again.

"No."

Mr. Zayvion Jones spent most his time looking like a pretty nice guy. He could do that street drifter, shy-boy smile that tugs the heartstrings, and he could do the unflappable Zen Master bit where his patience seemed endless. But right now, Mr. Zayvion Jones was angry—and he did angry like a caged animal.

"No is not an option." He took a step.

I mentally set a Disbursement—sweet hells, I'd pay for this—and traced a glyph for Impact.

It was not a spell I liked to use, but it was effective. I held off pouring magic into it. Which was not easy.

Zayvion stopped. "Allie. Don't think I won't fight you for this. You're being stubborn and stupid."

"You said you trusted my stubborness," I said. "The Binding stays. And you can leave."

Zayvion became very still, very quiet, as if all his anger and frustration were being drawn into a deep dark hole somewhere inside him. That was a bad sign. You can't cast magic in states of high emotion. Can't cast it when you're angry or panicked.

Zayvion Jones was cool, calm, and therefore more than capable of casting magic. Like I said, dangerous.

When he spoke, he was frighteningly Zen, frighteningly formal. Controlled. Just like at the graveyard.

"My apologies," he said, "if I have crossed a line. I am concerned for you and your safety. If Lon Trager is willing to risk Binding you with his own blood, he is willing to harm you. And he will do so. He is simply biding his time."

Biding his time, I guessed, because I didn't have Pike with me. But I would. This afternoon at the police station. Then me, Pike, Detective Stotts, and the rest of the police force could go pay Lon Trager a visit. With the glyph that was still on my leg as evidence, I'd charge him with magical attack with intent to do harm. A felony. Jail time.

"I know," I said. "I plan to use that against him."

"How?"

"I'm going to the police. The MERC."

Zayvion tipped his head and narrowed his eyes, as if that weren't an option he had considered. "And what will you tell them?"

"I'll show them the Binding. That's a felony. And it's my evidence to throw Trager's ass in jail."

"Do you really think prison will be enough to hold a man like him?"

"This time, I am the evidence. No one's going to tamper with that. His conviction will stand."

Zayvion looked at me, his eyes cool gold.

I looked him right back and said, "Unless you want to come down to the station with me, which I believe the police would like since they mentioned they're looking for you, you need to go now. Good-bye, Zayvion," I said. "Don't forget your coat."

Zayvion's jaw twitched, and his fingers rolled into a loose fist. But not to cast magic. I checked.

Just in case I was wrong, I didn't let go of the Impact glyph.

"No," Zay said as he reached over to the chair he had sat in yesterday. "I don't think going down to the station with you would be in the best of either of our interests."

He picked up something on the seat of the chair and placed it on the table.

A single long-stemmed pink rose.

He gathered his coat and draped it over his arm. Walked toward me. I moved to the side so he could pass, out of reach.

He paused in front of me. "Promise me one thing."

I raised an eyebrow.

"Promise me you won't take on Trager alone. Stay with the police, do as they say, and you should be fine. If, however, you do meet him alone—" He flicked his hand out from beneath his jacket and offered me the hilt of the thin silver dagger. "Use this to break the skin on your thigh and cut the tip off the outermost line on the Binding. Then pull the magic out of it— all of it. Doing that untrained will hurt like a mother. But it should break his hold on you. Give you a chance."

I took the dagger with my left hand—the hand I was not holding the Impact glyph with. "Thanks," I said.

"Thank me tonight, over dinner, after you have returned from talking to the police and not from Hounding down Trager on your own."

"I'll see what I can do," I said.

Angry Zayvion, Zen Zayvion, gently touched the edge of my right cheek, where marks of magic whorled. Even though he was angry, mint soothed through me, easing my ache and racing heartbeat.

"Be careful," he whispered. "I don't want to lose you twice." Then he walked out of my apartment and closed the door behind him.

Chapter Sixteen

The silver dagger was so clear and deep, it looked more like white gold, the blade tucked in a simple leather sheath. I pulled it free of the sheath. From the tip of the blade to the rounded top of the hilt were carved glyphs in the same colors as the metallic swirls on my arm. The center of the blade encased a thin strip of glass beveled in such a way as to control the flow of blood. I had no idea how this blade had been made, but it was clear exactly what its purpose was—to cast magic. Blood magic.

Zayvion Jones just got stranger and stranger.

Other than a couple minor spells, like Truth, I had no idea how to actually cast blood magic. I sure as hell had never used a dagger to uncast a spell on myself. And, yes, that worried me. But not enough to leave the dagger behind.

I put on my leather coat, tucked the sheathed knife into the deep pocket, and put on my gloves, scarf, and hat. I walked over to the table and drew the pink rose up beneath my nose, inhaling the sweet innocence of spring.

What kind of crazy did I have to be to kick out a man who brought me strawberries and roses and a big honkin' magic glyphed dagger?

I put the rose in a glass of water in my kitchen, grabbed my notebook and nonfunctioning cell phone, and locked the door behind me. I took the stairs down and pushed through the main doors. I paused before hitting the sidewalk. It was still early enough to be dark, but a silvery light reflected from everything around me. A light that had nothing to do with magic.

The stairs, the sidewalk, and every single twig on the trees were covered in a thin coating of ice. The rain had frozen last night, turning the world into something alien and beautiful. And slippery.

I stepped outside. The wind whipped down the street, biting at my exposed skin and shooting painful shivers through me. My fever and headache weren't gone yet. And sure enough, I'd forgotten to put the bottle of aspirin in my pocket.

Tree branches up and down my street clattered and chimed, a rattle of glass. I put my hands out to the side to keep my balance against the wind and carefully made my way over to the curb, hoping a cab would show up.

The city didn't get enough frigid weather to warrant the Proxy cost of permanent Deicing spells, so Portland relied on sand trucks to keep the hilly streets passable. A truck must have already made a run down my street, because cars were easing by.

I narrowed my eyes against the row of headlights and spotted a cab coming down the hill. I stepped out and waved it down.

The driver braked and slid to a stop. I got in.

"Have to be half penguin to be out in this weather."
The driver was a big man who sounded like he'd had
a bowl of extraperky for breakfast.

"Or just stupid," I said. "Kickin' Cakes, please."

The cab was warm and smelled soapy, like it'd just
gone through a car wash with the windows open. The
smell turned my stomach, but for the heat, I'd deal
with the stink. I tucked my nose in my scarf and closed
my eyes.

The cab eased to a top, and Mr. Cheery called back,
"Here you go."

I opened my eyes.

"Thanks." I dug in my pocket—the one with my
blank notebook, not the dagger—and pulled out some
cash. I paid him and made my way carefully up the
walk to the restaurant.

Kickin' Cakes was a bar turned breakfast joint, and
it still hadn't quite shed its former identity. A long row
of tables down one side of the single story building sat
opposite the curved black marble bar to the left. All
cooking was done behind that bar, and the restaurant
had an art deco feel: tables in chrome and black lino-
leum, booth and chair seats in turquoise and maroon.

I walked through the front door, and the smell of
butter, onions, sausage, and coffee, along with the
nutmeg-sweet scent of the signature dish, Kicking Pancakes, greeted me. They were good smells that got
through my pain and made me hungry. The restaurant
was nice and warm.

And busy, even with the icy roads. I scanned the
room for Violet. I spotted a pretty young redhead.
Next to her, sitting so he faced the front door, was
an unassumingly plain-looking bodyguard wearing a

henley shirt rucked up at the elbows. His name, I think, was Kevin. I knew of him, but if I had met him before, I could not remember it.

Kevin watched me walk in, held my gaze, and nodded to me. I took it as an invitation.

Violet glanced over at me, and since I was nearly at their table, I had to work on not letting my shock show. She was so young, we could have been sisters if she weren't my father's wife. And I was pretty sure I'd be the big sister.

Yes, I'd seen her in photos in the papers since my dad's death, and my friend Nola said Violet and I had met during the time I could not remember. She thought we had gotten along too, which was weird. I had never gotten along with any of my father's wives.

Violet had a petite build, wore simple but fashionable glasses, and had great cheekbones and a smattering of freckles. She wore a loose sweater, jeans, and sneakers. Put her in a lineup, and I would not point her out as a billionaire widow. She looked radiant, her face glowing and happy despite the dark circles beneath her eyes that spoke of sleepless nights.

"Allie," she said warmly. "Sit, sit." She pointed to the chair opposite where she sat on the booth bench against the wall. It put my back to the bar. I could see behind Kevin, and the windows and front door were at the corner of my eye.

"How are you feeling?" she asked.

"Good." I hadn't seen her since the coma that had knocked me out. "Better. Thanks. How's the coffee?"

Kevin was already pouring me a cup out of the carafe from the center of the table. Violet shrugged. "No coffee for me. I'm an herbal tea girl right now."

"Stress?" I thought about the pressure she must be under now that the duties of running my father's multibillion-dollar magic and tech integration company had fallen largely into her hands.

"Pregnant," she said.

The whole restaurant swirled under my feet. "Preg—what? Who?" I looked over at Kevin. He quietly picked up his cup and took a drink. He watched Violet across the cup's rim, and his gaze carried something—sadness? Jealousy? Then he tipped the cup down and smiled at me. Smiled at me for Violet, I realized.

Oh. I might be fevered, headachy, and struck dumb, but I could see a man who was in love and hadn't admitted it to himself. Or to Violet.

"Whose?" I repeated, looking at Violet.

She took a sip of her tea. "Mine. And your father's."

Wow.

At my expression she said, "I'm four months along. We had, well, just before he was killed." She didn't say any more, which was good. I was having a hard time sorting this out, and picturing her in bed with my father wasn't helping any.

Kevin had the right idea. I picked up my coffee cup and took a drink. Hot, bitter. I wished it were something stronger.

Violet, who was about my age, was pregnant with my father's child.

One part of me hoped maybe she was wrong—that it wasn't my father's child. That maybe it was Kevin's or some one-night stand she'd had. But Violet was a smart woman—the brains behind most of the newest tech coming out from my dad's company. If she believed it was my father's child, then I was certain it was.

"Wow," I said. "Are you happy?"

"I am. It was a . . . shock. I didn't find out until after. He never knew." She took a deep breath and let it out slowly. "I am. Happy."

"You and my dad were okay together?"

"Allie, I loved your father. Despite the age difference. I was the one who chased him."

It didn't take magic for me to know she was telling the truth. I didn't know what she had seen in him. My father was a controlling, driven, frequently angry man. But maybe this—the child—was what she had wanted.

"Congratulations?" I offered.

She laughed, a short, happy sound. "I'm sorry. Just . . . the look on your face is hilarious. Haven't you ever wanted a little brother or sister?"

Oh. Sweet. Hells.

"When I was a kid, maybe. I'm old enough to be this kid's mother." How was that for tactful?

But Violet laughed. "I know. Weird, isn't it? That's part of why I wanted to tell you before anyone else. Only Kevin and my doctor knows. I thought you should have a chance to get used to it a little before the gossip columns pick it up."

"You're enjoying this, aren't you?"

She slipped her fingers behind her glasses and pressed against her eyes. She was still smiling. "What else am I going to do? It is what it is. I'll figure it out as I go. That's life." She readjusted her glasses and placed her hands on the tabletop.

Kevin's fingers stretched slightly, almost but not

brushing her hand before he pulled away. I don't think Violet noticed.

For all her laughter, Violet sounded tired. Maybe even a little weepy. In her shoes, I'd be a big fat pile of panic.

"I'm happy for you," I said.

"Really?"

"Yes. And I'm happy for our family."

Sweet hells. I'd just told her we were family. Must be the fever. I mean, I did think I could like her someday—not as my stepmother but maybe as a friend. And if that kid was my father's child, then he or she had my father's blood—my blood. That made us family whether I liked it or not.

Violet smiled and her eyes got a little teary. "Thank you."

She reached over and gave my hands a squeeze just as the waiter showed up for our orders.

"Are you ready?" he asked.

"Sure." I ordered a stack of pancakes, sausage, and eggs. Violet went for eggs, toast, and fruit; Kevin chose the omelette and a side of bacon.

As soon as the waiter left, Violet spoke up again. "There are a couple more things I want to talk to you about. Nothing quite so . . . life changing, I think. First, I want you to take this." She pulled a cell phone out of her purse. "It's the same number as the one you have that isn't working. It's top-of-the-line."

I opened my mouth and she held up a finger. "This is coming out of Beckstrom Enterprise's budget, and it should. I want to be able to get a hold of you easier, Allie. So do other people in the company. Ethan has been trying to talk to you for days."

"Who?"

"Ethan Katz. Our accountant. He needs to go over some things regarding your father's estate with you."

I took the phone. Slick, black, and small. I flicked it open; the screen lit. So far so good. We'd see how long it lasted. I put it in my jacket pocket. "Thank you," I said. "For some reason, I'm not having much luck with phones lately."

Kevin shifted slightly. "Batteries going bad on you?"

"How'd you guess?"

He shrugged. "If this phone doesn't hold up, I have some other ideas."

Just as I thought. This man played in the magic sandbox with the big boys. Good for Violet. At least she'd have someone who could kick some magical ass and keep her, and my little sibling, safe.

The waiter came back with our food, and no one apologized for digging in. Kevin was attentive to Violet in small ways I don't think she noticed. Without her asking, he refilled the water of her tea and turned the jam carousel so that the huckleberry was within reach. They moved easily in each other's space. Something at least I and, when Kevin caught me watching, he was very aware of. I wondered why he hadn't told her he had feelings for her.

Maybe it was the recently murdered husband and unplanned pregnancy thing? Did they even make a greeting card to profess your love under such circumstances?

Yeah, they probably did. It was probably on the shelf next to the "sorry to hear you got groped by your dad's ghost, but running him down in the street isn't the way to pay him back, and by the way, dead people don't like you" card.

"I don't know how much thought you've put into this," Violet said. "But I want you to have a part in guiding your father's business."

"Interesting. So you don't like Beckstrom Enterprises?"

"No. I think your father wanted you to step in." She held up one hand and it cut off my smart-ass reply.

When did I start responding to hand signals? Note to self: work on that.

"I know running the business may not be your goal in life. With the present board and competent heads of all the divisions, things are going fine. Daniel didn't run the company single-handed, though that's what he would have liked everyone to think. He hired incredibly qualified and capable people."

"Sounds like all the bases are covered. What do you want me to do?"

"I want you to think about it. Do you want to follow your father's footsteps and take the company down the path he chose? Do you want to take the company in a new direction? You have a majority of the vote, Allie. Even if you don't want to do anything different from what is already happening, you need to at least lend your voice to the company's future. People are waiting to hear what you have to say."

Holy shit. I don't know why I hadn't ever looked at it that way, but she was right. I had the reins of my father's dirty, vicious, greedy company in my hands. To make, or break.

Violet ate the last of her toast and stared down at her nearly empty plate.

"Sick?" Kevin asked quietly.

"No." She smiled up at him, and he was very good

at not letting her see what her smile did to him. "Just happy I can eat breakfast again."

He nodded and went back to sipping coffee, watching the door, and ignoring my pointed looks.

Okay, so I wasn't just going to grind my father's company into the ground. Violet, and my soon-to-be sibling, depended on it. Not only that, she had cutting-edge magic technology copatented with Beckstrom Enterprises, and I would hate for the control of her own technology to be taken out of her hands. And I bet there were a lot worse hands it could fall into.

"Let me think about it," I said.

"Good. That's all I'm asking. So. How are things with you and Zayvion Jones?"

I carefully did not let my reaction show. "What do you mean?"

"I saw the security tape of you and him in the elevator. Looked like things were getting serious between you. Are you still seeing each other?"

Note to self: find security tape and figure out what she's talking about.

"We're going to dinner tonight," I said.

She smiled. "I think you would be good together."

"Wait—you know him?"

Kevin had gathered her plate and stacked it on his and then taken mine and done the same. Violet leaned back on the padded bench and tucked one leg up beneath her, cradling her tea in her hands. She looked over at Kevin, and he nodded.

Well, well. They shared secrets. How interesting.

"He's a part of the group your father was involved in," she said. "I'm not directly involved, but I am aware of the things that fall beneath their concern."

"Could you be more vague?"

Kevin brushed off his hands over the plates. It looked like he was getting rid of crumbs, but what he was really doing was casting a very subtle Mute spell.

Holy hells, he was good. This plain-looking guy with eyes that were too big and a chin that was too small was suddenly up there on my list of people I wouldn't want to meet in a dark alley.

That Mute spell would allow us to talk, and the people around us wouldn't even notice they couldn't understand what we were saying.

"Zayvion," Violet said, "is a part of the Watch. A branch of the Authority. Has he told you this?"

"We haven't had a lot of time to chat." Which wasn't entirely true. Zayvion had not told me he was a part of anything called the Watch. He had mentioned secret magic vigilantes. Maybe it was the same thing?

"The Authority is a private organization of people who do what they can behind the scenes to keep magic, and the people who use it, safe. Zayvion works for them."

"And my dad was a part of this too?"

Kevin answered. "He was a voice in the Authority. He had influence and sway among the members."

"Members like you?" I asked.

He nodded. "Members like me."

"So you're telling me there is a secret society of magic users, and that Zayvion Jones, and both of you, are involved in it to some degree."

"Yes," Violet said.

"Why tell me now? Why should I care?"

"I never agreed with your father keeping it a secret from you," she said. "Some of the board members in

Beckstrom Enterprises are also members of the Authority. I am not foolish enough to think you won't eventually find out. I'm telling you now because your father's death sent shock waves through that community."

"But if I'm not a part of that community, what does it matter to me?"

"*Shock waves* is a polite term," Kevin said. "Your father's voice held wide-reaching power and influence over the order of the group and the direction it was going. Not everyone agreed with him. Now that he is gone, sides are being taken. It is very likely there will be a . . . confrontation. And you, Allie, are a prime target. Beckstrom's child. Beckstrom's blood. Culpable."

"Whoa," I said.

But Violet spoke over me. "And that is why we would like you to move in with me. With us, at the condo. The magical wards and locks are beyond compare, unbreakable, and Kevin is an excellent guard. Please, Allie. For your safety. Until this . . . confrontation blows over."

It had been less than an hour since we'd admitted we might be family, and now she wanted me to move home with Mommy? There was no way she was talking me into coming home. That place had too many memories I would rather forget.

"No," I said. "No thanks. Absolutely no."

Violet gave me a hard look, and I raised my eyebrows, trading her stare for stare.

She finally looked away. "You are so like him. Stubborn."

I let that slide. See how nice I was to the pregnant woman?

I looked over at Kevin. "Is Zayvion 'watching' me? Hunting me? Is Zayvion following me around to decide if I'm a danger to magic or to myself? Spying on me for the Authority?"

Kevin blinked. His eyebrows knitted and he leaned forward a little. "Why do you ask?"

"Just a yes or no will do."

He didn't smile, but he looked amused. "No."

I watched his body language, which he patiently let me. He was hard to read. A lot like Zayvion, but without the Zen bit. Still, he didn't smell like he was lying.

And if he was any good at reading body language, he just saw how relieved his answer made me. Hells, I had it bad for Zayvion. Something deep inside me feared his interest in me was nothing more than a game of who got to keep the magic. Something deep inside me wanted us, Zayvion and me, to have a chance for something more. A lot more.

"Do you know who is watching me?"

"No."

Two for two.

"Do you know who Zayvion is watching?"

"Probably. If you want to know, you should ask him."

Fair enough.

"But let me tell you this," he said. "There are dangerous people and dark magics in this city, Allie. More than you can handle on your own. You should reconsider Mrs. Beckstrom's offer."

Mrs. Beckstrom? Wow, he was in serious denial. And he didn't have to tell me about dangerous people—I had an appointment with Pike and the police to take down Trager today.

"I'll keep it in mind." End of conversation. "Thanks for the phone, Violet. And for breakfast. Call me if you need me." I stood and put money on the table.

"Allie, I got it," she said.

"No. I'll pay my part."

And instead of acting like my dad and refusing to let me stand on my own, pay on my own, she just nodded. "I programed my number into your phone," she said. "Just in case."

Just in case I said no and didn't move in with her. See what I mean? Smart.

"Don't forget to make an appointment with Mr. Katz," she said. "His number's in there too."

"I'll see what I can do." The spiderweb tingle of the Mute spell brushed over me as Kevin deftly unwove it. I walked to the door without looking back.

Okay, that hadn't gone quite how I expected. Violet was pregnant. And secret magic vigilantes—the Watch, the Authority—were out to get me because I was my father's child.

If I believed Kevin and Violet.

And I did.

All the more reason to meet with Pike, go to the cops, and tell them about Trager attacking me and wanting Pike. Then the police could take care of Trager, and Pike could retire, and I could go on a date tonight and get information out of Zayvion so I could find a way to keep myself safe that didn't involve moving in with my father's widow.

I wondered if I could hire a bodyguard like Kevin.

Wondered if Zayvion would be my bodyguard. Right, like I wanted him all over me every second of the day. A wash of heat flushed through me at the thought of that. Okay, maybe the idea had some merit. Even if he said no, he'd know someone I could hire, at least until this "confrontation" blew itself out.

I made my way along the sidewalk, careful over the rock salt and ice. I didn't see any cabs.

The phone in my pocket rang. I jerked and almost slipped. I fumbled the phone out of my pocket, expecting to hear Violet's voice on the other end.

"Hello?"

"Allie, this is Detective Stotts. I've been trying to reach you. I thought this number wasn't working."

"It wasn't," I said. "What's up?"

"I need you to come down to the station as soon as you can."

Dread knuckled into my stomach and twisted. "Why?"

"Martin Pike is missing."

"Are you sure? He was helping a friend on the east side. Anthony Bell's mother."

"We contacted her. She hasn't seen him for several days."

"Days?" Hells, I'd seen Pike just yesterday. Home improvements, my ass. Unless Anthony's mom had a reason to lie. Which she might. Crap. "I'll be there soon," I said.

I pocketed the phone and took three steps toward the curb.

A sharp pain snapped electricity up my thigh. The pain shot through my stomach and then sawed up beneath my ribs. Something solid clamped my breastbone and tugged like an iron hook, biting hard and finding purchase.

Heart attack?

The pain faded, but I could not move, could not lift my feet. Could not swallow or blink.

The smell of sweet cherries wrapped around me, filled my nose, my mouth.

Blood magic.

"Come to me," a man's voice whispered.

A wash of sexual pleasure rolled beneath my skin, following the path of the pain. The pleasure blended with the echos of pain, creating a new sensation. Bitter and sweet. Oh. I wanted that. Wanted to feel that again. I didn't know where the voice was, or who it was, but I would do anything to hear it again.

"Ankeny Square." Words were cherry sweet in my mind, cherry sweet in my mouth, and they felt good. So very, very good. I shuddered.

The street, the city around me faded at the edges, blurring like a dream. I was panting now, too hot in the icy air. I held my breath, waiting, aching for the voice to speak again.

"Come to me."

And then the presence of the voice was gone. I was left empty, alone. But able to move.

Ankeny Square. I had to go to Ankeny Square.

I stood on the curb until a cab pulled up. I told the driver to take me to Ankeny Square. I tugged off my scarf, my hat, my gloves. I was hot, too hot. The hook in my chest throbbed and cut, an uncomfortable pleasure. The stroke of pain on my thigh spread heat across my hips and made me squirm.

"Can you go faster?" I asked the driver.

I didn't hear his answer.

The icy city slid past the window. I pulled off my coat and stripped out of my sweater. In jeans and a T-shirt, I still couldn't shake the heat, couldn't ease the lovely pain. What was wrong with me?

I leaned my head against the cool window and closed my eyes.

Was I dreaming? The vibration of the cab's engine transferred through the glass, and sweat stung my eyes and salted my lips. No, this was too solid, too real for a dream.

Why was I was going to Ankeny Square? Because I had to. Because the voice told me to.

Wait. I was following a voice?

Heat snapped out from the hook in my chest and zagged down to my thigh. The pain slithered over the rise of my leg muscle, soft threads of heat licking down the inside of my thigh.

I bit my bottom lip to keep from moaning.

This wasn't right.

This was blood magic. What had Zayvion said? Blood magic was *intimate*.

Trager. It was his blood magic, his glyph on my thigh, his voice calling me. It was his touch I wanted. His touch he was making me want.

Shit, shit, shit.

Inhale, exhale. Pain, desire. The blood magic glyph on my thigh throbbed with wicked pleasure. Magic in my blood rose in response, pushing to be free, to be used. No, no, no. That would be bad.

Blood magic bit, tugged, chest and thigh, a luscious ache that overwhelmed my senses. I hated it, and I wanted it. Wanted more of it.

And all the while a small part of my mind screamed at me to stop, to wake up, to run away. I leaned away from the window. Blinked hard. Focused on the seat in front of me.

I will not go to him. I will not be his toy on a string, his dog on a chain. I exhaled as another wave of pleasure shuddered through me. *I will not let him use me.*

I needed help. I needed my phone.

Pain, pleasure. I inhaled, tasted sweet cherries, and then held my breath as the blood glyph cinched tight again.

My hands shook. I pulled the phone out of my pocket, managed to open it.

Dead.

Maybe I'd pulled out the wrong phone.

I reached back into my pocket, and my fingers brushed over the dagger. Zayvion's knife. He had said I could use it to break the Binding. I exhaled. A stroke of heat pulsed through me again. I closed my eyes, waiting for it to pass.

Sweet hells. *Intimate* didn't cover it. Blood magic was far more than that. It was sexual. Orgasmic. Needful. No wonder people got hooked. And if they mixed it with drugs . . . Hells.

"This is it," the driver said.

I opened my eyes. Dawn was trying to wedge night aside. In the low light of streetlamps, the freestanding arched columns and cobbled bricks of Ankeny Square shone blue, black, and gold.

It was too early for any of the shops to be open yet.

My fingers were wrapped around the door handle.

Stop it, Allie, I told myself. *Don't open the door.*

Tell the cabbie to take you home. Tell the cabbie to call the police.

The hook in my chest tugged, and I bit my lip to keep from gasping. I had to get out of the cab. Had to go. Go to Trager.

I left money on the seat. Left other things there too, I think. My hat. My gloves. I got out. Stood there, trembling in pain and need in the ice-covered square. The cab pulled away.

The hook in my chest tugged again. Forced me to take a step. One step closer to Trager. To what I wanted.

No, what I didn't want.

I still had my jacket. Still had the dagger. Breathing hard, I pulled out both phones and opened each in turn. Dead and dead. Okay, that left me, the knife, and magic.

I could do this. I could break this hold. But if I pulled on magic to fight Trager, the Veiled would try to eat me. And it didn't matter how strong I was. I didn't think I could fight off dead magic users while I was trying to take down one of the most notorious drug and blood dealers in the city, who had his hook in my chest and thigh.

So much for magic. Okay, that left me and the knife.

I took the dagger out of my coat pocket and drew it free of its sheath. Light caught at the slim edges, pooled in the glyphwork that flowed from the hilt, down the blade, across the glass center, and slipped off the razor edge, glowing in the same metallic shades as the marks on my arm.

I didn't know how to break the Binding. Couldn't remember what Zayvion had told me to do. Fine. There were other things a sharp blade could be used for. Things like self-defense. And kicking ass. I gripped the hilt like I knew how to use the thing and scanned the square for Trager and his goons. A shadow detached itself from the pillars. He—I was sure it was a he—started toward me with a slow, limping gate.

I inhaled, sorted through the smells of ice and asphalt, and got a noseful of hickory and soap. And blood. Lots of blood.

"Pike?" I breathed.

He continued his slow, slow walk. Damn him. He *had* Hounded Trager without me, without the police. He'd broken his promise. Gone vigilante. I was so going to kick his retired ass.

"Pike?" I said a little louder. Still no answer. The hook in my chest stung and throbbed, until I took another step. Closer to Pike. That worked for me, so I kept walking, trying to focus on Pike and not the strokes of pleasure and pain. I picked my way across the icy uneven cobbles.

Pike trudged forward, swaying drunkenly. And the closer I came to him, I knew why.

A gory portrait out of a bad dream, Pike was covered in blood. A meaty, sloppy mess was all that was left of where his left eye should be. His cheekbone stuck out of his skin. His left arm swung and grinded with a loose gristle-over-bone sound. His T-shirt was so wet with blood, there was nothing of the original blue left. The front of his jeans were so heavy with blood, each grueling step he took toward me left behind a dark, wet footprint.

He wasn't breathing very well. Or very much.

"Oh, no. Oh, fuck, Pike," I said. "Where's Davy?

Who's watching you? Covering your back? Who has
a fucking phone?'' I tried to jog the remainder of the
distance, tried to reach him.

Just as I was almost close enough to touch him, pain
exploded in my chest. No pleasure this time. Hot
spikes rattled over my ribs, each one in turn until I
thought they'd break. I groaned.

Pike grunted, tipped his working eye up to look at
me, and then folded down to his knees. His exhale
wheezed with horrible wetness.

I stood above him, close enough to touch him but
unable to move, unable to bend in the vise grip of
pain and the damn Binding. I listened as his breathing
grew more shallow. I didn't know how he was getting
any air through all that wetness.

In the still air of the morning, where traffic moved
in the distance like a muted dream, I could very clearly
hear the soft snicking of Pike's blood falling onto ice
and stone.

I pushed against the pain, the need, against the
Binding that held me frozen. I couldn't even move
my fingers.

Then the pain eased and I could move. But I wasn't
the one in control of my legs any more.

I took a step *away* from Pike, a step past him.
Trager. The asshole was dragging me to him. Making
me leave Pike behind. Another step. Two.

I fought the pull of the Binding, leaned back against
it. Yelled as the hook shifted to catch at my lungs. I
couldn't leave Pike, couldn't leave him dying behind
me.

I still had the dagger. By damn, I was going to use
it. I forced my hands up, trembled as I turned the knife

to my chest, aiming for the hook. I had to use both hands to hold it steady, to press it against my chest. The tip slipped through the thin fabric of my shirt, nipped gently at my skin.

I took another step, heard the deadweight thunk as Pike fell the rest of the way to the ground. I couldn't turn to look at him. I pressed the dagger harder, broke the skin over my breastbone.

Wait. Something was wrong with this. Magic dagger or not, if I shoved a knife through my heart, I wouldn't be around long enough to do anything else.

Holy hells.

Think, Allie.

The glyph. The Binding on my thigh. I could cut the bastard's magic out of me.

I took another step and shifted the grip on the blade. Before Trager could make me take another step, I slid the tip—okay, more than just the tip, the whole damn length of the blade—across my thigh.

The knife sliced effortlessly through the heavy denim of my jeans. It sank into my thigh like heated glass. I yelled. Felt like barfing. Instead I jerked the blade out of my leg. I tugged at the hole in my jeans, ripping it open. I blinked sweat out of my eyes and looked down at the glyph.

What I saw was blood, my blood, pouring down the pus green venous ridges of the Binding glyph. I had to pull the magic out of it. Zayvion had said that. Pull the magic out.

But I needed magic to do that. Needed magic to see what I was doing.

Fuck it all.

I tried to calm my mind. I whispered a mantra over

and over: *Miss Mary Mack, Mack, Mack, all dressed in black, black, black . . .* I set a Disbursement—I was so done with having a headache and fever and went for a nice head cold this time. I jerkily traced the glyph for Reveal over my thigh and drew magic up out of my body to pour into it.

Magic responded strangely. It skittered beneath my skin like a rock over a pond instead of flowing smoothly. It took all the concentration I had to guide the magic into the spell I'd cast.

And doing that made everything hurt.

Trager yanked on the hook in my chest.

But my leg wasn't working so good. I stumbled forward and fell.

It is amazing how it doesn't matter how much pain I'm in, I can always feel one more thing. I hit the ground hard, banged my elbow, my hip, scraped the side of my face. Managed not to hit my head, break my hold on the Reveal spell, or impale myself on the knife.

Go, me.

I curled inward, fetal position, and wished I could stay there forever. Then pushed up to a sitting position. Made it too.

The Reveal I cast showed me the Binding's true nature. The glyph on my thigh glowed pus green and oozed black. I'd never seen anything like it. One part of my mind—the part I was trying very hard not to listen to—was screaming. The other part was getting pissed off.

Calm, Allie. Stay calm.

Pike rattled out a long, thin breath.

I inhaled, scented the rotten flesh stench of the

Veiled, who undoubtedly had invited themselves to my little private hell. I didn't take time to search for them. I knew they were there, around me, on their slow march.

Fast. I needed to work fast.

I opened my mouth, leaned toward my thigh, and inhaled the scent and signature of the spell. I knew Trager had cast it, but my Hounding senses sorted through the spell's subtleties. And, most important, let me trace the actual manner in which the spell had been cast.

With the knife in my right hand, I pressed my right fingers at the top of the glyph and traced it, dragging my fingers through the blood, drawing a new layer of pain along its twisted route.

Ow, ow, ow. Someone was whining like a kicked puppy. That someone was me.

My fingers probed at the spell, pushed at it.

There. Where the thinnest tendril of the glyph stretched out to connect to the knotted lump in the center. The Binding originated there.

Keeping my right fingers on the point of origin, I brushed my left fingers more lightly out from there, followed the twists and knots until my fingertip rested on the exit point of the spell—the last line drawn before the spell had been stabbed into me. That point was deep in the gash I'd made with the knife.

Good news, I told myself. I didn't have to make a second cut.

I gritted my teeth and stuck my fingers into the wound. Holy shit, that hurt. My fingers slipped across a very thin, glasslike thread in my flesh. That was the Binding, cast in blood magic, which had somehow turned solid beneath my skin. Or maybe blood magic always turned to glass. I didn't know. And I didn't care.

I pinched at the slippery thread, caught it between my thumb and fingernails. Then I tugged. The Binding slithered beneath my skin, unwinding with barbed pain along the path of its design.

Good, but not good enough.

I tugged harder, groaned. The glyph unwound some more. I could see the solid glass thread as it exited my skin, but as soon as it hit the air, it dissolved into ashy black smoke. And of course the harder I pulled, the more it hurt.

Pike was dying. The Veiled were closing in. I didn't have time to be subtle. I clenched my teeth and yanked. Fire scraped across my thigh, up my belly, shocked across my nerves. Pain gouged my chest and stabbed my heart and lungs. I yelled and yelled. Stars burst at the edges of my vision.

But I didn't stop pulling.

My vision narrowed. The only sound I could hear was the pounding of my blood. My world reduced to two things: pain and sheer determination not to stop pulling on the spell.

The Binding shattered, rising in the air like wisps of smoke from a sudden fire. I broke out in a heavy sweat, like a bad fever breaking. I was still sitting, my left hand pulled as far from my body as it could reach, the final ashes of the spell drifting away on the sweet-cherry-scented breeze.

Without knowing it, I'd pressed the dagger deep into my thigh again. Holy hells, that was going to scar. So much for wearing miniskirts.

Somehow I had managed to hold on to the Reveal spell. I blinked, looked up. The watercolor people—the Veiled, dead magic users—rushed me. Empty black eyes, mouths open, hands reaching, hungry for my magic.

I scrambled backward, turned my face away from their onslaught, and let go of the Reveal spell. The stink of dead flesh rushed past me, borne on an unnatural wind. And nothing more. No fingers, no eyes, no mouths.

I shuddered, gagged. Took a couple hard breaths. Then I dragged my ass back to where Pike lay.

Trager would now know the Binding was broken. He would now know I was not his little toy. And it pissed me off that I had just destroyed the evidence I had against him—evidence that would have thrown him in chains.

But when I made it to Pike, I didn't care.

Pike was curled up on his bloodiest left side— Hounding instincts to keep the most vulnerable side of yourself hidden, protected. It meant his good eye— the eye he still had—was toward me.

I brushed my fingers over his neck, searching for a pulse. A sluggish throb sent a slow gush of blood over my fingers.

Deep blood. Lifeblood. Pouring down to the icy street.

Even though I didn't remember doing it, Nola had told me I healed Zayvion with magic when the storm of wild magic raged over the city. Paying the price for that had thrown me in a coma and erased weeks of my life. It could have killed me.

But if I could do it once, I could do it again.

I calmed my mind, sang my little song, and shoved the panic to the side.

"Pike," I said. "It's Allie. I'm here. You're going to be okay." I ran my fumbling hands over his chest, his belly, looking for the deepest wound. His entire torso felt like ground beef—wet and pulpy everywhere. Someone had beat him physically and magically. I didn't even know where to begin.

I took a deep breath and, still holding the knife in one hand, pulled the magic up through my body. It responded better this time, spooling out through me like warm water over burned skin. I didn't know any glyphs for healing—no one healed with magic. The price was too high. Even doctors used magic only as a tool to assist in healing, not as a means to the end.

I closed my eyes and directed the magic through my fingers and into Pike's body.

Heal, I thought, putting my will and intent behind the magic. I held an image of him whole and well in my mind, and told the magic to make that happen, make him alive, breathing, healed.

Magic poured into Pike's wounds, and there were a lot of them. Magic poured through me fast, faster. But instead of wrapping around his bones, spreading through his muscle and veins, mending and healing, the magic poured through him and then sank, useless, into the ground.

I couldn't make it spread through him, couldn't make it catch up the pieces of him and knit him back together. It was like he was made of sand, and all the magic I pumped into him drained into the earth without touching him.

No, no, no. What was I doing wrong?

I smelled the fetid rot of flesh again, opened my eyes. The Veiled shuffled slowly toward me. I did not stop pouring magic into Pike.

Pike's eyelid flickered open. His eye roamed the flat, dark sky and then rolled down and focused on me.

"Al," he rasped. "Trag used"—he inhaled, a short rattling breath that made his body stiffen—"my blood. To kidnap girls. Trag used Ant to cast like me. . . ." He inhaled again, his one eye wide, as if there were more words trapped behind his broken lungs, as if there were more words trapped in his broken body.

"Doctor," he wheezed. "Has blood. Yours. Girls."

My blood? What doctor? What girls? The kidnapped girls?

"Don't let Trager free—" The painful inhale again.

"Easy, Pike," I said. "It's okay. I won't let Trager free. I'll take care of everything. You just hold on. Hold on, okay?"

A spasm wracked his body. His hand jerked out, gripped the blade that was still in my right hand. His blood mixed with mine, caught in the finely wrought runnels of the blade and slid down the liquid glyphs, turning the glowing symbols into a dull fire before dripping onto his chest.

"Not Ant's fault. I . . . failed . . . him. Look after"— the painful inhale again—"the kid. The Hounds. They're family. Mine. Yours."

"Hey, now. Don't get all soft on me. You and I can look after the Hounds together, okay? I promise." I poured magic into him—more, faster.

"Worth it," he exhaled.

Pike's one eye stared at me. I did not look away from him. Did not look away from him as the Veiled rushed me and shoved greedy fingers into my skin, burning, hurting, eating the magic out of my flesh. Did not look away from him as the last spark of life drained from his eye. Did not look away from him as he became unnaturally still, vacant, empty. Dead.

Only then did I let go of the magic pouring into him. Only then did I look away from my friend.

As soon as I let go of the spell, the Veiled faded. I stung from head to foot. Felt like my skin had been scraped raw by frozen sandpaper. My thigh throbbed; my chest throbbed. Every breath caught and burned, and, damn it, tears poured down my face.

But I was raging inside, seething. And way past caring about my own pain.

I was angry as hell. Trager was going to pay. Fuck the law. I was going to kill him with my own hands. I pushed up onto my feet, turned a slow circle. I couldn't smell Trager, but I could feel him like a dirty echo in my bones. He was here. Near. I followed my gut and my rage and walked toward the corner building. The wind picked up again, pulling ice off the skin of the river and slapping me in the face with it.

I felt alive. Focused. If this was the last thing I ever did, it would be worth it.

I strode along the building until I found a door that was partially open. The smell of blood came from that room—Trager's blood. I tightened my hold on the dagger and calmed my mind. I didn't hear anyone moving behind the door.

I pushed it the rest of the way open. Two rooms were divided by a wide arch in the center: an office. A large solid desk held down the back wall. Both rooms nicely furnished. Modern. Tasteful.

Except for the dead man with a slit throat on the floor. Lon Trager's goon. There was a trail of dead people, actually, and if I had to guess how they got that way, I'd bet on Pike. I walked past them all, noting their fatal wounds with satisfied detachment. Slit throat, bullet hole in the head, bullets in the chest, a knife still lodged in the carotid artery. The man with half a head missing, his buddy sporting a matching wound—probably from the big-ass gun in the river of blood on the floor. Six of Trager's men. The same six that had been on the bus with me.

Fuck, I thought. *What a mess.* Even though I was not accustomed to being this close to dead people, the numb rage that filled me let me note that I was going to have nightmares about this but also let me not care. All that was important right now was that Trager was not among the corpses. How could Pike have missed him?

Maybe another room, another office. I turned to leave. Heard someone struggling to stand behind me. I turned back around. Lon Trager stood behind the desk. Blood covered one side of his face, turned his crisp white business shirt red.

Looked like he and Pike had both gotten their hits in.

Trager white-knuckled the edge of the desk to stay standing. He held a gun in his other hand, leveled at my chest.

"Bye-bye, Beckstrom."

I threw myself to one side, yelled at the fresh tear of pain in my thigh. The bullet grazed my left shoulder, and my vision went black for a moment.

Trager fell back in the chair behind the desk, breathing hard. He wasn't moving. The gun clattered to the floor.

I pulled myself together and strode across the room, boots slapping in the blood of dead men. I walked around the desk and stopped in front of Trager. He watched me but did nothing more than breathe hard and hold still.

"You killed Pike," I said.

Trager, the bastard, smiled. "Won't be my last."

With a strength I didn't think he had, he lunged at me, a wicked knife in his hand.

Oh, hells, no. He wasn't the only person with a knife in the room.

I gripped the dagger in both hands and thrust all my weight behind it.

Pain rattled through me again. Trager had aimed low, stabbing my thigh.

I, however, hadn't. The dagger sank into his belly, catching against a scrape of rib on the way in. Trager went limp, heavy, his body dead weight against me, until all that held him up was my grip on the dagger in his gut.

"Yes," I said, "it will."

He gurgled and stank. I stepped back, pulling the dagger out as hard as I could. Then I watched him fall to the floor and move no more.

I was covered in blood. My blood, Trager's blood, Pike's blood.

Somewhere in the back of my mind, I was still screaming and screaming. This was a nightmare, and I wanted out. There was a dead man on my shoes. A man I had killed.

Killed.

But in the front of my mind, I was too furious to care.

I pulled my feet out from beneath Trager's dead weight and then knelt and shoved him over so I could see his face. The dagger wound added to the blood already on his shirt. I was no expert, but it looked like Pike's bullets, which had left three clean holes through his shirt directly over his heart, had done just as much damage—maybe more—as my knife in his gut.

I swore. Killing Trager, feeling him die in my hands, hadn't changed my anger. And it hadn't done a damn thing to bring Pike back. I stood and stared down at Trager, trying to make sense of it all. Pike had come to kill Trager, who had been waiting for him. Pike said Anthony had Pike's blood—probably sold it to Trager in exchange for blood magic and drugs.

But Pike had said something else. The girls and a doctor. A doctor had my blood. I didn't know which doctor. But I knew how to Hound. And I sure as hell knew what my own blood smelled like. All I had to do was track it—track the magic in it—and I'd have the last piece in this puzzle.

"Jesus Christ," a voice said behind me.

I swung around, dagger at the ready.

Davy Silvers, the hangover kid, stood in the doorway.

His eyes and nose were red, his cheeks splotchy. He'd been crying. He smelled faintly of alcohol and puke. He'd obviously been following me.

"You're up early," I said.

"Not early enough. Lon Trager?"

"Dead."

He glanced down at the bloody knife in my bloody hand and then looked me up from shoe to face.

"Did you kill him?"

I wiped the blade across the least gory leg of my jeans, staring Davy straight in the eye as I did so. "He was dead when I got here," I lied.

I had to give the kid credit. He didn't look away. He shifted his weight onto the balls of his feet, as if every inch of him wanted to turn and run from what he saw in my gaze. Still, he stood his ground.

"Good." His voice caught. "Wish I was here to see it."

Boy had a vengeful streak. That would probably serve him well in this business.

"Pike?" I asked, even though I already knew the answer.

He just shook his head. "I called 911."

I nodded. "When the police arrive, tell them I was here. Tell them I didn't see everything, but I'll give them my statement. If Detective Stotts shows up, tell him I'm Hounding a lead on the case I worked for him, but tell only Stotts that, got it?"

"Yeah."

"And if you follow me, Davy Silvers, I will kick your ass. Even if I have to come back from the dead to do it. Understand?"

He swallowed and nodded, and then moved out of my way.

Smart boy.

I strode out of that damn room, out into air that smelled too much like blood. I pulled a small amount of magic into my sense of sight and smell. And strode off toward the trail of magic in my blood that hung like a ghostly fire in the air.

Chapter Seventeen

Anger does wonders for all sorts of things. My pain—twice-wounded thigh, headache, fever, and every damn inch of my ghost-burned skin—didn't hurt so much. Walking—even if it meant all the way across Portland—seemed like a completely sane and reasonable thing to do.

And whoever was important enough that Pike had tried to tell me about them with his dying words was going to get a visit from me, whether they were girls, a doctor, or something else. And Pike said whoever that was had my blood.

No one stopped me as I made my way north and west, heading toward the heart of town. Maybe it was because it was icy and there weren't many people out. Or maybe I didn't see anyone because I was covered in blood and carrying a knife. Or it could be because the trail of magic in my blood led me down little-used alleys and footpaths hidden from traffic.

Whatever it was, I stopped at an old warehouse without anyone getting in my way. The old brick building's windows were boarded and broken. Red, black, and white graffiti twice as tall as me turned the crumbling brick and sagging doors into one flat canvas.

There. I knew my blood was there, inside that building. I didn't pull on magic, didn't want to draw the Veiled forward again, didn't want to alert whoever was in there with my blood that I was near.

A wave of dizziness washed over me. No, not now. I didn't have time to fall apart. I put one hand on the brick wall next to the only door on ground level and breathed until the world stopped rocking beneath my feet. When the dizzy spell passed, I tasted wintergreen on the back of my throat and I smelled leather.

My dad.

The last thing I needed right now was for him to show up and screw with me. I looked around the filthy alley, the dim light of morning glinting against the dark, ragged-toothed windows above me.

No ghost. No father. Good.

I lifted the latch on the door with my left hand, expecting it to be locked, rusted, welded shut. The latch released. I nudged the door inward on silent hinges. The warehouse might look abandoned, but someone had been using it enough to bother with oiling the door. The door swung open just enough that I could see into the shadows and wide-open space beyond.

Light filtered through grimy windows high on the wall to my left, illuminating the decaying brick and plaster wall in the back. Arcs of graffiti stained the wall, and in one slant of light someone had painted a face twisted in a scream, teeth crooked and white around a gaping black mouth.

The floor shone with a layer of water. The stink of

pigeon, rat, blood, and rot filled my nose. I paused but heard nothing but the traffic in the distance and my own uneven breathing.

I opened the door a little wider, put a little too much weight on my left thigh, and went dizzy with pain again. Damn.

In the light from the last window, I could see someone slumped in a chair, so near the screaming face that for a moment I wondered if the chair and person were part of the art on the wall. But then the person twitched, the head swinging back and forth at a strange angle.

I toed the door open a little farther, and my eyes, more adjusted to the light now, could make out the person: a man. No, a boy, head hanging forward, body and arms tied to the plain wooden chair with wide leather straps. I could smell his sweat, his pain, and his blood.

Anthony. The Hound kid Pike said had cast those spells to kidnap the girls with Pike's blood.

Sure, I promised Pike I'd look after the Hounds—all of them—and I meant it. But I felt a small dark satisfaction seeing Anthony tied up. It was all I could do not to storm across the room and shake him until he told me why he had betrayed Pike. Why he had let him die.

But chances were if there was someone tied up in a chair, the person who did the tying was nearby. And since I hadn't been grabbed or shot at yet, I figured that person was not currently in the room. Now was my chance to get Anthony out of there.

First, rescue the kid. I could kick his ass after I carted him down to the police.

I walked into the room, let the door swing silently shut behind me. The electric tingle of heavy Wards clicking into place as the door shut made me shiver. And without the extra light from the door, I suddenly felt like there were too many shadows in the room. Unnatural shadows.

I calmed my mind, set a Disbursement—I was going to be in the hospital if I kept this up—and silently wove the glyph for Reveal.

The entire warehouse changed. Dark burnt-ash glyphs on the walls flared to life. The walls dripped with pastel light carved in a mosaic of Life and Death glyphs just like the ones I had seen on the wall outside Get Mugged.

The light from the glyphs was bright enough that I could make out the rest of the room. To my right, a row of six cots neatly lined up along one wall. There were people on those cots, young women. The girls Pike was talking about. Maybe even the kidnapped girls Stotts was looking for.

Black lines of magic coiled around their still forms from head to toe like dark silken cocoons. More lines of magic extended from their chests, snaking and pulsing through the air to attach to two surgical tables in the center of the room. One of those tables was empty, and the other had a prone figure across it.

Next to four of the cots stood a ghostly copy of each girl. Not quite as pale as the Veiled, the transparent girls swayed in time to the pulsing lines of magic extending from their physical bodies, as if rocked by a gentle current. Just like the Veiled, they saw me and opened their mouths in hunger.

All of them stepped toward me, arms extended.

And then the lines of magic holding them to their bodies thickened, tightened, and thrummed with a bass-drum thump, jerking them back a half step, though their hands still wove in the air as if they could almost reach me.

Six cots, six girls, but only four ghosts. Did that mean the other girls were more dead or more alive?

Holy shit. I looked back at Anthony. No spirit stood next to him. Strangely, though I'd been holding Reveal for several seconds, there were also no Veiled, no pastel fog. I could only assume it had to be because of the pastel wards painted on the walls.

I hope they held.

I walked over to Anthony first. I tried to be quiet, which was near impossible in my boots over the uneven wooden plank floor and with my left leg hurting with every step. Anthony did not move.

I gently lifted his head. If I didn't know Anthony's scent, I might not recognize him. The kid was a mess. Blood poured out his ears. He was bruised and swollen like he'd gone through a meat grinder. And I knew it wasn't from physical violence. Thick ropes of magic wrapped around his neck and sent tendrils of ebony chains down to sink into his belly and chest, where they then reached upward to press over his face like an iron mask and stab deeply into his eyes, nose, mouth, and ears.

An Offload glyph. Someone was using him to bear a hell of a price for using magic. Dark magic.

I traced the fingers of my left hand over the magic chains, and Anthony twitched with every link my fingertip brushed. I didn't know how to break a spell this powerful without killing him. Only a doctor who was skilled in Siphon spells and knew how to slowly drain the magic off of him could break something this strong.

Shit.

Who would do this to a kid? I could probably answer that if I kept tracing, Hounding the spell around him, but every time I touched the spell, Anthony jerked in pain. I didn't know how long he'd been tied up like this. Didn't know how much more pain he could endure.

Just because I couldn't break the spell on him didn't mean I couldn't untie him from the chair. I'd carry him out of the warehouse, find a phone, and call the police.

"Allie." The whisper was close, a cold exhale against my cheek.

Holy shit. *That* was my dad. I spun toward the sound, holding the Reveal spell intact. Pain bloomed up from my thigh as my wound reopened and poured more blood. I gritted my teeth against making any sound and peered into the crosshatch of light pouring through the dust and dark webwork of magic that filled the air.

I didn't see my father. Didn't see his ghost. But I realized that all the lines of magic in the room—coming from the girls, coming from the glyphs on the walls—were connected to whoever was lying on that surgical table.

I took a step closer to the table. The figure was familiar. Two more steps, and I recognized that profile. And I should. It was my father.

Oh, hell, oh, hell, oh, hell. Reality did a sick little dreamlike swing, and I broke out in a sweat. Suddenly

I hurt everywhere: my head, my chest, my bleeding leg, every inch of skin and bone that the dead magic users had stabbed burning fingers into and torn apart.

This was too much. Too much too fast. I pressed the palm of my left hand over my forehead, trying to steady my breathing, trying not to let the part of me that was screaming and screaming take over.

Images of Pike's bloody body, his mutilated face, flashed behind my eyes. Trager's bloody smile mixed with that, his cold gaze as he shot me, stabbed me, died on me, a heavy stinking heap of flesh that I stabbed until his blood gushed down my legs. Stabbed until he was dead.

What did I think I was doing? I wasn't a cop. I wasn't a soldier. I wasn't a killer. I was a Hound. Good at tracking spells. *Spells*. My life wasn't supposed to be filled with dying, bloody, horrible, hurting, tortured people.

The part of me that was screaming took up a new chant. *What if he's not dead? What if he's not dead? What if Dad isn't dead?*

What if my father was still alive—right there, on that table, in this hell house? What if all those lines of magic leading to his body were keeping him alive?

A ringing started in my ears and I felt the room rock a little more. Hello, shock. Wondered when you'd get here.

Get a grip, I told myself. If that was my father, alive or dead, I needed to know. Needed to find a way to save him too. And Anthony. And the girls, if they were still alive.

All before whoever was throwing this little soiree came back to check on the guests.

I gripped Zayvion's dagger tighter and limped over to the tables in the middle of the room. The ghost girls to my left moaned and shifted, stretching to the lengths of their magical chains, hands still clawing the air for me. I didn't want to think about what would happen if those chains broke.

I stopped next to the table.

My dad—my dad's body—was strapped down to the table, leather bindings across the ankles, hips, and both wrists. Why? My mind raced with images from horror movies. Things people did to torture, to destroy. But none of it matched this. It was as if someone expected his body might get up, leave, go for a walk, escape.

Which was ridiculous. Because even I could tell he was very, very dead.

Black lines of magic from the girls draped down to play like wind-stirred mist across a large square lead and glass engraved plate on my dad's chest. From this angle, I could make out glyphs of Life surrounded by glyphs of Death carved on the plate just like the wall outside Get Mugged—just like the walls in here.

The acrid stink of chemicals—formaldehyde and something else—the rancid scent of something biological gone bad, like spoiled fat left in the heat, hit me. And the misty black spell rising like steam off of the plate stank of cloying licorice, so strong it made the back of my throat tighten. Magic. Not blood magic. Not any kind of magic I had ever smelled before. Something dark. Something bad.

"Allison." The whisper came from the other side of the table.

I looked up.

My dead dad stood on the other side of the table, his corpse spread out between us. Ghost Dad was transparent enough that even the dull light from the window poured through him. He cast no shadow next to mine on the floor.

"The gates between the living world and that of the dead are opening." His voice was the most alive thing about him, though his pale, pale green eyes still shone with a kind of light—anger, determination. He sounded like himself but as if he spoke from across the room even though he was close enough I could touch him.

"That's not my problem." I wanted it to come out strong, but only a whisper escaped my lips.

"Yes," he said. "It is. There are things you don't know, dark things, dark magics that dwell on the other side. If they are allowed into this world, you, the people you care for, will die."

I thought about Pike, already dead. Then I thought about Violet, who was pregnant with my father's child, my brother or sister. I thought about Davy, and then my mind turned to Zayvion.

Shit.

"I'm going to call the police," I said a little louder than before. "MERC can handle this. Fix this."

"Allison, listen to me. This is far more than the police or any of the uninitiated can handle. You must do as I say. Let me touch you. Let me use the magic you hold in your body, your blood to seal the gates. It is what you were born for, what you and I were meant to do. With your magic, I can break these spells. Close the gates that are just beginning to open. You and I together can keep those we love safe. Alive."

Okay, I liked it better when he couldn't talk. Maybe being so close to his dead body made him strong enough his words carried a little of the old Influence he used to use on me to make me do what he wanted.

Frankly, everything he was saying just made me want to run like hell.

"You want to use me?" I said. And yes, that came out indignant. I get prickly under extreme duress. We had a long history, my father and I. And most of it was him trying to use me for his own benefit. "For all I know you set this up. Maybe you're the one who wants to open the gates. Maybe you're the one who is hurting those girls and hurting Anthony." *Maybe you're the one responsible for Pike's death*, I thought silently.

"If that were true, I would not rely on chance to bring you here. I certainly would not rely on your cooperation for my plan to work. I am not that irresponsible."

He had me there. My father was a thorough bastard when it came to planning and executing his desires. It didn't seem likely he would implement anything, much less something that may involve a lot of magic, a lot of death, and me going along with it all, in such a haphazard way.

Still, he was dead. Maybe dying had dulled his edge.

"Fine," I said. "Prove to me I can trust you. Free Anthony from the Offload."

"Who?"

"The boy being used as a Proxy on the other side of this room."

He scowled into the distance as if trying to focus through a fog. "He is nothing."

"He's someone I care about. Someone I have promised to look after."

"Allie." He was getting angry. I knew that tone. "You underestimate the severity of the problem. One boy's life is nothing to give."

"You're wrong," I said. "One boy's life is too much to give. I am going to get the hell out of here, find a phone, and call the police."

I took maybe five painful strides away from my father's dead body.

"Oh, let's not ruin a good thing," a man's voice echoed from behind me.

I turned and spotted a movement by the darkest area across the room, which, now that I looked closely, was a doorway.

That movement stepped forward into the faint light.

Balding, thin, Dr. Frank Gordon ambled across the wooden floor, his dress shoes making solid clucks that echoed against the rotted rafters. As he walked, he rolled the sleeves of his dress shirt up to his elbows. He didn't look up at me, didn't look at my father. His glasses caught the liquid play of light and shadow from the windows, reflecting mercury and ebony. In his hand, he held a vial. A vial of blood. My blood.

"Do you understand now, Allison?" Dad asked. "This man is a very powerful magic user. He has done *this* to me. Used me, my death to open our world to magics that will destroy it. And you are going to help me put an end to him."

Fuck. How did I get in the middle of a dead-undead magic showdown?

"To bring the police here?" Frank continued like he had not heard my father, and I realized he *hadn't* heard him. So only I could see my dad; only I could hear him.

Frank pursed his lips and shook his head. "This is too sacred an event to expose to the uninitiated."

There was that term again.

"His name is Frank Gordon," my father said. "He is part of the Authority. An ancient order of men and women who are the caretakers of magic. Life magic in life. Death magic in death."

"I know who the Authority is," I said to my dad.

But it was Frank who answered. "Do you? And here I had thought your father kept you ignorant of such things. Protecting you." He shook his head. "Such an idealist. You belong to us, Allison. To our world. Both worlds. You always have. Even he knew it." He squinted to look up at me through his glasses. "Even he knew how useful you would someday be."

My father swore. Called Frank a dozen names in a dozen languages. I had forgotten how extensive his vocabulary was.

"My father didn't know me as well as you might think," I said.

Move over, shock. Fight, flight, and adrenaline had just kicked the doors down. My senses heightened; my heart picked up a runner's pace. Not because I was using magic, but because I was damned determined to get out of here alive. And I was going to take Anthony and the girls with me. I shifted my grip on the dagger, keeping it low, using the table that was still between me and Frank to block his view of it.

What I needed was a chance to throw a spell at him, something like Containment or Hold. Something to buy me enough time to run. Because unless I could knock him out—and I didn't think my physical reserves were up to bearing the price of that without passing out myself—my best option was to do just what I'd told my father. Run and get the police, the SWAT team, Stotts, and the MERC down here. Fast.

"And yet," Frank said, "blood calls to its own, Ms. Beckstrom, just as magic calls to magic. I have brought you here"—he gestured toward my father's body with the vial of my blood as if that explained everything—"and you have come. Welcome to the beginning, the birth, of true magic. Life and death as one. As magic, and the world, should always have been."

My father's ghost traced a very powerful glyph that had pain written all over it. His lips moved in words I could not hear. He threw the spell at Frank.

And absolutely nothing happened.

Okay, time to do the math. Frank had my dad's corpse. That made him a grave robber. And if he had my blood, it meant he was in league with Trager. He also had Anthony and the six girls whom I assumed were the kidnapped girls Stotts was looking for. I'd Hounded those hits, so I knew someone had used Pike's blood and cast the Glamour spells with Pike's signature. Even as I had Hounded them, I knew something was wrong with the glyphs, something that made me doubt it was Pike's hand that cast those spells.

Pike said he thought Trager used Anthony to cast those spells, but I didn't think Anthony was that good. He'd have to be a Hand—an artist who could forge magical signatures—and I didn't think Anthony knew magic well enough to do that.

Frank, however, looked like he might be very good at forging someone else's magical signature. Looked like he might be very good at all things magical. Hells, even my dead father said he was a very powerful man. Powerful enough to use my father. Powerful enough to be screwing around with the gates of life and death.

So I had it wrong. Trager was working for Frank, not the other way around. Working to help Frank with this horror-house magical ritual bullshit.

"He is working dark magic, Allison," my dad said. "It is forbidden. Magic that has been mutated by death belongs in death. He is using *my body*," he growled, "and the magic in it, not the magic beneath the city. He is using my body to open the gates to the dead. To free those who hunger."

Holy crap. Zayvion was right. Why hadn't my dad taught me this stuff years ago? Dark magic. Those who hunger. I didn't even know what they were, much less what they could do.

I was so screwed.

"So now," Frank said, "I will ask you once, politely, to come here and lie down on this table." He smiled and pointed to the empty table next to my father's corpse. "Please."

"No," I said.

"No," my father said at the same time. Well, at least we were in agreement on one thing.

The doctor shook his head. "I am so sorry to hear you say that."

He flicked his fingers fast and subtly enough he'd give Kevin a run for his money.

His spell radiated so much magic—dark, strange, twisting magic that moved on its own like snakes slithering through the air. I could see it, even without the Reveal spell. It was a huge spell. Strong enough it could knock a hole through a brick wall. And Frank had thrown it with no more trouble than flicking a speck of dust from his shirtsleeve.

From the corner of my eye I saw Anthony shudder in pain.

What kind of price did dark magic carry? How much more could Anthony take?

I held up the knife in one hand and wove Shield in the other, drawing magic from deep within my bones and pouring it into the Shield. I braced for the impact.

Instead my dad appeared in front of me and threw himself in harm's way. For me. It was the most selfless, noble thing I'd ever seen him do.

Unfortunately, it didn't work.

Frank's spell slammed past my father's ghost, slammed past my Shield, slammed past the bloody dagger I carried, and hit me like a train falling off a mountain.

The force of Frank's spell threw me across the warehouse. I tucked and rolled. Managed to land flat on my back hard enough to knock the wind out of me. Seriously, I should take self-defense classes one of these days. Maybe I'd find a way to stay out of these situations.

But, hey, at least I didn't eviscerate myself with the knife. Trouble was, I'd lost my grip on the knife. It was no longer in my hand.

My dad stood above me. "I will not see you fail in this."

Way to talk me up, Dad. That disapproving scowl told me I was in for a world of hurt.

He knelt. Shoved his hand in my head. My vision

went white for a second. I blinked. The warehouse was back, but I couldn't see my father. I saw myself— through my ghost father's dead eyes—on the floor of the warehouse.

No wonder Davy had been scared of me. Blood covered my face, following the strange leopard pattern burn marks from dead magic user fingers. Not pretty. Not even close to pretty. My eyes were too wide, hard and pale as cheap emeralds. I had a bad cut under one cheek and my lips were swollen. My hair was a mess. I looked wild. Angry. I looked like I was going to kill someone.

No coincidence, that. My father was pushing into me, into my head, taking me over. Oh, hells, no. There was no way I was going to let him possess me.

Problem was, I didn't know how to stop him.

I pushed with my heels, scrambling backward, scooting my ass across the floor but unable to get away from him, unable to get to my feet.

"Get away!" I screamed. "Get away!"

"You were meant for this, born for this," Dad chanted. "Your blood and mine. Beckstrom blood. The power you carry, the knowledge I carry. I have always known we would do great things, you and I. I have waited for this day."

And over my dad's babbling that grew louder and louder inside my head, I heard Frank's footsteps across the wooden floor.

Frank bent, reached through my father—right through him—and I moaned, because it stung me too, like Frank was reaching through me.

"Open your mind to me," my father said.

"I can't, I can't, I can't," I said.

Frank smiled. "Oh, you can. You can be everything I need."

He pulled me up through my dad and onto my feet. Stuck a needle in my arm.

Possessive ghost. Dark magic. Blood magic. Probably drugs on that needle.

Holy shit, could this get worse?

The pain in my body eased some, leaving my head a little foggy and slow. That would be the drugs. Sensual heat rose up my legs, and I tasted sweet cherries on the back of my throat. And that would be the blood magic.

Fabo.

Allison, my father said from inside my head. *Accept me. Let me use your power. I can stop him. Stop him from doing this to you. To us.*

"No," I whispered as Frank pushed me forward in a grip I could not shake. The drugs weren't helping my coordination any. Everything felt sluggish. Dreamlike. Slow.

"Out. Get out," I said.

"It will all be over soon," Frank said. He wrapped his arm around my ribs and held me up, because my legs weren't working so good. He shoved me over to my father's corpse. I threw myself to one side, but Frank was strong and didn't lose his hold on me.

"Be *still*," he said. The needle wound in my arm pulsed at that word. I could not move. No matter how much I wanted to.

Shit, shit, shit.

Frozen in place, I watched Frank let go of me and pull my left arm out over the plate on my dad's chest.

A slash of pain bit my left palm as Frank drew a knife—a pretty little thing a lot like Zayvion's—across my hand. He tipped my hand over the plate, letting my blood fall freely into the licorice mist.

He then poured blood out of the vial over my hand and over the tip of the knife he had used to cut me.

I might be frozen, but I could still breathe, could still smell. And that was not my blood in the vial—it was my father's.

Hatred rose like bitter bile and stung the back of my throat. The weird thing was it wasn't my hatred—it was my father's. He hated Frank. And hated that Frank was using him.

Using him to break open the gateway between the world of the living and the world of the dead. Using him to finally connect the magic of the living with the magic of the dead.

Horrors of what breaking the barrier between life and death and letting magic flow freely between the two swam through my mind—my dad's mind. Somewhere beyond that horror, I heard the cold, angry thoughts of my father wishing he were the one doing this exact ritual but with Frank's corpse on the table instead.

And it was then that I realized Frank was right about one thing. My dad did know how very useful I would be. And even now, in death, he was thinking about his missed chance of using me for his own ends. Thinking that he who opened the gates would be the one who controlled them.

I wanted off this crazy train. If I were going to get out of this room, get away from my father, from Frank, now would be a great time to do it. Except I couldn't feel my feet. It's hard to run when you have no idea where your legs are.

Anthony moaned.

Crap. I couldn't leave him. Couldn't leave him and the girls. I wondered if my father could feel my emotions, my thoughts like I could feel his.

Yes, he said. *I can.*

If I let you . . . use me . . . use my magic, you'll stop Frank? I asked.

Yes. And I knew without a doubt that he was not lying. Okay, that was one good thing about this. He was so close to me I would know exactly when and how he would try to screw me over. I might even have a chance to stop him.

And you'll help me free the girls? I asked. *And Anthony?*

Allison, there isn't much time. I don't know what I'll be able to do after breaking Frank's Wards and the Binding he has on my body. It is complicated. Untried. Half true. He might not know what the magic would do, but he had ideas, plans, of exactly what he'd be able to do: control me and all the magic at my disposal.

"Lie down," Frank commanded. He put some Influence behind it. Anthony, the poor kid, whimpered. Of course, I wasn't in that great of shape myself. Frank's command filled me with the desire to do exactly as he said.

Damn it.

I crawled up on the empty table, fighting it, sweating, hating him, hating myself, hating my father. Magic filled me, but if I pulled on it, my dad would be able to reach it—push me aside and use it, use me, and then he could make me do anything he wanted to.

But maybe it would be worth letting him use me if he stopped Frank.

I looked around wildly. Shadows, slanting light, webs of magic, moaning girls. I twisted so I could see the door. Maybe I could get out. Maybe I could still get away and call the police.

The door I had walked through was open. That was weird. I thought it had shut behind me.

A man moved into the light of the doorway, silent as a cat's dream. Dark and shadowed, his skin flickered with silver glyphs, his body crackled with dark fire.

Zayvion Jones.

Maybe I was imagining him. I really wanted someone to show up and make some sense out of all this. Make Frank stop, make my dad stop. Make this all go away so I could get away, and life and death and the world would be normal again.

But Zayvion said he wasn't following me. Kevin said Zayvion wasn't following me. So why would he be here?

He made his way silently to Anthony's side, and I looked away from him just in case he was real. Just in case Frank caught me looking at him. Frank was busy weaving a spell between my father's corpse and me with the tip of the bloody knife and his empty left hand.

This was not how I wanted things to work out. But if Zayvion could get Anthony out of here, maybe I could find a way to rescue the girls.

I moved my feet, felt the bite of a rope around my ankle. Not a physical binding—a magical one. Frank was a busy little bastard.

"You are much like your father, Ms. Beckstrom," Frank said in his nice-doctor voice while another rope of black snaked out to tighten around my legs. "Intelligent. Willful. And incredibly powerful. If you had simply returned my phone call, we could have gone about this in a much more civilized manner. It could have been very . . . pleasurable."

Holy crap.

Allison, my father growled in my head. *Now. Give me your power.*

Help me free the girls.

Allison, he warned. *If you will not give it to me, I will take it. And that will cause us both damage.*

Anthony grunted.

Frank noticed. Glanced up away from me. Saw, as I saw, Zayvion carrying Anthony on his shoulder, moving toward the door.

"Ah, Mr. Jones. The guardian of the gates has arrived. Please return my Proxy." Frank wove his hands in the air and pulled magic—from my father's corpse. The magic rose, sticky, wet, thick, not so much glowing as sucking light into it, leaving an afterimage of the rest of the room on my eyes when I blinked.

My dad groaned in my head. I felt it too. Frank sucked the magic out of me like a leech sinking teeth in my bones and sucking the marrow.

I yelled. From the pain, from trying to warn Zayvion.

One of the ghost girls screamed with shrill, childlike terror. I glanced over at the six cots. One of the ghost girls lifted away from the cot, away from the dark chain holding her there, and shot across the room toward Frank. She twisted, thinned, became a bolt of pure magic. Magic that Frank caught in his hand as easily as catching a ball. Magic that he twisted into a glyph and threw at Zayvion.

Zayvion cast Shield. Frank's spell, the spell made of the girl, skittered off it, sparking magic in black and gold. The stink of sulfur flashed through the air. There were only three girl ghosts left. He had killed her. Used her soul and spirit like it was magic. Holy shit.

Frank pulled more magic out of my dad, out of me. I yelled along with Anthony's moan. Since I was busy yelling, I missed seeing the spell Frank cast.

But Zayvion countered it. I turned my head in time to see the backlash from the two spells colliding. Bloodred flames flared from floor to ceiling and then fell and hissed like acid as they ate into the floor. That surge of magic made the glyphs on the walls flicker bright, too bright. Then the glyphs went dull. Dead. Nothing but pastel ash.

The Wards were broken.

Allie, now!

The glyphs on the walls dripped down, hit the floor, and then stood up—*stood up*—and became the Veiled.

Holy shit. Those weren't spells on the walls. They were dead magic users, somehow bent in ways magic was never meant to be bent and forced into the lines of glyphs, the warding spells of Life and Death. Frank had used the dead like they were nothing but fodder for his spells. Used them just like he used the girl's ghost. Used them like he planned to use me.

The room was suddenly full of the Veiled. Only they

weren't nearly as transparent as before. They were so
solid, it was hard to think of them as ghosts. Well,
except for their empty black eyes and slow, swaying
movements.

The dead people closest to the ghost girls turned on
the girls.

The three remaining ghost girls screamed as the
Veiled pulled at them, ate away bits of their spirits
with greedy fingers.

I was so done with this bullshit. Hells, yes, my father
could use me. Because I planned to use him right
back.

Yes, I said to my father. *Do it. Take my magic. Stop
Frank. Stop it all.*

And like inviting the wind into a room, my father
blew open my mind, settled into those parts of me I
thought of as mine—private, safe, sacred—and pushed
that aside. He pulled magic through my body, my
blood, as easily as water runs through fingers.

He chanted. I chanted. His words but my voice, my
body. And I understood the words though they weren't
in a language I had ever heard before. They were the
words of Closing. Killing. Ending Frank. Ending his
dark magic.

I could feel my feet. My legs. The Bindings still held
me down, but I could sit.

I sat, twisting so I faced Frank's back. Frank, who
was busy trying to kill Zayvion.

Zayvion stood braced, both hands outward in that
tai chi stance again. An amazing sort of Sheild glis-
tened with magic that flowed and changed in breath-
taking colors and shapes in front of him, taking forms
I had seen only in my dreams. Beautiful. Zay's magic

was beautiful, powerful. And so was the man behind it.

Anthony was on the ground behind Zayvion and his powerful Shield. It didn't look like he was breathing any more.

Sorry, Pike, I thought. *I tried to keep him safe.*

Frank extended one hand toward me, weaving a Sleep spell.

My father lifted my right hand. Now *that* was a weird sensation. He blocked Frank's spell, and I felt the weight of the impact and leaned forward from my shoulder to physically hold off his spell.

And still the ghost girls screamed.

So here's the thing. My dad was in the most private parts of my mind. And he was as open to me as I was to him. I sifted through his knowledge, found what I needed. A spell, a different sort of spell.

I drew on magic, traced a glyph with my left hand— the one my dad wasn't using.

Allie, my dad strained to say. *Do not use magic. It will damage us both. Kill us.*

And I knew he was right. But I already knew what my father was going to do to me. I'd seen his plan. Once Frank was taken care of, my father would either take over my body as his own, burning away the parts of me that made me who I was, or he would—and I'm a little shaky on the details of this one—use the magic in my blood and the core of my life energy to transfer himself into another body. Frank's body.

Both options would leave me dead.

So, fine. In the time I had left, I was sure as hell going to save those girls.

The image of the white cross on the building came

to me. The image of the words "my baby." There were families out there waiting for these girls to come home. People who loved them. Maybe I couldn't fulfill my promise to Pike by looking after his Hounds, but I could at least make sure these girls got home.

And if by doing so I screwed up my father's plans—then sign me up, baby. If I was going to die, I was going to take my dad down with me.

I threw every ounce of my will into that spell, threw it at the Veiled—all of them in the room, and it sounded like there were hundreds—howled.

"No," Frank yelled. "Do not destroy them. They are magic—true magic. Do not!"

He lifted his hand from what he'd been about to throw at Zayvion and leveled both hands, both spells, at me.

The room went black at the edges. I think I saw Zayvion bend, scoop up the dagger I'd dropped, and run toward Frank. I think I saw the Veiled let go of the girls. I think I saw the Veiled crack like old plaster, that strange dark light pouring out of them as they came apart like ice hit by a hammer. And I even think I saw my father's corpse on the table exhale, his last breath a mist that stank of licorice.

I know I smelled blood, fear, sweat, my father's wintergreen and leather, blood magic's sweet cherry, Frank's burnt almond, and Zayvion's pine.

I think I saw the ropes of magic that floated in the air, connecting the girls to my father's corpse and to me, turn to ash and scatter as if caught by a strong wind. And I realized, with sorrow, that there were only three ghost girls because the other girls, their spirits, had already been used up by dark magic.

But even though I saw all this, I didn't know how to get the remaining girls' spirits back in their bodies.

I trolled my father's memories, trying to find something I could use. My father was still busy pouring magic into the spell that was wrapping around Frank like a giant octopus and squeezing tight, tighter.

A Containment spell would work. A Containment to hold a soul. All I had to do was leave the smallest amount of magic wrapped around the girls' souls, and it would hold them in a stasis state.

I was having a really hard time breathing. I clumsily wove the glyph of Containment left-handed, filled it with a small amount of magic, creating an orb in my hand. I had no idea how to put the girls' souls into it. . . . No, wait, I knew.

I cast a quick glyph for each girl, a glyph of Healing, and Death, but more healing than death.

Balls of pastel light formed in my hands. I didn't know if the spell was right. Didn't know if it was done.

My heart was taking too long to beat. Much too long between beats. Everything was hazy and going black.

Somewhere in the back of my head, I heard my father intone the last piece of the Containment spell for me. He willed the balls of light from my palm. The orbs drifted off toward the side of the room where the girls' bodies lay. I hoped it worked. I couldn't see them anymore.

All I saw was Frank, eyes wide with fervor, chanting, his hand lifted in a spell I did not know, a spell filled with the unlight of dark magic.

And just before the spell left his hand, I used my father's hand—my right hand—to cast a Freeze spell.

Zayvion threw himself at Frank. And look at that, Zayvion did have the dagger. On that dagger was my blood, Pike's blood. Grim satisfaction filled me as Frank held very, very still in my Freeze spell and Zayvion slit his throat with one vicious stroke.

A wave of darkness poured over the room, drowning me, sucking me down. I fell so deeply into it that I knew I'd never reach the bottom.

But the last thing I heard was my father's disapproving voice. *Always set a Disbursement. Always. Every time you use magic. How many times do I have to tell you that?*

And I wanted to laugh. He hadn't set a Disbursement spell either. We were both so completely screwed.

Chapter Eighteen

"Allie," Zayvion said. "Breathe, baby. Come on. Come back to me." His words, heated with Influence, would have woken the dead.

I inhaled, not enough, but even that small amount made me want to scream. Breathing was a bad idea. Bad.

"Good," Zayvion said. His voice was calm, but a little high, like he was trying to hold panic in check. "You can do it again, honey. Breathe."

And because he was using Influence on me, I did as he said. And this time I couldn't stop breathing no matter how badly it hurt.

I wheezed and moaned. I had never hurt this much in my entire life.

"Open your eyes," he said. "Let me see your beautiful eyes."

Beautiful. Yep, that was just exactly what I felt like. I worked on opening my eyes. Managed to pry them open, but they were so swollen I couldn't see out of them very well.

Which was probably a good thing. I had no idea

where I was. But it smelled a lot—too much—like blood and death.

Memories brushed through my mind. There had been someone, a man doing magic. Right? Frank. My neighbor? That was as far as I could get before the memory slipped away. Holy shit, I hurt.

A soft stroke of mint washed through me, cooling and warming at the same time. I blinked, squinted up at Zayvion.

I was lying down?

"You are injured, Allie. You've been hurt by blood magic and dark magic. And you have a few other wounds. But you are going to be fine." The last he said with that careful emphasis of Influence, as if his words alone could will me to recover. And those nice eyes of his were more gold than brown. His hands were on me, though I couldn't quite tell where, and mint, strength, and peace flowed from him through me.

"I am Grounding you, because right now magic is raging through you so hard, you're burning up. Can you let go of the magic, Allie? Can you let it flow back into the earth?"

Oh, sure, why not? And right after that I'd get up and run that marathon I'd been meaning to get around to.

I licked my lips, tasted my own blood.

"Just try for me," he said. No Influence. Just him asking.

So I tried. Tried to calm my mind, empty myself of magic. *I am a river. Magic flows through me but is not me.*

"That's good. Keep doing that."

So I did.

Even though I heard sirens. Even though I heard footsteps.

"I called 911," Davy Silvers, the Hound who should not be following me, said.

"Good." Zayvion's voice was tight. Grim. "Can you check on the girls? Make sure they're breathing?"

More footsteps as Davy crossed the room. Sounds of him moving around. Finally, "Only three of them," he said angrily. "Who did this?"

"Him," Zayvion said. My eyes were closed, so I couldn't see which him he was talking about.

"He's dead, right?" Davy asked with just a little too much hunger in his tone. I was going to have to talk to that kid about how unhealthy revenge was.

"Very," Zayvion said.

Sirens, lots of sirens, became louder. I heard a mix of voices, of footsteps and other things that sounded like wheels on wood—maybe gurneys?—fill the room.

"Ambulance and police," Zayvion said so near me, his voice sounded like his lips were at my ear. It was a good sound. Good to know he was still there with me. That I wasn't lying here, trying not to burn up with magic, alone.

Heavy footsteps came closer.

"Jesus, Tita," Makani Love said. "What did you get into now?"

"She needs a doctor," Zayvion said.

"Yah, yah. They're here. You don't go anywhere, Mr. Jones. We need to talk to you."

I heard Love walk away, heard him talking to someone else—Davy, I thought.

"Zayvion Jones," Detective Paul Stotts said. "You've

been a difficult man to find. I'd like you to step away from her and let the paramedics take over."

"Do any of them know how to set a Siphon?" Zayvion asked. "Because she needs one, and so does the boy on the floor over there."

What boy? A memory floated through my mind. Anthony? Davy? Someone else?

Okay, I was getting tired of not seeing what was going on.

I worked hard to open my eyes again. Looked up. Saw Stotts and Zayvion sizing each other up. Stotts had a coffee cup in one hand, and the smell of dark roast was pure heaven. Both of Zayvion's hands were on me, one on my torn-up thigh, one on my breastbone. That was also pure heaven.

"I think she was used for a Proxy," Zayvion lied. *Lied*, because even though the exact order of recent events were sort of fuzzy to me right now, he had been here for enough of it to know I hadn't been used as a Proxy. I'd been used. Used by Frank. For something. Dark magic? Something about opening something.

I reached for it, but the memory skittered away, like there was someone on the other end of an invisible string, purposely pulling my memories out of my reach.

That was weird.

"Hey," I said, my voice quavering and weak.

Both men looked down at me. Even though Zayvion was trying hard to pull off the I'm-just-a-harmless-street-drifter bit, those burning gold eyes were a dead giveaway. That man was more than capable to cast magic. A lot of magic. What had Frank said? The guardian?

I wondered what kind of trouble Zayvion was in with the police.

"You're going to be okay," Zayvion said. "The paramedics are here."

Stotts nodded. "They'll set a Siphon if you need one. Just rest, Allie. I want to know everything that happened once you're on your feet again."

He shifted a little and an EMT, a woman about ten years older than me with a round, concerned face, stepped forward.

"M'okay," I managed.

"Good to hear that," the woman said. "My name's Lori. I'm going to shine this light in your eyes."

She did. She did that and a lot of other things, like pressing on my cheekbones and the bridge of my nose, both of which hurt like mad, and cleaning off the blood magic cuts I seemed to have everywhere, and pushing my filthy hair out of my eyes and pouring something in my eyes that made everything go blurry but stopped my eyes from scratching so bad. She spent some time doing stuff to my thigh, and then I think she put an IV in my arm, but I wasn't sure.

What did you know? I could hurt so much that I didn't feel a needle.

Zayvion didn't move away until another man, who had a wide, easy smile and was tall enough to be a basketball player, came over.

"So we need a Siphon set? Let's take a look at you." Zayvion stepped aside. The tall man placed his hands on my chest, and his fingers were so long they reached from my shoulder to shoulder without a problem. "My name's Marvin. I'm the medic with the magic, and I'm gonna take care of you."

He was joking, right? A soothing wash poured over my body, like water over all my stinging wounds.

Marvin the medic with the magic was very much not joking. I'd never had a Siphon set on me before, but I could feel the gentle lessening, ever so slowly, of the pain in my body—different from Zayvion's touch. Marvin was good. Very good.

"That your boyfriend?" he asked.

And it was such an utterly normal question, the kind of question you asked in an everyday sort of situation, not in a warehouse full of bloody, dead, and dying people situation, that I smiled, even though it made my mouth hurt. "Think so," I said.

Marvin leaned in a little closer. "Well, just so you know, he looks really worried about you," he said in a conspiratorial whisper. "But he doesn't need to be. I got you covered. What's your favorite flower?"

"What?"

"I'll make sure he brings you some when you wake up."

"Oh," I said. I was already feeling drowsy, but not in an overwhelming way. Just a soft, comforting, it-was-okay-to-let-go-now-way. "Roses," I said, even though my favorite flowers were iris. "Pink roses."

And then sleep—real sleep—found me.

Chapter Nineteen

I didn't remember getting to the hospital, but when I woke, I was cleaner, wearing a hospital gown and hospital bracelet, and was tucked into a hospital bed. An IV line ran to my arm, and the soft blue lacework of Marvin the magical medic's Siphon spell hung from a special glass and lead glyph-worked arm of the IV stand. Threads of the Siphon spell ran alongside the IV tube to my arm and then spread out to settle over my chest.

Marvin had done a great job on the spell. It pulsed with my natural heartbeat and made my injuries hurt a whole lot less. Even my head felt clearer.

But apparently Marvin had forgotten to tell Zayvion to bring me flowers.

Or Zayvion hadn't wanted to. There wasn't a single pink rose in the room.

From the light coming in through the small window, I guessed it was morning. Still? I glanced at the clock on the wall. Seven o'clock.

Wow. I'd slept all the way through the day and the night to the day again.

I still ached—inside and out—but the combination of painkillers and Siphon kept it at a distance. I did, however, really need to pee.

I pushed the blankets off, got a glimpse at my legs—still covered in fingerprint burns with some kind of cream that smelled like a diaper rash ointment smeared over them. I pulled my IV stand, IV bag, Siphon, and all, with me as I walked on feet that were still a little swollen into the bathroom.

I made use of the facilities, and as I was washing my hands in tepid water, I heard someone come into my room. Hopefully a nurse. I wanted to go home, take a real shower, and crawl into my real bed.

I walked out of the bathroom.

It was not the nurse.

Davy Silvers stood uncertainly in my room. He had on clean clothes—jeans and a denim jacket with a hoodie beneath it. He had both his hands in his pockets. But even though he'd had a chance to take a shower, the dark circles and bloodshot eyes told me he had gotten less sleep than I.

"Hey," I said as I limped over to my bed. "What are you doing here?" I felt stupid wearing a hospital gown in front of him, so I pulled the covers back over me again.

"Came to see if you're okay. You know." He shrugged.

"I've been here all night, haven't I?"

He pulled a chair away from the wall, sat. "Yes."

"Have you been here all night?"

"Not all night."

"Davy," I said. "I appreciate you watching my back when I Hounded for Stotts. And . . . and yesterday morning. With . . . Pike. But you don't have to do that any more."

He leaned the length of his forearms on his knees and clenched his fingers together. "Pike told me to look after you."

"For one night. One night, Davy, no more."

"Hounds stick together," he said stubbornly. "Watch each other's backs."

"Sure. When we're Hounding."

"That's not what Pike said. And it's not what he would want."

"Davy . . ."

He just gave me a long stubborn look. I so didn't feel like arguing with him. He'd been crying. And from the set of his jaw and tension in his shoulders, I knew he was angry enough to fight me for this. For his memory of Pike and what Pike wanted from him.

Hells. I was angry about everything too. The image of Pike's mutilated face flashed through my mind, and I pressed my fingers carefully against my eyes to try to free myself of it.

"I swear, Davy, if I see you peeking in my windows at night, I will call the cops on you."

"That's fair," he said. Though whether he meant it was fair that he not peek in at me, or that I not catch him doing it, I wasn't sure.

"Later," I said, "when things get . . . straightened out, I want to call a Hound meeting again. Do you have everyone's numbers?"

He nodded. "Did you see him do it?"

"Who?"

"Trager. Did you see him kill Pike?"

And there was that vengeful tone again. I tried to

line up my memories of the day. "No. Pike had already left Trager's office. He killed six of Trager's men. Mostly killed Trager too."

"And you finished him."

I swallowed back a mix of anger and nausea. I'd never killed anyone before. I wasn't sure I was comfortable thinking of myself in that way. Still, Davy needed to hear the truth. And I needed to hear it too. "Yes. I killed him."

Davy nodded, his gaze never leaving mine. "If you hadn't, I would have." And he suddenly looked much older, much more determined and cold than he had when he walked in the room a minute ago. "When you're ready, I'll call the meeting."

"Not today," I said.

He stood. "Anytime. We'll be there." He reached over and touched the back of my hand. I was a little surprised, because Hounds didn't do that, didn't leave their scent behind with anyone. "Feel better, okay?"

"I will. Thanks."

Davy Silvers strode out of my room, shoulders stiff, hands in fists. Pike's death had done something to that young man, changed him in a deep way. Probably changed both of us. I just hoped it hadn't done either of us permanent damage.

I took a deep breath and pushed those thoughts away. I wanted to go home. Take a shower for about a year then crawl into my bed and sleep the rest of my life away.

I pressed the call button for the nurse. I knew I had to make a statement to the police. Tell them what I knew about Trager, starting with him jumping me on the bus. And I knew I'd have to explain everything that had happened in Trager's office and the warehouse. I wondered if they'd consider me stabbing Trager as he stabbed me self-defense?

I tried to track my memories about what had happened in the warehouse and had that empty feeling I get when I realize I was missing memories. Anthony had been there—hurt—an unwilling Proxy for Frank Gordon's magic. And I remembered the six kidnapped girls and their ghosts tied by dark magic to their bodies.

And there had been more happening, some reason Frank was doing all that.

But like something had been pulled just out of my reach, I could not quite remember what else, or maybe who else, had been in that warehouse with me.

What I did know was I had used a lot of magic. And I hadn't set Disbursements. Which meant magic beat its price out of me any way it wanted. It had caused swelling, bruises, and I was pretty sure it had burned away some of my memories too. My hand itched for my blank notebook. I looked around the room. There was a plastic bag of clothes on the table by the wall, but I just couldn't bring myself to go digging in that bag. Not even for my notebook.

Sweet hells. Even over the heavy cleansers in the hospital room, I could smell the stink of blood in that bag. My blood. Pike's blood. Trager's blood.

I swallowed and tasted the faintest hint of wintergreen and leather on the back of my throat.

My stomach clenched with fear. Maybe I didn't want to know, didn't want to remember the details of the warehouse.

The nurse came in and checked my vitals. She told

me the doctor would be by soon and she was right. The doctor on rotation stopped in, checked my chart, asked me a few brief questions, and then skillfully unwove the Siphon spell. The nurse took out my IV line and shunt.

A bottle of prescription painkillers, some analgesic soap, and my promise that I'd make an appointment to see my regular doctor got me release papers to sign and a checkout time before noon.

My jeans were a bloody mess. My shirt too. Luckily, victim's assistance had some sweats I could borrow. I even managed to shove my swollen feet in my boots.

I called a cab and let the nurse wheel me down to the waiting room in a wheelchair.

Just as we were rolling into the hospital's main lobby, Detective Paul Stotts walked in through the door, talking on his cell phone. He saw me and held up his finger. "In about ten minutes," he said to the person on the phone.

"Ms. Beckstrom?" Another man wearing a dark suit and tie, about my father's age but shorter and heavier than my dad, walked over from the receptionist's desk.

I knew that voice, had heard it on my answering machine for weeks now. My father's accountant, Mr. Katz.

"Hello," I said rather lamely.

He walked over and offered his hand, his dark eyes sparking with curiosity.

"I'm Mr. Katz. It's my pleasure to finally meet you."

I shook his hand. "This is a bad time for me. I know there's my father's estate and business and everything to take care of. I've been meaning to set up an appointment to see you at your office."

"Of course, of course." He let go of my hand. "I understand. But it is becoming more difficult to hold the wolves at the gate, if you know what I mean. Stockholders," he said in case I didn't, "and other . . . people who have vested interest in the company are anxious to hear from you, Ms. Beckstrom. And I assure you, it will make both of our lives easier to take care of these things sooner rather than later. However, since I haven't been able to reach you by phone, I came by to let you know I've taken care of the hospital bill." He glanced at the paperwork in my hand and at my secondhand sweats. "And to remind you that your trust fund is available to you."

"How did you know I was leaving today?" I asked.

He smiled again. "We keep a close eye on all our important clients, Ms. Beckstrom."

I didn't know if I should be worried or grateful.

"I have also contacted your father's lawyer, Mr. Overton."

Stotts walked over, turned off his phone, and put it in his pocket. "Paul Stotts," he said, holding out his hand to the accountant.

"Ethan Katz."

They shook. Stotts looked like he already knew who he was. He looked over at me. "Is there something you and Mr. Katz need to take care of?" he asked.

"Not right now." I glanced at Katz, who nodded.

"Yes, that's correct. I was just settling her bill and telling her she has legal counsel." He handed a card to Stotts. "Mr. Overton can be reached at this number."

Well, well. Wasn't he smooth?

"If you'll both excuse me," Katz said, "I do have an appointment to keep." He shook both of our hands

again and then walked down the hallway, deeper into
the hospital.

"I forget you're rich sometimes," Stotts said, watching him go.

"Me too."

"How are you feeling?"

"The doctor said I need to take a painkiller and get
some rest."

"I'm not surprised. Would you like me to take you
home, or should I call your legal counsel?"

"Neither. I called a cab."

He looked off across the lobby. "I do need to talk
to you, Allie. It can be off the record, if you'd prefer."

"Now?"

"As soon as I can. And if you want your lawyer
there, I can arrange that too."

I held on to the plastic bag of my clothes, took a
deep breath and stood up from the wheelchair, careful
not to let him see how much that effort hurt.

"Will you tell me why you wanted to talk to Zayvion?"

"So you remember that?" he asked. "I can't disclose that information. Police business."

"Is he in jail?"

"What?" Stotts stopped in front of the sliding glass
door, so the door hung open and then jerked in and
out of the wall, trying and failing to close.

"Is Zayvion in jail?"

"No. I am curious as to why you think he might be."

"I . . . just . . . I don't know. After the last couple
days, nothing would surprise me anymore."

We started walking again.

"He's not up on any charges," Stotts said. "He was

just . . . a person of interest in a case I've been following."

The outer door opened, and wet, Oregon December wrapped around me. I was so not going to like the walk to his car.

"I'm over here," he said. And I guess that's one benefit to being a police officer. You get to park close to the hospital.

I walked as quickly as I could, shivering the whole way to his car, and got in.

Stotts got in the driver's seat and turned on the car so the heater was running. "Could you tell me the order of events as you remember them?" he asked. "Off the record."

And I realized Stotts looked tired too. There had been several deaths in the city—many of them because of magic. And all of those fell under his jurisdiction.

So I spent the drive reciting the events. I started with Trager on the bus, something Stotts didn't look surprised about. I must have talked to him about it earlier, like when I was Hounding for him.

I left out the Veiled. Left out the Death and Life glyphs outside Get Mugged. Left out the Hound meeting. But I told him all about the blood magic spell drawing me to Pike in Ankeny Square. Told him what Pike said—that he thought Anthony had been used to kidnap the girls—and told him about me finding Trager and his men. I included all the details I could remember, including the knife I had on me—which I told him I'd gotten from a friend. I told him about the gun I saw at Trager's and that I thought it might have been Pike's.

Then I told him about the warehouse. Anthony, the

Life and Death glyphs, the girls (but not their ghosts), and Frank having my blood and wanting to use it for some strange magical ritual I did not understand.

By the time I was done, we were parked outside my apartment building and my throat was sore.

"What about your father's body?" he asked.

I blinked. Something in my head skittered, as if avoiding the light.

"What?" I asked.

"In the warehouse. Do you know what Frank Gordon was using your father's body for? Do you know what the plate on his chest was for?"

I swallowed. "I don't remember that at all."

Stotts looked a question at me, but maybe my shock showed. "All right. When you do remember, if you do, I'd like to hear about it."

I nodded. My ears were ringing with a thin high tone. My dad's dead body had been in that warehouse. Frank Gordon had been using it for something. Something involving Life and Death glyphs and the girls he kidnapped.

Was it too much to think my father's ghost might have been there too? My stomach clenched in remembered fear. He had been there. Even though I couldn't remember it, my gut, my emotional memory of the fear, told me he had been there.

"Do you believe in ghosts?" I whispered.

Stotts nodded. "Yes, I do."

"Do you think my father's ghost was there?"

"I don't know," he said evenly. "Do you?"

"Maybe."

"You don't remember?"

"No."

We sat there, in silence, the car engine still running, which was burning gas, but it kept the heater warm. It was raining outside, and suddenly this little space, this crowded car wasn't nearly big enough for me. I needed out. I needed to breathe.

"I'm going home now." I pulled on the door handle.

"Let me walk you in."

"No. I got it. Really. I just want a shower and bed. Thanks for the ride."

"Call me if—"

I cut him off. "I will. I'll call if I remember anything else."

"I was going to say, if you need anything."

Oh.

"Thanks." I got out of the car and shuffled across the sidewalk. Someone, probably my landlord, had thrown rock salt on the sidewalk and stairs, so it wasn't even slippery anymore. Just wet.

I held my breath and dug in the plastic bag of my clothes. The clothes were stiff and damp with sweat and blood, but my hand came out a lot cleaner than I thought it would. I pulled the key out of my coat pocket and I let myself in the building. I took my time climbing stairs until the third floor showed up.

My head spun with thoughts of my father. His ghost had touched me twice. Had he touched me again in the warehouse? Had he done more than just touch me?

Even though I could not remember, there was an echo, an emotional memory. My father had done something to me. Something bad.

And I knew, without a doubt, that whatever it was, it was permanent.

What did you do to me, Dad? What did you want to use me for?

That skittery feeling at the back of my head triggered again, like a moth wing beating at the top of my spine—like something moving away from my concentration, dodging my notice.

I made it to the third floor and stopped. Down the hall by my door, stood a woman. She looked older than me by fifteen or twenty years, her faded red hair streaked with gray and pulled back in a loose bun. She had on a forest green wool coat and high heel boots.

I'd never seen her before, but she held up a hand and waved.

"Allie?" she asked. "Are you Allison Beckstrom?" Her voice had the slightest accent that made me think Ireland or Scotland.

And sure, it might be really dumb to tell a stranger who I was, but damn it, I was tired. And a little spooked. I just wanted to get home, and she was in my way.

"I'm Allie Beckstrom."

She closed the distance between us and stuck out her hand. "My name is Maeve Flynn. I knew your father."

I shook her hand, aware that mine wasn't very clean.

Her hand was warm and strong, and she shook mine firmly enough I could feel the bones beneath her flesh, but not so hard as to hurt. She had working hands, a little calloused, but her nails were professionally polished with a soft pink gloss.

"Business partner?" I guessed.

"No. More of an acquaintance than anything else,"

she said. "He and I didn't agree on many things, though neither of us were shy about our personal opinions on the use of magic. He wasn't pleased you went into Hounding, you know."

"I'm not at all clear why you are here to see me. Is there something I can help you with?"

She looked up into my eyes—I was taller than her by several inches even though she was wearing heels and I wasn't. Her eyes were the same color as her coat.

"Your father was a vicious and determined man. In life. And in death. I came by to see how badly he has hurt you."

"Excuse me?"

"I am a member of the Authority. I am here to see that his death, his spirit, has not harmed you."

What had Zayvion said? There were powerful people watching me, waiting for me to do something wrong with magic so they could kill me. Was Maeve my killer?

I took a deep breath and looked at her. Really looked at her. She didn't seem to be harboring a burning desire to off me. Which would put her several steps up from the company I'd been keeping lately.

"Maybe we can go inside and talk about it?" she offered.

"I thought you people were all about keeping a low profile," I said as I walked toward my door.

"We are. But I believe that no longer suits both of our interests."

I put the key in my lock and paused. "You aren't here to kill me, are you?"

She laughed—and I mean really giggled—like that

was the best joke she'd heard in years. "Where did you get that idea? I just told you I'm here to see that you are unharmed. Why would I kill you if I'm here to help you?"

"You're the people who have been watching me, right? Waiting for me to misuse magic."

"That's right," she said. "And we've seen everything you've done. Everything he did too."

"Who?"

She pointed at my head. "Your father."

"What does he have to do with this?"

"Everything."

At my look, she went on. "There has been a . . . review . . . among the Authority. A discussion of what to do with you. Mr. Jones has been fiercely insisting you be allowed into the group, that you be allowed the teachings your father denied you."

"Does Zayvion's opinion have that much sway?"

"He is not without a voice among us. And he brings up valid points. If what he says is true . . ." She shook her head. "Well, it's only logical for us to see that you are not judged unfairly. Are you interested in our offer?"

"To teach me about magic?"

She nodded. "To teach you the unknown about magic."

"I suppose it will cost me if I say yes."

"It will. The first price being to trust in me, so that I can see what sort of damage your father may have done to you."

I so wasn't up to dealing with this right now. I just got out of the hospital, for cripes' sakes. I should just tell her to go away. Go back to her little club and tell them I was not interested. The problem was, I was interested. I wanted to know what my father had done to me, wanted to know what the Life and Death glyphs meant. Wanted to know what Frank Gordon had been doing to my father's body. And to me.

And if someone in this city knew how I could keep from getting screwed over every time I used magic, I'd like to know. Even if it meant joining the secret clubhouse.

I unlocked my door and opened it, holding it so she could walk in past me.

I waved toward the living room. "Have a seat. I'm going to get changed."

I passed the bathroom and threw the plastic bag of clothes on the floor near the hamper. In my bedroom, I got out of the hospital sweats and into a pair of loose jeans and a thick wool sweater.

When I came back out into the living room, Maeve was sitting on the edge of my couch. The blanket Zayvion had slept under was folded neatly on the arm of the couch. The food we'd never gotten around to eating was still on the table, along with the single, dead pink rose.

"Sorry about the mess," I said.

"That's fine," she said in a sincere and motherly way. "And I promise this won't hurt. I'll tell you everything I'm doing as I do it, and you can ask me to stop at any time."

"I'm not made of glass," I said.

"Ready, then?"

No.

"Yes."

She patted the couch next to her and I sat.

"I need to touch your hand or your leg," she began patiently, like maybe she had talked a lot of people through this before.

I held out my right hand and she took it in both of hers.

No weaving of glyphs, no chanting; Maeve simply closed her eyes, took a deep breath, and opened her eyes again.

But instead of deep forest green, her eyes were shot with lines of silver. I knew, without a doubt, that she had called on some kind of Sight. And that she was using it to look *into* me. The weird thing was I couldn't feel the magic, couldn't smell the magic.

Very sneaky.

Maybe, if I pulled on my Sight, I could see what she was doing, but I felt as burnt out inside as a month-old forest fire. No magic for me for a while, if I could at all help it.

I wondered what she was looking for. Wondered if it was in me.

The moth-wing flutter started up in the back of my head again. Then went deathly still.

Maeve frowned. "There is much of you that is hidden, Allie," she said in an isn't-this-interesting way. "And much of you forgotten. Your father . . . he . . . parts of him are still with you."

"Parts of him?" I asked. "Like my memories of him, right?"

She didn't say anything.

"Pieces of his soul? Tell me I don't have parts of my dead dad in me."

And even though I would have sworn I was too tired to panic, I felt the clutch of fear in my stomach and my heart started racing. I didn't want anything to do with my dead dad, didn't want him talking to me, didn't want him touching me. And I sure as hell didn't want him *in* me.

Maeve blinked. The silver drained from her eyes. She let go of my hand and pinched the bridge of her nose. "I'm not sure."

"You don't know if bits of my dead dad are left inside me? Aren't you some sort of expert on this?"

She nodded. "Many would say I am. But your father, Allie . . ." She stopped pinching her nose and leaned back a bit. "He has always been a difficult man to pin down."

"Which means?"

"Which means I think your father left something in your mind, probably couched in your memories. I am not sure what it is nor how much of his own . . . soul . . . he left with it. It could just be an echo, an aftereffect from the massive amounts of magic you and he used.

"And he pulled that magic through you, using your body as his own. It is unheard of. . . ." She muttered, like maybe if she hadn't been just looking at me, she wouldn't believe it possible. "That it did so little damage to you—physical pain and some memory loss—is bloody amazing. Anyone should be dead from what happened to you in that warehouse."

It's great to be special. "Well," I said, trying not to show how crappy I really felt. "I'm not dead."

She smiled in a motherly way. "No, you aren't." She stood up. "And I think you will be fine between now and when you come to learn. I'll be able to see better just what you father has done when you come to my place. I don't want to keep you." She walked to my door.

Wasn't she in a big hurry all of a sudden?

"No need to show me out. Get some sleep, take your painkillers. And call me when you're back on your feet. Here's my number. I'll tell you how to find me." She put a business card down on the half wall between my front hallway and kitchen.

I stood and followed her, even though she had told me not to.

She opened the door. "And, Allie? You are healing. I hope you get well *soon* so your true learning can begin." She hesitated, like maybe she was going to say more, but then simply nodded, as if agreeing with herself, and shut the door behind her.

Weirdos. My life was full of 'em.

Chapter Twenty

The next few days went by in a blur. I took painkillers, slept a lot, and filled out the blank pages in my notebook. Small, disconnected flashes of what had happened in the warehouse came to me, mostly when I was falling asleep. I wrote those down too, dark magic. Something about hunger but they didn't seem to add up to anything. It was like trying to use pieces from the wrong puzzle to complete the picture.

My father, if any part of him were indeed inside me, was silent as a ghost.

Ha. Not funny.

Violet called a couple times, and I managed to convince her I wasn't up for visitors and still didn't want to move in with her. Detective Stotts called and I answered a few more questions for him, still off the record. I was sure there would be a couple official visits to the police department ahead of me. I promised not to leave town.

I didn't hear from Zayvion. Not a single pink rose.

I watched the news and read the papers, which was probably the first time I'd done either in five years.

The kidnappings were mentioned, and so were the deaths of Pike, Lon Trager, and his men. But while Frank Gordon was also implicated in the crimes, his death and the rest of the details—such as my father's corpse, me being there, the magical ritual Gordon had been attempting, and Zayvion's involvement in his death—were carefully omitted. It was eye-opening to see all that had been left out. Someone had pull over the media. I wondered if it was the Authority or MERC.

Five days after I'd left the hospital, Violet called again.

"There is going to be a burial for your father. I thought you might want to come this time." Her voice sounded tight. Like maybe she had been doing her share of crying.

"When is it?" I asked around the knot in my throat.

"Noon today at the cemetery. There will be a small gathering of . . . important people, and no one else. I thought you might want to know."

I unclenched my fists and rubbed at my cold left arm with my always-warm right hand. Did I really want to see my father's dead body again? I stared out at the bleak Portland sky. The ice had melted, but it was still cold and wet, and would likely stay that way until May.

Yes, I decided, I needed this. Needed to see him lowered into the ground. Need to know, once and for all, that he was gone. His body and, I hoped, his spirit.

"I'll be there," I said. "Thanks for calling."

She paused. "It means a lot to me that you're coming."

"Sure," I said. "No problem." I hung up the phone

and spent the next few hours staring out the window
and trying not to think too hard about anything.

Just before noon I changed into the only good black
I owned—slacks and a sweater—and then called a cab
and waited for it to pull up. When I saw it outside
the window, I grabbed my umbrella and headed down
the stairs.

Just outside my apartment, someone strode down
the sidewalk to catch me before I got into the cab.

I looked up, ready for trouble.

Davy Silvers, wearing his hoodie and denim jacket,
nodded to me and kept walking. He didn't say anything but just as he came parallel to me, he handed
me a card. I took it, and he continued on.

Very secret agent of him. Except then he sneezed
several times and swore, which sort of blew the cloak-
and-dagger bit.

I ducked into the cab and told the driver to take
me to the cemetery. I tipped the card to read it. Black
with white letters: The Pack. But on the back was a
handwritten note. "Pike's last meeting. Two o'clock,
O'Donnel's."

Great. Just what I needed. A meeting with a bunch
of twitchy, nervous Hounds right after I watched my
dad's body get sunk six feet.

Well, at least they were holding it at O'Donnel's
this time. A pub meant beer. And I had the feeling
I'd need a lot of that before the day was over.

The cemetery wasn't that far outside the city, but
enough that the push and pull of magic in me eased
just the slightest amount.

But driving up to the iron gates made my stomach
clench. This was where my father would be buried.

Again. For the last time. Death was final. Even for him.

A small gathering of people, maybe twenty-five or so, all in black stood on the crest of the hill in front of the mortuary. They each held black umbrellas against the slight drizzle in the air.

These must be the important people Violet had mentioned.

"Want me to take you up there?" the cabdriver, a thin man who reminded me a little of Anthony, asked.

"Yes." I smoothed my hair. No one had found my hat or gloves. I had started knitting new ones but hadn't made much progress. Which meant I was going to have to use my umbrella to keep my head dry.

My umbrella was bright yellow and had little duckies on the edge.

I totally knew how to blend in.

The cab stopped and I paid, took a deep breath, and then got out into the cold air.

Half the people were watching me. People who I had never met—men, women, lots of shapes and sizes and ages. A tingle ran down my back as vague memories of each of them came to me. Tall, temperamental Victor, who always thought his opinion was correct; mousy Liddy, who could tear a man apart with the flick of a finger; big, friendly Jingo, who had a thing for little children and their bones.

I blinked, trying to stop the flow of memories. Memories that were not mine.

I popped open my umbrella so I had an excuse to look away from the crowd for a minute. Yellow duckies filled my vision, and the memories were gone.

But the remaining thoughts that filled my head were mechanical as the workings of a gun.

These important people were magic users. The Authority. People my dad had spent a lifetime hiding from me. All here. Now. Gathered to watch my father's corpse get lowered into the ground, to be covered in dirt, once and for all.

Holy shit.

I scanned the crowd for Violet, saw her there by the top of the stairs, her guard, Kevin, behind her. She was talking to another woman with red and gray hair pulled up in a loose bun. Maeve.

She and Maeve knew each other?

I was so out of my depth here.

So I did what I did in any social situation that throws me. I faked the hell out of it.

I walked up like I had expected this. Like my dad had told me all about each of them and I knew their secrets. I held my ducky umbrella over my shoulder and practically sauntered, selling all-the-fashionable-grievers-are-wearing-ducks-this-season attitude for all I was worth.

And I took great pains to keep my mind, my thoughts, and the magic that flowed through me very quiet.

The crowd hushed. Not that they'd been talking loudly. But as soon as I was a few steps away, they stopped talking completely.

The other half of the crowd who hadn't been looking my way turned so they could.

I put on a disinterested expression and scanned the faces. I spotted Zayvion. He stood near Violet and

Maeve and a thin, pale kid done up in Goth couture. My heart raced.

The crowd shifted to make room for me, to allow me to walk up through the middle of them if I chose. Everyone waited. Everyone watched me. Like whatever I did next was important.

It is no fun playing a game when you don't know what the rules are, much less what is at stake.

From the tension in the air, I didn't think these people were all on the same side exactly. No, this felt more like a strained truce that would remain long enough to see their mutual enemy, or friend, buried.

It probably mattered a lot who I decided to stand by. But it wasn't a hard choice. I strode up the open pathway through the crowd and climbed the stairs to stand next to two people, Violet Beckstrom and Zayvion Jones. Just to make sure they got my point, I turned to look out at the crowd. We stood, Zayvion on one side and Violet on the other, shoulder to shoulder.

I liked that feeling. Liked the guarded looks of respect, and anger, and curiosity it brought from the crowd.

And no matter how much my logical mind doubted I was making a good choice, since I didn't even know what the hells I was choosing, my gut, my heart, knew I was right where I should be.

"Is this all of us, then?" I asked in a calm voice.

Violet, next to me, nodded. "We may begin."

The big double doors behind us opened, and a group of six men brought out a casket. Instead of carrying it on their shoulders, they carried it low, at hip height. And instead of the lid being closed, it was open, from head to toe.

We stepped to one side, and the pallbearers brought the casket forward and paused in front of us, letting us take a long look.

That was my dad. No doubt in my mind. That was my dad's overpreserved, leathery, gray, rotting corpse. He was naked except for a black blanket across his hips. Zayvion squeezed my hand gently in silent sympathy. Violet, on the other side, placed a lavender handkerchief on my dad's chest, over his heart.

The pallbearers moved on. They walked slowly down the stairs, pausing every five steps so those in the crowd could look into the casket and agree that the body in that coffin was my dad. Once everyone got a chance to see him, the lid was placed upon the casket, and the pallbearers began the slow, long walk to my father's grave.

We followed along behind, and no one spoke a word. Only the sound of our shoes on the grass and the rain on our umbrellas stirred the silence. Zay was beside me, his hand still in mine, no mint, but the scent of pine and a familiar warmth that was solid and real in this surreal moment.

We walked out to the thin gathering of trees, barren of leaves, stone angels grieving at their roots, black limbs spread against a stormy sky. A draped lowering device surrounded the newly re-dug grave.

The pallbearers placed the casket on the lowering device and lifted the lid on the casket one more time. All of us could see it was still his corpse. Wetter now, but still the same. A few people leaned in closer to get one last look. I did not feel the need to do so.

The pallbearers closed and locked the coffin lid and then worked the controls so the coffin could be lowered.

No one moved forward after that. Everyone watched as the coffin sank to the bottom of the grave, the equipment was removed, and the cemetery grave diggers—three of them wearing black raincoats and carrying shovels—cut shovelfuls of dirt and threw it into the hole.

No one sang. No one cried. No one gave words or comfort or remembrance. There was no sound at all except silence, raindrops, and the heavy thud of dirt upon pine.

After an unspecified time, the crowd began to break up. Each person walked past me and Zayvion and Violet. Some stopped and spoke to Violet in a low tone. No one spoke to me. Some made eye contact, looking for something or maybe trying to tell me something, and then looking away. Some turned so I never got a good look at them.

I tried to commit as many of their faces to memory as I could, inhaled to get the scents of them. Then they were gone, black coats beneath black umbrellas, beneath a dark sky.

The grave diggers were still filling the grave. Violet stood at the edge, watching each shovelful of dirt cascade down. Kevin, hands folded behind his back, stood by her side. I thought they looked good together, him painfully reserved but radiating strength and loyalty, her small, pale, and, I knew, fierce.

Violet's shoulders shook and she put her hands over her face.

Kevin lifted his hand, hesitated with it just above her shoulder, as if weighing the consequences. Then the moment was gone. He quietly drew his hand away and stood, once again as only her guard—near her, but not touching her, his hands folded behind his back.

My heart hurt. For her. For him. For what they almost had.

"Allie?" Zayvion's voice was quiet.

I looked over at him.

"Would you like to get out of the rain?"

What I would like was some kind of an explanation. Of where he had been the last five days.

But suddenly I realized I was really cold. My feet were numb from standing in the same place for so long. "Fine," I said.

I walked over to Violet. Caught Kevin's gaze. He sized me up.

Unreadable, that man. He tipped his chin down, just enough, I knew he was giving his okay.

I gently put my hand on Violet's back. She had both her hands across her stomach now. She was shorter than me, thin, petite. Standing this close to her, touching her, made me realize how small and breakable she was, and I felt an overwhelming desire to protect her, to not let her, or my sibling she was carrying, get hurt.

"I'm sorry," I said.

She did not look at me. Did not look away from the grave.

"So am I," she whispered.

"Are you going to be okay?"

She nodded. "It's going to take some time. More time," she said faintly.

"If you need me," I said, "I'll be here."

I wanted to say more, wanted to tell her words of comfort, wanted to tell her that I had spoken to him, to his spirit, but it seemed like the worst time ever to bring that up.

"Take care of her." I said to Kevin. He nodded. I walked back to Zay, and he fell into step with me as we crossed the graveyard.

"Where were you?" I asked. I hadn't meant for my voice to catch.

"Lobbying for you."

"With whom?"

"Them." He pointed in the direction of the people leaving the cemetery.

"Maeve stopped by."

Zayvion, the graceful, the unflappable Zen master, tripped on smooth ground. "She did?" he asked as he pulled himself back up and dusted his muddy hands.

"That worries you?" I asked.

He took a deep breath, let it out through his mouth in a cloud of steam. "Honestly? Yes. Yes, it does. What did she want?"

"She and I . . . talked. She mentioned some teaching."

Zayvion smiled and put his hands in his pockets. I could almost feel the tension draining from his body. "And you said yes, right?"

I shrugged one shoulder.

"Allie." He sounded worried. "You did say yes, didn't you?"

"You never asked me if I wanted you to lobby for me, Zayvion. You went out and decided my future for me."

He stopped. Looked off at the horizon, his breath coming out in steam. It was still raining and he hadn't removed his knit cap. He looked like he was trying hard to keep it together. Like maybe a lot was riding on this.

"You should have asked me," I said.

He turned back to me, Zen, calm. Ready to hear my answer. "I see that now. Did you say no to her?" His eyes were brown, but flecks of gold sprayed through them, as if he were trying very hard not to use magic. Or maybe that was what his eyes always did when he was worried.

"No," I said. "I told Maeve I want to learn. But don't ever assume you can make decisions for me, Zayvion Jones. Men who do that don't stay in my life. Period."

"I'll remember that."

We started walking again.

"Thank you, though," I said.

"Don't thank me yet," he said. "It is not an easy thing to learn. It means giving up a lot. A lot of your life. Paying the price."

Yeah, I got it. Using magic was hard. But if I wanted to survive in this new secret world of magical back-stabbing, corpse-stealing soul suckers, I needed to learn the moves. An image of Pike flashed behind my eyes. Maybe if I had known more about this world, about Zayvion's world, I could have kept him safe.

"Was it worth it? I asked. "For you?"

"It is now."

He unlocked the car door and walked around to the driver's side. I lowered my ducky umbrella and closed it. Then I opened the car door.

The overwhelming scent of summer—roses and

irises—wafted out of the car. Zayvion was leaning on the roof, watching me with those warm brown eyes of his.

I bent and looked in. Roses in every shade of pink filled the car. Interspersed with the roses were irises in soft lavender and deep purple. There was even a bouquet of roses buckled into my seat.

Wow. It must have cost him a fortune to get that many flowers in the dead of winter.

"Well, well," I said as I unbuckled the roses. "What would have happened if I told you I didn't need a ride?"

He shrugged one shoulder. "I had a good feeling about it." He got in the driver's side.

I got in too, maneuvering under the bouquet with one hand as I buckled my seat belt.

"I thought you were going to bring these by my hospital room."

"It was suggested. That didn't work out how I wanted it to." He started the car.

I stuck my nose in the roses and inhaled, long and deep.

Lovely.

"What didn't work out?" I asked.

"Everything. I should have known something would go wrong when I saw Trager's blood magic mark on you. I should have gone with you to the police, been there when you confronted Trager."

"Zayvion, you are not my guard."

He didn't say anything.

"You aren't. You know that, right?"

"Sure." He didn't sound very convincing.

"Did Violet hire you to be my guard?"

Nothing.

"Zayvion? Hello? An answer here?"

"Would you like lunch? I think I still owe you that date."

"Zayvion. Focus. Are you working for Violet?"

"No."

"So you're not my bodyguard?"

"Did you want me to be?"

"No." *Yes. No.*

It was confusing being me.

"We haven't even decided if we're going to date," I said.

"We can take care of that. Let me take you to lunch."

I suddenly remembered the card in my pocket. Davy's invite for me to go to Pike's last meeting. I glanced at the clock in the dash.

"You have plans?" Zayvion asked.

"No. Yes. Maybe. I have lunch plans. I think."

"You aren't sure?"

"It's Davy Silvers. He's a—"

"Hound. We met."

"You did?"

Zayvion looked over at me, frowned. "Ah. Memory loss?" he asked.

"I don't know. When did you meet him?"

"During the . . . in the warehouse with Frank Gordon. Do you remember that?"

"Some. Can you tell me about it?"

"Sure. How about over lunch? On our date."

Was there nothing without a price in this city?

"Fine. Take me to O'Donnel's."

Zayvion turned the car in that direction.

We found parking in the lot behind what used to be the old treasury building that had been turned into the pub. We got out of the car. A few patrons were smoking beneath the awning, and we walked past them through the haze of smoke and into the back door of the pub.

The place was small but had two levels. Off in one corner was a player piano. Velvet curtains sectioned off parts of the walls, giving it plenty of private booths. Everything was black walnut, red velvet, and brass.

Classy.

I scanned the room, looking for Davy. The flame of a cigarette being lit caught my eye. Jack, the Whiskey Guy, leaned on a door to an alcove area. He tipped his chin up, turned, and walked into the alcove.

I strode across the room. Maybe more like limped. My feet were numb in my wet boots, and honestly, I'd been doing a lot more standing and walking today than I'd done in the last five. I was feeling pretty worn-out. My stamina was shot. The doctor said I'd feel a little stronger every day. He was an optimistic fellow.

Still, it was a small enough place that I held my own and walked into the alcove area, Zayvion behind me.

The room was filled. Maybe thirty or forty people. Most standing, a few seated at the table. They were grouped by vice, as I suppose made sense. Hard drinkers to the right, street drugs in the back, prescription meds to the left, and smaller pockets of those who used special-ized pain-avoidance techniques—the cutters, smokers, sex addicts, exercise freaks, and gamblers—sprinkled throughout. Still, no matter what group they belonged to, everyone had a drink in their hands. Platters of food covered the table, and in the center of all that food was a plain black urn.

Oh. For some reason I didn't realize this would be about Pike's death. But that urn spoke volumes. I suddenly wanted to leave, wanted to be anywhere but here, face-to-face again with Pike's death.

Sid, the Hound who looked like he should program computers for a living, appeared from somewhere in the crowd. He was grinning, his eyes half crescents behind his glasses. His cheeks were red. Probably from that glass of tequila in his hand.

"Allie, I'm so glad you came," he said. "And you're Zayvion Jones, right?"

"I am."

"I'm Sid Westerling," he said. "Davy mentioned you. Welcome."

Well, that was not at all what I expected out of him. Hounds were notorious loners. Life did not let them make friendships. Life did not bring Hounds together. But apparently death could do both.

"Everyone," Sid said to the crowd. "Attention for a moment." He waited for the noise to die down. Someone pressed a glass of red wine in my hands. Zayvion had managed to snag a beer.

"We're here to recognize and honor the life of a good man and a good Hound: Martin Pike."

"Pike!" several voices called out.

"May he live on in our memories and hearts. To Pike!"

All glasses raised, and everyone drank.

"And that's the end of my speech," he said. "Someone else talk."

"I'd like to say something." All eyes turned to a younger voice. Davy Silvers slouched in a chair by the wall. Several people moved out of the way while Davy stood up on the chair. He bobbled his balance just a bit but did not spill the tankard of dark beer in his hand.

Was he even old enough to drink?

"Pike was . . ." He tipped his head back, closed his eyes. I could seen his Adam's apple bob as he swallowed back tears. "Not always a good man."

A few people chuckled.

"But he was what he was. What we are. And he accepted us for all of our faults. 'Cause face it, we're all a bunch of screwed-up losers."

More chuckling. Davy looked back down. He wasn't smiling. "And there was only one of us who was there for him when he needed it the most. Allie Beckstrom."

Glasses raised, all faces turned to me. I gave a small smile and nodded. See, I'm good under social pressure. Having a notorious father will do that to a girl.

"To Allie," Davy said.

"Allie!" the crowd agreed.

And then they waited. Waited for me to say something. Okay.

"Pike was my friend." Wow, this was harder than it looked. "And the last thing he told me before . . . before he died was: it was worth it."

Silence fell over the room.

"To Pike," I said. "The strongest Hound I have had the honor to know. I wish he would have had a chance to find his island away from it all. I'll miss him. We'll all miss him."

"To Pike," the crowd said somberly.

Everyone drank, and I did too, because my throat was tight with tears.

"Pike would have wanted a new leader for the Pack," Davy said. "A Hound as tough as he was. A friend. I elect Allie Beckstrom as the new leader of the Pack. All in favor, say aye!"

"Seconded," Jamar's baritone called out.

"Third—I mean aye!" That from bouncy, corpse-sniffing Beatrice.

"Wait," I said. "No. Wait."

Sid, standing next to me, was laughing.

"I'm not a leader. I shouldn't be your leader," I said. "I've only ever been to one meeting. I'd make a terrible leader. Vote for Sid, or Jamar or Beatrice."

No one heard me because everyone was clapping.

Sid, his arms still crossed across his chest, leaned toward me. "Give it up." His breath smelled of tequilla and lime. "They want you. And we need you. Pike's death will destroy the ground he worked so hard to gain. You're not gonna turn your back on your own kind, are you? What would Pike say?"

"I don't have a kind," I said.

Sid patted me on the shoulder. "You do now."

A motion near the back wall of the room caught my eye. The cutter girl, Tomi, Davy's ex-girlfriend, shouldered her way across the room. She stopped in front of me and looked me straight in the eye.

"Tomi," Davy called out from across the room.

She didn't turn, didn't look at him.

"Yes?" I asked.

She gave me a bored glare.

"Tomi," he said again, this time a warning. He got

down off his chair and pushed his way through the
bodies.

I was looking Tomi right in the eye, so I noticed
she waited until he was behind her to talk to me. And
it was clear from her expression that she didn't like
me much.

"Tomi, leave her alone," Davy said.

I don't think he knew what that single sentence did
to her. But I did. I watched as her eyes widened. Then
she searched my face as if trying to see what he saw
in me. Then she licked her lips and scowled.

Great. It didn't take a genius to interpret the flash
of jealousy that screwed her face into a sneer. That
woman had hate in her. And lots of it. For me.

"There's nothing between us," I said. Neutral. Calm.
Maybe some of Zayvion's Zen was wearing off on me.

"I don't owe you anything," she said loud enough
for Davy to hear it. "And I will never follow you."

"Tomi," Davy said again.

"Fuck you, Davy Silvers. I've had better than you.
Bigger than you." She flipped him off and pushed past
me. If Zayvion hadn't been standing hip to hip with
me, I think she would have tried to step on my foot
as she went by.

About a dozen people, all young enough I'd card
them if they tried to buy beer, filtered through the
crowd like strings being pulled out of the weave. Each
of them, about an even mix between men and women,
glared at me and then followed Tomi out into the pub.

I watched Davy's face slowly slide from confusion
to anger.

"Nice job, Silvers," Sid laughed. "Chasing away
members before we even get started again."

Davy smiled a tight smile. "Their loss."

Sid swallowed down his drink. "They'll be back. Give 'em time to cool off. We all need time to cool off." He angled a look at me and then at Davy, asking me to do something. Then he walked off to find more booze.

Great. I guess I was the guidance counselor now too.

"You know," I said to Davy, "I recently told someone that I don't like it when people decide my future without consulting me."

"Does this mean you're backing out?" He looked at me with that hollowed shock of betrayal. He looked lost. I knew how he felt. Pike had been my friend too.

"No," I said. "It means you better enjoy that beer, because I'm going to keep you so busy being my assistant, you're not going to have time to drink."

"Huh." He took a deep swallow of the beer. "I think you underestimate my multitasking abilities."

"I think you underestimate my ability to work your ass off."

That got a small smile out of him. "We'll find out, won't we?" He hoisted his nearly empty glass. "To tomorrow."

"To tomorrow."

We drank on that.

Okay, that was enough red wine before food. My head was feeling a little muzzy. "I think I'm done here," I mumbled.

Zayvion, who had been quiet, put his hand on my elbow and walked with me out of the room. "Home?" he asked.

"Please," I said.

Once we got into the car, drenched with the scent

of roses, I put the vase of pink flowers on my lap again. I closed my eyes and pressed my fingers over my lids. "How did it get so confusing?" I asked.

"What?"

"My life. Everything used to make sense."

"Did it?"

"No. But at least it didn't change every few seconds."

"Some things are the same," he said.

"Like what?"

"I still owe you a real date."

I rolled my head so I could see him. He looked good in profile, a strong nose and high-cut cheekbones that gave him that slightly exotic flare. Wide lips, and dark, smooth skin. The note of his pine cologne mingled with the roses and made a new, sensual scent.

"I thought O'Donnel's was it," I said.

He looked over at me. "O'Donnel's was definitely not it. How about we try it again. Tonight. I'll come by your place around seven. I have reservations at the Gargoyle."

That was one of the most expensive French restaurants in town.

"Wow, the Gargoyle? Being a secret magic assassin pays good, don't it?"

He shrugged one shoulder. "It's not about the money; it's about the health benefits."

I laughed. I mean, seriously guffawed. Sweet hells, it had been a pretty bad few days.

"Or maybe you'd rather have some time alone tonight?" he asked.

I thought about it. He was probably right; I did need time alone. But what I needed even more was to not be alone.

"Seven is great. Bring your wallet; I'm going to be hungry."

He looked over at me, and those beautiful brown eyes sparked with bits of gold. "I think I can handle that."

We arrived at my apartment building and he double-parked outside the front door.

"What are we going to do with all these flowers?" I asked.

"Let me take care of it." He got out of the car, opened the back door, and gathered up all the flowers.

"A little help with the doors would be nice," he said from somewhere in the middle of the giant bundle of flowers.

I giggled. "You look adorable, Mr. Jones." I think the wine had done some damage. Or, I don't know, maybe it was seeing my father's body buried or my friend in an urn.

"Door, Beckstrom," Zayvion growled.

"Hold on, hold on." I jogged up the stairs and opened the front doors.

"Only three flights," I said to Zayvion.

He grunted.

I walked up the stairs first, Zayvion silent behind me. I paused at the top of the stairs and looked down the hall. It had become a habit. A sort of dread hit my stomach every time I approached the door to my apartment. I couldn't help but glance over at the apartment where Frank Gordon had lived. So close. Too close. I hadn't heard anyone come to clean out his apartment yet. I wondered if he had family.

"Allie?" Zayvion said.

"Fine," I said. "I'm fine."

He somehow managed to sort the bouquets and free a hand. He gently touched the side of my arm. "I know," he said.

And that, a casual acceptance of me, of maybe even all the stuff I'd been through, made me wish he had his arms around me instead of those flowers.

"Okay," I said. "Thanks." I walked down the hall, unlocked my door, and strode in like I never worried about what might be waiting, lurking for me in my home.

Zayvion took the flowers into the kitchen and set them all carefully on the counter.

"Might need some more vases," he observed.

I came up behind him and looked around him to the sink.

"Maybe I'll just float them all in the bathtub." I drew back and he turned, leaning against the counter.

"If you want those flowers in the tub, you'll have to do it yourself. I am done hauling these things around for you."

"Aw. Being a hero is a tough job."

"It is. Especially when it involves you."

He tucked his thumbs in the front pocket of his jeans and smiled. Standing there, comfortable and smiling in my kitchen, smelling of roses and pine, and looking like he knew a secret I'd never find out about, he seemed . . . I don't know. Strong. A little dangerous. A lot sexy.

So I leaned forward and kissed him.

He put one hand on my hip and gently cradled the curve of my jaw with his other hand. I drew my right arm around him, tucking my fingers in his back pocket.

Nice. Very nice.

I tried to put my left arm around him too, but the

vase of flowers in my hand tipped and peed water on my floor.

Did I know how to do romance or what?

I righted the vase so I could turn my real attention on Zayvion.

My tongue slipped along his bottom lip, and he opened his mouth for me. Electric heat shot down my body and pooled deliciously in my belly as his tongue slid along mine, sparking desire, making my body want to stretch for him.

Oh, loves, I wanted him.

The kiss deepened as each of us explored, touched, and remembered, if even for a brief moment, what this meant, what we meant, together.

Then I pulled away. "We were going to wait for it to be real instead of just trauma sex. Isn't that what you said?" I was hoping he would say no, that was not at all what he had said.

And even though his eyes were burning bright, and even though the heat of passion from the kiss still lingered on my lips and in my veins, Zayvion Jones said, "It's never been just trauma sex. But yes. We're going to wait until we both know for sure what it really is all about. And I want to make good on my promise to take you on a date. First."

Promises, promises. "Then I guess you'll have to leave," I said.

"Yes, I guess I will."

We stood there, our shoes wet from the rose piddle. Finally Zayvion pushed away from the counter and walked past me toward the door.

Damn. That man must have put on his stainless steel willpower panties this morning.

He opened the door. "See you at seven," he said.

I leaned one shoulder in the kitchen doorway. "Don't be late."

Zayvion smiled. "Not a chance."

He shut the door behind him, and I strolled over and threw the locks.

Maybe things were looking up after all.

I hadn't been on a date for years. How did one do this? Shower first, and then I'd see if I owned any clothing that wasn't made of denim or wool. I walked into the bathroom and flipped on the light, trying to remember if I still had that little red dress I'd bought a couple years ago. I bet that dress could burn right through Mr. Jones' willpower.

I was still carrying the vase of roses. It was out of water, so I tipped it under the spigot and turned on the water.

Allie . . . A thought, a whisper, an exhale. Chills ran down my skin. I knew that voice. Only I hadn't heard it with my ears. I'd heard it in my head. Panic pounded my chest.

I looked up into the mirror. And saw my father's gaze looking back at me through my eyes.

ALSO AVAILABLE

FROM

Devon Monk

MAGIC TO THE BONE

Using magic means it uses you back, and every spell exacts a price from its user. But some people get out of it by Offloading the cost of magic onto an innocent. Then it's Allison Beckstrom's job to identify the spell-caster. Allie would rather live a hand-to-mouth existence than accept the family fortune—and the strings that come with it. But when she finds a boy dying from a magical Offload that has her father's signature all over it, Allie is thrown back into his world of black magic. And the forces she calls on in her quest for the truth will make her capable of things that some will do anything to control...

Available wherever books are sold or at penguin.com

Also Available

FROM

Devon Monk

MAGIC IN THE SHADOWS

Allison Beckstrom's magic has taken its toll on her, physically marking her and erasing her memories—including those of the man she supposedly loves. But lost memories aren't the only things preying on Allie's thoughts.

Her late father, the prominent businessman—and sorcerer—Daniel Beckstrom, has somehow channeled himself into her very mind. With the help of The Authority, a secret organization of magic users, she hopes to gain better control over her own abilities—and find a way to deal with her father...

Available wherever books are sold or at penguin.com